STORM FEVER

Currents dark with passion focus on the languid Caribbean lotusland of Nevis ...

When Ned Murdoch brings the cast of 'King' Heinlein's latest movie to The Sugar Mill, Nevis Island's premier hotel, tranquillity ends and a Pandora's box of prima donna jealousies, tempers and lusts breaks open.

Sultry Hope Parnell is the driving force behind The Mill. She's a woman in control of her own destiny — until she meets Ned and dares to love ...

Smouldering starlet Karin Genevieve wants him too. She's committed to King and it's a great relationship but Karin's hunger requires more than casting couch conventions.

Nevis is refuge for Veronica Marston after the break-up of her affair with a Cabinet minister. But the scandal of his divorce and political fall from grace sends out inescapable shock waves ...

STORM FEVER — an irresistible novel of elemental energy, divine luxury, violence and seduction.

STORM FEVER

VIVIEN LEYLAND

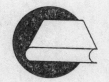

Printed and bound in Great Britain by
Robert Hartnolls (1985) Ltd, Cornwall.

*To Monahan who took me to Nevis and
Becky who brought me home.*

Chapter One

THE ISLAND, shaped like a ball beneath the baseball bat of St Kitts, rose threateningly towards the cockpit window. The pilot guided the little eight-seater craft towards the airstrip by the beach using her eyes rather than the unreliable equipment.

On the horizon, a thread of scarlet dawn broke the golden sheet of crushed velvet that was the morning sky.

For the sheer hell of it, Hope Parnell buzzed a couple of scrawny cows grazing on the side of the volcano, flashing them with her landing lights. The white birds she always thought of as ibises flew from the backs of the cows to flutter for a few moments in utter indignation before resettling to pick off more ticks.

The Islander landed precisely and coasted towards an older machine parked at the end of the runway.

Overhead, pelicans flew in formation like ace pilots.

Oz Lennox was unloading crates from the cargo hold of The Goose onto a pallet ready to be carted to customs. Hope swung out of the cockpit and unlatched her hold.

'How were the Virgins?' she yelled over the sound of the cooling engines, gasping from the stench of burning petroleum.

'Hell,' Oz yelled back, his voice whipped into the air by an aggressive wind blowing from the south. 'You can't move for dog-collars! There's a religious convention on the US Island, and every hotel in the Virgins is packed with pastors and their wives. And they don't believe in abstinence. There isn't a bottle of bubbly to be had.'

'For drinking or buying?' Hope asked.

'Buying. The Barbados order, remember? Can't fill it today – I'll have to fly over to Miami tomorrow to get it.'

Hope cursed. 'You should have bloody cabled over first, you bum. We could have arranged another pilot run today to Miami to cut time. There's some Medicals to pick up there too.'

Oz Lennox ambled round the plane's fuselage and threw a burly arm round her shoulders. 'Sorry, Babe. Should have thought.'

She pulled off her headscarf and a tangle of dull hair that ought to have been silver fell round her shoulders. 'You stink something rotten,' said Oz affectionately.

'Essence de Petroleum,' she grinned back. 'And how you can tell with the way you pong I'll never know. What was the consignment? Fish?'

'Dolphin. That was for Barbados too, but the refrigeration packed in, so I had to dump the whole frigging lot over Antigua. Couldn't stand it any longer.'

They both imagined the fat silver fish – no relation to the mammals called dolphins back home – floating through the air to land in unsuspecting hoteliers' grounds, ready to greet the tourists after their breakfasts. 'Another inexplicable phenomenon,' said Hope. 'Now it rains dolphins in Antigua. You realise the *Supernature* freaks will be onto this in no time?'

Oz hitched the pallet to the fork lift and started up the motor.

Hope loaded her final crate onto the back. 'Any other disasters I should know about?'

'Isn't that enough?' he called over his shoulder, and the fork-lift trundled off down the airstrip.

Tucking her hands in her pockets, Hope kicked gravel like a kid as she walked the hundred yards or so to the single storeyed shack where so much of her time was spent so uselessly.

Amos Bardram, the most officious of all the customs officers was standing in the doorway, legs spread wide apart and hands on hips to prevent either of them sneaking through the gap unnoticed.

'Come on, Amos, give us a break,' Oz was saying by the time Hope arrived at the wooden hut, 'it's too early for a row. We've been flying all night.'

Bardram's face was mule-like.

Oz was twice his size, but he wasn't the one with the trump cards. 'You know we haven't got any cocaine or arms or stuff. We couldn't afford them, man, even if we wanted them.'

'Don't you *mahn* me, mahn,' shouted Bardram. 'I got my job an' every time you come in you cause me dis same problem. Besides, I got a long memory.'

'That had nothing to do with me or Hope – '

Hope was sidling towards the back exit, planning to leave Oz with the paperwork and the hassles. 'An' you ain't going nowheres either *Miss* Parnell. You the boss-man, if this guy brung in drugs, you responsible.' His eyes opened so wide they grew stalks and popped at her.

'Amos, you know where I'll be if there's fines to pay.'

'I knowed where you'll be. You'll be right here in de customs house.' He smiled smugly to show he thought he'd said something incredibly witty and to prove he had the upper hand. As always.

Every crate was opened, every item of the cargo inspected.

It was two hours later that the crates were finally re-packed. Some of the linen brought in from the Dutch island, Saba, was ruined by the blue chalk that said Amos Bardram has checked and passed this consignment. The deep frozen meat, a survivor despite the refrigeration failure, had bled through its wooden packing onto the case of claret below.

'Nobody know de diff'rence,' grinned Bardram. 'Dey think the wine leaked over the label so no problem.' Flowers for Nelson Plantation, packed in ice in Hope's hold, drooped and were drowning in pools of steaming water.

She heaved a box into her arms and began to walk away.

'An' Miss Pansy say you contact her the minute you touch down,' he threw at her as a parting shot. 'She say it very important.'

Hope seethed but said nothing. Bardram had been known to order a body search as a reprisal for sharp replies.

9

Outside, they loaded the crates into the two Jeeps. Though they were parked under palm trees, the worn leather seats were covered in early morning dew, rapidly evaporating in the heat of the first rays of sun.

Oz started his motor with difficulty and waved as he drove off to make the deliveries. Hope went back to customs to wheedle for the use of the telephone.

Bardram had disappeared to his breakfast in the canteen, knowing from his schedules there'd be no-one else left to hassle till the next plane in at eight hundred hours. His assistant was anxious to make amends. After all, Hope Parnell may be only a woman, but she was going places and ran an airline. Someday he might want a right to Montserrat and Ms Parnell was a person to be cultivated. He even got the number for her.

'We got a booking, Hoape,' Pansy bubbled. 'Some film crew left over from the spy movie they made over in Barbuda. I didn't know to say yes or no.'

'So you said yes?'

'Was I right?'

'Give you a big sloppy wet one for it. When are they coming?'

'They comin' today, Hoape! One of dem phoned last night from Montserrat while you was in Trinidad. He say they makin' an overnight crossin' by boat.'

Hope made split-second calculations and worked out that yes might have been the wrong answer. She preferred to make meticulous plans before guests arrived.

'How many, Pansy?'

There were to be five of them. All in separate rooms. One had wanted the Mill Suite, but Pansy had said it wasn't available.

The hotel, Sugar Mill Plantation, and more specifically, the mill itself, was Hope's home. No way would Pansy see home being disrupted in the dead summer season. Winter was different when the boys and the Barbados woman took over the airline.

From Pansy's point of view, that was the best time of the year, when Hope concentrated on making Sugar Mill the most luxurious small hotel in the whole of the Caribbean.

Then, the Plantation sparkled and glittered, as every possible indulgence that could be bought was on offer to visitors. Only then was the suite in the old mill available for travellers. At a price.

So there were five unexpected guests. Maybe Hope could manage. There was food in the freezer and the rooms, each in separate bungalows dotted around the plantation, could be made up in next to no time. The staff could be recalled and the chef flown over from England. No problem. 'Get Jimmy to check over the pools, order lobster – are they Americans?'

'I think so.'

'Okay, so we're definitely going to need lobster. And order conch from the fish boy too. And ask Zeke to dig up plenty of fresh fruit and vegetables.

' – And phone Nelson Plantation to tell them I could only get half the wine they wanted and the flowers got ruined by Amos Bardram.'

She hung up the phone and ran – despite the heat – for the Jeep. Temperatures of over eighty degrees at before seven still took her by surprise, though she should have been used to them by now. This was her fourth summer on Nevis.

She drove out of the enclave with the Jeep's door still open, banging it to as she rounded the bend onto the lane. The roads to the isolated Nelson Plantation, thickly lined with coconut groves and manchineel trees, were deserted apart from the odd sheep or goat that wandered dazed and shell-shocked onto the shingle track. It was a short drive, all uphill, and one that Hope would have enjoyed had she had the time.

The night watchman on the gate, about to finish his tour of duty, opened the padlock agonisingly slowly for the Jeep.

Julian Winchester was waiting at the kitchen door, pointedly looking at his watch. Hope jumped out of the driver's seat and counted out exactly half the crates of wine for the manager at Nelson. She needed the others herself now and Julian would just have to make do.

To her credit, she gave him the bottles with the unbloodied labels.

11

Nelson Plantation Inn looked pretty much like the other hotels on the island. Old stones shrouded in heady blossoms, cobbled entrance ways, derelict arches and toppling chimneys.

It was located higher on the mountainside than any of the other Plantations. Though it was a long way to the beach, this disadvantage was outweighed for the regulars by the cool breezes that whisked up The Central without even rustling a leaf at the lowland hotels. Temperatures here were consistently ten degrees lower than anywhere else on the island.

English roses flocked in droves to The Nelson.

Its façade was a crumbling grey stone that suggested a sad neglect; inside it was pristine white marble everywhere, with overstuffed armchairs and settees from English stately homes sold off to pay death duties. They had seen better days but were as acceptable as old friends. Much like Julian Winchester himself.

The Nelson was the only hotel managed rather than owned. To their everlasting irritation, no-one on the island had managed to discover whose bank accounts the profits went into, despite the prolonged prying and delving that was a way of life in Nevis.

It had been a topic for much speculation ten or twelve years ago, and the subject's interest value was revived with the advent of each new hotelier.

Though Hope had been less interested in the intrigue than in what made The Nelson so successful, she too had formulated a few ideas as to the inn's ownership.

Julian Winchester looked at her disapprovingly as he signed for the wine and initialled the alteration she'd made. He had very strict ideas about how women should look and behave.

And this woman looked a mess. Black smears over her face, hair unkempt and dirty with engine oil. Tattered flying suit that had probably outlived its previous owner.

Hope was a woman of contrasts. In summer, she was only seen in the pilot's outfit. It was easy to forget how beautiful she actually was – only to be annoyingly and forcefully reminded in winter, when the other Hope Parnell

12

surfaced. That was the time when she really looked the part she was playing.

But for now he could peer down his nose at her with good reason.

They were sorting through the consignment, ticking items off lists. 'Sorry about the flowers, Jules,' said Hope. 'Were they vital?'

He shrugged. A stiff upper lip formed beneath his moustache.

'Veronica Marston's flying out from London today, complete with the entourage. I'd have liked a few Birds of Paradise for her room. Orchids. Suchlike.'

Summer guests were real prestige – maximum points, after royalty, on the scoreboard – even if they could be an inconvenience. If you were able to boast of filled rooms when all the other hotels stood empty, you could really claim to have arrived.

The hoteliers were a group on their own, mainly ex-pats whose community rarely changed. They played the points game, scoring for business acumen and unusual successes. It was a friendly hostility that only broke out into open warfare when one or other husband ran off with another's wife. For those who did not have a summer interest, there was little else to do. It was adultery or alcoholism or nothing. Actually, it was usually adultery *and* alcoholism for the one normally led to the other.

Hope chuckled secretly about her own arrivals and concentrated on taking the wind out of his sails for now. 'Times must be hard – if Veronica's coming out in the off season.'

Julian Winchester sniffed. 'It is her second trip this year, dear. I don't think times have ever been hard for her. And at least *she's* never any problem. I'm quite looking forward to seeing the old bitch.'

He signed for the last of the deliveries and tucked Hope's pen into his jacket pocket. A decent Parker. Jolly good.

He cleared his throat, enjoying himself. 'I gather her party will be the only one here once Manor Inn's Canadians go home at the end of the week.' Underlining

13

his status, crowing in the gentlemanly way he had.

'Well, Jules. I am surprised. Your ear is normally so firmly planted to the ground.'

'Sorry?'

'Perhaps you've been away or you'd have heard. I'm sure everyone else knows. I've got *five* residents coming in to The Sugar Mill this morning.'

He lifted an eyebrow questioningly. How had he missed this titbit?' What good luck. And what a pity you've got to work with the planes.'

He couldn't let her get away with stealing his thunder so completely.

The jibe caught its mark. Hope put an oily hand to her forehead and rubbed more grease onto her face. 'Oh God. You're right, Julian. I've been flying all night – that's why I might look a bit – '

'Disreputable?' he supplied helpfully.

She grinned. 'That's the word. Would you mind if I cleaned up here, Jules? Just in case they're there when I get back?'

'Naturally you may. Don't want you giving the Hoteliers' Association a bad name . . . And besides, it will be a pleasure to give an urchin a clean start.'

'Like Fagin did for Oliver Twist, you mean,' Hope laughed, running for the stairs up to Julian's rooms.

Though time was short – there was so much to arrange at the Plantation, and Hope was rarely so unprepared – she showered beneath the slow trickle of water in Julian Winchester's bathroom that heralded another breakdown in the island's water supply. 'That's all I need. No water,' she thought aloud. The breakdowns always seemed to come in the wet season. One of the quirks of island life.

She rubbed herself dry on a fluffy white towel, unaware of the amused gaze of Julian Winchester, watching her through an angled mirror from his bedroom beyond. Twelve years of life in a backwater had taught him to take his pleasures where he could.

She dressed in the flying suit and trainers and left the towel in a heap in the centre of the quarry tiled floor. Grime from the suit somehow managed to transfer itself again to her face, but Julian Winchester decided to say nothing.

On the other side of the island, at the empty hotel that was called Portlands, Terry Morelands called for more toast to go with the Coopers marmalade.

He didn't need to watch his weight. His panther body never gained or lost a pound. He had the best body on the island. It was one of his many assets.

He poured more coffee, but let the maid Hannah add the cream since she was already there.

It was a good day. Peaceful. Nobody telling him what he should and shouldn't be doing. Two weeks it had been like this. He could go out and feed his fighting cockerel any time he wanted, without comments about his so-called 'obsessive behaviour'. He could fly over to Barbados or Antigua for a little night life. He could gamble and screw as much as he liked and there was nobody – nobody – to start nagging at him.

Terry Morelands had married his wife for her money. It was no secret – even from Miriam Morelands. Seven years ago, he had had nothing but a room in town, a couple of beaten up fighting cocks and a job as an air steward with LIAT. Hardly the most glamorous lifestyle, hardly the most prestigious airline in the world. Locals called it Leave Island Any Time. Or Lost In Air Terminal, depending on circumstances.

Now look at him: the owner of Portlands Hotel, the champion Goliath, a Ferrari, maids . . . and a wife.

Seven years ago, Miriam Whitlock had liked his looks, his light, arrogant Tobagan features. He was so smooth faced you could use his chin to shine up your window. He fitted the job specification she'd drawn up for the post of husband like a glove.

They'd married in a hurry. Terry liked the idea of a whirlwind romance. It didn't give Miriam the time to change her mind or the chance to find out too much about him. For her own reasons, Miriam wanted a certificate signed and sealed by the Charlestown magistrate fast – before her relatives got to hear of her plans. No way would they approve of her marriage to the son of a Tobagan fisherman, no matter how 'rich' he was supposed to be.

There were no children from their union. There were no children because they had stopped sleeping together after their first four months of marriage, when Miriam became frigid with boredom. She made no allowance for his lack of maturity and expertise, cursing his clumsiness without ever telling him about the things that would have pleased her. She turned one of the staff rooms into a bedroom for Terry and consigned her own sexuality to the deep freeze where it lay forgotten and wasted.

The damage to Terry's ego did not show. He sowed oats wherever they were received, proving to his own satisfaction that he was not only great but that he was the best.

Knowing that lovers cost money, Miriam drank rum instead. She feared the dwindling of her wealth almost as much as she feared being alone.

They were perfectly mis-matched. The idea of a divorce never occurred to either of them. Terry liked his English-tailored suits, his silk shirts, his cars; Miriam was finally secure, partnered in a world that was hostile to single women, and firmly in control. What her husband did with his prick was his own business, as long as he didn't bring it anywhere near her.

And as long as he didn't take it permanently elsewhere.

For some time, Terry's on-going project had been the conquest of Hope Parnell.

The first time they'd met, Hope had been in winter costume, otherwise maybe he wouldn't have given her a second glance. It was at a house party for all the hoteliers and guests on the island. The Hoteliers' Association felt obliged to provide something to liven up the dead, black nights for the tourists. That was the formal excuse for the weekly get-together at any rate.

It had been Hope's turn to play host at The Sugar Mill during her first season. She was gorgeous. Icy blond hair, golden brown skin glittering and gleaming beneath a cutaway black silk dress that was more cut away than it was there.

Terry, several years younger than the fading Miriam,

16

looked at Hope, and was hungry as a wolfhound. Hope failed to notice as she handed out the champagne and the caviar, flown in from Miami by her own company earlier that day. Maybe he should have taken his chance right then, only Miriam was watching his movements too closely.

The year after that, there'd been Oz Lennox, though no-one really believed there was anything serious between those two.

But Terry knew when to jump and when to bide his time. That was the way he was. That was how he'd made his own personal fortune from a small initial investment out of Miriam's capital.

He chose then to bide his time. He wasn't into any more rejections.

Rumours about Hope were always rife because she gave so little of herself away. First, there was the Oz thing, then there'd been some freelance pilot who'd watched her every move. Trailed her like a tracker dog.

Later Jules Winchester had told him about the man in London, who had set her up in business. And that had sounded a helluva lot more realistic than the Oz stories: for a start, the existence of the rich lover explained all the mysteries. How could anyone who looked like Hope ever make it on her own?

The London guy had flown out a couple of winters ago, soon after the pilot had disappeared from the scene, and the set-up was obvious. Older man, wedding band on the finger. And he and Hope were very close. Very close indeedy.

Terry had tried to score with Hope just once, but he hadn't succeeded. It couldn't have been because of a lack of charm. He had enough of that to set up a school and give free gifts to the students. Hope had simply distanced herself from his advances in what Terry thought of as her delicious, 'maybe-later' way.

Now though, with no guests cluttering up his home at Portlands and a wife drying herself out in California, he had every chance of getting Hope into his bed. There was no-one around to interfere with his plans.

Terry dumped his napkin on his plate and dropped a

cigarette into the dregs of the coffee. He walked purposefully to the phone at the empty reception desk and called The Sugar Mill to make a dinner reservation. The time for Hope – he just knew it – was now. He licked his lips in anticipation and mentally wished his wife a long and happy convalescence.

Ned Murdoch arrived at Sugar Mill Plantation at roughly the same time as Hope. She was in the rusty old Jeep, he was in some kind of taxi. The boot was tied down over a collection of trunks with a rope. The driver – a grandfather of eight though he himself was only in his forties, as he had told Ned Murdoch twice already – was offering to take him round the island for a tour for only twenty dollars. Ned was looking bored. And very irritable. His denim jeans and open shirt were covered in sweat and salt stains. A scar ran down the side of his face, white against his nut brown skin.

Hope looked at him as she jumped from the Jeep and didn't like what she saw. He was the typical hard-man. Tourists you could get eating out of your hand most of the time. But this one had lived and worked in the Caribbean – you could see that at a glance. They were the ones who knew when wool was being pulled over their eyes. They had the ability to destroy the island magic Hope was in the business of creating with the same analytical thoroughness as a mechanic would strip away pretty bodywork to get at a car engine. How could this one work in Hollywood, where you needed to believe in fantasies to survive?

Ned Murdoch mumbled 'Yeah, maybe,' at his driver, and watched Hope standing hesitantly by her Jeep. She wasn't the sort of woman who normally hung around the plush resort hotels. There was oil on her cheek and her clothes looked as though they served a purpose. Women fell into three categories: bored housewives, bored ex-housewives and Women On The Make. At first sight, Hope didn't seem to fit. He hoped she worked around the hotel. It would make the prospect of a stay on the island much more palatable.

Zeke, six feet five and still growing, loped down the drive, looking from Hope to the new arrival and wondering

18

whom he should offer to help with the carrying. Hope beckoned him over and together, a combined force, they walked towards Murdoch who was paying off the taxi driver. There was no tip.

'I'm Hope Parnell,' she said brightly, extending a hand, grimy from the steering wheel, to the man. 'Are you with the film crew?'

Her grip was strong as a man's, but Murdoch returned it with compound interest. 'Ned Murdoch,' he said. 'The crew's using my boat, though they're not really a film crew any more. They're vacationing after a long, hard shoot and giving me a long, hard time.

'The wrecks off Barbuda and the salt pans of Anguilla have made them *mean*. You have been warned.'

They exchanged significant eye rolls and Hope felt encouraged. If there was any sort of animosity between him and his charges, it meant she could depend on him as an ally. A co-conspirator. Those in the know either enjoyed playing the game or spoiling it. Her job was to maintain the illusion of Caribbean calm – if he saw his role in the same light things might run smoothly. She might even get to like him if they had something in common apart from their filthy clothes.

'Are you staying here or on the boat?' she asked.

'Here. I've got a team repainting the schooner in the harbour. We're here till Friday – by which time the job'll be finished.'

'Only five days? The minimum's a week in the summer.' Hope's spirits sank. So much disruption for so little reward.

They started to walk towards the Great House, Zeke carrying two trunks in his long arms, Ned and Hope dragging a further two cases each along a stony path.

'They'll pay the extra, don't worry,' said Murdoch. 'They're crazy with their money.

'Nice place. Who owns it?'

'I do.'

Ned was a poor judge of character. Snap judgements were an asset at sea. On dry land they led to mistakes. He forgot the Working Woman category and re-filed Hope in the On The Make compartment. That or Rich Bitch. Pity.

The front of the Great House, a huge, collonaded edifice, was covered in the dried branches of a single, monstrous bougainvillea. In March it blossomed with coloured flowers like tissue paper, stretching all the way to the mill, along the covered walkway and down to the arbour that marked the divide between the sand and the newly fertile land. The flowers managed to change from white through shades of pink to deep purple at different times, creating the illusion of many varieties of the plant intermingling.

Like so much Caribbean magic, it was a disappointment to learn the truth. Hope never gave its secrets away.

The heavy oak door, due for a re-paint, stood open at the top of the flight of white stone steps. From the contrasting darkness inside came voices. Petulant, carping, niggling voices that sounded as though their owners were all suffering from the same migraine.

'That lot came up after breakfast about half an hour ago,' said Ned. 'They leave the cabin boy to carry the baggage.'

A blond woman, her hair frizzed into a halo around her head, was sprawled over a brown leather chesterfield.

She was saying: ' – as the maid will discover when she unpacks my trunk. I'll have a word with the owner. You just can't *move* in the dressing room.'

Pansy, behind the bar, was hidden from view by two men, both in white safari suits.

'If you haven't got Perrier, what *have* you got?' snapped one of them.

'You're going to adore my friends,' Ned Murdoch grimaced. 'Try to imagine these guys playing out their Hollywood dramas in Barbuda. I don't know how they survived it. No fans, no Press, no nothing.'

'Perhaps they're simply tired from the journey,' said Hope optimistically.

'Don't you believe it,' he growled back as they entered, obscuring the guests' view of the magnificent grounds, and the sunlight.

An old cat, Honest Joe, rolled off an armchair and made his way to Hope's legs.

'Hi, everyone,' Hope said enthusiastically. 'Everything okay for you?' The salesman's assumption, the question that begs a yes answer.

It didn't work.

'Could do with some Perrier,' mumbled the fat man at the bar.

'And my room is ridiculous,' piped the blond. 'Would you be so good as to ask the manager to do something about it?' Her face was vaguely familiar. It was one of those faces that you remember more for its sensuous lips and high cheekbones than for its character.

Ned and Hope moved into the cool of the room. Another woman became visible as the shadows vanished again. Nine o'clock in the morning and she was sipping a pina colada through a straw. It looked like an easter bonnet. She had to be insane to risk it. Even lunchtime was too early to be hitting one of Pansy's specials as this dark-haired girl would soon find out.

'Ned!' she shrieked. 'Have you brought my bags? I'm desperate for my sun creams. Look at my *nose*. And my *eyelids*. I'm in agony.'

Ned forced a smile to conceal his irritation. *Carry the luggage. Stop the boat rocking. Switch off the sun.* 'Sunbathing on the decks, Jewel. I warned you – '

'You an' everybody else,' cut in the man at the bar. 'If this had happened while we were shootin', babe, you'd have been on that first plane back to Houston.'

'Aw, Perce, you don't mean that.' She sucked on the straw again through pouting lips.

The blond didn't acknowledge Ned Murdoch, though she was very much aware of him.

'I'm sorry about the room,' said Hope. She turned to Pansy, who was now emerging from behind the bar. 'Which room is Miss . . . ?'

'Genevieve,' supplied the blond.

Karin Genevieve. That was the name behind the face.
' . . . Miss Genevieve in?'

'The Mary Room, Hoape.'

21

Diplomacy was called for.

'Shall we move her into the Victoria Room? I think you'll prefer that one, Miss Genevieve.'

Pansy knew better than to say it was identical in size.

Hope walked to the bar to look for the missing Perrier and crossed a downlighter. The girl with the Pina Colada giggled stupidly. The man who'd said nothing sniffed.

'Sorry,' said Hope. 'Engine oil. I didn't know you were coming or I'd have changed.' She located the Perrier but left it to Pansy to pour.

'Engine oil? Whatever sort of place have you brought us to, Neddy, darling?' said Karin Genevieve loudly, finally turning on her famous smile. 'It's a strange hotel where the mechanic decides what room the guests sleep in.'

Hope smiled good naturedly. 'We do have a few odd quirks, I must admit, but I'm sure you'll be extremely comfortable.' If you can relax and let yourself have a good time, she added to herself.

Karin's reputation preceded her everywhere. She was a bit part actress who somehow managed to get her name equally prominently into both the film credits and the gossip columns.

Hope had heard enough about Karin Genevieve to be wary. She knew that she carried trouble around with her like other people carry small change in case of crisis. But there'd been sufficient Karin Genevieve women at Sugar Mill Plantation for Hope to know how to handle this one. Kid gloves, all the way.

There were no shadows as the passengers boarded the Tristar for Antigua. The clouds over London were packed tight. A thin drizzle washed into pools across the tarmac, splashing grey stains over the sandals of the outward-bound tourists as a last reminder of home.

Andrew Dean clutched his snakeskin bag as he took his seat at the back of the plane.

Expressionlessly, he gazed out of the window, half-seeing the men and women trotting out to the plane, shrugging off the rain, anxious to begin their holidays in exotic places.

He was a small, bearded man with eyes that never

22

blinked and a soul that may as well have rotted through neglect. He spoke to no-one and no-one spoke to him.

It was his first flight since his release. But he was quite calm, perfectly confident, relaxed. He wished that he was doing the piloting, but that was all.

There was nothing to worry about.

It was going to be easy. Easy. Out there, they suspected nothing. They wouldn't know he was out of the hospital, let alone on his way back to the Caribbean. Hell! There'd been no fanfares, no bulletins, no anxious Pressmen ready to make the announcement that Andrew Dean was a free man again to the world . . . and why should there be? He was a nothing, a nobody, just one of eight hundred lunatics committed every year. He was forgotten, buried by more recent events and – he hoped – disasters.

His planning was flawless. Christ – and so it should be. He'd had plenty of time to work on it.

The only regret now was that the revenge would change nothing. There was no going back to those good times in London. Those blissful months that had given him everything that had – until then – been missing from his twisted, loveless life.

And that thought was like a crooked finger poking around in his wounded brain.

Inside, he rasped the words *Nicky, Nicky,* over and over again. But they had been robbed of their desperation by time. They were nothing more than a part of a ritual chant: a mantra.

Bitterness had magnified his relationship with Nicky; loneliness had idealised it, enlarged it until the loss was a more tangible, more poignant emotion than the love itself had ever been.

That which has been taken away is infinitely more precious than any gift. No great romantic heroes, no avenging angels, no marauding armies killed for love. They only killed for loss.

Andrew Dean stretched his legs out under the seat in front of him and glanced at his watch. He had boarded too early, giving himself time to brood, to dwell. His throat was dry and tight. He needed a cigarette.

23

The only addiction left. Nicotine. They said they'd fixed all his cravings, all his obsessions. And they'd pronounced him cured – with the comic's proviso that he kept on taking the tablets. He was certified sane. Guaranteed straight.

And what the hell did they know?

In their eyes he was a free man with no personality defects. And no fucking life.

Two years they'd spent fixing his head. Two wasted years of being a Pavlov's Dog. But he wouldn't think of it: that was over, gone, in the past, behind him. Here was the present and that woman was going to start paying for that wasted time, that wasted life.

Andrew Dean tucked his false passport into his pocket where it nestled against the old one.

Andrew Dean, meet Alan Walker. Walker – Dean, he chuckled to himself as the engines of the big plane blasted, being tested, and were cut again.

He'd taken every precaution, planned every contingency. To be on the safe side, he'd had the fore-thought to bring a gun as well as the knife. But he hoped the gun wouldn't be necessary. Where was the fun, the satisfaction, in a bullet?

Some old habits don't die, even when bombarded by Electric Shock Therapy.

My knife and I are on our way, Hopie, he thought. *Will you be pleased to see us again?*

A woman crashed a vanity case into his shoulder as she pressed close to reach into the locker above him.

'Sorree . . . ' she sang out and he quickly looked away from her.

She was ash-blond, like Hope, and it brought the memory of her vividly into his mind. Green eyes, cats' eyes, treacherous eyes that missed nothing; long, strong pianist-hands that moved like a foreigner's; endless silver hair like a siren's, like a mermaid's. No, like Medusa's.

There was no life in Dean's vision of Hope. In his mind's eye, she was already a corpse. A blind corpse with its tangling, ensnaring hair still growing.

She might have had a future to look forward to. A scarred future with that heart-shaped face touched by the

24

mark of a knife, but a future all the same. Still, silence had never been Hopie Parnell's way. It was something she couldn't learn for herself. She needed help.

She was the Venus fly-trap and she had to be eliminated before she could trap and suffocate anybody else with her spying and her marble-slab truths

He had been her victim. Now he would be her judge and her executioner.

She might plead with him, beg him, bargain with him; that would be amusing. And he might let her play out the scene to the full. It could just possibly affect the way she died, but it would do no more.

He slipped on a pair of mirrored sunglasses and the transformation was complete. There was no way for outsiders to get into his mind through the windows of his eyes.

Not that he had anything to hide. His motives were pure enough. What was revenge but a spiritual cleansing?

A baptism in blood, he thought self-righteously. *A redemption.*

Chapter Two

VERONICA MARSTON was not the old bitch Julian Winchester had described. Though she was unmarried, she loved men. Really loved them, with a passion that, had she had power instead of a pointless title, could have caused wars.

She was a latter-day Helen of Troy.

It wasn't just one or two men Veronica felt this way for, it was all men. It gave her a reputation she didn't deserve.

At the age of forty, she lived a life that most intelligent and attractive women would find unsatisfying to say the least. Veronica however considered her round of house parties in the country and missions of mercy, as she called her affairs, extremely rewarding.

Her life was financed by a small legacy – family money had gone with the major titles to her four brothers – and by her old lovers. They felt they owed her more.

Of course there had been offers of marriage. But Veronica, who was embarrassingly honest – even with herself – acknowledged that she would never be able to remain faithful to just one man. If another needed her, she would have to go to him. It was a question of instinctive priorities.

It was a conflict of emotions that took her now to Heathrow to board the British Airways 10.05 to Antigua. She travelled light, one single case to last the two weeks she planned to stay at Nelson Plantation. Her companions, Charlotte Wolff and Jessica Collier, were just about the only women in the world who shared Veronica's interests without finding her personally threatening.

Veronica fled when the going got tough.

And her liaison with Stuart Wilding had definitely got

tough. He had made demands on her that she simply couldn't fulfil. He had tested the mature relationship she'd assumed they'd had. Strained it, pulled it apart until it had burst.

Dr Stuart Wilding was both a married man and a Member of Parliament. It meant discretion should have been even more important to him than to Veronica. For years they'd met secretly and the trust between them was never broken. But that went without saying for Veronica was a woman who could be depended on never to tell tales out of bed.

Three weeks ago, they had made their final journey to the hotel in Devon where they had spent so many weekends. Neither of them had known it would be the end.

The room they were in was richly furnished in rose pinks and gold brocade. They lay together in a brass-railed four poster bed, looking out of the box bay window onto the desolate heaths of Dartmoor. Less romantic than she, Wilding reached for the television control and flipped through two channels to find cricket.

Warm and silky from sex, Veronica phoned reception for afternoon tea. It arrived after two no-balls and the silver tray was placed discreetly at the foot of the bed.

The teapot was too hot to handle, so they killed time by spreading sultana scones with thick clotted cream and raspberry jam that oozed onto their bare bodies and made the sheets sticky.

'I'm going to divorce Jannine,' said Wilding, a crumb of scone balancing on the ledge that was his chin.

'Don't be silly, darling,' said Veronica. She had heard the line more times than she could remember from one or other of her lovers. None of them meant it, it was just an expression of their love for her. She accepted it gratefully, knowing it for what it was.

'You don't believe me,' he smiled. 'But I mean it Veronica.

'Jesus, did you see that stroke from Gatting? Bloody brilliant. Actually, I've already been in touch with the solicitor.'

Her hand stopped in mid-air as it was approaching to

27

brush the crumb from his chin. The man was serious – this wasn't some convoluted flattery.

A cold chill crept up her spine till it reached the nape of her neck. Emotion wasn't Veronica's strong point – it was carefully buried beneath several layers of what passed for thick skin. But the panic she felt now was a recognisable emotion. It took the form of a rushing in the ears and blurred vision – a psychiatrist would have described it as a physical attempt to close the door on the world.

She looked at him and saw the threat to the order of her life. His own eyes never left the television screen and his voice remained casual – offhand almost. As though what he was saying had no significance whatsoever.

Shut it out, shut it out, she screamed inside.

Blindly she flew out of bed and headed for the bathroom, almost overturning the tray, scrambling into a gushing shower to cut out further discussion, to drown out the sound of his voice, her thoughts.

'Ron – what's the matter? What are you doing?'

Now he was in the room, moving anxiously from sink to door and back again. Through the water and the bubbled glass screen, she could see his hazy shape drifting. How could he fail to see what he was doing to her?

'What's up love? Say something.'

Yes, she loved him – but more than the others? They were all wonderful: all kind, considerate men who satisfied her body, amused her mind, provided for her material needs. They all needed her in their own way, but normally they acted in the set pattern of courtship, passion, cooling and friendship.

That was what she craved more than anything. To be liked – not loved. Not in the way she loved them. That would be far too consuming.

'Ron-ee. Hey, I can't work out what's going on – '

Still ignoring him, she rubbed Crystale soap between her legs into a lather and groaned with misery.

She had let the affair with Stuart Wilding last too long.

She had never broken hearts. She had always had the rare gift of being able to end a relationship without her partner realising what was happening. But Stuart had taken it too far. There would have to be an abrupt ending now and there would be no easy way to retain his affection afterwards.

His monkey-face appeared over the top of the screen. Veronica looked up and swept wet, dark brown hair out of her eyes.

'I know I've talked about it in the past, but I didn't think you'd believe me until I'd actually taken some sort of legal steps. You do love me, Ron, don't you?' He *still* didn't know.

Damn him. She viciously spun the taps and the water faded to a trickle. 'I can't hear you over the water,' she snapped.

If you can dry yourself angrily, that is what Veronica did, rubbing her white skin with such vigour that red blotches appeared from the friction. She turned her back to him in self-defence. Suddenly her nakedness was private.

'I want to marry you,' he said, placing heavy hands on her shoulders, turning her again to face him. He was doing *everything* wrong. 'I thought you'd be pleased.' But her expression was blank, silent. Without saying anything she had refused him. 'Ron, look I'm sorry. I don't know what I've done wrong. I want you and I thought you wanted me?'

She snorted. 'What was the matter with the way it was?' she demanded, clutching the towel tightly to her body. 'We've seen each other regularly. Jannine wasn't causing any problems. You've liked the way it's been, haven't you? Why bloody spoil it then?'

Anger wasn't something that came naturally, it was used for effect. But on this occasion it wasn't forced. It was genuine disappointment that her way of life, one that she had found more than pleasant, was about to be changed completely and – from her point of view – unnecessarily.

She said: 'You've had your cake and eaten it – you're one of the few men in the country who can have a wife and a mistress without either of them carping about the other. Most men would envy you.' She pulled on grey tights over white Janet Reger pants and reached for a cashmere sweater she had left hung up on the back of the bathroom door. 'Stupid bastard.' She disappeared into the sweater. 'Stupid, stupid bastard.'

He stood naked and limp in the huge, black-tiled bathroom. 'I thought you'd want to marry me. I thought that was every – sorry I don't like this expression – but every "Other Woman's" endgame.' He didn't understand. 'I thought you were playing me along when you always said no before.' He followed her back to the bedroom where she was pulling a jersey skirt over her hips, fastening pearls round her neck, slipping long, narrow feet into court shoes. 'I thought you were forcing my hand by keeping your relationships going with the others. That you were trying to make me jealous.'

She stuffed underwear from the drawers into a battered suitcase that had accompanied her round the world.

'But they do matter to you, don't they?' Now he was frantic, shouting, waving arms above his ludicrously naked body. 'You have been playing a game, you bitch, haven't you? But it's been with me. You've been using *me* to make somebody else jealous!'

'Stop it – stop it, Stuart!'

'Who is it you really want, Veronica? Do I know him?'

The crowd in Jamaica roared its approval as Gatting was caught for forty-five.

She scurried a brush through her hair as tears sprang to her eyes. 'You're being absurd.' There was no-one else who mattered more. Many who mattered equally, but none *more* than Stuart Wilding. 'You can't believe that I won't marry you because I don't want to? In your view there has to be *one* man who means more to me? That's the only reason you can accept?'

His scowl darkened because this was the truth.

'But I can't lie, Stuart, even to make it easier. There's nobody.' *Or rather there are hundreds of men in my life* . . . She had thought he'd known that instinctively. And had understood her well enough to see why it was so.

It was exactly the sort of scene she could cope with least. She was unprepared for emotional outbursts that weren't an expression of utter, undying adoration. She owed him an explanation but all her treacherous mouth would do was tremble.

She poured herself a vodka and tonic from the fridge in the room. 'Want one, Stuart?' She spoke softly and he nodded. When she turned he was dressing.

'I love you more than life, Ron,' he said. 'It just takes me more time than most men to realise these things.

'There's no point saying I've got the best of both worlds – there's only one world I want.'

She hung her head, speaking to the floor instead of to him. 'I'm sorry, Stuart. I don't trust myself to make the commitment you want. I can't be your wife, you know that.

'The publicity . . . Hell – you're an MP, and I haven't exactly got an untarnished reputation. I'd let you down, and I wouldn't be able to help it, love . . . It's the way I am. I'm safer with married men.

'But you know I'll always feel perfectly happy about being your mistress – that way there's always someone for you to go home to.'

'Home?' he erupted. 'Home? What are you talking about, woman?' He flung his glass, still half full, onto the carpet.

'Hush,' she warned, terrified of the knock on the door. 'Don't.'

'I can't bear sharing you. I can't see why you don't mind sharing me? Though in fact you don't share any part of me. My love is all yours. I haven't slept with Jannine since the first time – '

'Oh for Christ's sake! Don't start that first time drivel with me. Why do all men think women want nothing but security, romance and nostalgia? It just doesn't cut ice, Stuart.'

They were both packed now and they stormed out of the room leaving cricket still on the television and a full pot of tea, cold on the bed.

He paid the bill by cheque, not caring that the name he signed was not the one they'd booked in. It was not questioned by the hotel manager, who had recognised the face anyway.

31

Their fury subsided to sadness during the long drive home to London.

It was during the drive she decided to call Julian Winchester in Nevis to seek sanctuary.

The Alimony Wives, as she called Jessica and Lottie, would be happy to take any excuse for an impromptu trip to the West Indies, even if it wasn't The Place to go out of season. And God she needed them with her. They were her balance and her security though never her confidantes.

Escape, think things out. Disappear and hide. They were the only things Veronica knew how to do when it was she who needed help.

The women waited in the first class boarding lounge for the call. Jessica, the ex-wife of Joseph Collier (Sugar Importers) Limited, ate chocolates. Swiss ones out of the sort of box other people get as birthday presents from adoring sons. Neither Jessica nor Lottie had perpetuated their lines. Jessica had bought the chocolates for herself and sod the consequences. She had every excuse. She hated flying.

Lottie, married to assist the Wolff-Armstrong takeover bid in the late seventies and divorced two years later, when the papers were signed, shook her head as Jessica offered her the box. She closed her book on computer programming with a snap. It was too technical and never seemed to get down to the meat of the matter. She left it on the seat as they were called to board the Tristar and would remember to claim it as a loss on her insurance.

Veronica had drunk too many vodkas at the airport. And she did not intend to decline the proffered champagne on the plane.

Since their return from Devon, she and Stuart Wilding had not communicated. Yes she had seen him. Rather she had seen his car, his black Jaguar, parked on the opposite side of the street to her Kensington flat, late at night, after the House had finished sitting. He had not tried to ring her – there had been no inundations of flowers, no letters, no suicide threats passed on through friends. He was far too subtl or that.

But she had seen him waiting and had not known what he was waiting for.

One night, she turned off her light and stood by the parted curtains at her second floor sitting room window. Nothing happened. The car didn't move, Stuart didn't switch on his engine or go. Was he sleeping across her doorstep or something? Was he tailing her, watching her movements? Waiting for her to change her mind and staying so close to her that he could actually see the conversion taking place? She watched the dark, lifeless Jaguar for nearly an hour before she finally went to bed. In the morning, it was gone.

Every night, the car was there. Every morning, by seven, it had disappeared.

It was a threat she couldn't define, though Stuart was no danger to her. He was incapable of violence. Even anger – despite all the righteous show in the House – left him drained and empty. But still it invaded her privacy. She had made her decision. He should have the grace to accept it.

Lottie and Jessica knew there was some sort of emotional crisis going on. They both knew not to pry. They both ached to do so.

Jessica consoled herself with smoked salmon and quail from the luncheon menu and felt the millimetres accumulating around her hips. What the hell, she could starve tomorrow. Lottie read the Financial Times to watch the progress of Wolff-Armstrong. When shares were rising, it meant there was no excuse for a delay in the maintenance. Not that she needed it, it was the principle of the thing.

Veronica was sick in the lavatory.

'Who's the latest man-friend?' asked Jessica while she was gone.

Lottie shrugged. 'Perhaps it's not man-trouble. Perhaps it's something completely different. A business crisis. Or the Menopause.'

Jessica chuckled, forking up another pomme parisienne then wiping her wide mouth delicately on a napkin. 'Business is out. She wouldn't care less if the whole of Wall

33

Street and the Stock Exchange collapsed. And it couldn't be the change. She'd have pooled her knowledge on that one.'

'Well I can't ever remember seeing her so down before,' said Lottie, fiddling in her bag for a pack of cards for Patience.

'I'm telling you, it has to be a man. The question is, which one?'

Lottie grunted. 'Who knows?'

Veronica, composed again from a wash in cold water, emerged from the lavatory cubicle. Physically, she was fine now and would stay that way till the next drink. But her mind was a mess of confusion. Had she done the right thing in running away? She was missing him, missing his shadow. But characteristically, as School had taught her, she brushed her feelings aside the way other people brush a dusty mark from a jacket. It was too late. What was the point of worrying about things one couldn't change?

At the back of Tourist Class, in the section reserved for smokers, Andrew Dean cradled his snakeskin holdall on his lap like a baby and looked out of the window. They were over the Azores and a thick mat of cloud obscured the Atlantic. Weather forecasts in July always talked about a depression over the Azores. That was it – building and swirling over the gingerbread houses of the capital. And he was the depression above the depression.

He must be more tense than he'd thought. His head was filled with that crazy music again, those familiar dischords and ominous rhythms from The Crooked Mile that drove him mad with their monotonous pounding.

The beat confused him, made him forget his purpose, his mission. The only way to silence it was with the pills. If he went too long without them, he knew his whole world would slip into an eighth dimension, taking his brain on an endless, inescapable bad trip.

'If you find yourself stranded without the Largactils for any reason, Andy,' said the psychiatrist patronisingly, 'there are mind-tricks you can use for yourself. With practice they'll be more effective than these tranquillizers.

34

'*Try humming Christmas carols. Or nursery rhymes. Something comforting from your childhood.*

'*You'll be okay. Don't mix the pills with alcohol. And don't fall back on the speed, all right?*'

It showed how much that fucker had known about Dean's head if he thought some nightmare hymn from the black depths could drown out the cacophony that ruled him.

He'd like to tell him about it sometime. He'd like to tell Doctor Colin Harte how reassuring the treatment had been before he wired him up to his own EST equipment and fused his brain.

The punishment should always fit the crime.

He twisted the cap off the bottle of Largactil tablets and threw four into the back of his throat, swigging them down with Scotch. Easier that way.

The plane was a silver speck, a microscopic arrow in the sky over the empty Atlantic as Dean finally slept. A stewardess reached across him to pull down the blind. The light during the in-flight movie was making the other passengers complain.

Injection! screamed his inner alarm.

His eyelids flashed open like shutters and he was awake, expecting one of the hard-faced male nurses, grabbing her outstretched wrist and twisting it unnecessarily. He held it motionless for long seconds as reality filtered through. 'Don't lean over me,' he hissed at her eventually. 'Ask nicely next time.'

She was stunned by the nastiness in his tone. People on this flight – in Tourist at any rate – were normally excited to be flying out to the Caribbean. They were in good form. Drunk sometimes, but this one wasn't. She looked down at her wrist and watched red welts appearing.

'I'm sorry, sir,' she muttered. 'I was closing the shade. I'm sorry.'

He ignored her, closed his eyes and left open the blind.

In the stewards' cabin, the staff decided to leave him alone. The film was nearly over and they would have to serve tea soon. Who needed a loony freaking out when there was still another four hours' flying time? They could

35

have cabled through to Antigua, warned them, or reported the assault, but they didn't. It was only a job.

The big plane touched down smoothly in Antigua. The modern airport, concrete and glass, sweltered under the sun though black clouds were billowing on the horizon, heralding a summer storm.

Passengers emerged at the top of the steps, paused to feel the heat that first-timers to the tropics put down to the jets, and adopted the natural, slow gait that moved you from place to place with the least possible effort. The first-timers gasped as their feet touched the tarmac. The hot, damp blanket of heavy air – like opening a bread-oven – was no less once you were away from the jets.

Veronica Marston and her friends were already safely in the transit lounge, waiting to be told their plane was ready for takeoff. If you've got money, moving around an airport can be remarkably easy.

Andrew Dean was the only other passenger to Nevis. In the queue through customs, he was at the back. He watched as a tiny plane, one of Hope Parnell's small fleet, taxied in from the runway. Jesus what irony – that was *his* plane. His own little Cessna.

The woman in front of Andrew Dean hadn't filled in her immigration papers. 'I'm only staying for a week,' she whined at the official on the desk. She was already drooping from the sudden change in temperature and longing for air-conditioning.

'You gotta do de form, mahdam,' he grinned at her, glancing surreptitiously at the pile of identical green forms he'd already processed into the waste basket beneath the counter.

Dean stepped towards him, his feet tap-dancing with impatience and irritation. He was a big man in a beige uniform and a peaked cap.

'Back behind de line, mahn!' he barked.

Dean looked down. His toe was across it by one inch. He settled his face into an amiable mask. 'My plane's in,' he called. 'I'm in transit.'

He rubbed his thumb against his fingers and the customs

man nodded and beckoned. A five dollar Eastern Caribbean note was exchanged.

Andrew Dean was waved over to collect his bags from the Heathrow plane without his passport being checked, without the immigration form, and without a hand-luggage search.

The Goose wasn't in any fit state to fly passengers. Oz Lennox was flying the neat little Cessna in a round of island hopping. He handed down the Canadians from Manor Inn as they climbed out for their overnight stop on the island so they could say they'd 'done' Antigua when they got back home.

Oz looked towards the airport for the next lot back. There were four according to the list, three for Nelson Plantation, one independent. It left four empty seats but he was too far behind schedule to go touting for more customers.

And there they were, coming over now.

The Honourable Veronica Marston was the willowy brunette sweeping along the tarmac with a linen coat flapping around her shoulders. One arm grasped a jewel case, the other held on to a wide-brimmed white hat. Jess Collier, an even more frequent visitor to Nevis, was blooming despite her irrational fear of flying. Lottie Wolff waved to him in recognition. She'd changed, gone sharper, more angular: yet she'd been a real looker a few years ago. Oz remembered she had once been involved with the other wolf on the island – Terry Morelands.

The man was a puzzle. Small, thin, bearded and hidden behind mirrored sun glasses. The name on the list said Alan Walker. The name didn't mean anything to Oz, but there *was* something familiar . . .

He threw open the door to the hold amid cries of 'lovely to see you,' and let porters stack the luggage inside. Andrew Dean loaded his own trunk, propping it between the rear seat and the stack of lifejackets as though it was fragile.

Jessica Collier struggled with the step into the plane's body. She wrinkled up her pencil skirt till Oz's eyes popped at her long expanse of bare thigh. With any luck, getting out would be just as good.

Jessica saw his eyes and tried to angle her body to hide what she thought of as her fat. Once in, laughing to cover her embarrassment, she settled into the two seats nearest his own. The others boarded quietly.

He spoke briefly to control at Antigua and told the passengers to put their belts on. Jessica leant forward nervously to peer through the front window.

'Shouldn't there be a co-pilot?' she worried.

'Never has been, Jess. All the flying you do, you should be used to it by now,' said Veronica.

Andrew Dean lit a cigarette – he could do what the hell he wanted in his own plane and let this bastard try to tell him different. He remembered the black pilot vaguely – he'd flown passengers while Dean had shipped dry goods and their paths had rarely crossed. Oz would never remember him.

Jessica sniffed smoke and gaped in horror as the neon fasten seat belts, no smoking sign winked at her in mockery.

Oz said nothing, right now he fancied a roll-up himself; he gave further co-ordinations to Antigua and received clearance for take-off.

Easy-easy the plane slipped into forward thrust and the little bird soared into the dense, impossibly blue sky, fierce sun blazing on its wings and currents bobbing its light carriage upwards.

For five minutes there was nothing but sea. Emptiness.

Then there was a shadow on the water, gleaming like moss, changing as the sun shifted, until its shape finally identified it as St Kitts. Where the water touched the sky, to the west, a thread of storm clouds was growing and billowing, spreading tentacles towards the Cessna which slipped away faster than it could be snatched.

In twenty minutes, the sky had nearly caught up with them, but they were crossing the short channel from St Kitts to Nevis, skimming round the volcanic jungle. There was no traffic control at Nevis. But where Hope used her eyes for landing, Oz preferred the dials and instrumentation – when they were working.

He located the runway by sight and reduced altitude and speed to give a soft landing on the bubbling tarmac below. The customised retros blasted satisfyingly, thundering behind his slipstream. Oz felt like a god, like Thor.

The passengers unloaded themselves – Jessica Collier in a blur of flashing thighs, blue lace and seams; Veronica accepting his hand gracefully and Lottie refusing any help despite the four foot drop. Andrew Dean jumped out easily, like a pilot, and Oz began to wonder again. He unloaded the cases, Dean's last, and stacked them ready to collect on a trolley.

Together they walked to customs as the rains caught them. First there was a splash of water that no-one outside the Caribbean would describe as a raindrop. Then another: 'Terrific start!' sniffed Lottie. 'Bad as London. Two drops of rain the second we get to Nevis and we're soaked!'

'How long will it last?' gasped Jessica, jogging uncomfortably for the shelter of the airport building.

Oz looked up to the sky. It was a big cloud, alright. He'd been watching it since just after take-off and hoping they'd get to Nevis before it could start buffetting them. 'Could be an hour – could last overnight. It should rain itself out by morning. No problem. Have you a car waiting?'

Veronica told him Julian Winchester should be waiting in his big Datsun.

With just a few yards to go to the customs hut, the skies opened. The rain fell as if it regretted being birthed in the sky instead of as a waterfall. Everyone hurried into the bare room but Veronica.

Oz turned to see where she was. Her arms were outstretched, her head thrown back. Rivulets of water streamed through her hair and over her face. The hat was lying in a pool of water by her feet. And she was laughing joyously.

'It's *hot* rain! Lovely warm, warm rain,' she cried, twirling and pirouetting till she was thoroughly soaked.

Jessica and Lottie stared with open mouths. Oz roared with laughter. 'There's one sensuous lady,' he thought to himself. Shame she wasn't staying at Hope's place. Shame they weren't all staying at The Mill come to think of it. Might relieve the summer silence.

There was no-one in the customs house. The ramshackle wooden building reverberated to the sounds of the unleashed elements and pools were already forming on the floorboards. At the start of the rains, whichever officer had been on duty had decided nothing was worse than being 'stranded, maybe overnight, in the leaky hut and made a dash for home.

Oz thought ruefully of the consignment of marijuana he might have brought in under the circumstances. He could have foiled Bardram yet again.

He shepherded the women out to the waiting Datsun and turned to find the man registered as Alan Walker.

He wasn't there. And no-one could remember just when he'd disappeared.

Chapter 3

GRECIAN GOLD sandals wound their way round Karin Genevieve's calves like snakes. They were several shades lighter than her luscious skin tone.

At the entrance to the top pool, she saw Ned Murdoch. He'd skipped lunch to recuperate from the voyage, lying full-length on the sun-bed, soaking up the sun's rays like a hunk of blotting paper.

This was the first time she'd managed to get him alone. On the boat, there were always the others. And the crew. And, of course, King.

Well King could go and screw himself. Did he think he owned her?

She felt over-full from her meal of grated carrots and lettuce and pulled in her stomach muscles.

Somebody called 'Byee!' and Karin stood on tiptoe to peer over an enormous hibiscus. She watched as an open-topped Moke roared out of the drive. The director, Jimmy Percival, was driving the others round the island before the predicted rains came. Hope Parnell had told them they had at least an hour, though how the hell could she know? Shee-it, she was as bad as a Detroit cab driver.

Karin sat on the beach bed next to Ned and angled her bare breasts towards the sky.

He didn't look up at her; just lay there, with his eyes filtering the sun.

He must have known she was there – felt her presence. His silence irritated her. She felt provocative, sexy. If he didn't want to notice her, she could make him.

'I suck cocks better than anyone in the entire world,' she cooed.

Ned Murdoch stiffened, but it was his body, and not the

41

specific organ intended that was reacting.

'Is that what you think I want?' he said sleepily.

'Well of course it is. Isn't it?'

Dolphins' mouths, carved out of the natural rock of the cliff spilled gin-clear water into the oval pool. From there, a waterfall flowed down to the two lower pools.

'Let me get you a drink, darling, while you think about it,' she said, moving her feline body sensuously off the sun-yellow couch.

He watched her walk to the open bar, cut into the cliff like a cave. She was long and thin, with those bare, conical breasts tipped by little pink nipples that pointed at her chin. Her waist could be spanned by a necklace; her tight buttocks swelled like polished ostrich eggs beneath the wisp of ecru silk. What a pity he didn't like her very much.

Being played with didn't amuse Ned. Sex games and mind games weren't his scene. If she wanted to put out, fine. If she was out for her own ends and it happened to satisfy him into the bargain, that was fine too.

And that body, if it was on offer – what man could resist? Not even Ned Murdoch.

Just as long as there was no bullshit.

He had realised the situation between Karin and the producer, King, the second day out of Barbuda. They had an off and on relationship. It was off when they boarded, on when they'd sailed, and off enough now for her to be chasing Ned. That lady was screwed up. Either that or she wasn't screwed up enough.

Karin ladled out rum punch from the silver tureen that stood in the cool of the bar and added an extra measure of rum for Ned. She fluffed out the blond hair and strolled back lazily, pelvis first.

He'd turned over and was lying with hands propping up his chin, shaggy hair curling into the apex of his shoulder blades. He was peering through the slender branches of a blossoming shrub to watch Hope Parnell at the mill below. She was sitting in the shade of the old building at a white wrought-iron table, going through documents and signing papers. By her side was a bottle of white wine from which she refilled her glass as he watched.

42

Karin slipped off her sandals and looked over to see what was drawing Ned.

The Mechanic.

She popped an ice cube down the back of his trunks to regain his attention.

There was nothing like a bit of premeditated spontaneity.

With a yell of indignation, he spun round. Karin put the drinks delicately on the tiled pool surround and licked droplets of water from her fingers, running her pointy tongue from her palm to the finger tips. Her nipples hovered two inches away from his teeth. 'Shall I dry you?' she murmured, running her tongue over her upper lip.

Ned rolled his eyes and fiddled down his pants to remove what was left of the ice cube. Her eyelids closed to a slit, the way King had told her to pose for the advance publicity shots. 'I might do that again if you like it.'

'I didn't,' he said, grinning despite himself and aware of his growing sexual interest.

'I might do it again because you didn't like it then,' Karin pouted, jiggling her breasts sulkily.

He moved in a flash, making a grab for her long thighs, snarling at her, and she was into the pool, diving gracefully like a bird into the deep, sun-warmed water. She surfaced, shaking droplets from her hair like a wet puppy in time to see him leap in after her.

With a little scream – the director, Perce, would have said it was very realistic – she twirled and swam for the far side as Ned snaked like a torpedo after her.

Coming up for air, he said: 'There's only so much I can take.'

She arranged herself on the top pool step with the leg facing Ned lower than the other. The three-quarter angle was the one she most favoured. At the moment he reached her, she pulled the tiny silk strings at the side of her pants and they fell as easily as autumn leaves.

Her hand traced lines with sharp, red fingernails on her inner thighs, stopping as they reached her naked pubis. She looked into his eyes to see whether he was shocked or excited by her depilated body and read excitement. The

43

fingers slipped out of sight and the water lapped at her passion's centre.

Ned, holding onto the chrome rails squirmed towards her. He could taste her before his mouth was there. His mouth was open, ready to suck in her smooth flesh, run his tongue into her oily warmth. But she was sliding downwards, between his legs, under the water, to fasten her lips on the hard cock she was releasing from his pants.

For a long time, he could feel the pressure of her cool mouth, rubbing up and down him, seeking out his most sensitive points, then she was bobbing before him, gulping air before another wave of exquisite sensation overtook him as she submerged again.

This is crazy, he thought and laughed aloud.

The warm water of the pool lapped around them, into them. Karin came up for another deep breath and his arms were around her tiny waist, clasping her to him as he angled his cock into her vagina.

As the wisp of ecru silk descended the waterfall to the lower pool, Karin cried out. The hilt of his penis scraped against her clitoris in agonising ecstasy. She wrapped her thighs around him, pushing out from the side of the pool into deeper water. Coupled like porpoises they wove through the blue waters in absolute unison, weightless, blind to anything other than the feelings in their greedy bodies and the look in each other's eyes: the look that says I love you, whoever you are, and I love me and I love us together like this. But only for the moment.

Then he was coming, her muscles twisting around his organ so that it felt like a hand milking him to an inevitable climax. And she was coming, pushed over the edge by thoughts of the new situation, control over another man, a delight in her own body, her own skill.

Ripples from their orgasm echoed in their flesh and the water bubbled around them from their turbulence.

As Karin opened her eyes she looked straight into Hope's. She was standing by the pool dangling the bikini bottoms from an outstretched finger. Ned's back was to her and he was unaware of Hope's existence, let alone of her presence at that moment.

Karin thought she'd better have another climax in case Hope had missed the first and writhed around on Ned's cock to create the necessary effect.

Hope placed the pants on the sun-bed and walked away, adjusting her sunglasses.

'Damn, she missed the best bit,' thought Karin, who hadn't yet reached full song. She gave up and wriggled away, leaving Ned to regain his own balance and composure.

Hope had had the starlet moved into the Victoria room as soon as she'd finished dealing with her guests in the bar that morning. All the bungalows were the same though all looked totally different inside. The Victoria room was one that she particularly liked and, in fact, occupied during the winter when one of the guests specifically wanted her own Mill Suite.

Like all the rooms, it was split-level, taking advantage of the contours of the cave- and flower-strewn cliffs. The bedroom was at the back, where the coolness of the rocks penetrated the limestone walls most effectively. A gallery at the end of the room, completely dominated by an elderly, mahogany half-tester bed, draped in a gauze mosquito net, looked out onto the double-storeyed window.

The view was incredible. As one of the highest of the bungalows on the estate, it commanded a spectacular panorama. On a clear night, you could see the lights of Montserrat and Barbuda, if you could distinguish them from the fireflies in the frangipani trees below.

The marble-floored sitting area, furnished with good English reproduction antiques was at ground level, screened off from the dressing room and twin bathrooms by a fixed Chinese screen. Outside was a terrace where guests could take breakfast privately or shelter under the ceiling of clematis vines from the hot sun in the afternoon.

Hope felt the Genevieve woman should be pleased with the room. She had even arranged Nelson Plantation's Birds of Paradise flowers in a crystal vase for her and placed it by the bed. The flowers weren't completely dead; they could easily last another two days with care.

But she hadn't even looked at the new room yet, thought

Hope, as she walked away from the poolside where she had seen the starlet with the cocksman-yachtsman. She felt an unaccountable pang of annoyance. She had sensed intuitively that Ned Murdoch did not like his passengers. What kind of game did he play?

If she hadn't seen their frenzied activity for herself, she wouldn't have thought it a likely pairing. She decided to go and make trouble in the kitchen to take her mind off what she'd seen. Her annoyance was countered by an unpleasant sense of arousal that both disturbed and confused her.

Rachel, the cook, should have been baking bread ready for dinner, but the kitchen was empty and the stove cold. Hope looked anxiously about the spotlessly clean room. Lunch dishes had been washed and put away, mounds of fresh fruit - yellow bananas, green bananas, pawpaws, prickly pears and soursop - were washed and stacked on serving plates.

Sticky coconut cakes, covered in muslin to keep off the flies, were heaped into pyramids for afternoon tea. The lobsters and conch were alive and lumbering gloomily around the old water storage tank, meticulously scrubbed out for the purpose.

Her eyes fell on the evening's guest list. Four of the film party, Ned Murdoch, the lecher Terry Morelands, herself and Oz, who was treating himself on his housemaid's night off.

Hope always dined with the guests. For a start, it helped when they were a small party to make people feel relaxed. It also gave the impression that guests were staying with friends rather than paying for a holiday. It made the outrageous bill easier to face when it came.

Outside there were noises. She left the Great House kitchen and walked into the garden, where vegetables and fruit grew in profusion.

Pansy and Rachel the cook, together with three of Rachel's youngest children, were bent over a thymus bush, making the sort of noises senators make to babies.

Rachel looked up at Hope: 'Kipper have her kittens,' she called. 'She eat two but they four left. What we do to stop her eating the rest?'

Hope heaved a sigh. She didn't feel mad enough any more to make a scene. Kipper's pregnancy had been a source of so much interest to everyone – especially Rachel's children.

'We could take them indoors? Give Kipper some proper food? I don't know, Rachel. I don't know that much about that sort of thing. Are their eyes open?'

She went back indoors and packed an old fruit crate with newspapers to load the new-borns into. They'd need warmth and milk. If they were outside and vulnerable the wild dogs might get them, though it wasn't to become the general policy to have animals in the kitchen, she told Rachel and the children.

The kittens squeaked like mice as they were loaded one by one into the box and transported to a warm place.

Outside, the sky was darkening. Hope wished it would rain properly before the seductive Karin had managed to get herself back to her room.

Rachel began the process of bread-making while Pansy laid tables in the lounge for tea. All the tables were set whether anyone turned up or not. There were pretty, white lace table-cloths spread with linen napkins and silver cake knives and forks, Dresden china cups and saucers, dishes of jams and conserves flown over regularly from Harrods; the Sugar Mill was an English country house in the heart of the West Indies.

Hope wandered back to the mill and her plane schedules, mentally checking that all the arrangements were satisfactory. She'd fixed up the chef, Robert Lane. She'd phoned through to her friend, Esme Little, who had agreed to take over her flights till the hotel was emptied of its unexpected visitors.

She wished she could use her regularly. Esme could do with the cash after her recent separation. Her *and* the two kids. But sadly on Nevis you had to put your own interests first. And summer on the island would drive Hope mad unless she had an excuse to leave it.

It would drive her mad, too, she thought, to never return.

Tom Parnell had been a BOAC pilot till he launched IN-Flight from Nevis, back in the sixties. Hope rarely thought about him now, keeping him out of her head deliberately, the way you forget a nightmare.

It was a technique she had perfected through practice.

It wasn't that she hadn't loved her father – far from it – it was simply that when he invaded her mind, she was incapable of dealing with the present. The now. The memory of him was a destructive thought, a sadness that could consume her, in direct contrast to the person he'd been. The grief did him no justice at all.

It was while she was in her final term at boarding school that he was killed in a crash in St Vincent, overshooting the airstrip there and ploughing headlong into a palm grove.

A Press photographer had been on the spot. There were pictures. Pictures of a fireball.

Hope's stepmother, Stella, had been heart-broken. They said you couldn't die from a broken heart? Tell that to Stella.

Enough money was put in trust for Hope to ensure she never wanted for anything – finishing schools, secretarial college, an allowance, a home in the country . . .

Balls to that, Hope told the executors and she used a part of her legacy for flying lessons, not knowing whether or not she was doing it in defiance of – or to please – her father. Their mutual love of planes was the one bond that could never be broken; and that one thought had spurred her on. Subconsciously, she was still looking for his approval when there was no more to be given.

Hope had originally taken on the hotel to give herself a base. It started as a whim but grew into a passion.

In the beginning, when she first came over to handle the West Indies side of IN-Flight, she had lived in one of the rented houses, built like Roman villas around central courtyards in the Cliff area. But it had seemed too temporary, that vast, white building with the staff appointed by the villa's Canadian owners. It was wasted on her.

She and the senior partner, Nick David, had talked about her diversifying to give herself an extra income. Nick

48

had his London-based accountancy practice. She had nothing but the minority shares in IN-Flight and the remains of the trust fund.

He possessed the financial know-how, she could fly planes and manage people. As long as she could continue to control operations from on the spot, Nick saw the sense in arranging the money for the investment in Sugar Mill Plantation.

They restored the Great House, flew in linen and china, Osborne and Little fabrics, hand-cut Mexican tiles, Persian carpets. Neither Nick nor Hope believed in half measures. They both had the same desire to be best at whatever they did.

Hope turned out to be a natural. After just one winter season, Fisher's Guide rated Hope Parnell's country estate: *'Deluxe. As comfortable as your own home, and better service.'* By the next edition the Sugar Mill was printed with five red stars next to its name and hyperbole followed hyperbole. It was now described as *'BEST of the best. On a par with Young Island. Wear Dior to dinner.'*

Had someone tried to force Hope at knife-point to make a choice between the Plantation and flying she would have refused. They were equal loves that kept her as firmly tied to Nevis as chains might have done. But that was the beauty of her situation: there *were* no chains when you could fly.

By the end of the last season, they had virtually bought out investors. The only loans that were left were kept on for tax advantages.

It was a perfect arrangement. Nick had the minor share in the hotel: it was enough to keep him sufficiently interested to watch over its finances like a hawk. Even a minor shareholding in the two-point-two million dollar estate secured its priority among Nick David's other interests.

Though speculators on the island thought of Nick as Hope's sugar daddy when he came to stay at the Plantation, they were wrong. There had never been any intimacy between them. For a start, Nick was Hope's much older step-brother. Secondly, he was, though married and the father of two future accountants, a part-time homosexual.

He was also the only one who knew the truth about her fading scars.

Hope folded the schedules back into the file. The four-plane fleet would be well-occupied over the next month with private runs for the rich ex-pats to the shopping centres of Miami and St Croix in the Virgins. The island dwellers could no more do without their YSL gowns and their Givenchy aftershaves than the relatives they'd left back home.

IN-Flight's reputation was built on efficiency and immediate attention – it was rather like an air-borne taxi service.

The third pilot Gem Welch – a dab-hand with electricals – would have fixed The Goose by now and it would be in good order and ready for Oz's champagne and pills run to Miami tomorrow.

She checked her watch and glanced into the sky. Right on cue, the Cessna appeared round the side of the mountain, heading for the airstrip. A spot of rain fell onto the one letter Hope had left out for posting, spreading the fresh ink into a dizzy, translucent swirl on the envelope. Her weekly letter to Nick. He was possessive, over-protective these days. Hope didn't need him to be this way, but she allowed him the luxury of worrying for his own sake. If the trans-Atlantic phone calls and the letters made him feel good, if they helped him to get over his guilt, then it was the least she could do. She wiped the envelope absentmindedly with the back of her hand and slipped it with the others into the folder.

Above her, by the top pool, Ned threw a sweatshirt over his head. He had fallen asleep in the sun after his love-making with Karin Genevieve. He glanced over to the couch next to his. The woman lay full-length, breathing deeply. Her back was a uniform golden colour, unbroken by any white bikini marks. Her hair streamed silkily downwards, perfectly dry and golden, the colour of corn.

She did not move him and he ignored the gorgeous, sleeping figure to hurry back to his room. He did not intend to be caught in the rain that was about to fall. This time it was going to be a real squall.

He was stopped in his tracks, again, by the sight of Hope Parnell, bending over a briefcase, draining a glass of wine, slipping feet into strappy sandals.

Their eyes met and he waved. Hope thought for a split second then lifted her glass to him, pretending to drink a toast though the glass was empty. Ned missed the irony of the gesture. But Karin Genevieve, woken by the sounds of movement around her, did not.

The 'Mechanic', as she thought of Hope, had cleaned up and looked far too smug for someone who had recently witnessed a perfect demonstration of how the ideal sex-symbol should behave.

She reached for her bikini bottoms and asked Ned to serve his obeisance by passing her a towel. There was no reply and she looked round, annoyed. Ned was already making his way down the cobbled path to Hope.

The maxim 'win some, lose some' didn't occur to Karin. Mainly because lose wasn't in her vocabulary. Sooner or later an opportunity would arise for her to make Hope look the prissy Miss Moffat she suspected she was, preferably with the great lover-boy's help. If she put a foot wrong, Karin would be ready to jump.

The taxi, a very ancient Mercedes, drove out of the airport car-park towards Charlestown.

'Dis rain won't last,' announced the driver to Andrew Dean. 'It comin' early today – it usually rain at night and then de days are nothing but sunshine.' He ignored his passenger's indifference.

'See over there on de right?' He waved towards a coconut grove and a small beach where old oil cans and newspapers nestled between gargantuan bull rushes. The clouds appeared to touch the tops of the trees as they bent beneath the sheets of rain, now falling by the gallon from an ugly, bruise-coloured sky.

Dean looked over, despite himself.

'Dat's where Admiral Nelson first come ashore. You knowed he married Fanny Nisbet on dis island?'

51

There was no reply.

He tried again: 'How long you stayin' in Nevis?'

Dean ground his teeth: 'I don't like prying.'

'You had a bad flight over?' Driver Arthur Arthurs was never discouraged. He had softened up more hard guys than any government P.R.O. – and he did it for free. That was the way he was.

'You want me to pick you up tomorrow for a tour of the island? I knowed the whole history and ev'ry jack-rabbit by name.' As if to prove his point, he slowed down as another car approached on the same side of the road and each pulled over to the side they should have been on. Arthur Arthurs flashed his headlights, hooted and waved. The other driver did likewise. They exchanged a few fast words in patois.

'I show you the penitentiary where dere's still ghosts, an' de bath-house. Everybody want to see de bath-house,' he said as they drove on again.

'I've seen it.'

'You been in Nevis before. I knowed it when I seein' you.'

Oh yeah, Andrew Dean knew island people. They were the same throughout the Caribbean. They 'knowed' everything with hindsight.

Dean glanced out of the window again, watching trees like telegraph poles steaming in a short burst of sun between the rain. For a moment, a doubt crossed his mind. Could he maybe have been recognised?

No! Impossible.

Throughout his exile, he'd been in Nevis only three, maybe four times. He'd insisted on being based in Miami and the Turqs so he could be well in the swing of the money and the deals.

Nevis had had nothing to offer him.

His own memories of the island were hazy; they were limited to little more than the airport, a few of the tourist spots and Sugar Mill Plantation itself. But how reliable *were* his memories, while his mind was still playing those weirdo tricks on him?

The car took a bend in the road at fifteen miles an hour

and below them stretched little Charlestown, the capital of Nevis, the prettiest harbour town in the world.

The brightly painted wooden houses, some no bigger than chicken shacks, lined the two main roads, one leading to the St Kitts ferry, the other to the indoor market. Dazzling material that could have been shirts or skirts or dresses, for they were of an indeterminate shape, adorned washing lines that reached from hooks on the houses to little picket fences that marked out territory. Every now and then, an abandoned ruin of someone's home stood neglected in what appeared to be a building site, for further back in the garden, behind the ruins, men were piecing together breeze blocks. Some of the new houses were further advanced than others. Some had reached the roofing stage with low slatted beams covering the tiny rooms created below. The new houses didn't look much different to the old, abandoned ones.

Andrew Dean, lean, hungry and rational as Cassius while the pills were still working, wasn't aware of any of this. Nor was he aware of the open-topped Moke heading towards them, or of its passengers, two men and the budding movie-star Jewel Dankworth, shrieking with excitement from the rain's lashing as they careered down the narrow streets. He was too busy cursing himself for betraying the fact that he was no stranger to Nevis.

Arthur Arthurs pulled up outside the stairs to the apartment Andrew Dean had rented. Opposite, little Jenny Smith, the newspaper seller and evangelist, waved a greeting and called to Dean to be sure and be at the One God Church on Sunday. She knew all strangers needed to be made to feel at home.

Dean let the driver carry in the heavy case that had escaped the attention of authority. He carried the holdall himself and together they climbed the sagging stairs to his apartment above the police station.

He had packed in a lot of reading while he was in Broad-moor, and *The Purloined Letter* had given him the idea. He was going to be right on top of the cops. It would be the last place anyone would bother to look for a killer.

Chapter Four

THE BRAND new orange Datsun glided between the stone pillars that marked the entrance to Nelson Plantation. On the top of the pillars were the heraldic symbols that Julian Winchester claimed were Admiral Lord Nelson's family crest. He told Americans it was something to do with the US Secretary to the Treasury, Alexander Hamilton instead, knowing that Nelson was of no interest outside Europe.

The white stone walls, traced in patterns by monstrous campanula and golden saxifrage, had been there even before Nelson and were of far more interest to Veronica Marston. The Great House stood, reassuring and tranquil, in its hiding place of jacaranda and tulip trees.

'Thank goodness,' she breathed.

'Everything's the same,' said Jessica. 'Excellent.'

'But you're here for the blossoms this time,' said Julian Winchester, pointing to the glorious, scarlet and rather wicked-looking flowers dripping from the tulip tree. 'That's got out of hand. The more you cut it, the bigger it gets. They always say that growth follows the knife.'

'It's put out another six branches since March,' said Jessica. 'You wouldn't believe it possible.' Petals from the flowers had dropped onto the grey cobbles lining the court-yard to be swept by the torrential rains towards discreet gullies.

He drove to the front door, where three, blue-uniformed maids waited with open umbrellas.

'What, no red carpet?' said Jessica, swinging out from the back seat. 'Watch that puddle, Ron.'

Inside, tea was already waiting for them, Earl Grey in proper china pots, its delicate aroma beckoning them.

'Shall Suzannah unpack for you ladies?' asked Julian.

'Mm, please.' Veronica was handing her soaked hat and coat to one of the maids while Lottie poured the tea.

Comfortably, she settled herself into a familiar armchair, a gold velvet Parker Knoll that might or might not have been one of her uncle's, shipped over when the old Viscount died. There was a painting of her great-grandmother, stern but beautiful, even in the high-necked black dress worn in mourning for Victoria. A Chippendale chair was placed before the Bechstein piano she had been allowed to play early in the evening at family gatherings as a child. Now she could play it any time she was in Nevis, but she had no wish to do so.

Though Julian knew of her connection with the Cambridgeshire estates from which Nelson Plantation had been partly furnished, it was never referred to. It would have been unutterably bad taste since Veronica's childhood home was now owned by the National Trust.

Veronica never regretted the past nor lusted after the trappings of wealth that Jessica said should have been her heritage. What was gone was gone. And besides, it was here for her pleasure – so who cared who legally owned it?

She sipped the fragrant tea, relaxed and stretched long, bare legs that would soon be brown to wriggle her toes in the pile of the Axminster carpet.

'Let's hope it brightens up,' said Jessica, walking over to the expanse of glass that overlooked tropical jungle and, far below, the desolate black beaches and stormy waters of the Atlantic side.

'What does it matter?' said Lottie, overcome by a sense of bonhomie and luxury. 'It's hotter than England, even though it's raining. And it's a darn sight more beautiful than London.'

'What are we going to do while we're here? Shall we go over to Montserrat? And St Kitts?'

'Jessica!' gasped Veronica. 'You've been here precisely thirty minutes and you're already anxious to be on the move. You can't sit still for a moment!

'I, on the other hand, shall relax. Read. Swim when nobody's looking. Walk to keep me from putting on too much weight.'

She's here to convalesce, thought Lottie. Aloud, she said: 'I have lists of things I'm *not* doing. I'm not watching television. I'm not reading any English papers. I don't want to know if Reagan blows up the whole world. Or even if Capital Gains Tax is doubled. As long as the Caribbean's all right, that's what matters to me.'

They each went to their rooms. Veronica's was simply furnished – a wooden-framed bed covered with a sunflower-embroidered counterpane, a bentwood chair and a cane dressing table were the only things in the bedroom. Patio doors led into a private little garden where a stone fountain was surrounded by star-shaped flowers that were heavy with the rain. Under an awning were stacked three folded chairs and a wooden slatted table.

A second door from the bedroom took her into an enormous, cool dressing room. She slid open the doors to the wardrobe and saw her clothes hanging and pressed in perfect order. Her coat and hat were missing. They would be returned to her when they had dried out sufficiently.

The bathroom was almost all bath, sunken into the Italian-tiled floor. There were mirrors everywhere and they reflected a Veronica Marston that looked like her own ghost. Her hair had dried straggly from the rain; there were circles under her eyes. Though her headache and nausea had vanished, she looked her age, possibly for the first time in her life.

'I should have spent a week at Champney's before my week here,' she thought, running water to fill the bath. It ran slowly, but that didn't matter. Quickly she stripped off her travelling clothes, putting them straight into the linen basket to be cleaned.

There was no air conditioning – not even a fan – at the Nelson. It didn't need it. Through the open patio doors, the cool breeze filtered into the rooms, bringing with it the scent of jasmine and honeysuckle.

Despite herself, her thoughts kept returning to Stuart Wilding, wondering whether he was a survivor. Her emotions were in a turmoil. To hurt someone she loved should have been unthinkable – beyond her. And it hadn't been. She had deliberately turned him away – perhaps at

56

the moment he needed her most.

He must have known she had seen him, waiting outside each night. He must have interpreted it as a final rejection when she refused to acknowledge him. She doused her hair in cold water and vigorously lathered on shampoo.

She'd known he hadn't loved Jannine from the start. When men thought they were pulling a fast one, they behaved differently, cockily, sneakily. Stuart Wilding had never done that. And it was a relief.

But it was different when he had first confessed that Jannine actually knew about Veronica. That she was aware of their affair and *didn't mind*. It was freakish - perverse. Unnatural. And Veronica had called the whole thing off immediately, only to return to him after she'd worked out that in fact this made the situation even more honest and open. Even more acceptable.

It was an open marriage, he'd said. Chains destroyed rather than bonded people together. That revelation had taken her by surprise; it was outside her experience. But eventually she had reconciled herself to the fact that this relationship did not have to be concealed from the one person most men dreaded finding out.

They had still been discreet, of course. The Press was their main danger as mutual friends were no threat.

Even so, Veronica told no-one. Why break the habit of a lifetime?

The only other people who knew about the liaison were fellow MPs at the House, where a camaraderie existed to prevent such scandals reaching the ears of the electorate.

Veronica had always been brutally honest with Stuart Wilding. When she told him she loved him, she meant it deeply. But her love for him did not exclude her love for any of the others who had claimed a piece of her to keep for eternity.

On occasions, she had gone to them when they were lonely, ill or sad - even when it had meant cancelling an arrangement she had already made with Stuart Wilding. She knew when someone else needed her more, and in her openness, she expected him to see it too. She never went without a qualm of conscience, but she went because it was

57

something she simply had to do. Sometimes she slept with them if it might make them feel better. Sometimes she didn't.

When Stuart stopped asking questions about her disappearance, she felt that he had grown accustomed to her ways and had understood. And because of this 'understanding' she assumed he would never have put her in the position of being forced to end what had been the longest-enduring love of her life.

She rinsed the creamy soap from her hair and climbed into the now-full bath, submerging beneath the softness of the water.

Now she missed him; now it was she who was suffering. She wondered which of her lovers she could call on for the sort of comfort she had given them undemandingly in the past. But there was no one who would not see it as a weakness, who would not take advantage of her distress to turn it to emotional profit for himself.

Did it all come down to self-satisfaction then? Was there a motive behind every kindness, every smile?

Perhaps she had not given so unselfishly of herself as she had thought. Look at the ways in which she had been rewarded . . .

She ran through the list of jewels, dresses, holidays, cars and homes she had received from her past lovers, and wondered just how much they had been her incentive. Then she dismissed the thought utterly. Everything she had done had been performed willingly and without expecting payment.

No, there was no ulterior motive behind friendship, behind love.

She reached forward and pulled the plug release handle and felt herself as well as the water being drained.

Karin Genevieve turned her back to Jewel Dankworth to allow her to pull the zip up to the back of her neck.

'Your nose is hideous,' crowed Karin. 'How could you be so silly as to let it get in that state?'

Jewel peered into the gilt-framed mirror in Karin's dressing room and stroked the offending organ tenderly.

'It's not that bad. If you want to see something *really* bad you should look at Perce's legs.'

Karin yelped. 'Perce has *legs*? Beneath that great body there are legs? And me to look at them? No way. No thank you. I'm far happier basking in the sunshine of King's adoration.'

This was a lie. At this moment, Karin had no interest in the producer's adoration. And despite the delectable prospect of destroying the budding affair between Jewel and the powerful director, Jimmy Percival, she had no interest in him either. Ned Murdoch was the one. And Ned Murdoch had not succumbed. She would have like to crow: *Abandon Hope all ye who enter here,* but it would have been inappropriate.

He had screwed her and gone, mentally, if not physically. And Karin had no doubt that he would have left her physically too if he had seen an opportunity for himself with Hope. It didn't please her at all. Once they'd bitten, they were normally hooked for ages. Months, sometimes.

'Have you got any Clarins aftersun?' said Jewel, still inspecting the rosy nose. 'I ran out and nothing else suits me.'

Karin pointed to the dresser where there were enough cosmetics and sun preparations to rival any pharmacy.

Jewel rifled through the pots of nail varnish, boxes of false eyelashes, body shiners and powders.

'This is auto-tan!' she shrieked triumphantly. 'You've got a fake tan. I wondered why you never burned!'

'Crap!' Karin snatched the bottle out of Jewel's hand. 'I only use that for blotting out bikini marks. If you want the aftersun find it and use it. Stop poking around.'

She admired herself in the full-length mirror, her sleek body sheathed in leopard-skin patterned crepe as thin as paper. Every contour of her perfect curves was beautifully revealed by the clinging material. She ran long fingers through her corn-coloured hair, making it stand out at the sides the way she liked it and fastened enormous black coral ear-rings into her ears.

Touching the mascara brush to her lashes, she said: 'What do you think of the cabin boy?'

'Ned Murdoch? Luscious. Droolsome. But a bit beneath

59

you, don't you think? No connections that might be useful. I'm surprised *you're* interested.'

A little smile played over Karin's full lips, outlined in gooey, scarlet lipstick. She loved speculation and gossip, especially when they were about her.

'He is a little different to the usual type, I have to admit it. But actually, I suspect he's a little in love with me,' she added airily.

They all are aren't they, thought Jewel spitefully. Goddam hooker. 'I find his attentions flattering,' Karin was cooing. 'He's really Mellors-ish. The rough and ready, up and at 'em sort. Between you an' me, I think The Mechanic's dying to get her hands on him, but that's completely off the wall. He was very attentive – while you were escorting the boys round the island this afternoon.'

Jewel had also found Ned Murdoch desirable and took the bait. 'How attentive?' she asked casually, rubbing the Clarins over her burnt arms as well as her face.

'Don't use too much of that. It's *very* expensive. It would cost *you* a year's pay-check. You know what attentive means. It means he *seduced* me.' Her eyes were wide and wicked. 'In the pool! It was absolute *bliss*, Jewel. You should try it sometime. But not with the Cabin Boy, okay?'

Jewel pulled a face behind Karin's back but resumed her normal expression as Karin turned to drawl: 'Hey are you ready yet? You look an absolute dreamboat now your nose has calmed down. Somewhat.'

The girl, tiny against Karin Genevieve, wore a white satin frock with leg o' mutton sleeves. Though her petite frame looked fabulous in simple clothes, she had absolutely no dress sense whatsoever. The satin creation she now wore highlighted her crimson face and made her look as wide as she was tall. How she ever got a part in the spy movie they'd just finished filming, thought Karin, she would never know. *And* she'd had five more lines than Karin herself.

The Mercenary Trap had been her most prestigious movie to date. The others had had titles that still made her shudder: titles like *Self-Help, Daughters of Damon* and *Creature Comforts*. Yich.

She and Jewel had both bedded King, separately and simultaneously, though they'd only been rewarded with minor parts for their trouble. Still a minor part in *Mercenary* was better than the lead in *Hot Rod* anyday. This was the real reason for their both being on the vacation with King and Perce now. More gratitude to be shown all round with the lure of better parts maybe next time. Anyhow there was no hurry to get home. Back in Detroit, Karin's agent had said there was nothing doing.

Karin ushered Jewel out of the room and carefully locked the door behind her.

Outside, the path down to the Great House was lit with chinese lanterns, all painstakingly and individually lit by Zeke at nightfall. They served three purposes – to frighten away the wild dogs that roamed the beaches at night, to distract the larger flying insects that would otherwise head straight for the rooms and to light the way for the guests.

As soon as Karin and Jewel stepped out into the evening, their ears were assaulted by the sounds of the tree frogs, no bigger than your little finger nail, celebrating nightfall with their piercingly shrill whistles. The rain had stopped and fireflies made a brief, flickering appearance like faulty Christmas tree lights before winking out forever.

The air was fresh, though it still couldn't be described as cool. The sound of the waves lapping then crashing onto the rocks by the beach occasionally managed to drown out the frogs and the cicadas.

Suddenly Karin screamed. Her foot probed something that looked like rock and she twisted away at the last moment. The rock turned great, luminous, saucer-like orange eyes at her before hopping resentfully away.

'Oh that is disgusting,' shuddered Karin. 'What in hell was that? I've never seen anything like it before. Like a huge bloated toad.'

They recounted the story in the bar where Pansy – who never took any time off apart from to go to church twice on a Sunday – was mixing frozen rhum, banana daiquiris and the power-pack fruit cocktail she passed off for a pina colada.

She dropped the ice shaker as Karin said how the thing

61

had blinked at her, as though it was trying to hypnotise her.

'Don't laugh, Perce,' said Jewel. 'It was big as a cat and totally terrifying.'

'Dat was a crapaud, Miss,' Pansy said. 'Dem's de spirit of de dead. Dey was usually an Obiman when dey was livin'.' She shook her head, horror stricken that the obeah had come to Sugar Mill Plantation.

Karin hooted with laughter and relief. 'Thank God it was nothing serious then!'

In the corner of the room, Ned slammed his rum punch angrily on the table. 'You shouldn't laugh about island taboos,' he warned. 'The appearance of a crapaud in an area like this has its effect – even if there's nothing in the so-called superstition. I've known times when a house has been abandoned for years because the locals wouldn't enter it after seeing a crapaud. To kill one means death, and you should respect island people's feelings, even if they don't mean anything to you.'

Karin snorted and took the glass of Perrier waiting on the bar for her. She put an arm round King and drew him close as an ally.

Her affections swung like a weather vane in a gale. 'Well I didn't kill the shitty thing!' she swore vehemently. 'I only nearly stepped on it. I didn't actually do anything.'

'It's just the attitude,' he replied. 'Typical American tourist. Learn some respect and don't talk so smart about things you know nothing about.'

Hope chose this moment to appear in the doorway that led to the dining room.

Silence greeted her as the guests took in the latest trans-formation, Karin and Jewel with annoyance and the men with quite obvious lust and desire. Though she might not have looked anything to write home about in the flying suit that morning, or the plain batik skirt that afternoon, Hope believed in dressing for dinner. The surprise on the faces of her guests always rewarded her effort.

Whatever she wore looked a million dollars. Tonight's gown was a simple tabard of emerald-coloured spun silk, edged in Greek gold braid. Pansy had run it up for her in an afternoon. To know that would have made Karin – who

62

spent a fortune on her own clothes – absolutely livid. Hope's hair, clean, shining and twisted into a French plait that lay heavily over one shoulder, was silver to Karin's gold. Hope's might have been natural. That was the difference.

Honest Joe followed her licking his lips after raiding the lobster. Hope had rescued it before it was too damaged and had excused him on the grounds of his being a father with a new family to support. The damaged shell-fish could be resurrected. Terry would never notice.

Ned stood as she entered and her eyes were drawn to him. Dressed in a dinner suit and white silk shirt and tie, he looked totally unlike the deck hand that had arrived earlier in the day. She smiled at him and thought of the rippling muscles of his back and shoulder blades, the damp coils of black hair in the nape of his neck, and of the strong arms that had clasped Karin Genevieve to him in the pool.

'Good evening everyone,' she smiled. 'I hope you've all settled in and are perfectly comfortable.' She reached over to Karin like a conspirator and said sotto voce: 'Is the Victoria Room better, Miss Genevieve? I do hope so, it's one of my favourites. And I put the anthuriums in your room to make up for the initial mistake.'

Karin was disconcerted. The woman was so frigging *nice*. Surely she must be angry about the pool incident? Pissed off about the room switch? Still, nice or not, she was to be no friend of Karin's. Some people you just couldn't get along with and Hope was one of them; a natural rival. Despite her initial dishevelled appearance, she had class and style.

The compensation was that she obviously had to work hard for her living. If she turned up at breakfast looking as though she'd done the night-shift on a truck assembly line, the owners couldn't pay her very much to be their frontman.

Terry Morelands' car, the only Ferrari on the island and completely wasted on the roads, pulled up outside the Great House. The liveried doorman, Elisha, summoned back from his summer building work for the benefit of the guests, opened the door smoothly for the young man. He

63

climbed enthusiastically into the driver's seat and parked it precisely by one of the Plantation's fleet of Mokes, blasting the accelerator a couple of times before reluctantly turning off the motor.

Though she was irritated by Terry Morelands, Hope welcomed him with her usual sparkle. Pansy poured him a vodka martini without being told.

Quick as a snake he wound one arm round Hope's waist while the other reached for the tall glass. He planted a kiss firmly on her lips as she twisted around, trying unsuccessfully to avoid his mouth.

'Am I on your table tonight, darling?' he said, still holding onto her possessively. Ned watched them, unable to hear what was being said. He felt uncomfortably pissed off by the West Indian playboy and hoped he wouldn't have a good reason to sock him one.

'I'm sorry, Terry,' she apologised. 'I need you as a stand-in host. I have a small party here and I really wanted to split us between them. They'll want to know so much about the island . . . Let me introduce you . . . '

She turned to Karin, feeling that she would be the best diversion, and then to Jewel.

King and Perce, deep in conversation by the log fire that was burning for the sake of atmosphere, looked up and smiled. Ned shook hands formally and King, mistaking Morelands for someone famous, simply *oozed* conviviality.

There was the sound of Oz's motor as drinks were being finished. Hope watched from the door as the battered composite of Ford, BMW and more Ford crawled into the grounds. Oz waved Elisha away and drove it to his parking spot.

He didn't see the grey, bubbling creature in his way. He didn't see its orange eyes like beacons, like spotlights, blazing with agony.

The crepaud, crushed beneath the front tyre, screamed its dying curse at the big man. No-one but Pansy heard it above the other night sounds and recognised it for what it was. She crossed herself quickly as a glacier chill moved up her spine and wondered how long it would be before Oz Lennox paid his death dues.

Chapter Five

IT WAS pure co-incidence that led the dinner parties at both Nelson Plantation and Sugar Mill to be discussing the same topic.

Julian Winchester who, like Hope, dined with his guests, suggested the excursion because he was a betting man.

Five miles away, Terry Morelands, tucking into his lobster creole, rice and peas, brought up the cock-fight more to be outrageous than for any other reason. Being the owner of a champion fighting cock made him dangerous, sinister. Women looked at him in a new way. The ones who were really into sex found it exciting. All that blood.

Karin shuddered and licked her lips. 'Isn't it illegal?' she asked.

He leant back in his chair, savouring the hot pepper sauce and breadfruit which was cooked to perfection. 'All gaming on Nevis is illegal,' he said, taking a sip of the chilled Montrachet. 'But I can get you in on it if you're interested. Doctor Doom – '

Karin shrieked with pleasure.

'Really, Doctor Doom. He's always been known as that. He rolls the dice and he holds the cockfights. There's other things too – '

Hope threw him a warning look. He was giving away insider secrets to tourists.

Terry Morelands took the hint.

'He's also rumoured to be the wealthiest man in the Caribbean,' she said, interrupting to prevent Karin asking questions.

Ned said: 'Must be the same guy as the one who ran the unofficial casino in Trinidad?'

Terry nodded. 'That was closed down because of tax

avoidance. Now he's here and no one in the government could give a toss. He's put too much money into the economy. He has an interest in all the cotton here and in St Kitts.'

'Did you hear all that?' Karin called to Jewel and Perce's table. They had. 'When's the next fight?' she said breathlessly to Terry.

'Tomorrow,' he replied, wiping his mouth on a white napkin. 'Eleven. Back my bird – Goliath, okay? We could go dancing first.'

Hope said: 'I wouldn't if I were you. It's very unpleasant.'

'The dancing or the cockfight?' whispered Ned in her ear.

'The *cock*fight,' she hissed back, emphasising the 'cock', narrowing her eyes at him.

Karin said: 'I'm not chicken,' laughing to show the joke hadn't been accidental.

'You got some more Perrier, Hope?' boomed Perce jovially. 'This rich food's gonna murder my ulcer.'

'Of course.' She rang the bell for Pansy and added: 'I'll see you get plenty of greens from tomorrow.'

He pulled a face but didn't object.

'So who's comin'?' asked Terry, fearing that he was losing centre stage.

Karin said: 'I am, for sure. And Jewel will. Won't you, Jewel?'

The younger girl nodded. It'd be a new experience. And it sounded a terribly sophisticated way to spend an evening. Very *risqué*.

'See how we feel about it tomorrow,' said Perce, wondering whether it would be too much of an interruption. Proceedings with the kid were going very nicely, thank you. And if all continued to go well, they'd be occupied in another action replay while the others were at the fight.

At Nelson Plantation, Veronica eagerly agreed to go to the cockfight. She had ridden to hounds since she was a child. She rather enjoyed the excitement of blood sports. Other people said it was out of character with her CND views, her radical politics, her education. She didn't try to justify herself and simply accepted that she was, as they said, a cotton-wool commie.

In fact cockfighting seemed less deliberately cruel than hunting. It was all over so quickly, there wasn't really any time for the birds to suffer. A halt was always called at first blood.

It had been a long time since she'd been to a cockfight and she remembered only vaguely the smoky atmosphere, the smell of fear and the sweating brows of the birds' owners and the gamblers. More vivid was the memory of lovemaking with Stuart, afterwards.

Lottie and Jessica both felt they had better things to do: cockfighting didn't stir either of them. Trivial Pursuit was much more fun since Jessica was such a good loser.

After dinner, a sumptuous rijstaffel served up by the Nelson's Indonesian chef, they drank Armagnac while looking through the hotel's photo album. There were pictures of Deva Romaine, James Mason, Henry Mills sitting in the gracious lounge, swimming in the outsized pool.

'No new ones, Julian?' called Jessica to her host, who had settled himself down by the window with a port and a three day old edition of *The Times*.

'There's more in the cabinet.' He waved to the black, Chinese lacquered bureau and Jessica opened drawer after tiny drawer all studded with polished mother of pearl till she found them.

She arranged herself back on the sofa with Veronica and passed her the loose photographs one at a time as she'd scanned them. 'Yes, I've seen some of these. There's Oliver Reed,' she said. 'And that one's Alan Hughes Rothwell, with his first wife. When was that taken, Julian?'

'Last winter, I think, Jess,' he said vaguely, concentrating on the obituaries.

'But weren't they divorced years ago, in the sixties? And he remarried? Twice?' She pulled a mocking, scandalised face. 'What would happen if that got out in England? And look – who's that? Wasn't he involved in the – '

She stopped abruptly and tried to put the next photograph back in the box.

'That's not very good,' she said to cover her confusion.

Julian Winchester had suddenly risen from his chair. He walked anxiously to the couch. 'I think you've got the wrong box, Jessica.'

Veronica held out her hand impatiently.

The sudden tension caught Lottie's interest. She put her thumb between the pages of The Sound And The Fury. 'Well? What's the next one?'

'It's no one important. Not recognisable, really.' Jessica's fingers twisted the photograph anxiously.

'Don't be silly, Jessica. I know you well enough to realise that this picture is one of particular interest if it's got you all hot and bothered.'

Veronica felt a sinking feeling.

Lottie rested the book on the arm of her chair and rose.

'It's one of Veronica,' Jessica said miserably.

Veronica took the photograph. It was a picture of her and Stuart Wilding, taken in April. They were sitting by the pool. Holding hands. Between them on a little garden table stood a Scrabble set they hadn't used and a bottle of wine that they had.

'Let's see,' said Lottie. She passed it to her reluctantly, knowing there was no way out of it.

'And in case you don't recognise him, it's Doctor Stuart Wilding,' said Veronica.

Lottie studied the picture. Her friend, normally serene at the best of times, glowed with happiness. Stuart Wilding – she had recognised him immediately as the former Cabinet Minister – looked at Veronica with a tenderness she herself had never known from any man. Lottie felt a pang of envy that she immediately suppressed. She glanced up at the real-life Veronica, drawn and pale, and knew instinctively that this was the reason they were all together in Nevis. Out of season.

No, she didn't envy her after all.

I can't bear her to be like this, she thought. Aloud, she said: 'I'm sorry. I've upset you, haven't I?'

Veronica dismissed it with a shrug.

'Why did it end, Ron?'

Julian Winchester sensed the need for drinks and brought over full bottles and clean glasses from the cabinet before leaving the women on their own.

Veronica didn't tell all. With the evidence of the photograph before them, she could not lie, but she did pass off the whole affair as a trifle. It was very unconvincing.

She said they'd parted so he could concentrate on his work. He was expecting a return to a Cabinet post. They were on good terms, she said.

Lottie, who knew a little about everything and enough about politics to know that Wilding was not in favour currently, did not contradict Veronica.

Neither did Jessica, who knew the agony of rejection and also believed that this was what had happened to Ron.

After Veronica had retired to bed, pleading exhaustion but really escaping, Lottie removed the photograph from the box.

'How could anyone hurt her like that?' she said, angry and bitter with years of similar experiences behind her. They always said Lottie was too clever by half.

Jessica shook her head. 'Politicians. They're all the same. They don't really care about anything apart from their political careers.'

'Well this bugger's had it,' said Lottie. 'It's not going to harm Veronica - if anything, it will enhance her reputation.'

'What will?'

'This photograph. I'm going to cable the picture over to the *News of the World*. It'll absolutely ruin him politically. Then we'll see about this "return to the Cabinet".'

Jessica knew it was wrong - that it was more than wrong - immoral, wicked even. The repercussions could be unthinkable. 'No! I don't think you should interfere. Veronica would absolutely hate it.'

'No she wouldn't,' snapped Lottie. 'Anyway she doesn't have to know. Can't you see the way she's been looking? She's really hurt. She must be terribly angry.

'If she hates anything, it must be him. Doctor Stuart Smart-Arse Wilding. She wouldn't do anything about it herself, but she'll be glad. You wait and see. Everybody likes a bit of revenge, no matter how *good* they might be.'

Lottie slipped the photograph into her handbag and snapped the clasp closed as tight as her lips. 'I'm glad you mentioned St Kitts earlier on, Jess. I'll come with you. We'll go tomorrow.'

In London, Stuart Wilding announced his resignation at the emergency constituency party meeting. He said he would continue as their elected member until the next general election but that was it. He would not stand for re-selection. He did not give his reasons and would not bow to the pressure of questions.

It was an informal meeting that turned into a wake, and party officials swore each other to secrecy, knowing that the announcement to the Press would come later on, when a new candidate had been chosen. When it was a *fait accompli*.

He drove home the long way, passing Veronica's flat and looking at the closed curtains. Where in God's name had she gone? He needed her – he needed to know she was there and all right, and happy, maybe. This continued absence was driving him crazy.

What he planned to do with his future he wasn't sure. He had begun the divorce proceedings, and that would be out soon enough – probably as soon as Jannine received the writ. If he couldn't have Veronica then he would have no one.

The life he'd led with Jannine had been a shambles, a pretence at civilised marriage. They shared nothing but their bed; they had nothing in common but the children and their name. Even Jannine couldn't still be satisfied with so little. She had moved away from him as he had from her. They had different circles of friends, different interests. She was so tied up with her WRVS and he was so into his politics, where could they bridge their lives?

They didn't need to waste themselves on each other. They needed to call it a day, to accept they had been beaten by change and time.

In his forties he had become a romantic. Veronica had

done that much for him. He liked the new Stuart Wilding, and wondered now whether it would survive without its source, or would it simply dry up like a river in a drought?

He wanted Veronica more than anything, wanted her with a desperation that was as strong as his will to live.

Without her, he couldn't even dream.

Until he had her for his own, everything else was unimportant: his career, the grown-up children at university, his life.

The summer recess would give him the time he needed to find her. And find her he would, though she had apparently disappeared without a trace.

He had never really believed there was another man more important to her than he himself was. When you love someone so passionately, it is returned, nurtured, and thus grows ever stronger, otherwise it ends soon. Unrequited love was the sole prerogative of lovers in the middle ages, where overwhelming emotions were more an intellectual exercise than something that came from the soul.

Courtly love be buggered.

His outburst in the Devon hotel had been anger and jealousy exploding irrationally in the heat of the moment.

But Stuart Wilding was no fool. It had taken time, but now he understood Veronica's reasons for flight. He probably understood them better than she did.

If she had gone into hiding, she had done so because what he had suggested was what she really wanted. For some reason, she felt that what they both honestly desired was wrong. And Veronica was an extremely moral woman, despite her apparent promiscuity.

There were several possibilities. She could have fled to another man, one with whom she felt safe. If that was the case, his chances of finding her while her emotions were still high and she was at her most susceptible to persuasion were remote, as no one knew who her past lovers were. No one except perhaps a friend of hers, Jessica Collier. That was someone she'd spoken of with affection.

He turned his car into the long drive where a distant lamp shone from the porch. There were no lights on in the house. Jannine would either be in bed or at bridge. He

71

parked on the loose gravel and opened the door quietly, through force of habit.

Though it was late, he called connections in the City to track down the director of Joseph Collier, Sugar Importers. He and Jessica had been divorced long ago, but you never knew. He might still keep tabs on her. And it might narrow down the options.

Even thinking of Veronica brought back the dreams.

If it was all done quietly he'd eventually be able to return to politics. If there was no fuss, he might even get back into the Cabinet. At least he could rely on her silence to buy him the time he needed.

Andrew Dean weaved his way along the road from the Rookery Nook where he had consumed a vast quantity of planter's punch and a small helping of peppery fish soup and stale sweet bread.

His head was spinning. He had washed six Largactil tablets down his throat with the alcohol.

Funny that, his whole life had been ruled by pills of one sort or another.

It had even been the pills that had given him away to that bitch. That wrecking, destroying bitch.

The sky above Charlestown had cleared, the stars looked like sequins set into a black curtain. He was looking at it horizontally. Didn't remember lying down.

'But I will always remember you,' he said menacingly to Hope.

The policeman, a wide grin stretching over his burnished chestnut face, said to the prone Andrew Dean: 'No need for that, mahn. Just doin' mah job.' He slipped a brawny arm under him and hoisted him to his unsteady feet.

'Bitch!' spat Dean.

'Sorry, mahn. I didn't know my own strength! C'mon, where you stayin'? In town?'

Andrew Dean's watery eyes focused on the policeman. His peaked cap looked like a duck's beak.

'She hated me, you know.' His words were slurred. 'She was jealous of me an Nicky. An' I'm going to kill her.'

'Sure, mahn. Dere's many a dronk feel like killin'. De good thing is dat when they feels like dat, they not capable of killin' a Jack Spaniel fly. When they's sober, they don't feel like doin' all dat killin' no more.'

The policeman began to guide him along the narrow pavement. Gettin' him movin'. Walkin' him around some. They headed in the direction of the police station, because that's where the policeman needed to go.

Suddenly Dean was alert, wary. 'How did you know where I was living?' he asked sharply.

The officer was confused. 'I doan't mahn. I'm gettin' some fresh air into those lungs of yours. I'll make you some coffee an' you can get your head together.'

From somewhere, the sounds of Bob Marley drifted into the still night. The policeman's hips swayed involuntarily.

Okay, thought the policeman. Dis guy gonna sober up quick so's I can get out again.

He steered him through the door, past the desk sergeant with a shrug and into a cell. By the time he came back with a mug full of steaming Nescafé, Dean was unconscious, stretched full-length on the cot beneath a hairy grey blanket.

Though his body was inert, his mind took him down the black alleys of his adolescence to The Crooked Mile where the music played and his brothers laughed.

'You gonna do he for drunk and disorderly?' asked the sergeant, shuffling papers around in anticipation.

'No,' said the police officer. 'He totally harmless. I gonna see what de Rastas doin' so late at night playin' de music fit to waken de dead.'

'If dere's ganja, don't you go havin' some, mahn,' he said. 'You remember you is owin' me.'

'If dere's ganja, I plannin' to impound it, like you already tol' me,' replied the younger man earnestly. *After* he'd had a blow.

Hope sat with Oz at the bar while the rest of the guests took coffee in the lounge or messed around in the games room.

'You don't remember anyone called Alan – what was it – Alan Walker, do you?' he asked her.

73

Hope thought and shook her head. 'Name doesn't mean anything to me. Why?'

'Just a weird little guy on the plane run from Antigua this afternoon.'

'Should I know him?'

'Dunno. I just thought I recognised him as a flier. Thought maybe we'd come across him before, though maybe not.' He drained a glass of Banks beer. 'Veronica Marston came in from Antigua with Mrs Collier and Lottie Wolff. Does Terry know she's here?'

Hope looked round to see Morelands sliding an arm behind Karin's devastating back. 'Would he want to?' she said. 'That was over years ago. And he's always got new fish to fry.'

Ned Murdoch, who'd been playing bar pool with King, joined them and ordered a straight rum. 'I lost,' he grimaced. 'I was The Raiders, but I still lost. I owe the guy ten dollars.'

'I'll play you for the debt,' said Hope.

Oz eased himself off the stool and stretched. 'Okay,' he said. 'I should make a move. See you when I see you. Don't suppose I'll be back early tomorrow – Miami first then Barbados. Do I get to stay at Sandy Lane overnight on expenses?'

'No way,' said Hope, laughing. 'You'll stay with Esme Little as you always do. She's doing short hops for me over the next couple of days, so she should be around when you get there. If not – '

'The key's under the fire coral. I know.'

Downstairs in the pool room, where old fishing nets looped from the ceiling and threaded shells hung in strings like curtains across the windows, Ned broke first. 'I'm Raiders again, okay? Blacks.'

She shrugged, amused. He couldn't just be Ned Murdoch, he had to be a whole, damn football team. 'Then I'm The Lions,' she said.

Taking aim, he scattered the balls wildly out of their triangle. 'That your boyfriend, up there?' he asked nonchalantly.

The green silk tabard opened as Hope leaned forwards

74

over the table to reveal a long, lean thigh. Ned was tempted to run a hand up its length to feel the softness of her hip. Instead, he watched her score a cool thirty for The Lions. It wasn't a football team he'd ever heard of, but she was welcome to any name she liked.

'Hardly,' she eventually replied, losing her concentration and missing the next shot. Ned bent over to cue again. He was rather nice, after all. And what superb buttocks he had. 'Oz is just a bloody good pilot who works for the same company as I do.'

Another Lion disappeared from the field.

'I thought *you* owned the company?' He was watching the curve of her breasts instead of the action on the table. He wanted to run his fingers over their outline, feel their warmth through the silk. They rippled as she pushed the cue forwards.

'No. Only the hotel,' she replied. 'Damn. Missed the bugger. I just have a small share in the airline.'

They brushed against each other as they swapped places.

'*Only* the hotel. Thank God for that,' said Ned, wondering which ball he was supposed to be going for. 'I thought you were rich.' He could smell her perfume. She was taking unfair advantage of him. The cue dabbed first in one direction, then the other, as he tried to remember whether he was Black or White.

She wanted to brush the unruly hair back from his eyes. They were dark brown, almost black. Like pits.

'The hotel is worth a bit,' she admitted. 'Why are you carrying on with your turn, Ned? You just put one of my team down again.'

'I slipped.' He had a five o'clock shadow and a midnight expression, even if he couldn't play pool.

She could feel him behind her, watching the flare of her hips. They burned beneath his gaze. 'Is it your boat?'

'One of them.' Her whole body was smooth. Ripe fruit. He could take a bite out of her. And there was more: he actually liked her.

'Thank God for that,' she said. 'I thought you were penniless.'

'Not,' he said with the remnants of satisfaction, 'any more.'

'I used to do up wrecks in the Keys. Pick 'em up cheap, sell 'em for a packet. Turned boats as ugly as a headache into ships people wanted to buy. That was in my spare time.'

'Karin describes you as the cabin boy.'

'Karin is a woman unloved.'

'By you?' She miscued entirely, thinking of rippling shoulder muscles, nut-brown skin, coils of wet, black hair. It aroused her again. Could it be the thrill of the chase? The challenge?

He took off the bow-tie and unfastened the top two buttons of his shirt. She watched him, fascinated. 'Most certainly by me. Can't stand her.'

Hope frowned, wondering why she was always drawn to men whose appetite for variety and whose ability to kiss and move on were equally great. He gave out all the old danger signals, and she was not even trying to resist them. Situation normal.

'I think I win,' he said, potting the last two balls. Neither of them knew the score.

'I think I did,' she replied.

'Give you another. Or do you want to quit while you're behind?' Her nipples were like pencil erasers. Her hair was coming loose. Soft and loose around that lovely face. It had an extraordinary quality about it – determined but not hard. Generous. Natural. Quite beautiful in some lights.

'Set them up Ned Murdoch,' she challenged. 'Though I shall thrash you again.'

'Do you ever lose?' Right this second, he could reach out and touch that warm skin. It glowed like a magnet. He knew it would respond to his fingers.

'Never. I cheat when necessary.'

He let her break first, breathing in her scent as he leaned very close to watch her angle. 'We shouldn't fight, then, Skylady. Because I don't lose, either.'

Her cue scratched the baize table covering and she looked into his eyes.

'You won't win that way.' He wanted to kiss her, she

76

was so close. Instead, he took the cue and potted five Raiders with precise strokes.

Impatiently, she watched the poolcue glide smoothly in and out of his fingers. Why hadn't he kissed her then? She wouldn't have minded. Couldn't he tell?

'Do you like boats?' he asked, retrieving the balls from the pockets.

'I'm not wonderful with them,' she confessed, matching his score. Concentrating now. 'They leave too much to chance. I'm more mechanical. I prefer the planes.'

'I'd rather have the sea than the air any day. The air's like magic – you can't see it, hear it or touch it. But you can with the sea.' He was quite lyrical. It was his passion. 'You can even hold it in your hands.'

'Not for long.'

He was back at the table, flashing the cue, potting everything in sight.

Hope said: 'Only the pelicans are at home in both the sea and the air. They're strange birds. Any-element birds.'

He missed his target, but couldn't have cared less. His heart was racing. She had that effect on him. 'Why don't you come for a sail tomorrow?' he asked. 'I thought I'd go over to St Kitts.'

She ran a hand through her hair, pulling another piece of the plait out from its clasp. 'I thought the boat was being repainted in the harbour?'

He shrugged. 'They'll get it finished. I was being over-generous giving them till Friday to get it done.'

Boats, waves, churning stomachs. Was it worth it?

She tried to work out which of the two remaining balls was easier. He placed a hand tentatively on the top of her spine, imagining he might get an electric shock. Now he could breathe again.

'I'd like you to come,' he said, feeling but not knowing how to put 'I want you' simply.

She straightened and turned to face him. 'Is this to distract me?' Her eyes were almost level with his. 'Are you cheating?'

'I – '

'Goodnight!' called Terry Morelands from the stone

stairwell, his voice chipper as a longshoreman's. He was visible from the knee downwards. Ned and Hope sprang apart like guilty teenagers. 'You coming to the fight tomorrow?'

Hope looked at Ned and said: 'Depends.'

Bridges were burning. Ned growled: 'Might see you then.' He hoped he wouldn't. Perhaps he should kidnap her on board the Maria Juana. Put some distance between them and him.

They racked their cues and left the balls where they were, forgetting there were two left to pot.

Upstairs, only Jewel and Perce remained. Pansy had left them to fix their own drinks. Jewel had been giggling captivatingly but she stopped as soon as she saw Ned and Hope. 'Sleep well,' she called slyly.

They walked through the gardens to the place where the path forked to the sugar mill or to the bungalows.

Ned's loping stride was matched by Hope's exactly. They were rhyming couplets.

She didn't fit into the compartments. Rich bitch was definitely out. She worked too hard for someone who'd had it easy all her life. She had too much enthusiasm for someone who'd seen it all and done everything. There were tiny lines around her eyes that she didn't try to hide. There were faint marks on her throat, hairline scars maybe as the result of a road or a plane crash long ago. They made her strong beauty all the more interesting and compelling because they showed she'd had her share of suffering too.

Maybe Hope is real, Ned thought wistfully; a person, not a cut-out cartoon character as the other stereotyped beauties have all been. It's too soon to tell, and five days is too short a time to find out.

He should give up trying before he started.

Instead, he touched her hand briefly and said: 'Will you sail with me tomorrow?'

'Yes. I think I will.'

'Shall I see you at the harbour? At eleven?'

She nodded. 'How do I recognise the boat?'

'There's only mine in.' There was only room for the schooner, but he failed to warn her of its size. Years ago he had stopped thinking about material possessions and status symbols in relation to himself. Everything he had achieved had been hard-earned, and once he'd become used to the trappings of luxury, he didn't want them any more. In fact, there was nothing he needed that he lacked. Absolutely nothing.

But he looked at Hope and wondered why he was so sure.

'Do you like opera?' he asked, suddenly, wanting to keep her talking.

'Only Rigoletto. Brings tears to the eyes.'

'Rock music?'

'Yes.'

'Californian wine? Nectarines?'

'Yes.'

'e.e. cummings? Brian Patten? Whales? The colour red?'

'Yes-yes-yes-yes!' she laughed. 'Why all the questions?'

'I thought you would, that's all.' He lit a cigarette and the flame danced in his eyes. 'Is there anything you don't like?'

She thought for a moment and then grinned. 'Karin Genevieve films.'

They didn't kiss goodnight and went to their separate rooms, each of them wondering why.

Chapter Six

JULIAN WINCHESTER had once been Veronica's lover. Now he looked out of his bedroom window in the early hours of the morning to see if she had yet put on her light.

It was still twilight, neither night nor day. The sun could choose to go either way, up or down. It still hadn't made up its mind.

He was an early riser and had never adapted to Nevis time. He glanced at his Rolex watch and calculated it was already eight in England. The streets of Oxford would be crowded with students riding their bicycles, staying in the city though term was over.

There would be the sound of the bells, motor cars, John Timpson and Brian Redhead on Radio Four, birds with dull songs, not like the showy, vulgar creatures in Nevis.

Maybe it was time he went home for a while.

It was at Oxford he had met first her brothers and then Veronica herself. It was during the turbulent sixties and they found themselves on opposite sides of the political fence. Veronica in her hippie dresses breathing peace and love everywhere. Where was the future in that? They all changed once they grew up. No more love around, was there? And the people in power, the people who could have stuck to Veronica's ideology, where were they now?

Were they still growing hashish in their allotments back home or were they bankers, accountants, stockbrokers?

Where had even Veronica got to with her gentle voice, her Crosby, Stills, Nash and Young albums, her *laissez faire* attitudes?

On the shelf at forty, that's where.

They had had a brief affair – Julian was the first to admit sex wasn't his strong point, though it wasn't for a lack of trying – and it was no surprise to him when their little romance had petered out. They had, of course, remained friends. That was the civilised thing to do. Though Veronica was a Red, she had breeding. She would never have behaved in an uncivilised way.

He had read Classics, she was History of Art. He'd passed with an Upper Second. He tried to think what Veronica had got, and remembered with annoyance that it was a First.

Outside, the boy with the goats was waving a stick madly at his herd, trying to persuade them to stay away from the kitchen garden. He was riding a donkey, his bare feet trailing along the stone pathway, occasionally using the leverage from his feet to push the donkey along, as though he was astride a trolley.

Julian, dressed only in a flown-over Marks and Spencer bathrobe, flung open the door at the top of his outside staircase.

'Keep those goats off the beets!' he shouted.

The boy pivoted round and poked a tongue at him. He spoke in the patois Julian still couldn't keep up with.

'I'll have you, Ranson, if just one of those beasts puts a foot on a plant.'

Ranson put his middle finger up to Julian Winchester and whistled at the goats, flicking one of them nonchalantly with the stick.

As he turned away again, he called: 'Dey's sheep, mahn. Y' guddah tell de sheep from de goats or you is nowheres.'

Julian watched as he drove them onwards to the field beyond the estate. Well, maybe I is nowheres, then, he thought.

The sun had made a casual appearance over the horizon without Julian noticing. Already, an inch of canvas sky was egg-yellow, and the grey of twilight was turning to an appealing powder blue.

There'd be no rain today, there was no hint of the murky gold expanse that heralded a summer storm. Already it was hot, though not as bad as it would be down on Portlands, by the airport, or at Sugar Mill Plantation at beach level.

Veronica's light was on.

Julian ran a comb through thinning hair and swiftly razored his beard stubble before slipping into his swimming shorts. Yes, he still liked her. Of course he did. She was a damn attractive woman, even if she looked strained after the bloody Wilding affair.

He'd never liked that chap.

The first of the church bells was ringing as he strolled casually down to Veronica's room to see if she fancied an early morning swim.

She was already wearing her bikini, waiting for him, though neither of them allowed the encounter to appear anything more than by chance. It was a ritual they always observed when Veronica was at Nelson Plantation and manless.

'It's lovely and warm,' called Veronica, bright and enthusiastic, gazing into the blue waters of the pool.

She was first in while Julian pretended to shiver on the steps. They each managed a few lengths, though Veronica gave up first, still tired from the journey the day before.

'You'll get back into it, darling,' said Julian.

'I feel as though I've been back years,' she said. 'Really, years. Or as though I'd never been away.'

'Why don't you come and live here?' asked Julian, anticipating the answer he'd heard on countless occasions.

Veronica dried herself vigorously and hauled up her tiny bikini pants. She had lost weight again. 'I would if there were more men!' she laughed.

'But Veron – there are four thousand of us! How can you want more than that? Sheer nymphomania!'

He picked up the phone by the pool and rang the kitchen to summon hot coffee and croissants.

'It very early, boss,' said Fransis.

'We shall have a very early breakfast then, please, Fransis. By the pool. Hot coffee, lots of it. And heaps of hot croissants. Put them in the microwave if they're out of the freezer. Don't mess around trying to light the oven.'

Turning to Veronica who was wrapping herself up in a gorgeous silk kimono, the colour of the sky, he said: 'What can I do to help you?'

Veronica gave it careful thought. She herself never

offered help unless prepared to do virtually anything suggested. She took Julian's question very seriously.

'You could phone Stuart Wilding and tell him I'm here,' she said. 'Or you could phone Stuart Wilding and tell him I'm dead.

'I don't know, old love. I'm so confused I don't know what I need, let alone what I want. I feel like an infant, waiting for more responsible people to attend to the things I need to keep me alive.

'Actually, I feel completely rotten. And I don't know whether I'm just feeling guilty – it was me that finished the relationship, by the way, not what I said last night – or whether I made a mistake.'

'What was that song you used to be so fond of – something about taking it to the limits?'

'The Eagles,' she said.

'Yes,' he said. 'The Eagles. Maybe that's what you've got to do. Test out the limits. Feel the absolute end to despair and happiness and come up knowing where you are.

'Sometimes pleasure and pain are indistinguishable, you know.'

He reached a hand out to take hers and kissed the back of it.

'So some of the things I taught you didn't get filed under irrelevant,' she smiled.

'Why don't I tell Fransis to bring the breakfast things to my room?' he asked.

She shook her head, no. 'I don't feel very sexy, Julian,' she said.

'Christ you are off colour, aren't you?' But he didn't mind: it was only his way of offering what comfort he could.

In the cool light of dawn, Hope climbed lazily out of her bed. She slept naked, cocooned between the sumptuous white percale sheets.

She showered, folded her hair under a wide-brimmed rush hat and padded, barefoot and completely naked apart from the hat, into her kitchen to make coffee.

Her suite was in what had been the mill when slaves and plantation owners turned the fertile land from wild jungle into cotton and sugar crops. From the outside, the two-storied mill – like a windmill without sails – still looked like a ruin. Completely circular and built of five foot thick slabs of stone, the old building was smothered in vines, mutations that had evolved over centuries from imported African flowering shrubs.

The oak doors – originals – led into a sitting room and library with windows to every side. Books, many of them hand-bound in leather, reflected the literature of the islands: Jean Rhys, Bassett Ferguson, Bob Shacochis – these were the people who had understood the essence of the Caribbean. Lived and breathed it. There were books on Leeward Island birds, Windward Island flowers, politics and folklore.

Small steps led down through an opening to an ante-room where Hope had installed a circular bath carved out of jasper. A stone spiral staircase to the top floor was lit by a skylight in the hidden roof, built beneath the jagged external roof structure out of mahogany slats. Here was where Hope had her bedroom, shower room and kitchen.

The mill was one of the oldest surviving relics of the slave era, built in 1684 by the ruthless landowner Breaker Bussenius. He had begun in business as a pirate trader, bringing beautiful men and women together – each sex from different tribes in a divide and rule philosophy – from the west coast of Africa. The ones who survived the horrendous journey in filthy, plague and parasite-infested holds like so much breathing cargo, were landed at the same creek where much later Admiral Lord Nelson was to arrive on the island. They were then herded to the Breaker estate to be bred like prize stallions and mares in his so-called stud-farm.

It wasn't long before Bussenius returned to the more profitable pastime of piracy, raiding the Spanish and English galleons that strayed into the Caribbean sea carrying their Aztec and Inca booty.

Countless casks of treasure – priceless silver necklaces, pendants, bullion, ingots – found their way into the underground cellars at the Bussenius Estate.

It was on one of these forays against a Royal Navy galleon that Bussenius was finally captured, taken to England, tried and convicted of piracy.

He returned ten years later, granted a knighthood by the whims of a fickle monarch whose estates had been populated by Bussenius's beautiful, strong slaves.

He was made an Island Governor and died in the odour of sanctity, surrounded by adoring children, grandchildren and two too many wives in 1710. It was during his son James's 'reign' on the estate that the legend of the ghost began.

James had six daughters, all beautiful, all elegant, and untouched by the harsh rays of the sun or by man. One of them, Catherine, was unlike the others. She had been given a strong and powerful nature that was kept in check with difficulty. Her overwhelming need for passion and physical gratification – it was said – caused her to fall in love with a Mandingo. They met secretly, hopelessly trying to conceal the violent passions that had erupted between them. The Mandingo, of course, was executed immediately they were discovered making love beneath the thick stalks of cane that grew at the estate. He was burned alive, his blue-black skin flayed by the horse-whip James himself had used on him.

A marriage between Catherine and the son of another one-time buccaneer was swiftly arranged. But on the night before the wedding, at a feast for some one hundred guests, an argument erupted between the groom and his best man. The reason for the dispute was trivial. There was a challenge to a duel and at dawn both men lay bleeding and dying beneath the manchineel groves of Gingerland.

Catherine, driven to madness, was shipped back to England and an asylum where she spent fifty years in the company of lunatics, paupers, and other fallen women. She herself managed to produce three children, one of them born with only slightly less black skin than that of the Mandingo. Her body was finally laid to rest in an unmarked grave somewhere near Hastings, though her spirit never left the island.

Hope was a descendent of the Bussenius family. To have

the estate back in the family was like returning to her roots. Going home.

Pansy and other workers on the estate had said they had heard Catherine crying and Hope saw no reason to disbelieve them. She had a healthy respect for island beliefs. Anyway, she too had seen shadows where none should have been. And during the excavation of the mill, an Aztec chain, studded with precious jewels, was found beneath the ground. It looked in mint condition, belying its age and history.

It became Hope's property.

Hope pulled on a one-piece terry cloth shorts and top and drank her coffee black and without sugar. Humming a medley of Jim Reeves, Bing Crosby and Dire Straits songs, she whipped up an egg and dunked bread in it to fry in butter and serve with maple syrup.

She carried a tray set with her breakfast things outside to the wrought iron table where she sat to watch the night clouds being beaten away by the force of the sunlight.

Today, the proper chef would arrive, Robert Lane, from England. The troops were rallying. Esme Little would meet him in Barbados this afternoon and the homely island food cooked by Rachel would be replaced by the exquisite nouvelle cuisine created by Lane. Her guests would be even happier. And grow fat, she thought smugly.

She devoured most of the French toast rapidly, anxious to be finished by the time the sun had risen over the side of the volcano. She left the empty plate and mug for later, feeling replete and lazy, and taking the remains of the bread for the birds.

All was quiet. It amazed her, the way other people slept. She herself could take or leave sleep, napping when necessary to preserve her alertness for night flights, parties or whatever other demands were made of her nocturnally.

Still barefoot, she picked her way over the cobbles between the carefully planted groves of bushes and flowers to the path that led down to the beach.

Already, gardeners in their smart overalls were raking the sand, sifting it, to keep it powder fresh for anyone who ventured onto the private beach.

It was one of the few stretches of white sand on Nevis, most of the beaches being the typical black sand created when the volcano last erupted. It would have been a tourist trap, a place for cruisers to head for, had it not been strictly reserved for Hope's guests.

'Good morning, Sam,' said Hope.

'Looks like a bad storm brewin' Miss Hope.'

Hope looked at the sky and disagreed. The sky was perfect. Tendrils of gold spread into the sky like a fisherman's net, scooping up the last of the stars to save them for a night show.

There was a white, plastic-framed beach chair under a dead tree, a skeleton of a growth that sprang lifeless from the sand, like just another piece of washed-up coral. She settled herself into the chair to relax and make herself ready for the day, the cool wind blowing through the strands of hair that had escaped from the confines of the cane hat.

It was a luxury to do this – one that came all too rarely these days.

This was her special place, the place where she nursed her hurts and her joys. It was where she'd spent a lot of her time after she'd come back from London, two years ago, with her face still mending and her fears firmly suffocated beneath the blanket of her willpower.

Her mind emptied and she was receptive to all smells, sights and sounds. There were the waves, gentle ripples of blue, sweeping up onto the white – impossibly white – sand around the bars of the beach chair. If she wriggled her toes off it, she would be able to feel the ripples of the sea as they ran over the sand in their hopeless attempt to claim back the land.

Then there were the birds. Hope had brought down the remains of her French toast for the big black birds that looked as dull as starlings but sounded like nightingales, and the chi-chi birds.

They knew the routine. They gathered around her chair as though she was Snow White and sang for their breakfast, the black ones with their dull eyes, fanning out tails, thinking they were peacocks and shrieking: 'Chew-eee'; the red-breasted chi-chi birds in their groups like gossiping

87

fish-wives, waiting for the left-over crumbs.

Waders, oblivious to Hope and her beneficience, ran over the smooth wet sand, ahead of the tide, racing the waves, ridiculous with their long legs tripping over their pointed bills. They disdained the breakfast titbits; they were after the silly land-crabs that you only saw at the last moment, as they tilted their white, sideways bodies, ready to slip down the right hole at the right moment. Every now and then one's life ended as it was snatched by a grey wader that flew off into the dawn sky, remembering after all that it did have wings.

Suddenly there were the pelicans. After four years in the West Indies, Hope had still not become blasé about the great, brown birds with their ungainly bills. She was filled with the same excitement there had been at first at the sight of them. One landed on the reef that stretched from the sand to fifty foot out into the sea. Its mate circled it lazily, on bulky wings that would have got The Goose airborne.

The female preened on the breaker, her huge beak nipping under wings, around her belly, reaching impossibly over her back, paying no attention to the male. He was soaring in the dawn sky now, watching the shoals of fish with X-ray eyes. He flew to cloud level, till he was merely a speck in the sky, then his body was angled like an arrow, like a suicide bomber, like a bullet, aiming for the little fish only he could see.

His body hit the surface of the water like just another wave, disappearing beneath the sea without causing a ripple and after a gasp, the holding of a breath for just a split-second, he was back, floating like a decoy duck, raising his impressive bill to swallow God knew how many fish in a single mouthful. Then his head was down, peering through the translucent, sapphire waters before diving yet again, this time to catch the little fish for his waiting mate.

She took the fish from his crop, opened to her as though she was a chick, and greedily took the morsels from him.

Then together they rose, flew into the sky and were heading toward the cliff, two halves of the same mating machine. Existing only to produce more pelicans to feed, mate and produce more pelicans.

88

The air was alive with birdsong now. No frogs singing in the trees, just birds, the first of the buzzing insects and the lapping of the waves. A sugar bird landed on the broken, plastic bed and thought about making its way across Hope's body to take the tiny piece of French toast she was extending to it as an offering. At the last moment, it realised this was far too dangerous an escapade for so early in the day when there were hens to be wooed, nests to be built and easy fruit bushes to be raided.

The sky was pink in the east, slurring into a pale watery blue in the west. Hope watched two land crabs escape from the waders and thought to herself just one more, laughing at the birds as they ran on stilt-legs, afraid of getting their feet wet. One was caught, the bird cawing in triumph and losing it as she opened her beak. That one was too stupid to survive. Hope didn't count the descending crab as an escapee, and watched out for just one more.

Around the curve of the bay was Charlestown and then, in the distance, St Kitts, its high mountains and uninhabited southlands dark, like an inkblot against the lightening sky. The lights of the capital, with its white-washed houses and their red roofs, winked out as daylight crept into the corners.

Ned Murdoch, unmoved by pelicans, white sand beaches, thoughts of fresh paw-paw (again) for breakfast or even the need for a first coffee, turned the starter motor in one of Sugar Mill's Mokes.

The engine was as reluctant to start as any other motor in the West Indies, complaining of a combination of damp, humidity and neglect. It creaked, moaned and groaned in protest, finally bent to his will and chugged into life, granting him its grudging permission to drive to the harbour where he planned to check his boat, the Maria Juana, was seaworthy.

By breakfast, Veronica was sparkling, looking and behaving like someone in her twenties. Lottie and Jessica were relieved, but it didn't alter Lottie's resolve to contact the Reuters chap in St Kitts. He owed her a favour from last time, in Berlin, when she'd divulged some hot City stuff about Wolff-Armstrong, particularly about the Wolff part of the partnership.

'What are you doing, girls?' Veronica beamed. 'Any plans?'

Jessica coloured and spread maple syrup thickly over her French toast, adding a bit extra on the thin, crispy bacon for good measure.

Lottie said: 'I've decided I will go over to St Kitts with Jessica after all. I'd enjoy the boat ride, if nothing else. Want to come?' The Brer Rabbit ploy. She prayed for the right answer and got it.

'No thanks. I'm just going to be an absolute sybarite today. I'm going to sleep and eat, eat and sleep. For your information, this is already my second breakfast.'

Jessica glowered. 'Thin bitch,' she said. 'Don't rub it in.'

'You've got no problems, Jessica. Though you will have by the time we go home if you carry on like that.

'I think I might book lunch at The Sugar Mill. I'd like to see how Hope Parnell's getting on. Haven't seen her for a while. Super lady. What the Americans call up front.'

Jessica took this as a sign she and Lottie had been found out and blushed furiously again, mopped her brow and said: 'Hot today.'

'It will be cooler on the boat,' Lottie snapped pointedly. 'You go and get Julian to order a car for us while I finish my Ryvita. How you get through your food so quickly I do not know.'

'Nerves,' said Jessica. 'From tomorrow, I starve.'

Veronica shared their taxi, with Arthur Arthurs pointing out familiar landmarks to them on the way to Charlestown. There was Fig Tree Church and the Jews Cemetery; there, a seventeenth century ruin where the ghost of a plantation owner's daughter was still said to roam.

They got out at Charlestown where Veronica headed for the little bookshop that sold only Caribbean books and Jessica and Lottie bought return tickets for the short crossing to the bigger sister island.

There was already a huge queue lining the dock, though

the Island Queen ferry was nowhere to be seen. Obviously it should have left Basseterre by now.

There were young men, in t-shirts saying Montserrat Is Paradise and Bob Marley Lives On. There were women, their hair plastered with sickly-sweet smelling coconut oil, or wearing strange polythene bags over their heads, to keep off the salt spray. There were old men with brightly dressed children in their arms, men with birds in cages. Rastas with enormous transistor radios blaring out Eddie Grant.

Despite the poverty of the place, Nevis people had pride and dignity. Their clothes might be rags, but they were clean rags.

When the boat came, Jessica and Lottie sat in the lower deck, thinking it would be cooler out of the sun. The boat rocked alarmingly and there was a heavy smell of diesel and coconut oil. It was overpowering. Lottie leaned her arm out into the murky waters through the open side of the ferry and tried to breathe fresh air.

'Got the photo?' Jessica asked, half-hoping it had been left behind.

'Stupid woman,' cursed Lottie, already feeling ill. 'Do you think I got where I am today through being inefficient?'

The spray began to slop into their faces and Lottie threw back her head to enjoy the sensation.

Veronica emerged from the bookshop in time to see the Island Queen making two channels in the calm-as-a-mill-pond sea as it headed towards the next island. Its blue and red striped blinds were being rolled down, closing the sun, the salt and the fresh air out from the lower cabin.

She waved in case her friends were on the top deck and were looking back to Nevis. She clutched two books and six post cards, one chosen with Stuart Wilding in mind, though she didn't yet know whether it would ever be posted.

Andrew Dean's body was drenched with sweat; cold streams of it ran down his skin finding its crevices and indentations and spilling over the planes of his face.

His clothes were wet, as though he'd spent the night in a sauna. The hairy grey blanket lying over him was brittle-stiff and smelled of urine.

The world swam around him. A barred window, high, near the ceiling, swirled in and out of his consciousness as he tried to clutch for sanity. The gloss-painted green walls were all too familiar and with a sickening certainty, Dean realised that he was still in the prison hospital. His release had been nothing more than fantasy. A delusion.

Like a thief in the night, the music crept in on him. It was a heartbeat, a rushing, a roaring. It was a part of him and so much so that it was as though he had never been free of it.

The faces of the men at The Crooked Mile floated tanta-lisingly before his eyes, broken teeth and blood spurting from the ribbons of their flesh, their skin running and metamorphosing like crazy amoebas . . .

'Noooo!' he screamed, throwing off the cover and flailing his fists wildly at their images.

The faces cracked, shattered like plaster of Paris – fragments of bone ripping in every direction – to be replaced by more and more horrific visions of the past.

The tablets – where were the nurses with the pills? He must have gone way over time for the Largactils – this sort of thing didn't happen when he was given his regular dose. He began to scream for the doctors, howling and viciously banging his fists against his head to shut out the halluci-nations.

The bastards were ignoring him – allowing him to torture himself with his head. They knew. They knew what happened to him when he was left alone –

'Come and get me you cunts!' he screamed, howling at the monsters of his mind.

Dean knew they were a trick, a deception – but if he saw them, if they were in his head – they they were far worse than reality. They were closer.

He collapsed onto the floor and sat huddled and weeping into his knees – the faces, the faces of men he had torn apart at The Crooked Mile – floated onwards and inwards, stealing behind his closed eyelids into his very soul, for his guilt had given them birth and now welcomed them with familiar recognition.

It was worse than the methadone, when he had cried himself hoarse trying to cut out those non-existent wriggling grubs from under his skin – as bad as the acid trip when he'd been able to see single cells, running riot like cancer all over his body – 'Help me!' he screamed. 'Don't leave me here – ' And then there was Hope's face, mobile and alive and changing like seaweed in the current, laughing at him, mocking him, and bleeding as his nails reached out to rake the smooth, tanned skin.

Station Officer Mollina lumbered through to the cells. That hollerin' was gettin' him down and no way was any prisoner goin' make *that* sort of racket in *his* respectable jailhouse.

'Quiet!' he bellowed as he unlocked the door to the cages. 'Yuh heah? Quiet!'

A thin brown pool of liquid trickled from under the barred door that led to the cell housing last night's white drunk. Moodily Mollina toed the ooze and decided it was nothing worse than old Nescafé.

'What you callin' for, mahn?' he asked, pleasantly enough.

His voice cut into Andrew Dean's brain like an ice-pick. The apparition of Hope vanished as swiftly as it had appeared.

And reality swept in on Dean to leave him reeling. There were no black nurses in peaked caps at the hospital – there were no bars on the door in solitary – only thick padding.

This wasn't Broadmoor – this was Nevis. It was okay. The release, the flight over – they hadn't been a delusion. Only the faces had been conjured up from within . . .

It dawned on him that somehow he'd got himself into jail, and he needed to find out what he'd done to get himself there.

The music was quiet enough for him to form the words, though he'd have to get hold of the Largactils soon because any respite from the faces would be only temporary –

'What did I do?' he asked brokenly.

'Nothin', so far as I knowed.'

Dean hauled himself up till he was sitting on the edge of

the hard metal cot. He wiped his wet forehead with his palms and concentrated on keeping the officer in focus. 'Why am I in here?'

'You very, very dronk, mahn. You not capable of movin' yesterday night an' I think you still in de same situation.'

'I did nothing?' said Dean incredulously. He almost laughed. 'Nothing?'

Mollina shook his head slowly. This didn't sound like some innocent drunk. Maybe there should have been some charges laid after all.

'You mean I can go?' Dean went on. 'I'm free?'

'Well, slow down, heah. First I got to take a note of your name an' address. Den I ask you some questions to ascertain whether you is an undesirable a-lien. If you is, den we get you sent home, wherevers dat might be. Can you walk?'

'Sure,' said Dean, straightening up shakily and lurching for the opening to freedom. 'I'm not hungover – '

'Sure you ain't!'

'I'm not, officer. I'm epileptic, see. I need to have tablets regularly and I must've overslept my time.'

Mollina was almost convinced. He supported the swaying man to the front desk where he took down the information he needed. 'You livin' heah, Mistah Walker?' he choked as Dean gave his address. 'On top of de station? Ha! Den we knows where you is sure enough. An' we be keepin' an *eye* out for you, mahn. All de time.'

The room was hot as a cellar and the sound of water boiling in rusty pipes echoed from the kitchenette.

Those pills, those goddam pills. Where the fuck were they? Dean ran through to the bathroom and flung open a cupboard over the sink where a dead, brown cockroach lay belly-up.

His hands trembled as they twisted off the lid to the bottle and he crammed six white pellets into his mouth, crunching them because he couldn't bare to touch the tap with the dead thing lying so close. They were bitter as quinine and his body rebelled at their taste, heaving and

94

retching but losing the battle to reject them.

For a while, he leaned against the green-painted wall, resting, panting, knowing that soon he would be in control again.

Being alone didn't help. And he'd been alone since Nicky had turned away from him. Because of the bitch.

He'd been isolated for two fucking years. When he hadn't been confined to solitary, he'd been shipwrecked among the crowd of lunatics that couldn't tell their arses from their elbows in the main ward.

At least he'd never been a moron, he thought with satisfaction. At least his particular brand of mental disorder hadn't been due to a congenital defect that would have made him unfit to be called a human being. His own *imbalance* had been man-made, through drugs and ill-treatment. Oh no, Andrew Dean was in no way responsible for his fucked-up head. You can't blame yourself for getting a habit.

He was calmer now, walking softly, catlike across the dusty linoleum. His thoughts were straight. The music had gone. Now he could concentrate.

He opened the snakeskin bag and tucked the pistol that had been concealed there into his pocket. He took out a stiletto knife and a fading photograph of a woman in her mid-twenties with shoulder-length blonde hair and eyes like jade. Here she was, right in his hands. The woman who had had him locked away for two years. The woman who had made Nicky despise him.

For the first time in two years, Andrew Dean had an erection. It had to be the feel of the knife in his hand. It certainly wasn't the thought of Hope Parnell that was arousing him. The only way *she* could get him worked up was by dying.

Slowly and very carefully he cut the irises out of the picture with his blade as his excitement mounted. Each slice he removed quickened his pulse, stiffened his penis further.

But because there was no blood, he could not reach a climax. And eventually he flung the streamers of paper back into his bag in an agony of frustration and hatred.

Chapter Seven

THE STORY Lottie Wolff told to the Reuters man in Basseterre, St Kitts, was not strictly accurate. She was made more fluent in her vehemence by an hour-long sea journey that had felt like a year in hell.

According to Lottie, Veronica Marston, 40, society woman of independent means, was considering her engagement to former Cabinet Minister and the Right Honourable Member for Tiswick East, Dr Stuart Wilding. However the unfortunate woman was destined for an extremely long betrothal as father of two, Wilding, had yet to separate from his current wife.

It was neatly summarised, even if it was all guesswork: but Lottie wasn't one to admit that. Veronica's behaviour and her undisguised misery were all the proof she needed.

'Standing this one up's going to be tricky unless either Marston or Wilding will talk,' said the Reuters man, tapping his front teeth with a Bic.

Lottie delivered her coup by presenting him with the photograph. 'This was taken last week,' she lied.

He took the photograph, whistled, and made a few swift long-distance calls. The call to the Commons established Wilding had not been in the Divisions Lobby for an important vote the previous week. A second conversation with a contact in Wilding's constituency revealed that the MP had secretly announced his intention not to stand for re-selection at the next election.

It was enough to start work on, said the Reuters man, and Lottie left the upstairs office feeling relieved that the co-incidences had rolled in her favour. Had Veronica's ex-lover attended Parliament when he should have done, she'd have had to think fast to invent a cover story. Thankfully,

Stuart Wilding had played into her hands, though Lottie was unaware of why these events should have taken place so fortuitously.

She met Jessica outside The Golden Lemon Boutique. 'Poor Ron,' she sighed. 'I knew it was all a lie. That bastard Wilding's about to resign – he wasn't expecting a return to the Cabinet at all. It was just an excuse to dump her.'

Jessica looked puzzled.

'He's got rid of Ron and now he's ditching politics. It can only mean that his wife's found out and given him the ultimatum.'

They were strolling down to The Circus, where a gingerbread clock struck a doleful eleven. Jessica stopped and fiddled with her Minolta to get a picture of the square. 'There are other possibilities,' she said, adjusting the focus.

'No way. It's the threat of The Elbow.' She was so sure. So convinced. It was Lottie's stock in trade to formulate theories. 'What's the first thing you do when you know your husband's got a fancy woman? What did you do?'

It was still a painful memory. A failure that nibbled away at Jessica's insides like a disease. It had been less than a year after their marriage that Joseph Collier's first affair came to light. Okay with hindsight maybe she'd deserved it. She'd been immature and silly; a yes-kid in a twenty-five year-old's body; a live-in ornament when Joe had wanted a thinking partner, not a Barbie Doll.

She'd learned a lot since then, though city-sharp Lottie would be the last person to see the changes. People you'd known all your life never realised you could grow up.

'It's a long time ago. Fifteen years.'

'It doesn't stop it being relevant.'

'All right, Lottie, if you want to grind old bones, I'll admit that I did make Joe sell the house, move to a new area and all that. But I didn't persuade him to pack in his career, as you're assuming Wilding's wife has done.' She grunted and fitted the lens cover back into place.

'No, but you got Joe away by *moving*, didn't you? Wilding's wife is getting rid of the Veronica factor by making sure he won't be in London all the time, so there'll be no chance of him bumping into Ron by accident.'

'Well that tactic didn't work with Joe.'

'No. And I'm sure it won't work with this bastard Wilding. And don't forget it's poor Ron who's suffering.' Lottie glanced nervously at her watch and wondered how long they'd got before the horrendous trip back to Nevis. Two hours and nine minutes, that's all, Hell. In more ways than one. 'What have you got there?'

Jessica passed her the green bag she carried. Inside was a pair of aquamarine earrings set into an enamel clasp.

'Pretty. For you?'

'No. For Ronnie.'

'You're not feeling guilty are you, Jessica?' Lottie asked patronisingly.

Jessica flushed. Lottie had struck unerringly home yet again. 'Guilty? No, not that,' she said. 'Anxious. I'm just worried about the consequences.

'You know you might be right when you say Veronica would appreciate a bit of revenge. Hell hath no fury etcetera. Then again you might not. You never can tell with Ron. I just think you should have warned her what you were planning to do, that's all.'

Caught off guard, Lottie snapped: 'I'm not the only one. You're as much involved as I am by association. You could have told Ron yourself, though that would have been an end to the matter. You know her. Let well alone.

'You either think that I have done the right thing, despite what you say, or else you can't wait to see what happens. Something exciting is about to happen in your quiet life. But you've either got to be with me or against me.'

'Quiet?' Jessica was indignant. God – just because she didn't bleat about her successes, her investments and her achievements –

'And I don't count jet-setting, Jessica. That's sitting doing nothing, letting other people whisk you from A to B.'

For the first time, Jessica considered upsetting the status quo by telling her just how wrong she was. How ill-founded was her assumed superiority.

But Lottie forestalled her, ploughing on, speaking in

capitals. 'This is a Turning Point. You have to remember that if Wilding is disgraced, he could be forced to stand down straight away.

'It's a *hung Parliament*. His seat is *vital*. If he goes – the whole Government could fall.' She paused to let her friend take it in.

'So if you really are against me, you've got the power to do something about it right now. Go and tell Don Derby I've lied. Go and say I'm nothing but a malevolent scandal-monger. Only you'd better hurry.'

They were in Cayon Street. They'd walked back to their starting point without even noticing. Lottie stopped short, blocking the pavement, waving her arms like windmill sails. Crowds of shoppers, business people, tourists, parted as they approached the two women there, like currents at a reef.

'Well?' demanded Lottie. 'Make your mind up. Are you going up to that building – ' she gesticulated at the office above the antiques shop across the road where at that very moment the West Indies correspondent was already cabling the News Editor of the *News of The World*, 'Or not?'

Jessica frowned. A general election? She and Lottie might be about to bring down the Government? Impossible. It was a private affair. Lottie was being melodramatic. Absurd.

Jess Collier was used to relying on her army of professional advisers in her business life. She paid other people to buy and sell, manage and direct on her behalf. It made her susceptible to Lottie's persuasion now.

'Let's go and have a coffee and a cake at the Palm Restaurant,' she said at last. 'I don't want to go and see your newspaper man.'

Lottie grinned in relief. 'Thank God for that. You nearly had *me* doubting myself.' She hesitated, remembering something that had occurred to her a few minutes earlier. 'Hang on, though. Let's nip back to the shop where you found the earrings first,' she said. 'I want to see if there's a matching bracelet.'

Hope left Pansy in charge of the Sugar Mill and told her

she'd be back by dinner. Pansy thought it odd that she should take the time off when she'd gone to a great deal of trouble to arrange cover for her flights and extra staff in for the unexpected guests and said so. Pansy was not one for concealing what she thought.

'Ah think you has taken a shine to dat boat-man. An' ah think you is not right in de head.' She banged her own head with a fist and it wagged self-righteously above a large, brightly coloured bosom.

'It's okay, Pansy,' said Hope. 'I just felt like a bit of time to myself. I'm not terribly interested in Mr Murdoch.'

'*Meestah* Murdoch!'

'Will you stop worrying about my welfare? Please?'

Pansy grunted and swung on her heel, her red, green, orange and purple skirt twirling around her large hips.

Hope didn't feel guilty – well, no guiltier than she had when she habitually skipped Cookery lessons at Bridelands, all those years ago. She used to hide in the lavatories reading about faraway places, her feet propped up on the loo-roll opposite so that any prowling prefects wouldn't notice the shoes beneath the door.

The escape made her feel sneaky, like Snoopy playing at being Joe Cool.

She drove down the coiling drive between the coconut palms, a hamper filled with cold chicken in mayonnaise, conch fritters, bread rolls and fresh fruit, balanced on the seat next to her.

She hadn't brought wine. Or plates, or napkins, or a table cloth, or any of the bits and pieces that the romantic associate with picnics. She wasn't sure whether she wanted a romance with the casual Ned Murdoch anyway. He was just someone who happened to be around, that's all. Just an unattached man who looked quite pleasant, played pool as badly as she did and had a scar on his cheek. And eyes that creased in the corners from spending most of his time squinting into bright sunlight. And fantastically strong back muscles.

She pulled over at the little shop in the village, where men stood outside, drinking beer in long glasses; women hovered at the counter to look dubiously at the morning's fish which was spread out in the full sun, and children played marbles around their ankles. She bought a rum and raisin ice cream, made with real rum and plump, juicy raisins and thought: Let him wait.

In town, she bought a newspaper from Jenny Smith, who told her about the bearded man living above the police station who was coming to Church on Sunday, and about her son Charles who was maybe going to be a magistrate, and about Lady Veronica Marston who had been into town that morning.

'*Miss* Marston,' corrected Hope automatically.

'You comin' to de Church of De One God on Sunday, Miss Parnell?' asked Jenny Smith hopefully.

'Don't think so, Mrs Smith,' said Hope, scanning the paper for a weather report.

'Dey say dere's another storm comin' from de west,' said Jenny.

Hope looked at the sky and shook her head again, as she had earlier to the gardener. 'No chance,' she said. 'Not a wisp of a cloud, and no wind to blow one in.'

She handed the paper back to the old woman, careful not to crease it so it could be re-sold.

Hope walked towards the cinema that was showing something that sounded fairly far-out: Lolita's Return From Domination. The poster had a portrait of a young black woman dressed in chains and surrounded by men with whips and wearing nothing but black leather cod-pieces. The film itself though would be totally innocuous, and quite probably nothing at all to do with either the title or the advertisement. It wouldn't even necessarily star the actress on the poster.

The hamper was quite heavy and she cradled it in her arms as she neared the harbour behind the little houses, glad she had kept the rush hat on as a protection from the fierce sun.

Behind Hope, at a discreet distance and so casually even Jenny Smith hadn't noticed he was trailing her, Andrew Dean dogged her footsteps.

He had seen her from his window. Two years of waiting and here she was. She was unmistakable. Maybe his

101

chance was coming sooner than he'd expected. His heart pounded and drowned out the rhythms in his head.

As she cut across the wasteland to the tiny marina where the Maria Juana was anchored, she glanced over her shoulder, feeling uneasy.

Quick as a flash, Andrew Dean jumped a picket fence into somebody's garden to hide behind a bush. Where was she going, all alone like Little Red Riding Hood with her hat and her picnic hamper?

Excitedly, he watched her standing uncertainly by the jetty and saw the man leaping across the deck, over ropes and furled sails to get to her. Not so alone, after all, then.

She hadn't seen her lover yet, but Andrew Dean had. God must be on his side, pointing this man out to him. What poetic justice. An eye for an eye.

Hope shook herself, putting the nebulous shadow out of her mind. She stared at the only boat docked. So this was Ned Murdoch's yacht. What an understatement. The Maria Juana was an enormous ocean-going vessel, not one of the usual grey schooners that did the tour of the islands.

Unreasonably, she felt she'd been deliberately deceived. Ned Murdoch wasn't what she'd expected. Or perhaps even what she wanted.

The telephone rang, resounding through the bright, airy rooms at Longthorpe Manor.

'Mrs Wilding?' said Tim Nesbitt.

'Yes?'

'Jannine Wilding?'

'Yes.'

'Sorry to disturb you. My name's Tim Nesbitt, *News of the World*. I wondered if I might ask you a few things about your husband?'

'Of course,' said Jannine Wilding, thinking how did they get hold of the resignation so fast? A mole at Constituency?

'Is it true Doctor Wilding no longer intends to fight the next election?' He knew he was on safe ground. Start with the easy questions. Get them flowing. On your side because you're so sympathetic.

'You should probably ask my husband – he's upstairs. Shall I get him?'

'No – no. It's the woman's angle I'm after here. What *you* think about the resignation.'

'Oh I see. Well, since you already know then, I'll tell you that he has my full backing. I think it was essential under the circumstances. We discussed it of course. His business commitments are very heavy, Mister Nesbitt.'

Ha! Resignation confirmed! The other reporter listening in on the audio-only extension winked and put his thumbs up to Nesbitt to show he'd got it written down.

'What exactly are those business commitments, Mrs Wilding?' There was a silence. 'Just the engineering?' he prompted. Mustn't let her seize up.

'That's right.'

'Are you happy about this, no longer being in the public eye?'

She relaxed. 'Oh yes – it will be a great relief not to be trailed round by security men and photographers. Though, you know, we haven't been so public since Stuart left Defence.'

'There's no other reason for the resignation?'

'No, why should there be?'

Here was the biggie. 'What about Veronica Marston?'

Jannine Wilding's gasp was perfectly audible on the other end of the telephone.

Stuart had said it was over! That he wasn't seeing her any more! That she had gone away! It had been hushed up for so long . . . Three, maybe four years. But now everyone would know what a fool she'd been, when there was nothing left to know.

'I gather she's his mistress,' said Nesbitt coolly. Hit 'em when they're down.

'Mistress?'

He'd promised there'd be no scandal. He'd kept his word till now. Veronica Marston was supposedly out of circulation, out of Stuart's life. Out of her life. 'No,' she cried. 'No not any more . . . '

Nesbitt glanced excitedly at the other reporter. 'So there's to be no divorce, Mrs Wilding?'

Divorce? What was this man talking about?

'Of course there's no divorce! That's all over. Done. Finished.'

'And that's not why Doctor Wilding resigned to the Constituency on Tuesday night?'

'No!' Jannine Wilding was almost screaming.

'Or why he didn't attend the crucial vote on arms to Chile last week? Or why we've heard he has been seen sleeping in his car in Kensington on and off for a fortnight? Or why he's been pictured in the West Indies with Miss Marston?'

'Stuart! Stuart!' Jannine called.

'And can I ask your age, Mrs Wilding?'

'Take this bloody 'phone. It's the Press and they say you're divorcing me. That you and Veronica – '

Stuart Wilding, haggard and still in his dressing gown, took the receiver from her. He had already been on his way, hearing the alarm in her voice. The panic.

Wearily he said into the 'phone: 'Call me back. Give me two hours.' And hung up.

Two reporters at Wapping danced a victory dance. 'We've got the lead!' they called, prancing over to the subs desk. Tim Nesbitt said: 'All confirmed. Well nearly. And the wife didn't know but she does now!'

The panic was gone. It was as though her emotions were smothering between cushions. 'You lied.'

'I'm sorry, Jannine, I never lied.'

'You told me it was over.'

'It is. You know that. I was – I am – devastated, I haven't tried to hide it from you.'

She turned her back on him and stared out of the leaded windows. 'Then how do *they* know? And what's this about the West Indies? And – Stuart – a divorce?' Her voice was rising, cracking.

'Sit down, please. Please. I can't think when you pace.' He knew he was being unkind. Betraying her like this made him cruel. 'Yes it's over. Her and me. And you and me.'

No-no-no-no. Why did she feel he was hitting her? Strangling her?

104

'I have to find her Jan, I'm useless without her. I'm a wreck, I don't sleep – '

'You want my sympathy? You want me to understand that your mistress has left you broken-hearted? And then ruined you by going to the Press about your affair?'

'She didn't – '

'Explain it then.'

'I can't, Jan. But she wouldn't. You know her – you like her.'

'I *hate* her!'

'But I love her,' he shouted. 'And if I've screwed up my life because she's gone, it's because I don't care.'

'Not your life, Stuart, you're a survivor. Mine. And David's and Natalie's – God she's got her degree next year.'

'All right, but don't you want the truth?'

'No!' she screamed. 'Not if it's going to destroy my world! I want lies – I want deception. Tell me anything but not the truth!'

Stuart shook his head. 'I can't do that. I've had enough of wasting your life and mine. Jan I love you, but not in the right way. We love, but we're not *in* love. We're like brother and sister. We were too young, sweetheart. We changed. We were comfortable. Never exciting.'

Jannine said sadly: 'I like comfort.'

But deep down she knew that was just another pretence.

The reporter rang back when the two hours were up, to the minute. It was another witnessed interview, though Stuart Wilding didn't know and would not have cared.

By the time the copious short-hand notes were typed out as a memo to be directed to the paper's legal department, Jannine was sitting in the back of a taxi, heading for the railway station to buy a ticket to anywhere.

Karin Genevieve was a late riser, and why not? For all she cared, it could be nearly lunchtime.

What luxury. No dawn calls any more. Nobody yelling at her to dive and dive again for data from the wrecked nuclear sub.

105

No Perce screaming: *'Cut! It's not hard, Karin. You just gotta make sure the machinery's facing the fuckin' camera. We don't need another shot of your fuckin' ass.'*

No thinly-disguised Soviets holding her hostage in the wastes of Anguilla for *six whole days* while Mister Big Shot decides whether the mercenaries are going to attack from the left or the right.

No barking stars complaining about her 'trying to steal the limelight.' She'd never imagined that making serious movies was such hard work.

Stretching languorously she felt linen sheets, smooth as silk, against her toes. Above and around her, the gauze mosquito net made everything in the lovely room look as though it was under water. Yes, it really was a lovely room. In fact it was quite a lovely life, now that the hard work was over. Such a pity the other half of the bed wasn't occupied by some gorgeous stranger for her to seduce and to fall madly, passionately in love with her. Such a pity Ned Murdoch was playing so hard to get.

She dived to the edge of the netting and wormed her way through a tangle of material to reach for the 'phone to order coffee to be brought to her terrace. Then she dialled Ned's room to see if he too was a late riser when he was on dry land.

Someone answered: 'Hello dere.'

Only the maid, she said to herself reassuringly and hung up without bothering to speak.

She bathed in the left-hand bath, pouring lashings of Chanel into the stream from the faucet, soaking herself in oils and creams to ensure her skin would be peach-smooth, silky perfect. Her completely hair-free body glistened and she admired it lovingly, touching, petting herself, remembering the West Indian, Terry Morelands, last night.

He had followed her back to her room in the hope of getting some. Hard-ly, she thought. He reminded her of some pimp she had known back in Highland Park before she had made it. Just no way was Terry-the-pimp going to have any.

Better to screw somebody who can do something for you if you're not going to have a good time. Somebody like

106

King. Or Perce, at a pinch. She'd done it before, she could do it again . . . as long as she kept her eyes closed.

She climbed out of the bath and into the huge fuschia-coloured towel that hung warming on the heated rail. She rubbed more auto-tan into her body, all over, between her legs, rubbing the cream round and round over her hyper-active clitoris, dipping her finger inside herself, carefully so as not to drag the tender skin with a finger nail. No one else could do it this well.

She sat on the edge of the bath, careful not to disturb the set of the autobronze. She watched the long, thin hand moving in rapid motions over and into her body. The mirror opposite reflected her tension, her trembling thighs, her quivering mouth.

So many cameramen had watched her do just this. She could control her own orgasm perfectly. Reach the height of passion in ten seconds or ten minutes or ten hours. She was the perfect skinflick star, producing climaxes to order.

And here it comes. Here comes that climbing sensation, the moment when the clitoris and the vagina take over and the rest of Karin Genevieve sinks into a complete oblivion for however long it takes to fall from the peak of the highest cliff in the world.

'That's better,' she sighed to her adoring reflection and reached for the Factor 15 total sun-block cream. She needed to protect her delicate skin from the sun's natural rays.

Zeke and Jimmy the pool boy, their eyes popping at Karin Genevieve's open bathroom window-slats, silently exchanged obscene facial expressions and arm movements before blending into the background of the garden.

The coffee was still hot on the cane table outside. She left her room, dressed in a virginal, white swim-suit, jewelled sandals and a neat little beach robe made out of feathers.

Oz Lennox loaded the six cases of champagne, five Moets for the Barbados Beach Club, and one case of Lanson for Hope, into The Goose and under the watchful eye of the Miami customs official. He checked his watch, and decided he had time for a beer before the long flight back to Barbados. Then he would see Esme Little, his long-time lover, she of the ebony breasts, the coal-black thighs and the red, red mouth.

Things should be easier between them this time. There were no conflicts of interest any more.

Esme had had two men for too long. Now she'd just have to make do with the one. Shame Bill hadn't made his exit sooner.

He knew Esme's flight schedule for the day and worked out that she'd be back in Barbados in time for them to spend the night together.

He drank two beers with the customs guy, and they swapped anecdotes about women who tried to smuggle jewellery into the country under labels in their clothes, inside make-up jars and inside their bodies.

'You've only got to watch the way they walk,' shrugged the customs man.

Oz thought about the Moroccan Red in the heel of his shoe, a present for Esme, and concentrated on laughing in the right places. When he'd drained his glass, he walked very, very normally out of the long, low hut out to The Goose and prepared himself for a smooth take-off.

The dials flashed their willingness to get the craft airborne, the radio crackled and confirmed a clear air-space. Oz eased the plane into the runway and as it gathered speed, he pulled back the yoke to which the other pilot, Gem Welch, had attached the insulting note 'This one takes you UP'.

Ned Murdoch was hauling ropes, calling instructions to his crew who ate, slept and lived on the boat dreaming that they too would one day own their own.

Seeing Hope below, he loped over the boards and waved, shouting: 'The ramp's over there.'

Hope looked down at her hamper and thought ruefully that she needn't have bothered. He had probably got one of the Roux brothers on board as his personal chef.

She climbed unsteadily, aware of the boat's rocking on the tide. Hope was no sailor. Every time she had been on a ship, she had vowed it would be the last. That old remark of her stepbrother's, made when she got a splinter in her finger or a cut leg as a child, that 'worse things happen at sea', had impressed her deeply. Then, and now.

The ramp ended abruptly, hanging over the edge of the ship with a three foot drop below her onto the deck. 'I bet he puts down a proper ramp for the tourists,' she thought, annoyed.

He was balanced on top of a cabin, doing something with sails, hoisting them up the mast or something. 'Good day for a sail,' he shouted to her, his eyes sparkling and crinkling, even at that distance. 'There's a wind going to pick up.'

'I know,' Hope shouted back. 'Big storm brewing.' If you can't beat them, join them. Everyone else was determined that today the sun shouldn't shine, that there shouldn't be a blue sky. Who was she to kick against the pricks?

'You were late. Thought you weren't coming.'

Hope shrugged. 'Well I did. I brought a hamper. Chicken and stuff.'

Ned jumped down from the roof of the wheelhouse to land next to her like a buccaneer. 'You needn't have worried. I've got a chef on board. Or I thought I might fish and we could grill it over an open fire in a cove.'

Oh very romantic and twee, thought Hope, no longer in the same good mood she'd woken up with. She wasn't sure what had spoilt it. The size of the boat, maybe. But she shouldn't have been in awe of it – she'd had many millionaires staying at Sugar Mill. She herself would be one if all her money wasn't tied up in property. Why should she worry if Ned wasn't what he'd at first seemed? Did money make a difference?

'This is just *one* of your boats, is it?' she asked pointedly, following him downstairs into a galley, where, sure enough, a chef in a white uniform and toque worked at a counter, dicing vegetables, slicing avocados into fans, shelling prawns faster than any machine could do it. At least it wasn't Albert Roux.

'Yes,' said Ned. 'There are three, but this is the big one.

109

Come on, I'll show you round. Leave the basket on the side, Michel will put it in the fridge.'

There was a state room. In the centre, an enormous rosewood table took up half the available space. There were bedrooms that were as luxurious as those at the Sugar Mill. There were two dining rooms, one casually arranged for buffet meals, the other laid formally. Tapestries and wall-hangings were suspended between the huge windows looking onto the deck.

There was one lounge, very modern in pale blue and chrome and rainbow-coloured metallic wallpaper that rippled as the light reflected onto it from the sea.

'I'd have dressed more appropriately if I'd known,' said Hope, looking down at her bare legs and her worn leather sandals.

'Hey! What's up?' laughed Ned. 'Am I in full dress uniform?' He wore nothing but a pair of very faded cut-down Levis.

She smiled. 'Sorry, I think I wasn't perhaps expecting all the grandeur. I should probably excuse myself and say I've got something to do back at the hotel.'

'The hell you will,' said Ned. 'We're not turning back.'

Turning back?

Hope looked out of the window again. St Kitts was nearer. She was on a boat and she hadn't felt it move. Her stomach wasn't churning. She tried the ultimate test of remembering what she'd had for breakfast and still didn't feel bad. She brightened visibly.

'We really are moving, aren't we?' she said in amazement.

Ned didn't understand. 'You think I sent the fitters away just so we could sit in the marina at Nevis?' He took her arm to guide her to the front window. She felt a charge of electricity shoot through her at his unexpected touch. He felt it too and didn't let go.

'We're going to an uninhabited part of the island,' he said. 'Boats often moor in the coves, but we'll just move around until we find one that's properly deserted.'

'Shouldn't you have a moustache to twirl as you say that, and call me m'dear?'

'Would you send out an SOS if I did?'

They went back to the deck, where the Grenadian deck-hand was setting out two chairs. 'You sitting, Ned, or you workin'?'

'You drive,' he said. 'I want to watch the world go by and see if I can read this lady's mind.'

Despite the sunshine, the virgin forests and unnamed mountains of the south were dark. Every now and then, they lit up briefly to look like faded moss.

'They say there are still Caribs living there,' said Hope.

'More likely Rastas lighting fires,' said Ned. 'Cookin' a little vegetable stew, smokin' a little weed.' He did the accent very well.

A wind picked up the sail and it billowed, pregnant, to speed the journey. Every now and then there was a puff of cloud, brilliantly white like a floating snow-capped mountain against a cobalt blue sky.

Keith the Grenadian cut the engine and there was no sound apart from the rushing of the sail, the lapping of the water.

Hope, feeling brave, leaned over the rail to peer into the sea. 'You can see the bottom,' she said.

'That's at least twenty fathoms down,' said Ned. 'I hope.'

There were great coral reefs off to starboard, populated by animal-flowers, tiny psychedelic fish nibbling at the coral, the occasional sailfish, red snappers and tuna. 'Lunch?' asked Ned, pointing to one of the snappers.

'What do you do, clap and it jumps into your arms?' said Hope.

'No, I whistle,' he said, squaring his shoulders, attaching bait onto the end of a line and slinging it over the edge. 'These fish are dumb,' he said. 'They're not street-wise. They'd have no credibility at all in the tough waters of the Atlantic where it's every snapper for himself.'

Keith manipulated the sails to hold the boat steady. *'Feel all right,'* wailed Bob Marley from the tape, suddenly audible in the silence of the sea.

Almost as soon as the bait hit the water, there was a turmoil. Sand was kicked up from the depths of the sea, a

111

shoal of fish seemed to rise like lemmings from nowhere, all anxious for one last meal before the fires of a barbecue could take them.

Instantly, the line jerked taut. The rod bowed and bent into a u-shape, straining, almost hauled out of Ned's hands.

Then he was reeling it in, going with the snapper as it swam in the opposite direction to its captor. They danced a duet, the man and the fish. They shadow-boxed, the man winning as the ratchet on the rod tightened and clicked firm.

'You've got him!' said Hope.

'It's a her,' Ned gasped as the fish, a flash of silver lightning, was swept up into the air. It thrashed uselessly as though it were trying to fly.

'How can you tell the difference?'

The fish thunked onto the deck, heaving at his feet, its eyes seemingly crazy with panic, its body flapping like a shoe gone mad.

'Women never come quietly.'

Chapter Eight

'SEE WHAT dat sign say, whitey?'

Andrew Dean read it and nodded sullenly. It was a large sign, written on cardboard in several different coloured felt-tipped pens. *'Josiah Newcastle, Undertaker. Keep yore ass OUT'* it said.

'So what is you doin' in me garden?' said the man, patiently bending down to Dean's level to peer into his eyes with an understanding that Dean at once felt threatening.

'I knowed you,' said the man. 'You is de guy livin' over de sta-shun in de town. I seen you last night at de Rookery Nook.'

Dean toyed with the idea of trying out the pistol, it was right there in his pocket, but the man was big and ugly, and too close for comfort. You never knew how fast big guys could move. So instead he told the truth. It was always his last resort. 'I was following a woman.'

'Ah,' said the man. 'Womahn.'

'I didn't want her to see me.'

'If you got troubles wid ah womahn, I unnerstahnd.' Josiah was a keen student of female behaviour, with three wives behind him and sixteen children who didn't know their pappy from Adam. 'You comin' in de house, boy, an' I tell you about womahn.' Josiah's eyes rolled to show Dean just how much he was going to tell him. Dean glanced back at the marina then followed the disappearing blue overalls reluctantly. He shrugged. There was nothing he could do about Hope Parnell right now.

The shack behind the corrugated iron door smelled of dog shit. Two pups emerged from under what had been a sofa thirty years ago. In the corner of the one room stood what used to be a bed where a mongrel, a skinny old bitch, lay curled asleep.

There was a two-ring stove against the wall, a mat on the floor. There were no windows but the room was light because there was hardly any ceiling.

'What do you do when it rains?' said Dean.

'I go into de garden,' said Josiah. 'If I gettin' wet, I may as well be watchin' God's love pour heself over de plants an' de grass an' de trees.'

He paused to see whether the bearded stranger would chip in with an Amen. He didn't. 'You drinkin' a little rum?' He poured a two-finger measure into a plastic tumbler without waiting for a reply. 'I keep it in for de bereaved.'

Dean took a sip of the moonshine and it hit the Largactils like lightning. His pulse raced alarmingly; he was short of breath, as though he'd had a double dose of adrenalin.

'You know somethin'? I had many women,' the undertaker was saying. 'An' dey all gived me pain fit to make me heart burst.

'Den I found de ways of De Lord.'

Jesus Christ. Another evangelist. First the newspaper hag, now this one. If they had their way, Andrew Dean would be reborn many times before he'd killed Hope Parnell. Maybe he could be reborn *afterwards* he thought to himself and started to giggle.

'What you laughin' at, mahn?'

Andrew Dean composed his face again. 'Joy, brother,' he said.

Reassured, Josiah said: 'Praise de Lord.'

Wowee. This one was a real sucker.

'I buried one wife when she was only fourteen years. She died in givin' birth to me eldest son. She de only wife who never given me problems. An' we *knowed* why.'

Josiah took a swig of his rum from a plastic bottle and dragged the back of his hand over his mouth. He belched loudly and with satisfaction, enjoying himself. Nothing he liked better than someone who hadn't heard his life story.

'I found out dat de only way to keep a womahn is to poke

114

she all de time. Keep she full of babies. Den no odder mahn int'rested in she. Dat your problehm?'

Andrew Dean ignored the question.

There had been no women. Not a single one, thank you. There had been only men. Brutal men who'd made him scream while he was a kid; and men he'd later brutalised in revenge. That was why the blade had changed his life. Vengeance. It took years for him to find out that that was how he was getting his kicks. The knowledge had come as a surprise: a shock. It was the blood that was turning him on, not the orifices and the willing bodies as he'd at first assumed.

No one ever squealed to the cops. Not in those days, when it was still an offence to be a homosexual. So the fags had kept tight-lipped. They just passed the word around and shut him out of their little twilight zone.

His two older brothers had first taken him down to The Crooked Mile when he was fifteen. It was a place where strobe lights flashed like an acid attack and the Velvet Underground and Beefheart tracks hammered through your spirit as well as your head.

Even now, if he let himself go again, he could be back there, in the midst of the grunts and the moans; the dew-drops of blood and the jism. His head throbbed as if in sympathy and he groaned from the pain . . . But the face he'd so long been unable to recall, the image that he'd struggled unsuccessfully to recapture, floated at last like a ghost into his brain. Nick David's face.

Andrew Dean, in a different world to Josiah Newcastle, whimpered with joy. He knew it was an illusion, but it didn't matter. It didn't diminish his exhilaration. He could picture Nick again! It meant he was breaking through the conditioning. He was Pavlov's Dog no more.

There'd been the erection earlier, at the touch of the knife, and now this vivid memory of Nick! He'd won! He'd beaten the bastards. They hadn't destroyed his real self at all. His memories ran riot, now they were an open book to him. Nick's grey eyes. Nick's face. Nick's athletic body, that was his – only his.

Dean had met him after he'd been discharged from the

Air Force for drug running, and he'd found Nick while he was at his low ebb. Nick had been stoned out of his head, nursing a gin in a bar in Mayfair.

Maybe it was because Dean had needed him in the beginning that things had been different. He hadn't felt the old aggression – hadn't wanted to beat the shit out of this one, the way he had with the others.

And Nick had *really* loved him, hadn't he? He'd given him his own plane and the IN-Flight contract after that first six months. Okay, so it had been a crummy idea. That wasn't Nick's fault. He just hadn't read him right. The only thing Dean had wanted was to be close to him. Every minute of the day.

Dean had reluctantly flown five thousand miles away, consoling himself with the customised Cessna and the thought that this was just the next stage in their relationship. It wasn't anything permanent. It was a temporary separation that was simply grooming him for a partnership in IN-Flight.

Dean snorted ironically and Josiah the undertaker frowned, puzzled. Where was dis guy's head? Not in dis house, dat for sure.

But women wreck, Dean thought bitterly. Women destroy. Women kill emotions with their spying and their jealousy and their self-righteous testimonies.

And now it was all over for Nick David's pretty little step-sister. He had never hurt Nick but now he'd do it to Hope Parnell instead. Properly. He'd smash his knife into that soft face like a mallet into butter and he'd wash his hands in her blood. Just wait till the sailor's out of the way.

He laughed mirthlessly and the forgotten glass in his hand dropped to the floor, shattering his chain of thoughts. It took a long time for him to remember where he was. This stinking room with the big black guy sitting squat-legged on the bed opposite, the bottle of moonshine tipping in his hands.

The world was swimming underwater. He had to get out.

He was half-way to the door when he stopped. What had

116

he been thinking about? What had been on his mind to throw him off balance just now? The boat. No, not the boat. It was the man on the boat.

Maybe the black guy could be some use after all. People in the islands tended to know everybody else's business.

'You know when the big schooner's due out of the harbour?' he demanded.

Josiah shook his head, his mouth still open from having stopped in mid-sentence. He'd been telling the sad tale of his unfaithful third wife till that final pistol-shot laugh and he hadn't yet bothered to close it. 'I can find out. I drink wid de crew at de Rookery Nook ev'ry night.'

Dean pounced. 'You seeing them tonight?'

'Sure, mahn. As always.'

Did that mean the boat was left empty?

'You're seeing all of them? The whole crew?'

Josiah's confused face crinkled like a withering plum; something didn't feel quite right. 'All 'cept de boss. He stayin' at a Plahntation. Why? You wantin' to hitch a ride?'

'Maybe.'

'Dose men doan't take no free-loaders – but if you wantin' to see for youself, dey'll be dere tonight. I guess you can ax dem, no harm tryin'.'

Dean smirked to himself. *This was going to be easy. Like smothering a new-born babe, but more satisfying.*

Josiah watched him go and shivered. He was a small man, five-eight, five-nine maybe, not in peak condition – that was for sure – but there was something about him that could make your blood run cold. Those weird private jokes all the time, like he had a personal comic strip going non-stop in his brain. He hadn't listened to a word of the advice that Josiah had offered. He was a blank, like one of the corpses that were sometimes in the morgue behind the shed; he was empty, like a glass with no beer.

Josiah shook the Big Ben alarm clock on the chest of drawers, decided it was about time for a break and lumbered off to The Longstone Bar. There was nothing he could put his finger on, but he was uneasy. A good day had turned bad for no damn reason, and it bothered him.

Ned watched the dinghy bobbing on the sea as the men scudded round the bay, scuba-diving, fishing.

He'd buried the bones of the snapper in the sand, and felt greasy from the fish.

'Swimming?' he called to Hope, who was drawing crazy patterns in the sand with a piece of the burnt firewood.

'Again?'

He walked towards her, feeling the sand burning the soles of his feet. 'Why not?'

'Indigestion, on top of all that food. I hadn't noticed your appetite last night. But now . . . I'm amazed you can move.'

Keith leaped from the dinghy, like a black star with his arms and legs splayed.

Hope pointed to him. 'Is that how you got that?' she asked, tracing the livid line of the scar down his face with a finger. 'Leaping like a maniac out of a boat?'

'Nope. It's a coral scratch. Fairly new – that's why it looks so bad. It'll fade.' God, she was lovely. If it wasn't for that boat . . . 'I'll just swim out to the dinghy and back. Won't be long.'

Taking a run at the water, he plunged in, feeling that time was precious.

He hoisted himself up into the boat and looked back at the sand. Hope was stretched out on her back, the brim of her hat lowered to shield her eyes from the fierce sun. Keith's snorkel was zooming towards him, reminding him of a periscope.

'Get this dinghy out of sight, Keith,' he said as the Grenadian's face bobbed on the sea like a buoy.

He leered, knowingly. 'Round de cove or back on board, Ned?'

'On board. But listen out for me to yell if we want a lift back from the shore. Later.'

He dived back in the Caribbean and struck out for the beach, feeling the currents running around him, seeing the coral, well below.

118

She was asleep. Should he waken her? He could do. He could run his hand along her body, kiss her awake, make love to her. Tentatively, almost afraid, he reached out to feel the dark brown skin beneath his fingers. It was soft and smooth and dry. Golden girl.

There wasn't much air in the cove. It tended to stick in pockets in the West Indies, and this was one of the places it had decided not to hang around. So much for the predicted gale.

He stretched out by her side and let his hand flow along her warm arm, closing his eyes. There was no urgency after all. Things were very easy with Hope. No pressure.

It was so quiet. Even the sea didn't make too much noise out here.

A breeze at last escaped from the places where breezes usually flock to and licked over him like a warm blanket. How wonderful it would be to roll over on to his side and enfold her in his arms. How perfect to press his lips to hers and share her breath. Instead, he dozed, stroking her in his sleep.

And when he awoke, she was gone. He twisted onto his elbows, peering through half-closed eyes to filter out the white light. What was she doing?

Gathering shells. There were good shells on this beach. Large pieces of brain coral, conch, tiny molluscs. It was a good place for treasure hunting.

If he hadn't felt so laid back, he'd have gone poking around in the sand himself, to watch the vongole dig themselves back into the depths as soon as he uncovered them.

He stretched his long body and flexed his toes. A sand fly emerged and tried to bite the sole of his foot but the skin was too tough. Too many years of working everything from racing yachts to ketches for rich men. Too many years, now, of running his own fleet.

Ned could see the tiny figures of Keith and the guys, dancing around the Maria Juana, monkeying up the masts, blasting out ska. Occasionally, he could hear the strains of the music.

Clouds, like camels, like dragons, appeared from the left

119

hand side of the cove, scooted – in a hurry – to the right hand side and disappeared without ever obscuring the sun.

Hope had kept her clothes on. All of them except the sandals. That absurd hat. It made her look like an English country lady gathering roses for the hall and the morning room. She had even swum in it, with her blond hair, unruly wisps framing her face, tucked up inside the crown. Her clothes, soaked with salt water, dried rapidly in the sun, leaving strands of seaweed emerging from pockets.

She was bending over now, scooping water up into the hat.

'I'm sifting the sea!' she yelled, aware he was awake.

She aroused him every time he looked at her. Her long legs tapered perfectly from her slim hips. What had Betty Grable insured her legs for? A million? Hope's were just as beautifully formed. The shorts, tight from the water, ended high up on her hips. Her breasts were outlined by the terry-towelling top – more so when it had been wet, when the chocolate circles of her aureoles showed clearly through the damp material. He'd have loved to stroke them, treat them gently, lovingly. Smooth them with the palms of his rough, working hands to feel them swelling under his fingers, moving with her breath.

She was coming back to him.

'Look – how many of these could you fit in a matchbox?' she said, crouching down, holding the hat out to him, showing him the millions of tiny shells that mingled with the sand. 'I like doing this. I always liked shells. Ridiculous living in the Caribbean and never having time to hunt shells.'

He asked, were there any vongole, but his voice was whipped away by a sudden gust of wind. 'Clams, if you don't eat Italian,' he shouted, competing.

She shook her head, no, aware again of his flexible, muscular and powerful body. He was like that, coming over her in guerrilla raids. Close up, talking about something completely innocent, she'd be alive to every movement of his body, drawn to touch him as though she was his puppet. She stood up to get out of range of his laser stare.

Last night she had looked so sophisticated, Ned thought. Today she could be any age. 'When's your birthday?' he asked.

'April. I'm Aries,' she replied. 'But not typical.'

'Yes you are. Fiery lady.'

Fiery lady, she thought, with the laser man.

'We should get back,' she said.

'Or we could stay here forever.'

'Simple as that. Forever, the man says. But I can't clean fish.' She turned to the sea. It had faded to a dark blue, its phosphorescence clouded by currents bringing in bigger waves as the wind swirled the Atlantic somewhere out to the west of Antigua.

He rose to stand with her, the heat from his body tangible even though she stood away from him. He glistened, shiny, with perspiration. There was sand on his forehead where he'd put his hand up to shade his eyes. White against the almost-black of his skin.

'You look Arabian,' she said. 'Apart from the nose. Which is definitely Roman.'

'Very patrician,' he said. 'And your face is like a cloud. It changes every time I look at it. I shall never remember what you looked like when we leave Nevis. Or rather I shall remember fifty different women, all of whom said they were called Hope and lived at the Sugar Mill.'

'We should get back,' said Hope again, but she was thinking: he will remember me.

'Right now you look like a kid.'

'Well I'm not.'

'I saw that last night. How old are you?'

'Oscar Wilde said no woman should ever admit to being over thirty. Next April I'm planning to start lying.'

Ned shook his head. I've wasted this afternoon. Talked, dozed, watched her. I didn't touch her, not in the way I should have done. Too late. Wasted. And I want her.

'I want you,' he said.

'Too late.' There was a sadness in her voice, and a silence, like regret.

'So we have to go then?'

'Yes,' she said.

'Swim out or get Keith and Spencer to bring the boat?'

'Swim, it's cooler.'

'Or stay?'

'Swim. Ned, I have things to arrange. My chef's coming out. And there's this blasted cockfight that I shall have to go to after all because they'll need transport. And I have to change and get ready for dinner. And Pansy will be going mad and – '

'Okay, *okay*.' He looked at the moored Maria Juana and said 'Race you.'

He was running at the water, sailing through the air, angled to hit the surface like a cross-Channel swimmer.

'Bastard cheat,' thought Hope and stuck the hat with the shells still in it onto her head before wading out into the warm waves.

There was chaos at The Sugar Mill Plantation. The chaos was centred on Karin Genevieve.

She was on the beach, surrounded by black traders, the beach dwellers who depended on the treasures of the sea to make their livelihoods. She was wearing nothing but a striking pair of tiny, royal blue pants. Her breasts, tipped by their pale pink nipples like strawberry ice-cream, were bare.

She had spent a happy hour with King over lunch, chasing pieces of grated carrot, lettuce and cucumber across a plate. She had declined any protein because she was still watching her waistline.

So were the beach traders now, when they could take their eyes off her breasts. She was asleep. The men and women, who had approached initially to sell her their coral necklaces, mother-of-pearl earrings, sharks' teeth, island-print sundresses, fresh coconuts and bananas, sat quietly in a circle around her, watching the magnificent chest heave peacefully with the rhythm of her breathing.

Every now and then, one trader would whisper to another.

She sighed contentedly in her sleep. King had fallen under her spell again, as she'd known he would. No sweat getting this one wrapped up. On a pretext, she had

122

declined the planned trip to the Bath House that afternoon with Perce and Jewel and had persuaded King to stay and keep her company.

'Then I'll stop here too,' said Jewel, peevishly, wanting to spoil things.

'Don't be silly, darling,' said Karin, on to her game immediately. 'You go an' have A Ball. I'll be just fine.'

They hadn't had sex since their last row, back on the Maria Juana and Karin was determined to make King pay for it this time. She wanted firm commitment. Or better still – a firm contract. Perhaps she just might give him a reminder after the cockfight, when all their passions were bubbling ready to spill over. She'd be ready for anyone then.

As she slept, now, in the sun, she dreamed of the coming cockfight. But there were no birds, only cocks.

The men and women surrounding her had edged nearer. They were so close they could hear her breathing, smell the strange flowery smell of her.

The Rastafarian, Jumar-which-means-Gathering, felt his seed leading him to his destiny. He was very into the spirit-combined-with-the-body philosophy. If his seed said do something, Jumar-which-means-Gathering did it.

His seed now said 'Take This Woman', and cautiously, balancing his wiry body on pipe-cleaner legs, he rose from the circle to go where no good Rasta boy had been before. She sat waiting for him, her legs partly opened, ready for his hands to reach for her body, ready to open herself to him and to the seed. Jumar-which-means-Gathering knew this. His penis was Active.

Her lips were parted, moist and succulent, tempting him away from what his seed said he was to do. Her breasts, like the volcano in double vision, beckoned him as they jiggled to the rhythm of the soka music in his head. He swayed his hips in time to the music and his shoulders worked in counterpoint.

It was at this moment that Karin awoke. Slowly, like the Sleeping Beauty. Faces swam around her. Black, brown and almost blue faces. Eyes that were ivory from the salt in

123

the wind. Lips moist and hungry. Black hair under woollen caps, headscarves, bandannas.

The tall, tall, man looked at her with eyes that made her feel like a human sacrifice. There was a huge bulge in his cut-off, deckchair-striped pants.

Karin took in the scene in an instant, and opened her mouth to scream – not the cute, realistic little shriek that had become her trademark – but an ugly siren of alarm that echoed through the groves along the beach and up to the great house.

Jumar-which-means-Gathering stopped in his tracks. His hands on long arms hovered uncertainly in front of her breasts. His cracked teeth, yellowed from the ganja, were close to her face. She could smell his garlic breath. In close-up, his hands were enormous with long, curved black nails. He could smell her fear, a much more natural smell than those flowers he'd smelled before on her skin.

Karin screamed again.

And Rachel came running, swathed in her long white pinny, slippers two sizes too large flapping dangerously at the heel, waving a meat bat as she emerged from the grove onto the sand.

Jumar-which-means-Gathering followed his seed's new advice. He ran. His lanky, lithe body leaped a breaker, scudded on a stone, wove in and out of trees until he was a tiny vertical line, a black hairpin man on the white sand bay.

'You come wit' me, Miss Genevieve,' she said to the shaking woman.

'Ahn' you leave dis place,' she said to the traders. 'Or Miss Hoape Parnell gettin' rid of de tradin' licences.'

Slowly, they climbed to their feet. The action was over.

As Hope arrived back at the hotel, she was greeted by the sight of Rachel, sitting at one of the garden tables, feeding sweet tea to Karin. King was standing behind her chair, hands protectively on her shoulders.

'I was raped,' croaked Karin.

'Now, Miss Gen'vieve. No need to pile on de story.'

Rachel told Hope how it had been. And to Karin, she

124

said: 'You doan go an' sit on de beach wit' no clothes on.

'Dese Rasta men have one powerful nature, and dere's nothing wrong wit' dat. It's just dat dey doan't see de white boobies before. We have ah law you know, says you doan go on de beach topless.'

'I thought it was a private beach,' said Karin sulkily, to cover tears.

'He didn't actually touch you, did he?' asked Hope, praying that he hadn't.

Karin shook her head.

'Well then. Come and have a brandy,' said Hope kindly, taking the trembling blond up the stone steps and into the cool hall of the Great House.

She poured them each a huge Remy which Karin drained in one.

She held out her glass for another. 'Couldn't you put a fence round the private part?' she spluttered.

'It's only private because I paid for it,' said Hope. She meant that it *morally* belonged to the beach people: it was their birthright while she was the interloper, but Karin was more interested in the 'I paid for it'.

She clasped the down beach robe to her and leaned forwards: 'You paid for it? The beach is yours?' Her voice was sly.

Hope said yes.

'And the hotel?'

'Yes.'

Karin sat back in her chair. She could have spat at her. No wonder she wasn't in awe of Karin Genevieve. The beautiful bitch was rich. Independent. In control.

Karin hated her. 'Then I shall sue you. Personally. For a lack of security and endangering your guests' lives. There should be armed guards on the beach. Like in Jamaica. And barbed wire.'

'It's not like that here. It's not necessary. These people were only interested.'

'Interested?' Karin screeched. 'Do you have any idea what my body is worth?'

'I'm sure it's very valuable to you, Ms Genevieve.'

'It's *Miss* Genevieve. And it's not just *me* that my body is valuable to. There is a lot of money invested in me. I am insured for millions. Or I will be soon. People *pay* to look at my body.'

'I see,' said Hope slowly. 'You mean you'd have been happier about the incident this afternoon if somebody had passed round a hat.'

'How dare you?'

Hope bit her lip. She had gone too far. It was the first time she'd ever insulted a guest and there'd been plenty of provocation before today. 'I apologise. I shouldn't have said that. And I'm sorry the traders distressed you.'

'You,' said Karin, jabbing her finger at Hope, 'Are going to be more than sorry. You'd better get *your* plantation on the market now. Because you're going to need every cent you can lay your hands on once my lawyers get a hold of this.'

Chapter Nine

TWENTY-TWO years of marriage and Jannine had gone out of his life. Still Stuart Wilding felt nothing: no sense of loss, no regret, no shame, no guilt. It wasn't right to admit it, but if there was anything, there was only a sense of relief.

He was dressed now. A suit at night, a bath robe for the day. His timing was all wrong. Perhaps it always had been so.

He switched on the television to see the county cricket scores, and discovered that he wasn't really interested after all. Sitting and taking in information was too passive a thing to be doing at a time like this. Positive action was needed.

His career was in ruins of course – he'd be forced to resign as soon as the story was published in the *News of The World* instead of waiting for the election. Really he should call his agent and tell him now. But that was too much like crossing the Rubicon. It looked a long way to walk to the phone. The island of Nevis was closer than the desk.

So he'd have to accept it. There was no wife and no career. He looked around the room and briefly felt lord of all he surveyed. King of The Void, because there was no one left to share it with. Longthorpe Manor: all his. But empty of him – no little touches to show this was his home. No mementoes. No special room that was 'his'. No trophies, old school photos, certificates.

He laughed aloud and the sound echoed around the walls. Who was he fooling? – it wasn't his at all. Never mind that it was he who had found it and paid for it. Everything he looked at said 'Jannine' to him: the elegant taste in furnishings, the cool decorations, the Limoges, the Harrods seal of approval. He didn't like it at all.

He drained the vodka from his glass and poured another.

Anyway, the house would have to go – half to Jannine, if not more.

So no house either.

And no mistress. What a lovely, archane expression. He played with the word, rolled it around his tongue. Mistress. Beautiful, frightened Veronica, the person he'd always thought of as courageous. Well, if the fear of causing a scandal had been what was preventing her from making the commitment to him, she needn't worry about that any more. Ha!

He flicked through the evening paper again. There was no mention of him. Yet. So he had till Sunday before the truth was out and the electorate could condemn one more immoral MP.

How the news had got out, he couldn't imagine. He'd been puzzling over it since the first call from the reporter, Nesbitt.

He was beginning to feel the alcohol slugging away at his brain now, and knew he'd end up with a hangover. Served him right.

Perhaps Ron was unhappy and had finally confided in a friend. She herself could never have talked to the Press, he was sure of that. The so-called friend must have done, perhaps for financial gain.

It was ironic. He'd said once that he wanted to shout his love for her from the top of the highest building, and Veronica had gasped in mock-horror. Well, the News of The Screws was the next best thing. And good might even come from all this. At least he'd found out where she was.

The reporter had refused to believe him when he said that they hadn't been together in Nevis only a week ago. What had made Nesbitt so sure?

It really was the obvious place, now he came to think about it. It was Their Place. Their Special Place. Veronica had run off to cosy old Julian Winchester, wouldn't you just know it.

A swift call to Emigration would confirm the theory and Veronica wouldn't even need to find out he was on to her.

All he had to decide now was whether to face the flak, as

any good, ruined MP should, or whether to escape immediately. The idea of picking up the phone to his secretary and saying 'Book me the first available flight to Nevis' appealed. It was the sort of thing desperate men should do. But somehow he wasn't desperate any more. There was an inevitability about it all. Things would take their course.

And if he were to disappear, to do a John Stonehouse, there was no doubt his Party would lose the by-election to replace him. A lost seat in a hung Parliament – to a political animal such as Stuart Wilding, it was tantamount to treachery. There was a time when he'd have died for his Party, and even now, he couldn't let it die for him. That was a good line, he'd have to use it in a speech some time.

Party loyalties. Strong as ever. Do the decent thing. Call the agent. Get together a press release. He could even make a statement to pre-empt the Sunday paper's story.

If you're taking charge of your own destiny, the consequences can't be as terrible as if someone else is pulling the strings, he thought.

He looked out of the leaded window in the sitting room. It was quite dark, just a sprinkling of stars between the tops of the pine trees. No lights from cars passing by the boundary wall. Too late to call the agent. But it was time for some sort of action.

He took a piece of paper from the bureau and started to scribble notes for a press conference. And after the ordeal was over, he really could be ultra-dramatic. He pictured himself saying, hand pressed to forehead: 'I want an immediate flight to Antigua and Nevis. One way only.'

He knew what he needed – and he knew what Veronica needed, though she would take more time to come to the same conclusions. But the knowing was the important thing. It was only one step away from getting.

Wilding worked out his plan with the same precision as he would have plotted an election campaign in the early days, before Veronica became the most – the only – important thing in his life.

It was nearly sunset by the time Ned Murdoch got back to

129

Sugar Mill Plantation, an hour after he'd said goodbye, quite casually, to Hope at the marina. He hadn't felt very casual, he was moodily counting the hours till he was due to leave Nevis and cursing his luck.

Wednesday tomorrow. They would be going Friday morning, if the painting and servicing of the Maria Juana ran to schedule. Off to Puerto Rico where the film crew would board the plane from San Juan.

His next passengers weren't due for a week after that, they were cruising the Grenadines from St Vincent. That would be a good run out – even better if he had Hope's company. The lunatic thought occurred to him to ask Hope to take the week with him.

Why hadn't he made a move? Was he becoming all talk? A guy with two pool cues – one in his hand and one between his legs – and he didn't know how to use either of them? The hesitation was certainly nothing to do with a lack of desire. Just thinking about those lips that smiled so provocatively – without doing so deliberately – turned him on. The shape of her would fit so precisely into the space between his arms. She would mould beautifully beneath him, not fighting or out to impress, just there to enjoy and be enjoyed.

Even her character was like his. And she was an Arien too. Bet she read her horoscope when she noticed it and said crap, the way he did.

He wondered if her hair was naturally blond. That was one thing you'd never be able to tell with Karin Genevieve. No give-aways.

His Moke took the bend fast and a mongoose scurried out of his path.

He turned the Moke into the driveway and yelled 'Hello there' at Zeke who was heading for home. The gangly young man waved something that looked like a sack of potatoes at him and grinned.

Hope was walking through the car park on her way from the great house to her suite in the mill.

'Wonderful evening,' he called.

She shrugged, thinking about Karin Genevieve's threat about legal action. 'The storm didn't come then,' she said.

She was still in the shirt and shorts she'd worn at the beach, though the hat was missing.

He turned off the motor and hurried after her. 'You've brought some beach home with you,' he said, brushing a shell out of her hair with tingling fingers.

'I know,' she said. 'I'm going to shower. See you later.'

She seemed abstracted. Not the same. He guessed she was pissed off with him, because he hadn't tried to make love to her till it was too late. Even then, it was only a half-hearted attempt. Not serious, though ˙the wanting was serious enough.

'I'll come to the cockfight tonight,' he said. 'If it's okay? Say yes, Hope.'

'Of course,' she warmed to him, putting Karin and lawyers firmly out of her mind. 'That will be lovely. To have your company, I mean. Because I don't like the violence, you know.'

Terry Morelands had had a letter from his wife. Miriam was fine. The weather in California was fine. The food was fine. Everything seemed just dandy – apart from the fact that she hadn't touched a drop for two weeks and was feeling well enough to come home.

So this would be Goliath's last fight for a while. And Miriam's arrival would put an end to the terrific time he was planning to have with the movie star and, later, with Hope Parnell.

Last night, the luscious Karin had played hard to get. Okay, some women liked a chase and it added spice. The finale was inevitably more rewarding.

Or at least it would have been.

Miriam was landing in Antigua tomorrow. She asked him to arrange a pick-up through IN-Flight or one of the other island-hoppers. Just like that. Fix it Terry. Not much notice, nigger-boy, but do as you is tole.

Okay, Mrs Morelahnds, ah'll get you hoame. You keep pickin' up de tabs.

There was nothing worse than a black woman who'd forgotten the colour of her skin, thought Terry.

Moodily, he dressed and shaved and splashed Givenchy

131

Monsieur liberally over his smooth, milk-chocolate face.
Time to pay up, Miss Genevieve, he thought. No time left
for the endless chase.

Jake 'King' Heinlein was in love again. As he dressed for
dinner, he decided to forget about his diet with the arrival
of the master chef, Robert Lane, who'd flown over all the
way from Huntingdon, England. Just for him. He licked
his fat lips with anticipation and gave a quick blast of 'If I
Only Had A Heart' from The Wizard of Oz. He liked the
sound of his voice.

Tonight he felt frisky. Ready for a good meal and a good
time.

Karin was into King today. Some days she was on, some
days she was off. It was her way of doing things. With a
body like that she could afford to play around a little.

She should remember what he could do for her though.
In bed and out of it. He had the biggest cock she'd ever
seen, a monster of a thing that towered like a flagpole
above his belly. And he'd give it to her good and proper
tonight.

Then, maybe, he'd see about talking to Jimmy Percival
about that next contract. There would always be a part in a
Perce movie for a great pair of tits. And Perce himself had
had a piece of the action with that cute little Karin so it
shouldn't be too hard to arrange.

The thought of Karin doing the same things with Perce
as she did with him didn't please King too well. But a girl's
gotta make a career for herself.

And a man's gotta take what's on offer. He tied a dickie
bow perfectly, first time, shook a black jacket and worked
his arms into it. An extra splash of Givenchy Monsieur.
Check the nose to see it's none too hairy. Ears. Terrific.

And if Karin didn't come across, he could always fall
back on the kid, Jewel. Perce looked kinda peaky an' he
might welcome the break.

She was willing to learn, that's what he liked about
Jewel. When he said suck it, she sucked it. When he said
twirl that tongue around the helmet, she twirled the
tongue, just right. When he said sit on my face, the kid

132

showed the right amount of protesting and then giving in. She could go far.

Jewel sat on the bed and sipped the pre-dinner Pina Colada she'd had brought to her room. The gypsy dress she wore kept slipping down her arms, giving her pert breasts too much freedom in its downward passage. It was bright red, with a pink silk rose pinned at her cleavage. She manipulated the pin so that it pierced the strapless bra she wore underneath to keep the front of the dress at a safe level.

She'd tied her jet-black hair back tonight, holding it up with an ivory comb. For extra effect, she fastened in a hibiscus blossom from the bush outside on her terrace and felt really gorgeous. Especially now all the red bits were peeling off her nose.

She'd had an Eventful Day, and couldn't wait to tell Karin about it. She'd go simply gr-een. For some reason, the old bitch hadn't been around when she and Perce had got back from the drive that afternoon. And now she wasn't even answering her 'phone. She was playing 'I want to be alone'. The neglected star no doubt. Still, it would be good to see Karin's face fall, even if Jewel had to wait a while longer for the privilege.

She and Perce had seen Hope Parnell getting off the Maria Juana at the marina. *'Ned Murdoch's a little in love with me . . . '*, she'd drawled. So *that* would be one up the ass for her.

It was quite obvious what *he'd* been after with Karin. And now he'd had it, he wasn't interested any more. Served her right.

But that wasn't the only good news.

Jewel had met a man at the Bath House this afternoon, while Perce was stuck on the roof taking snaps of the surrounding countryside and moaning on about how in hell was he supposed to get down again.

But she'd ignored him. It gave her more time to make a lasting impression on drooly Georges Deneuil.

Georges wasn't in movies, but he was rich. Very very rich. And as gorgeous as Ned Murdoch himself.

Jewel believed in second strings to her bow. And Perce

133

was about to be relegated to the number two position: he was such a bore with his great paunch and his miserable ulcer.

She was planning to see Georges Deneuil tonight at the fight if she could slip away from the rest of them. That was the best part. It would blow their minds. They all thought she was just a kid. They didn't guess she was capable of independent thought and action, that she was all grown up like they were.

Her life was a whirlwind, it always had been. Changes in plans were necessary to her existence, especially if other people did the planning and the changing. It was much easier that way. So far she'd got to see a lot of the world by being open to suggestions.

She had no ambition, no real aim in life.

Nevertheless Jewel had acquired a great deal of experience for her nineteen years. She had made her own money – not a lot, but enough to be envied. She had been in a movie – her third – in which she'd had more lines than the great Karin Genevieve – *and* she'd never had to stoop to porno to get there. She had once modelled swimwear in *Cosmo*. She had acted in two commercials for slimming aids.

Yeah, she'd done plenty for a nineteen-year-old. She hugged her knees in smug self-satisfaction and contemplated her rosy future.

Perce's belly yawned wide enough to swallow up the rest of his innards and he made a grab for the Perrier.

'Yaaah!!' he roared, 'Yaaaargh!' and his voice echoed around the Catherine Room. That was better – immediate relief. It always did him good. Plenty of cabbage an' yelling to release the pressure. Thank the homeo for that solution.

He looked at the Camels on his dressing table and didn't light one. It'd bring back the groans so it was a question of the lesser of two evils. And Perce knew where *his* priorities lay.

He'd been ready for dinner for the last half hour and had written three cards to his wife, separately dated so he could say he'd had to wait for shore leave to post them.

He tried to imagine Greta back in Hollywood and couldn't. Shit – he couldn't even remember what she looked like. Perce had a lot of sympathy for the Red King in *Alice*. People only existed through his eyes. Life was one long complex dream that revolved around him, The Sleeper. Characters only had meaning in as far as they related to Jimmy Percival. When they were off-scene they went into a kind of limbo, waiting for him to call them back into the spotlight.

Or maybe they just winked out like candle flames when they were out of sight. How would he know?

He lit a Camel, forgetting, and inhaled deeply. *Mercenary* had gone real good. That British guy – Robert Powell. Nothing less than a-mazing.

And the kid. Jewel. Now she really had something. There were always surprises in the movie business. And one of the biggies this year was the fact that that girl could act. *Jewel Dankworth* could be a Star. The thought stunned him. Again.

Maybe it was because she was so devoid of character and experience that she could take on any personality he dictated. She was like an empty vessel you could fill up with the liquid of your choice.

He'd have to see about something bigger for the future – something they could shoot away from the tropics where she'd turned this weird shade of scarlet.

Yeah. She'd need working on, but Perce was the one to push her right the way to the top. With firm direction, that girl could go far.

The searing pain in his gut dismissed Jewel from his mind as completely as if she'd walked off-stage. He jumped into the air and ground his teeth, stubbing out the cigarette viciously.

'Yaarggh,' he bellowed into the still night air.

'Lazy boy.'

Honest Joe climbed onto Hope's lap in four easy stages: from dresser to open-dresser drawer, from drawer to stool and from the stool it was just a short stretch to the lap of his dreams. Honest Joe believed in economy of movement.

She loved the smell of his warm fur and buried her nose in it. 'What about mice for those children of yours?' she admonished him.

He looked at her as though she was a goddess, yawned and rested his chin awkwardly in the crook of her elbow, just as she was about to put on the mascara.

Her hair was loose and unadorned. If they were dancing, and she really ought to show willing, it would get messy enough without hairclasps falling out all over the place. It hung in a glossy curtain of rippling waves to below her shoulders, almost concealing her completely bare back.

'Off, Joe,' she said, and heaved him sideways. He left grey fluff on the sunshine-coloured silk of her dress. She turned to look at the back view in the mirror and was well pleased. She hung a string of pearls round her neck. Backwards, so the topaz clasp dangled low-down between her shoulder blades, flashing as it occasionally caught the light that filtered through the thick hair.

If Ned Murdoch didn't make a move tonight, maybe she'd tackle the problem herself. It had been too long since there'd been a man in her bed. She was lonely for comfort. 'And you don't count,' she said to the cat.

There is something about the freshness of the air, the heavy scents of blossom, the rawness of nature in the smaller Caribbean islands that drives me mad, thought Ned Murdoch. I feel poetic. Romantic.

It's not like being at sea, when you have to work with and against the elements. When you always know you are at risk from your own mistakes. When the illusion of safety you create for the passengers can be shattered by a gust of wind that takes you by surprise. When you have to be constantly on your toes. Sweating from the sheer energy you expend in hauling ropes or holding a boat with a will of its own steady.

Here you have time to slow down. Nevis is bliss. Nothing happens here. The rest of the world only creeps in with the tourists and even they forget about it after a day or so.

I could stay here forever, he thought. *Spend my days watching hummingbirds. Pass a little time playing dice. Live on plantains and pawpaw. Grow my own avocados. Spend my nights with Hope. Have breakfast with Hope.*

Perhaps it's Hope that's bliss.

He pulled the white silk bow-tie over his head and set it dead in the middle of the collar. It was on elastic.

He pulled down the mesh at the windows to stop the mosquitoes getting in through the open vents and lit the coil to kill off the ones that would beat him through the door as he left to go down to dinner.

Veronica, Lottie and Jessica took drinks on the trellised verandah that surrounded the dining room at Nelson Plantation.

Veronica wore a white two-piece with high padded shoulders and threaded with silver and gold and crystals that might or might not have been the real thing. Her hair was wound round her head and covered with a gold silk turban that on anyone else would have seemed ridiculous.

'You look like someone out of ''*Women in Love*'',' said Jessica.

'I feel like someone out of ''*Women in Love*'', Hermione. Or worse.'

She was not wearing the bracelet and earrings they had bought for her in St Kitts. The old Veronica would have chosen her outfit for the night just so that she could have done. Jessica took this as A Sign and felt wretched.

A waiter came round with more cocktails and canapes of smoked salmon and cream cheese on rye bread.

'The show's beginning!' called Lottie, who was leaning on the rustic pole that separated the terrace from the sheer mountain side.

She looked good tonight and felt terrific. Her short crop was pinned back with a gold clasp and her body looked almost voluptuous in a Medici shift. She had noticed Julian Winchester's admiration with pleasure as she arrived at the terrace.

The first frogs were singing, the sun was sinking fast. 'Watch out for the green flash!' she said as Jessica joined her.

137

One minute it was daylight, the next the light was fading and the sun was zooming down to the horizon, getting bigger and redder by the second. Blink and you might miss it. It shot scarlet horizontal streaks low in the purple sky as a parting shot and was gone.

'Damn!' said Lottie. 'Why no green flash, Julian?'

'To do with the level of phosphorous,' said Julian knowledgeably. 'It only happens as the sun shines through whatever irridescence there is. It would have been there tonight, but it had disappeared before our poor, slow brains had time to register it.'

'The subliminal green flash,' said Veronica, sipping the gin and coconut water that was described as being an acquired taste.

'But, do look, it's still quite splendid,' said Jessica.

The ghost of the sun lingered as the whole sky flushed from purple to an angry crimson. 'It looks like the sky's bleeding,' said Lottie. 'It's like the aftermath of a nuclear explosion.'

'God's cross,' said Jessica, poking Lottie meaningfully.

'Poetry now. You are so *literary* tonight, Jessica.' Veronica felt irritable, nasty. A leftover from a frustrating day.

'Go an' fuck yourself, lady,' the man in the shop had said.

She snapped back: 'Better than screwing you sunshine,' and felt much better for it.

People had stared and Veronica wasn't used to the public eye. She was ashamed of herself as soon as she'd escaped from the dockside jewellers where she'd refused to pay the equivalent of seventy pounds for a coral bracelet that might have been plastic. She had sat dwelling over the incident with a coffee upstairs at The Rookery Nook for over an hour.

She was beginning to feel she could see the shabby conjurer behind the Caribbean magic.

'You're preoccupied,' said Julian, waltzing over with another gin and coconut water in his hand.

She looked at the glass. 'No thanks. One of those is enough.'

138

'Make you frisky,' said Julian.

'Lottie will have one, then.'

'Bitch-y,' snorted Julian. 'The new you has more spikes than a punk. I rather like it. You were always so bland, Veron.'

She pulled herself together and forced a laugh. 'Only on the outside.

'Now tell me what's for dinner. I'm starving.'

He looked at his watch and said: 'Quarter of an hour to go yet. Hope you're not too desperate. It's lobster salad for starters, madame. We then proceed to Seafood Crepe filled with Dolphin. *Apres ça*, we will sample what I am told is an exquisiteDuck à l'Orange.'

Veronica shrieked. 'Duck à l'Orange? In Nevis? Where did you find ducks out here?'

Julian pulled himself up to his full height. 'I am told, madame,' he said in his best butler voice, 'that my Duck à l'Orange is the finest in the world. I even have it written down as a comment from an American in the guest book.

'Actually, the devil knows where the duck's from. Like the Cornish hen we're having tomorrow.'

Veronica smiled. 'The Cornish hen will probably be the result of tonight's cockfight.'

'Oh no,' said Julian. 'This one's already in the freezer. It was flown in by Hope Parnell, only last week.'

'Talking about Hope,' said Veronica, 'I went over to The Sugar Mill for lunch.'

'Traitor,' snapped Julian.

She ignored him. 'She wasn't there, but what an exciting group she's got staying. They've been filming some secret agent-type thing in Barbuda and Anguilla. I think perhaps I will have another gin, after all.'

Julian signalled to the waiter and asked her if she'd seen anybody exciting. 'Sean Connery or Moore?' he said hopefully. Julian tended to be star-struck on occasions.

'No one like that.' She took the fresh glass and sipped at it, letting the fires burn her throat. 'But there's a devastatingly beautiful woman who took a leading role, though I'd never heard of her, and I'm afraid I can't even remember her name now.'

'No one else?'

'There was a producer, a Jake somebody or other. Mean anything to you?'

He shook his head sadly.

'No, I thought not. But the filming off Barbuda sounded wonderful. They were diving around the wrecks off the coast. What a lovely, glamorous life they must all have.'

'Some would say yours isn't too bad,' said Julian.

A receptionist came through to call Mrs Wolff to the telephone. 'Call from St Kitts,' she announced, knowing that even the smallest scrap of news would be heard with relish and discussed as though it were a world crisis. So the more information she could supply, the better.

Jessica paled beneath the beginnings of her tan. St Kitts could mean only the Reuters man. And that had to be trouble.

'Who's calling you from The Big Sister, Lottie? If you have contrived to have an affair while you're staying with me, I shall be madly jealous,' said Julian.

Lottie hurried out of the room to take the call without speaking to anyone. She exchanged a look of horror with Jessica in passing.

'Mrs Wolff,' said Don Derby. 'Hope you didn't mind my calling you at your hotel?'

Lottie said: 'Not at all.' She was trembling.

'Just thought I'd let you know that the *News of The World* has confirmed the story you told me.'

– *They had?* –

'Dr Wilding is apparently about to announce his engagement to Miss Marston.'

'Wait a minute, Mr Derby. You've lost me. He's already married.'

'That's what you told me. And indeed it's confirmed. As I said.'

'He's admitted the affair then, or what? I'm sorry, I didn't quite expect – '

'Let me explain. It seems that the *News of The World* inadvertently broke the news of the relationship to Mrs Wilding. And she has now walked out.'

Lottie's blood boiled. This was worse and worse – the

man hadn't been given an ultimatum by his wife at all. He didn't even have emotional blackmail to use as an excuse. He must have just dumped Ron for convenience. So, he'd been keeping Ronnie in a cupboard for appropriate occasions and simply tired of her. How that poor woman must be suffering.

Derby was saying: 'He's confirmed that he's had an affair with Miss Marston, and that his marriage is now over.'

'Just a moment. Does he say he's still seeing Veronica?'

'No, he hasn't confirmed that. He says he hasn't seen her for some time. Though we know he's lying, don't we?'

'Yes,' Lottie said quickly.

'But he did admit that he's going to propose to your Miss Marston as soon as possible.'

Lottie nodded, though of course Don Derby couldn't see that.

It all made sense. Threatened with scandal – the man was going to use her again. He was going to hide behind her. He'd probably claim she was to blame for the whole thing. That she'd seduced him with her cunning wiles.

He'd seen there was no reconciliation with the wife and had gone for the one-in-hand option.

But – oh God! – if Veronica was still in love with him, she'd be duped into going back to him, only to be ditched again when a new model, Mrs Wilding Marque Three, came along.

What a complete bullshitter the man was.

'I see,' she said, not seeing anything at all. 'So they are running a story, are they?'

'You bet. And I want to fix up an interview with Miss Marston.'

– Oh. Here it comes –

'I'm going to network it. Too big to hold as an exclusive. It's Sarah Keays with no pregnancy to clutter up where the sympathies should lie.'

'Oh dear. Where should they lie?' asked Lottie, dreading the answer that she knew she'd made inevitable.

'With the wife, of course. Poor woman's really been taken for a ride. I rang to ask if you could arrange the interview.'

'Oh, no. Not possibly. It's quite out of the question.' She cleared her throat. 'Miss Marston is very ill.'

'That adds a new twist. Suicide bid?'

She hung up quickly before she could make matters any worse than they already were. And matters, she realised, were very bad indeed.

They had gone into dinner, but only Jessica was ready seated. Lottie slid into the chair next to hers.

'That wasn't the Reuters man, was it?' asked Jessica.

''Fraid so. He wanted to come and interview Veronica.'

Jessica gasped. 'That's awful. What did you say?'

'What do you think I said? ''Roll up and she'll give you a signed photograph''? I said that she was ill, but I shouldn't have said that either, Jessica – he's going to release the story everywhere. He said he'd network it.'

'So that means even the local papers here might carry the story? And Ronnie will find out what you've done.'

'What we've done, Jessica. I thought we had all that sorted out. She'd have found out anyway when she got back to England.'

Jessica looked up anxiously, afraid that Veronica might overhear them though they were talking in whispers and Veronica was deep in conversation with Julian Winchester.

'But that's not the only problem – Veronica is to be painted the scarlet woman, not the spurned one I thought she'd be.'

'Oh no, Lottie! It will ruin her. She'll kill herself! That sort of thing matters terribly to Veronica – and her family.'

Lottie glowered. 'I'm aware of that. So what do we do?'

'This time, Charlotte Wolff, it's what do you do, not what do we do. I've never been one hundred per cent convinced you were doing right. And don't interrupt me. You've got to tell her what you've done. She has a right to be warned.'

Lottie glossed over it. 'That wasn't my point – '

'Telling her is *exactly* the point. She has to know.'

'Well not yet,' Lottie pleaded. 'Let's sort this mess out first. Please. We've got to keep her away from the Press till all the outcry's died down. We must.'

'But has it occurred to you that Veronica might deserve

him? That she *has* stolen him from his wife and now she *should* have to face the music?' Jessica popped a stick of carrot into her mouth, remembering how Joe and his lady friend had got off scot-free while she'd been in an agony of despair and misery. 'That's only one idea, mind, I'm not saying it's the case.'

Lottie gaped at her, open mouthed. 'How can you be so disloyal?'

Jessica grunted. 'Me disloyal. That's rich.

'Talk about people in glass houses throwing stones. You've got to learn that your precipitous actions have repercussions. All I can say is thank God you're not in the White House. Or the Kremlin.

'Tell her what you've done and let her make her own decisions, Lottie. For heaven's sake, she's not some retarded child that needs your constant protection. Stop playing God for a day or so. Give yourself a break.'

Karin Genevieve looked maliciously at Hope over the lamb in raspberry and lavender vinegar. It was English spring lamb, chilled, never frozen.

We do everything so perfectly, don't we, Ms Parnell, she thought. And we get what we want, too. Look at the cabin boy. If he isn't drooling at you then I'm Marie Osmond. Well I bet I know a few more tricks than you do and you're going to be a big anti-climax.

She delicately swept most of the lamb to one side of her plate and sighed as if to say it's not up to the Fontainebleau Hilton.

Then she winked seductively at King. Just look at that guy, she thought. Now there's a man and a half. He knows which side his bread's buttered on. Eating out of my hand. Yes, Karin, no, Karin.

But it didn't take her in. She knew what he was after. She'd just have to see, then. Depended which way the wind blew.

She embraced the table in a smile that could have caused weak men to swoon.

What a pity Jewel was so peculiar tonight. It was disconcerting. She was ridiculously overdressed, so why wasn't

143

she pouring with sweat in all those ruffs and flounces? And red! What a colour to wear in the Caribbean. She should be dripping inside. Still, at least the dress matched her face.

Karin sipped her Perrier and covered her wine glass as King tipped the Pomerol towards her. 'Certainly no more, darling,' she said. 'One was *quite* enough.' Then, to Hope, pointing to the label: 'It wasn't a very good year, was it?'

King said: 'Seventy six was excellent for clarets.'

'Oh,' said Karin. 'I'm surprised. But then I'm so used to choosing my own wine. It's odd that you should choose it for us Miss Parnell. Was it a bin end that you couldn't get rid of?'

Hope didn't rise to the bait.

'And anyhow,' Karin shrugged, 'I prefer whites to these pretentious Burgundies.'

'Not so many calories,' said Jewel unhelpfully.

'Bordeaux,' said Hope. 'Not Burgundy.'

'That,' said Karin, 'is beside the point.'

She smoothed the black Zandra Rhodes dress over her body, arching her back and watching contentedly as every man in the room stared in admiration at *the* bosom.

Plastic, thought Ned.

Those shoulder pads make her look like The Refrigerator, thought Perce.

Hope looked around to see that everyone had finished and rang the bell for the staff to come and clear the tables. Tonight the party of Canadians was dining at The Sugar Mill as well as the regular guests, and they seemed quite high on the wine and the food. So far so good.

There was mango sorbet with passion fruit coulis or a sticky English sherry trifle to follow. Hope pigged it and had a helping of both, as did almost everyone else when they saw it was permissible.

Karin refused either. 'Have you any Jack cheese?' she said. 'I'm still starving.'

Terry Morelands arrived with a screech of tyres as they were finishing coffee. He looked quite dapper as he swung out of the room with King for a quick game of pool while everyone else made their final preparations.

To Karin's annoyance, he offered Jewel and Perce a lift,

144

leaving her and King to travel in Hope's beaten up old Jeep. Typical. That filthy old thing would ruin four thousand dollars worth of Zandra Rhodes.

Terry winked at her as he clasped King's arm. He knew how to get a woman's interest. She'd be seething that she wasn't travelling with him in the Ferrari And the longer she simmered, the faster she'd boil

Chapter Ten

RICK'S BAR, on the hinterland between Charlestown and Gingerland, was buzzing when the Ferrari skidded to a noisy stop on the single track road outside. The sound of the fifties bee-bop had Jewel shaking her shoulders around, snapping her fingers, even before Terry had cut the engine.

Perce said: 'I thought it would be ska music, Terry.'

Terry pulled a face. 'Ska isn't hip. Only the Rastas and the back-to-the-roots boys play ska. This is much better for dancing.' He looked in the mirror and saw the twin head-lamps of Hope's covered Jeep drawing up behind him. In the back there would be the blond Karin with King. Good bloke that: for a whitey he was *aw-right*. Great at the pool table. He'd buy him a drink. It might make up for him losing his chick.

The bar looked run-down or unfinished. It wasn't clear which. Anyway it had an air of neglect that was emphasised by the smooth characters that were already mooching around inside the room. It was more of a compound than anything else. There was no roof, though there were walls with holes at irregular intervals, where windows might one day be or once, perhaps, were.

The floor was part parquet, part bare earth. Strobe lights played on a youth who was dancing like a skeleton, like a silent movie, in the flickering of the acid white flashes.

'Ain't too keen on this,' said King to Karin, as they walked in. 'Brings back embarrassing memories.'

But she was already twisting her hips sensually to The Crickets. 'You don't remember this ol' thing, do ya, babe?' he laughed. 'You must be near my age if ya do!'

King was thirty seven and looked it. Karin was also thirty seven, but didn't. 'No way. I just like the beat,' she

146

said evasively. They took over the centre of the dance-floor and King whirled her around, throwing her out to a full arm-stretch and rolling her back towards him. They looked good together, jiving like the rock-'n'-roll teenagers they'd been.

'Neat, but not what you might call ace,' said Terry, knowing he was the best dancer in Nevis. He was probably the best dancer in the whole of the West Indies. In the world.

'Wanna hit the floor?' he said to Hope, but she said no. 'I can't do this,' she said. 'I think the Shake was the first dance I could manage, and I was only a kid then.'

Score one to Miss Parnell, thought Karin, overhearing. That makes her around twenty-eight, thirty. Shame she's let the sun get to her. A tan is so very ageing.

Perce had made for the bar and ordered drinks. Already the ulcer was beginning to play him up. *Raspberry vinegar.* It was his own fault. He should've said no. Fuck it. Double fuck it.

King had an erection and it showed. As Karin Genevieve twirled the dress à la Marilyn Monroe, her crotch winked at him for an instant. That lovely naked pussy. All his. He imagined he could smell her, taste her, already.

The music changed to Jim Reeves, slowing down the action and clearing the floor. The beat wasn't the right one for Terry, but he clutched Jewel to him easily enough while Perce's back was turned and they floated around a bit till she said she was thirsty.

Ned and Hope were talking to Rick, the bar owner, about business. Rather, Hope was talking to Rick and Ned was listening. The woman was a workaholic.

– How's trade? Many tourists this season? How was he coping with the new import tax on the records? –

Ned wanted to hold her and here was a dance-floor, the perfect excuse, and it was another opportunity wasted if he couldn't touch her now.

'Come on, Hope,' he said. 'Let me dance with you.'

This was it, thought Hope. Suppose my breath starts rasping? Suppose I tremble? Suppose I can't think of anything to say? Suppose he knows how much I want him?

147

Anyone would think this was her first lover, the way she felt. Her noisy heart. His eyes like fathomless pits. His hand, lightly on her arm that felt like a ton weight. They were on the edge of the floor now – his hand had moved carelessly round to rest on the swell of her hips. She could feel the warmth of him all around her. The place underneath his hand was rising involuntarily, to fuse with his flesh.

He tingled with the contact from her, not wanting to move the hand from her hip though it was too obvious to leave it there. His fingers wanted to move down, not up.

She was turning to him and looking at him. Obviously she felt something. She must do. This had to be a two-way exchange.

She looked away to duck a laser beam and put her hands on his shoulders, keeping three inches between their bodies. His hands were around her waist, moving her as though she was flimsy, from side to side, in time to the music. She could feel his breath against her face. Was it rasping? Was hers?

Their thighs touched, and they jumped back from the contact. Then his hands found bare flesh at the waistband. 'Lovely dress,' he said.

'Mmm,' she sighed.

If he could just move that hand up another few inches, she'd feel naked in his arms. He released her completely, shook his hands. 'Pins and needles,' he said. Then the hands were back. Higher. Not on the dress. He'd known what she wanted. Both of the hands were there, on the smooth velvet skin, rippling more sensuously than the silk itself.

Was she trembling? 'Do you remember Jim Reeves?' he said.

'My father used to play him a lot,' she replied, looking straight at him by mistake and feeling weak. The hands behind, pressing her to him. The eyes in front, dragging her further in, the rope-hard muscles of his shoulders beneath her own hands. Would it look accidental if she let a hand drift to lie in the nape of his neck, play with a strand of his hair?

It was Ruby Tuesday. The Stones. Ned and Hope

continued to dance to Distant Drums. Karin found it very irritating and started a row with King, whose erection subsided under the first onslaught.

Terry saw his chance and snatched her away, shaking his body in a soka rhythm totally unconnected with the beat of the Stones. It looked quite right. Better than Jagger almost.

'You're very warm,' said Ned.

'Hot night,' said Hope. 'No wind to cool the air.' She looked up, momentarily diverted. The sky looked like a void, which it was. The stars looked bigger and brighter. Not a shadow of a cloud. But there was an upside-down moon, a lazy one that you could lie back in like a deck-chair.

Deck-chair. It reminded her of Karin Genevieve. 'Did you hear about Karin Genevieve and the Rasta?' she said.

'Don't talk about her,' he replied.

– Does he blow hot and cold so easily? Arms clenched around that tiny waist, his face pressed down into her shoulder. Wet hair dripping onto the shuddering blond woman. Her, crowing her ecstasy –

'You've gone stiff,' he said.

'We're out of time,' said Hope. 'The d.j.'s playing soka.'

The record had changed again. Terry Morelands, forgetting soka wasn't hip, was as fluid as a strand of melted toffee. Karin was dancing round him.

'Is this a flamenco?' said Hope innocently. 'If not, why is the woman doing that stomping and clapping?'

Hope wriggled out of his arms and Ned died a little. She moved with an easy rhythm, flowing in that strange off-beat way the natural West Indians had. Her hair was looking wilder, her eyes had a flash about them. Arousal? It could even be anger. Uneasily, Ned took up the music and wished Jim Reeves had still been playing.

'Yaargh!'

'Good grief, Perce, what's the matter?'

'Friggin' ulcer again. Blame your bastard chef for cooking irresistible fuckin' food.'

'Your ulcer? Do you need a doctor?'

'They got any homeos on the island?'

149

'Homeos?'

'Homeopaths, Hope, for Chrissake! *Homeopaths*!'

Hope shook her head. 'No, I'm sorry, there's only one doctor – and he's all amputations and tranquillizers – '

'Doesn't matter – forget it. It'll pass. Just get me back to somewhere I can lie down. And get your chef to cook me some greens. Pronto.'

Shit, thought Perce, as he looked around at the whirling bodies. The night was really screwed up.

'You comin' Jewel?' he yelled. If she soothed his brow real nice, he'd get round to telling her about her Future.

She shook her head. 'You don't mind if I don't, do you darlin'? I'm just dyin' to see this cockfight.'

'I'll come for the ride,' said Ned. And the hell with it if I'm making a fool of myself, if it's obvious I only want to be with you. How else can I tell you, woman?

Terry said: 'I'll see you up at Doctor Doom's – no later than eleven, mind!' He hoped the big guy, King, would fit in one of the *back* bucket seats in the Ferrari with the kid Jewel. That way he could have Karin by his side.

Hope drove the Jeep with the windows down, the canvas roof flapping. She turned the radio to Montserrat and hummed along with the West Indian music being broadcast. There was a hurricane warning but the announcer said it would go just east of Barbados when it finally hit the Caribbean. They'd get the tail end of it, if any, when it passed by the Leeward Islands.

'Hurricanes aren't what they used to be,' she said to Perce reassuringly. 'We're warned about them days in advance now. Everyone has plenty of time to prepare. And buildings are designed to withstand terrific wind velocities. There are really tough building regulations.'

'But we won't be able to sail,' said Ned. 'Not even in the tail end of a hurricane. We could run before it, but not in its wake. The tides would be too high.'

Perce frowned. 'Gotta get that plane out of San Juan,' he said.

'Even Air Jamaica's not going to take off in a hurricane, Perce,' said Ned.

Hope sighed, exasperated. 'It's *not* coming our way. Don't be so alarmist.'

Ned wondered about that. Hurricanes were unpredictable. Capricious. He thought: maybe I am meant to be here, stranded.

But no. There was no inevitability about anything. No such thing as pre-ordination. You could circumvent any situation with planning and forethought. You could even dodge the wind.

And how would he like to be trapped in Nevis? No way. Not by circumstances outside his control. He could choose to stay landbound, if he wanted. That was a different matter altogether. But it was just about as likely as Hope learning to clean fish.

Veronica and Julian left the Datsun parked at the bottom of the winding path up the mountainside.

'Damn these high heels, Julian,' said Veronica. 'I'd forgotten the stones.'

There was a high wire fence. What looked like an armed guard stood on the door, checking the faces, cop-spotting.

'Dis a privaht party, mahn,' he said to Julian.

Amos Bardram, the customs officer, came over to the guard. 'Dis Julian Winchestah,' he said. 'He's okay. My problem if he's not.'

There was music in the grounds, proper ska music. 'Ex-o-dus,' sang Julian.

'I'm not the only one around here who's changed,' said Veronica.

All around them, muscular black men danced, writhing their bodies cleanly, leanly. There were a few women, sitting on the cool grass, drinking Coke and rum in tall glasses through straws.

A girl danced between two men. She wore a red and yellow bandanna in her hair, sweeping the black curls away from her face, a tight black t-shirt that was invisible, and a pair of white Bermuda shorts.

As the rhythm of the music changed, she rolled towards one of the men, her hips leading her body as though she was about to limbo. Behind her, the other man snaked up

151

against her, trickling his fingers up and down her sides, up to her breasts, down to her hips, back up again, in time to the music.

She pouted and brushed her crotch against the first man, rubbing against him slowly and deliberately. His hands extended towards her, cupping an imaginary outline of her bosom with fingers kept tantalisingly at a distance.

The second man, the chaser, bent his body into hers to feel her swaggering buttocks rotate over his erection. She pressed higher, encouraging the tantaliser to press down on her simultaneously.

Like this, the three of them gyrated, heaved.

'That's erotic,' said Veronica.

'Wonder if her mother knows where she is and what she's doing?' said Julian.

'You amaze me,' she said. 'Doesn't it turn you on?'

'It will do. When they take their clothes off. This is just the warm up.'

'You've seen it before? They're paid to do it?' Veronica was let down.

'No, darling, they're not paid – it's all spontaneous. But I have seen these three in action before, so I know what comes next if they really get going.'

The tantaliser was raising the girl's t-shirt. Her breasts swayed and shone in the moonlight. Around them, the other dancers took no notice. Many of them jigged to the music with their eyes closed, in another world.

He avoided touching her, even the most casual contact, lifting the thin material so that it shouldn't scrape against a nipple to give any relief to a body aching to be fondled. She looked as though she was in a trance, her shoulders rocking to the rhythm of the night-sounds, her hips rocking to the rhythm of her sex.

The chaser clasped her hips firmly to his pelvis in shiny-knuckled, bony hands. He appeared to be thrusting into her, though that was impossible because of the clothing that separated them.

He heaved and her feet were almost off the ground, balanced as she was as though he were a table and she spread out on it. The tantaliser lifted her legs and

152

supported them as she began to moan. And he was rubbing harder against her pelvic bone so that she was arching, out of control, moaning louder.

Another dancer lolled over to the three of them, grinned at the tantaliser and bent down to take a nipple between white white teeth. All the while, his feet kept in perfect time with the music.

Veronica groaned. She was giving off a musky odour that was more powerful than her perfume. Julian's hand took the opportunity to slip down from her waist where it had been resting protectively. He rubbed his hand downwards, finding the crevice between her buttocks and insinuating himself. She backed further onto his hand, instinctively. Her head was tilted up. He ran his tongue over her throat.

The black woman was turned around and she stood, supported by three pairs of hands, one on her breasts, one on her shoulders, one on her hips as the chaser knelt before her to rub his face against her hungry pussy. The t-shirt hung around her neck, her shorts were unfastened and slipped slowly, oh agonisingly slowly, down and she stepped out of them, unconsciously keeping the beat of the music in her movements.

The bandanna was removed from her hair and her head fell back on the tantaliser's brawny shoulders. The dancing man took another bite of nipple before tying the bandanna tight around her breasts, holding the knot as a leverage to make her supple body bend to his swaying.

Veronica groaned again. Julian felt a dampness spreading across the back of the Dior gown where it came into contact with her body. He pressed his hand harder against her, wishing she was naked.

The pursuer had his hands buried somewhere inside the woman. She was rocking backwards and forwards. His teeth, clamped firmly onto her heaving, damp flesh, guided his head to follow her movements.

She climaxed suddenly, her eyes opening abruptly to coincide with a howl that broke from her lips. A few women looked up from their seats on the grass and grinned.

'Dat Sherry she goin' strong,' said one.

'She get herself pregnahnt again if she not careful,' said another.

'Yuh doan't get pregnahnt like dat. If de mahn keep de clothes on you is safe,' said the first.

'There you are,' said Julian. 'There's the ultimate contraceptive advice.'

Veronica shook herself visibly and looked around her. Everything was the same since she'd disappeared into her head. The men were still dancing, though the three – no – four protagonists from the dance floor had disappeared. She looked for them.

'They'll have gone for a hot-dog inside,' said Julian, reading her mind.

'Hey-hey! Jules!'

Julian turned to see Terry Morelands rolling across the dance floor with three people he didn't know. They slapped palms in a ritual Julian enjoyed. It let everyone know that he was accepted.

'Meet my friends,' said Terry. 'King, Karin and Jewel. This is Julian and – it's Veronica, isn't it?'

'That's right,' she smiled. 'Yes I met Karin and King over lunch.'

'Small world,' said King.

'Small island,' quipped Terry, and laughed. 'Come an' have a drink, King,' he said. 'Get a preview of the champion.'

They were already pissed, Terry and King. They reeled over to the wooden steps that led to the hut where the bar was. They each had an arm around the other's shoulders for support.

They emerged, hooting, after a couple of minutes.

'There's a mean-lookin' son-of-a-bitch in there I'm backin',' roared King. 'An' it's not Terry's bird.'

'Are they on show?' asked Karin.

'Sho' are,' drawled Terry. He lurched towards her, remembered he'd forgotten King, went back to throw his arm round him again, and lurched back with King in tow.

'Forget King's Sweet Romance,' he hissed confidentially at her.

'Pardon?'

'Sweet Romance. The cock. Forget 'im. Just remember Goliath's the winner.'

Karin put on a Southern Belle accent, 'Why, Mistah Moah-lands. Ah ain't a gamblin' lady.'

King snorted, beery breath coming at her from two angles, his and Terry's. 'Yuh sho' will be, honey-chile, when y'all see this birdie.'

They went inside to survey the fighters. There were six birds, chained to the part of the counter that the men were staying away from. None could move their feet or their wings more than an inch or so, but the beaks weren't restrained sufficiently to risk an approach.

'That's Goliath,' said Terry to anyone who'd listen.

He was a massive, muscular cockerel, black and white feathered with the killer glint in his eye. Terry pulled on a leather glove and reached out to pet him, gingerly, knowing that to startle him could cost him a finger. Though he'd owned Goliath three seasons, he still treated him with respect.

Karin shuddered with delight. 'How can you touch him?'

'He knows me, don't you Ol' Mahn?'

The bird shook a red wattle angrily and tried to lift a silver-clawed foot capped with bone spikes long enough to rip out an elephant's eye. 'Disgusting,' said Karin, feeling hot and excited.

Another bird, mottled white and black, stretched its neck threateningly at Goliath but couldn't reach.

'That's my bird,' said King. 'Sweet Romance.'

'Are you betting, Veronica?' asked Julian.

'I don't think so,' she said. She was still trembling with passions aroused from the scene on the grass outside.

Karin said: 'If I wanted any of them, I'd back the one with blue in his feathers. What's his name?'

Terry peered over shoulders in front of him. 'Night Moves.'

– Oh yes, he thought. Very appropriate –

Hope and Ned had returned and were behind King, pushing their way through the people at the bar.

155

'Look at that big boy,' said Ned. He was pointing to Sweet Romance. 'Je-sus, look at those steel spikes!'

Hope looked and the metal held her gaze in a trap.

Steel. Knives. Blades. Violence. Blood . . .

She closed her eyes quickly to shut out the steel. Two years. Two whole years ago . . . her last visit to London . . . That man at her face with his knife . . . Nick pulling at him . . . No!

The memory had invaded her mind because it had attacked at an unexpected moment. She had let down her guard and the memory had sensed that it could sneak in there while she was unprepared.

The colour drained from her face to leave it ashen. 'Ned,' she said. 'I don't think I can bear it.'

'Hey,' he said, putting his arm round her shoulders, holding her close for a moment. 'Hey.'

'Perhaps we could go back outside? And dance? Please?'

'Sure,' he smiled, holding her closer, puzzled. But it was what he'd wanted anyway so he didn't ask questions.

'Place your bets now,' said Doctor Doom. He wore a trilby and an anorak, and on his hand he carried a gilt-framed birdcage containing dice. Stakes had been won and lost already on the dice. Doctor Doom always won in the end.

'Doctor Doom take only fifty per cent of de winnings.' He smiled beatifically around him, embracing everyone in his jackal jaws. 'Doctor Doom give de best deal on de island. In de whoale Caribbean.'

Terry and King had come to an amicable arrangement. They would back their separate birds which were scheduled to fight each other. They were playing for high stakes. A thousand dollars apiece.

And just to make it interesting, the winner would get Karin for the night.

Chapter Eleven

THE SMOKE-FILLED room behind the bar was already crowded.

In the centre was a twenty-foot pit, covered with a rush mat and sawdust. The wooden shack was unbearably hot and dimly lit by paraffin lamps, the stench of which was overpowering.

Doctor Doom strode in, his narrow hips swaying jauntily, despite the rest of his body's considerable bulk.

'Tonight we have de Battle Royal,' he said.

'Oh shit,' said Terry. 'Battle Royal. I wouldn't have entered him if I'd known.'

There were no seats. The gamblers squatted at the ringside, arguing between themselves, flashing coins and money, making strange hand signals to spectators across the room.

Veronica said: 'I feel like an outsider.'

A man in front of her, sweat pouring down his broad nose from his forehead, looked at her with black eyes. 'You is outsider, honey.'

'Place yo' bets wid Doctor Doom,' said the man himself, beaming like a hunting dog. 'An' if I catch any one o' you mudders takin' cash on de side, I have you out, mahn.'

'This is unbearable,' said Jewel, sticky in her limp red dress. 'The stink in here. And the heat. And the noise. It's too much.'

Everywhere there were shouts, hissing, braying. All eyes for the moment seemed to be trained on the white women.

'I'm going outside. See you later.' She had a man to find, anyway, and sod what Karin might think.

'You all right?' asked Julian. 'It is a bit feverish in here.'

'No, I'm fine. I like the excitement and the tension,'

replied Veronica. 'Even if I am an outsider.'

Karin said nothing. She was standing between Terry and King, the black dress damp with her perspiration and clinging between her thighs, under her breasts. Terry had an arm lolled over her neck, King steadied himself by holding onto her waist.

Terry put his mouth close to her ear, so close she could feel his lips moving. He whispered something to her, but it couldn't be heard over the noise in the arena. All Karin could make out was wish-wish-wish. Then he looked close into her eyes, asking for an answer. She smiled and he took it as agreement.

King, seeing the deal – as he thought – being clinched, came close to her other ear, nibbled the lobe and said: 'Better put your money on Sweet Romance, baby.'

The two men disentangled themselves from Karin and marched up to Doctor Doom who was surrounded by a disorderly queue of men trying to back their chosen cockerels at favourable odds. Doctor Doom was known to switch the odds during the fight and if you didn't have your written placing, you didn't even get your stakes back.

There was a group of men arguing over Sweet Romance, and Terry strained to catch the words.

'Tree to one, mahn, dat's de best I do for you. Dat bird a real winner if I seen one.'

'He sick, mahn,' whined the punter. 'I seen him crowin' and dat bird got no voice, mahn. He real sick. Five to one?'

'No way,' said Doctor Doom. 'Tree-to-one you get a real good pay-back. Dat's de St Kitts champion you backin'. An' I tell you somethin' for free, boy. Dese odds is narrowin'. I already takin' too much on dat bird. If he come hoame, I got a starvin' wife an' six children.'

'I'll get through for you King.' Terry elbowed into the crowd to lower the odds on Sweet Romance and raise them on Goliath. 'A thousand dollars on Sweet Romance.'

Doctor Doom turned back to the first man, who was still holding out his twenty dollar bill anxiously.

'You see what ah mean, mudder? Now you lost your tree-to-one. De odds on Sweet Romance is now evens.'

158

'Shee-it,' said Terry, looking back at King in feigned exasperation. He'd achieved his objective.

Doctor Doom turned to a blackboard, hung on the wooden wall behind him, and changed the odds officially. 'Now how I hopin' to cover a thousand dollar bet, mahn?' he said to Terry.

'You'll take it,' said Terry, watching with satisfaction as the receipt was painstakingly written out with a gold Waterman fountain pen. 'You could always hock that, for a start. An' I'm taking a thousand on Goliath,' he added. 'I'm his owner. That'll cover you for Sweet Romance, won't it. There's only one winner. But I want three-to-one.'

'For *Goliath?* You havin' a joake, mahn.'

'Take it or leave it.'

Doctor Doom made a quick decision and held out his hand for the notes.

The lights were dimmed. Someone called: 'You said dese were scheduled fights tonight.'

Doctor Doom smiled in the greenish glow. 'I changin' de rules. I already said we was havin' de Battle Royal.'

King and Terry fought their way back to their place. It seemed that the entire population of Nevis had managed to pack themselves into this shed.

'What's a Battle Royal?' asked Karin.

'It's to the death,' said Terry, swallowing hard. 'I'd have pulled Goliath out if I'd had warning. But he's good. He'll be okay.' He shrugged, feeling sad.

Julian looked at Veronica, anxious for her. Her face was flushed and she was breathing fast. 'They let all the birds loose together, you know,' he said. 'It's like a world war with the last one standing the winner. Are you sure you can take it?'

She nodded.

Terry hustled out of the shed to the bar where, already, other owners and handlers were wrestling their birds into cages. Sweet Romance, the champion from the sister island, was the only one Goliath hadn't faced before. Terry measured the look in his eye and was satisfied Goliath had him marked.

'You got the cage, Grenville?' he asked the man who worked as his handler.

'Here, Mister Moahlands.'

'Okay, Ol' Mahn. Easy now. Your time comin'. Look at dat son-of-a-bitch. Dat's who you is after, boy.' He pulled on a second glove and went in slowly to take hold of Goliath's neck, to immobilise that lethal beak. Then swiftly he grasped the bird's feet, pinning them together, staying out of the reach of the spurs that could flash and maim in seconds, keeping them separated enough to prevent Goliath doing himself any damage. 'Okay, loose the chain, I got him. In you go. I'll take him through tonight, Grenville. It's a Battle Royal.'

The handler nodded, understanding.

Terry made his way back through the spectators to the sawdust ring. He could feel the tension in Goliath, the adrenalin tearing through his veins and ready to explode. Inside the cage, the bird was quivering, but it was not with fear. Goliath never needed taunting – he had enough natural aggression and territorial instinct to go for the kill straight away, without any unnecessary cruelty first. That was the best thing about him.

The six owners crouched by their imprisoned fighters, waiting for the word. 'This is to the death, Goliath,' said Terry. 'You do good, you hear? Or I'll end up missin' you.'

'Main on!' shouted Doctor Doom, and the boxes were opened.

Terry jumped backwards, out of range of the beating wings, and loped back to King and Karin.

Goliath was first out of his box, two-inch long bone spurs tipping his own talons.

'He is mean,' said King in grudging admiration, watching the beady eyes peering over the hooked beak, stretching, angry, ready for the fray.

Other birds emerged – there was no sign of Sweet Romance.

'There's Night Moves,' sang Karin. 'Ooh . . . Do you think a bird can be sexy, King?'

He looked at her and wondered if she was really as dumb as she acted.

Then there was a rustling in the one box left. First wings appeared, and then the box ripped apart as Sweet Romance found the leverage he needed to make his grand entrance.

'Supercock!' hissed King. 'My namesake!'

'He like de devil heself,' said Doctor Doom. 'De odds for anyone bettin' on dat fighter now is tree-to-one *on*.'

'Why didn't you back anything, Karin?' asked Terry.

She shrugged. She hadn't wanted to press herself into the throng of men surrounding Doctor Doom, with their hot hands, their sweating faces. But she didn't want to admit it. Not to Terry.

'Night Moves is ten-to-one, Goliath three-to-one, Dream Heart twenty-to-one, fifty-to-one bar,' said Doctor Doom.

Terry groaned. If Doctor Doom was offering threes generally on Goliath, it meant he didn't like his form, didn't think he could beat the St Kitts champion.

'Damn,' said Julian. 'I only got evens on Goliath earlier on.'

There was a skirmish between Night Moves and Buffalo Soldier that didn't amount to much.

'They're just testing each other,' Julian said to Veronica. 'Sizing up the opposition.' His Goliath ticket was damp in his hand and sweat rolled down his forehead.

None of the birds threatened Sweet Romance as he strutted among them, his steel tipped spurs clacking on the rush mat.

Then there was a sudden flurry. Night Moves had gone for one of the smaller cocks. The two danced up and down, as though they were on a see-saw, steel flashing every now and then as the spurs caught the light. There was a crowing and a screaming. The see-saw display ended as if a signal had been given, and their corner of the arena erupted into a maelstrom of whirling wings, flashing feathers, spurting blood.

'Da's ma bird,' cried a man from the front of the arena. Braving the angry talons of the smaller cock, Crazy Little Thing, he fought to rescue the bleeding Night Moves. It

161

hung limply in his arms as he carried it out of the arena like a baby. The incident had taken less than ten seconds.

'You never can tell. Good job you didn't waste your money,' said Terry to Karin.

'Crazy Little Thing now fives,' said Doctor Doom. Punters pushed through to make new mid-fight bets.

And all hell suddenly broke loose. Sweet Romance went in for the kill. He'd worked out where the weaknesses were and he went for them. Crazy Little Thing and Buffalo Soldier, no more than shabby old feather dusters, were carried out amid screams from the audience: 'He still alive! He kin still fight! He still a strong bird, mahn!'

Dream Heart, ruffled like a fledgling, lay heaving in the pit, blood pouring from his breast.

And then there were two. Goliath was minus an eye. It broke Terry's heart to see him like that. Sweet Romance was ruffled but not bloodied, apart from the dark red streaks that came from his beak and his spurs.

Terry's eyes swam. He was stone cold sober now. That bird meant a lot to him.

Sweet Romance stepped onto the body of Dream Heart and faced Goliath. Goliath stretched up his neck but did not crow. And then the whirlwind exploded – talons sought flesh and found it, frighteningly human screams rang around the arena.

It was impossible to see whose blood was flowing, whose flesh was being ripped by the weapons fastened onto the birds' claws.

'Jesus, Ol' Mahn!' screamed Terry. 'Come on through!'

Abruptly, they broke apart.

Sweet Romance backed away, bleeding for the first time, huddling into himself, protecting his shredded wing with his body; Goliath, black and white and red, stretched up high on legs that suddenly seemed thick as a man's wrist. The bird was a monster. He had grown to terrifying stature, filling, it seemed, the whole pit. Blindly, he crowed out his cry of victory.

Terry's face crumbled into a grin and he found himself slumping over Karin as though she'd been a mantelpiece.

He'd been drooping through the whole main and hadn't realised it. But suddenly he was alive, and Goliath would fight again. He let out a whoop and called to the handler to get Goliath patched up and back to Portlands. 'I'm gettin' my winnings,' he said to Karin, feeling like a prince.

'Goliath win,' said Doctor Doom.

'Shit,' snorted King. A thousand bucks, *and* Karin. It wasn't his night.

Sweet Romance's owner protested: 'Romance still fightin' mahn. He still angry. He mad as a tiger! You said it would be to de death!'

'Doctor Doom decisions is final,' said Doctor Doom, thinking of the money he'd made out of the St Kitts champion. 'You doan't question de judge.' He'd collected more than enough to cover the Goliath pay-out and now he was tired. He wanted to close down, go back to the sweet arms of the new woman, Blossom.

'That's it, then,' said Julian. 'Good. I made fifty.'

'What an experience!' said Karin, wriggling in her damp silk.

Terry came back with his winnings, flicking the notes: 'Bastard took fifteen hundred dollars off me,' he swore.

Julian smiled. 'Course he did. You know the rules. You pay over fifty per cent as a winnings tax, he returns the rest with your stake. Doctor Doom never loses.'

'And you win two ways, remember?' leered King, recovering his good humour.

Veronica was high. The cock-fight had been over almost before it was begun, but the atmosphere had taken her out of herself.

It was violent. Some people would way it was obscene. But it was the essence of the West Indies. This cruel exploitation of land, animals, and man had always existed here. And, Veronica thought to herself, no *real* harm was ever done in the quiet blue waters of the Caribbean.

Outside, Jewel had found her 'millionaire' who had extricated himself from his wife for the evening on the pretext of betting on the birds.

Jewel didn't know about the wife.

Georges Deneuil was a Canadian. He worked for the Trust Bank in St Kitts. Jewel thought he owned it.

Ignorant and blissful she whirled around the dance floor with him, ready to promise anything. She'd simply *known* he'd be there tonight. She'd been so sure he'd found her utterly captivating. And here he was, the man who could take her on a new, unexpected voyage of hope and destiny. Compared to Georges, Perce was a big no-no. She'd made the right decision.

Her life twisted and turned more than the Colorado River. And it was good that it should be so.

Hope was in Ned's arms again. She wanted more. Now she was close to his body, letting him press his thighs against hers, closing her eyes and breathing what seemed to be cold air as his hands roamed over her bare back.

Ned shivered with the touch of her. She had her hands around his neck, resting her head against his shoulder. He wanted more. He buried his face into her flaxen hair and smelled the essence of her. She was musky. His cock grew and he stepped back slightly, so he wouldn't give himself away, wouldn't frighten her.

She felt his disentanglement and clung more tightly, frightened of losing him, rolling her body sensuously within his arms. He had an erection. She pressed towards him, touching his heat lightly with her own body, wanting to say something, not quite knowing what.

Their body temperatures matched perfectly, they felt as though they were holding themselves instead of each other, so exactly did they fit. Two halves of a jigsaw puzzle.

His hand moved upwards and brushed against the side of her voluptuous breast. Hope worried that his touch might be accidental, that she was reading too much into it. Now it was lingering there, his thumb pressed close against her ribs to feel the weight of the breast that heaved and trembled. Slowly the thumb moved, independent of the rest of the hand, a millimetre this way, a millimetre that way. It could be unconscious – not deliberate. She moved slightly so that her breasts were lower. The hand stayed, the thumb now in reach of the nipple and it was stroking again.

Ned realised she had pressed against his cock. Surely she must know he was hard with wanting her. Could she feel it? Did she know? He put his lips to her ear and, not knowing what to say, kissed the lobe tenderly and so softly it could have been mistaken for breathing or whispering.

He kissed her again, and she *was* aware – aware of everything – the thumb that was running over her erect nipple, the hardness of him that throbbed for her, the desire that was sweeping over him, out from him like something with an uncontrolled life of its own.

'Can we go?' he said, nuzzling her neck, pressing his thumb against her with more urgency.

'Yes,' she said, knowing Terry would take the others back to the Sugar Mill, not noticing that Jewel had become estranged from the party.

They walked back to the Jeep and drove silently, fast, along the dark, dead streets of Charlestown and Gingerland, along to the beach, not the hotel.

'I'll leave it here,' said Hope, parking beneath a manchineel tree that sparkled as moonlight fell on its beautiful, poisonous golden apples.

They took off their shoes and walked barefoot along the cove. The moon, low on the sea, now, shone a silver path over the top of the gentle waves.

'It looks like an airstrip,' said Hope. 'I could land on that.'

Ned took her hand, and at last it was spelt out, their desire for each other, their need for the physical bond they'd both been drawn towards from the first moment.

The sand was cool and damp under their feet. White sand crabs, bold now in the night, scurried ahead of them, around them.

'I think you are beautiful, Hope,' he said.

She smiled. 'I think you are too. Really. A quite beautiful man with your eyes like coal and your sinuous body.'

'Ha! Sinuous, am I? No one's ever described me as that before.' – And beautiful, Hope? – 'How far is it woman, why have you brought me the long way home?'

'I didn't want Pansy to know I was back,' she said. 'There's bound to be a crisis. There always is. And I don't think I want to know about it just yet.'

Ahead was the beach chair where she'd sat watching pelicans that morning. No pelicans now. Only the bony little crabs getting under your feet.

They turned beneath the avenue of coconut trees where the sand became grass. A coconut crab, big as a cat with one long, functional pincer, shot up a palm as they approached, disturbed by the unaccustomed night movement.

They were under the arbour, the trellis of tangled bougainvillea and clematis and passion flowers framing them like a bride and groom on a wedding cake, when he stopped and pulled her to him, kissing her lips, tasting her mouth which said yes, Ned, only yes.

Her eyes were closed, her breath shallow.

'My room,' said Hope, and they took the left fork, unseen by the people at the great house.

Like thieves in the night, like smugglers, like escapees, they entered the mill and its old stones groaned in recognition of them. Filtered starlight, impossibly bright, came through the windows to light the stone steps. As they reached the bottom of them, Hope flipped on a downstairs lamp that glowed orange, and they climbed the stairs, shadowed by the glow, two meteors leaving the sun's gravity against all odds.

In the bedroom they held onto each other tight, finding kindred spirits in the dark, absorbing each other. Ned released his grasp on her, held her away from him at arm's length. He slipped the threads that served as straps from her shoulders, and the sunshine silk fell around her ankles in one swift, rustling movement.

She was reaching for his tie, trying to undo it.

'It's on elastic,' he said, letting go of her to pull it over his head.

'Bastard cheat,' she whispered.

Her breasts shone like moons in the glow from the light downstairs. Chocolate nipples, burnished by the sun, stood out and beckoned to him. As she tried to free his arms from

166

his jacket, he bent to place a kiss lightly on each of them. She shuddered with delight and her arms fell limply to her sides, leaving him to shrug off his own jacket.

Their clothes lay unwanted and irrelevant on the Persian carpet. Hope, naked now, moved to the bed, and he followed, still in his trousers and shirt, though the shirt was being peeled off to reveal that glorious chest, covered with a light sprinkling of soft black and gold hair. She ran her fingers through it, smelling the scent of him, on fire for his touch.

He knew it, and still he lingered, though he was desperate to bury his head in her flesh, hold her breasts in his hands and play with them gently.

'You are my violin,' he said. And there was the hardness that was aching for her. She touched first, less restrained, less cool than he was. Touching lightly, with feather fingers skipping over his erection, ruffling oh so gently the soft, hair, stroking the smooth skin that was stretched tight as cellophane.

'You are my harp,' she said.

'Making love to you will be like making love to all women,' he said.

She understood and her legs parted for his hand to stroke her silky inner thighs, to knead and maul the flesh, to die in.

Now he buried his head between her breasts, pressing the firm, glossy mounds to his face, nipping them, licking them, a lion with a lioness.

Now his tongue was snaking down her body, longing to feel the touch of the marvellous golden pubic hair on his lips, the soft skin between his teeth, the sweetness of her juices. He was greedy for her.

Her sensations were intense even before he reached her. As he hit nerves with his slow, sensuous tongue, she arched her back, opening to him, giving herself as a gift to him. He stroked a finger inside her. His hand was quivering with the same sensations he'd have expected to feel in his penis. But now he was all fingers and tongue, so finely attuned to the sensations he was creating that he could feel their echo in his own body.

167

Then she was coming, a mountain climbing, hang-gliding, an eruption, Krakatoa, maybe, waterfalls, waves on the shoreline. May blossom in the wind, the Pastoral Symphony, trickles of rain.

He could have screamed with her. He felt he too had climaxed.

But Hope was softly caressing him and he realised it was just a trick of the mind, for he was hard and longing for her. She took his cock in her mouth, the softness of her enveloping him, coaxing and persuading him to a higher peak, her wet hand oily from her own body, gliding silkily along his length. Her tongue moved in slow, sensuous movements, finding his most sensitive parts, drawing him till he could bear no more.

'Stop, Hope,' he cried. 'Come to me.'

She climbed astride him, impaling herself, moving around and above his body with slow, coiling rhythms that echoed deep in her vagina and through his cock and into his very heart. 'You *are* me,' he said.

'I am,' she replied, for she could feel through him how she was.

'This is perfect,' he said.

'Yes,' she said and laughed with the joy that raced through her blood, pounding through her veins, hitting her brain like fire, her core like ice.

Then he was clasping her waist, turning her to lie beneath him, resting on his elbows to fall deep into her eyes.

'Lie still,' he said. 'Don't move a muscle. Just feel.'

'I can't,' she said.

'You can.' He pushed gently into her with the rhythms of the sea, sweeping her farther on through her own inactivity, pushing her slowly over to the point where she cried out: 'Ned, I'm coming.'

And he was with her, feeling that same drawing emotion he'd felt while he was licking her, buffetted higher and higher by her sensations transmitted to him through her vagina. Or was he transmitting these sensations to her?

But Christ, this was power, this was submission, this was forging irons, being blown by the wind, dropping an atom

168

bomb, drowning helplessly, victory and defeat.

It was all there. The flowing and the ebbing, the throbbing and the scream that welled up inside him, the absolute relief, the collapse.

They were one complete being – not two halves at all. The beauty with two backs.

'You're heavy,' she said, much later
'Did I sleep?' he said.
'Comatose.'
'Sorry. I'll move.' Reluctantly he rolled away from her.
'I'm pretty drained, too,' said Hope. 'And starving. What about a cheese sandwich?'
'And some coffee. Black, no sugar. I like it strong.'
'I noticed.'

They lay in bed together, side by side, his hand on her thigh that was still moist from his sperm, her juices, their loving. They dropped crumbs in the sheets.

The cat, Kipper, climbed on to his side of the bed and nestled between his spread legs.

'She had a litter this week. But she has no maternal feelings whatsoever.'

'That's why I like cats,' he said. 'They don't have any sense of responsibility.

'I had a ship's cat for company when I first sailed on my own. When I was a one man band doing the donkey work for rich men. Used to take parties out on the ketch to fish for barracuda.' He bit into the sandwich thoughtfully.

'You know, Hope, I really envied them. They'd got it so easy. They'd get pissed on deck and haul in their catches while I was stuck in the wheelhouse. But it was a living.'

'And you were quietly doing up boats and getting rich on the side, so where's the problem?'

'No problem. It just seemed to take so long.' He reached down to scratch Kipper behind the ears and she purred like a sawmill.

'What happened to the ship's cat?'
'He died eventually. Old age.'
'You should have another. They keep the roaches down. You could take one of the kittens if you're around when it's

old enough to leave its prodigal mother,' said Hope. – I know you won't wait, you're going soon. But come back sometime, Ned. Any old excuse will do –

'Maybe I will,' he said. And he reached across her to fondle a breast, in the unhurried way of a man who is sure what he wants.

Chapter Twelve

NIGHT-TIME was louder than the day in Nevis. Okay, so there weren't the shouts of the people on street corners, trying to sell their fish and their fruit, or the sounds of the cars with their broken silencers. Or the yells of the school-girls in their brown uniforms like wardens' outfits. But there were other sounds: the music that blasted out from the upstairs rooms in every other house; the songs of the drunks by the jetty; the crashing of metal as moonlighters welded pipes or beat out car panels.

And there were the indefinable noises – the shrieks and cries of unnameable insects; the bellows of strange animals; the glugging of discarded objects that bobbed on the coal-black water in the harbour.

Andrew Dean, covered in oil, clutching the remnants of his shirt, waited till the two kids were out of sight. They were kicking an empty Coke can backwards and forwards across the wasteland, aiming for telegraph poles, falling lop-sided in hopelessly inaccurate tackles that led to a scuffle every few minutes.

He watched as they took a final aim at the can and sent it scudding into the inky black water, shattering the reflection of the moon into a thousand jagged pieces.

Dean crouched low, listening for other sounds, peering over the edge of the deck intermittently to make sure no one else was around to see him. When their footsteps and laughter had died away, he threw the shirt and its contents into the water before climbing silently down the ramp of the deserted Maria Juana.

'Alan Walker,' he said, sliding into the chair next to Josiah Newcastle's. He'd cleaned up back at the apartment. He looked perfectly normal. Respectable, even. 'Remember me?'

'Sure.' Josiah felt that same creeping uneasiness as he'd felt last time he'd seen the man. 'You come to meet dese guys?'

Dean shrugged. 'Maybe. What are you drinking?'

'Banks.'

'And your friends?' He glanced round the formica table at the five other men whose faces were just visible in the dim light of The Rookery Nook.

'We all drinkin' beah.'

The atmosphere in the cellar bar was clammy. Sweat stains like maps stretched across the front of the men's t-shirts. They were unsmiling, silent, though they'd been laughing before Andrew Dean had joined them. The centre of the table was filled with row upon row of glasses, empty but for a trace of froth. It was gone midnight and they'd been drinking since seven, though none of them felt drunk. Not now.

'Dis is de crew from de boat in de harbour,' said Josiah. 'Cinnamahn Hicks, Keith, Spencer, Gonzo an' Michel.'

'You leave your boat empty at night?' Dean asked in mock horror. He already knew the answer.

Keith turned suspicious frog-eyes on him. He was built like a boxer that couldn't lose; even so, he watched where he trod. 'Nevah. Dere's other men on dat boat right now.'

'Quite right,' said Dean pleasantly, seeing straight through him and laughing inside. He'd only come here to gloat. 'I imagine even big boats go missing in a place like this.' He caught the barman's eye and ordered beer all round.

No one smiled, no one said hey, thanks a lot, man.

'So what're you doing in Nevis?' he asked. 'Fishing? Holidaying?'

Gonzo answered: 'We're crewin' for Ned Murdoch. Cruisin' some passengers.'

Keith the Grenadian flashed him a dagger look. He was wary of all strangers, especially the ones who opened a conversation with a question.

'Ned Murdoch,' Dean repeated softly.

'You said you lookin' for a ride,' said Josiah, feeling the tension round the table as though it was solid.

'Perhaps I did. But I don't need it any more,' Dean smiled. 'I'm planning to take a Cessna plane out to Antigua.' He offered cigarettes round the table. The men shook their heads and rolled their own. Dean slid the edge of his Three Fives packet through his fingers, thumping it down on the formica in a slow, circular rhythm. They watched him in silence.

'So how long you guys staying?'

'They sailin' on Friday,' said Josiah.

So soon! Good job he'd got down to it straight away –

'They goin' to Puerto Rico,' he added. 'San Juan.'

Dean drained his glass. 'Shouldn't take you long to get there in that baby. Big engine, has it?'

'We doan know nothin' mahn,' snapped Spencer. 'We just poor sailors keepin' we noses clean, doin' as we tole an' not axin' too many questions.'

'Cool it,' said Josiah. 'He means no harm. He got womahn problems, dat's all. He ain't no cha-cha.'

'I ain't no cha-cha,' Dean mimicked.

Spencer pushed his beer to one side. 'Ma beah turned sour. You keepin' some strange company, Josiah. Perhaps it's spendin' yo' days wid too many stiffs.'

'Hammerin' all dose coffins,' said Keith.

'Send a mahn crazy,' said Hicks, standing up, ready to leave.

Gonzo shuffled anxiously in his chair. 'We goin' Keith?'

'Better get back to dat boat. Doan want it goin' missin', right?'

They were all at the door, leaving their beers unfinished and their roll-ups burning in the tin-foil ashtrays on the table.

They could at least have finished their drinks, Dean thought. After all, it had been his farewell gesture to them.

'You comin' Jo?'

Josiah looked at Dean and saw emptiness behind the mirrored glasses. His own reflection, bloated in the lenses, seemed uncertain, unsure of itself.

173

'Well then, are you goin' too? Mister Josiah-the-Under-taker,' said Dean.

Josiah leaned towards him and spoke quickly. 'What you doin' heah mahn? Talkin' so strange, takin' on de world. You doan fit. You doan belong heah.' He didn't wait for any reply. He didn't want to know the answers. He put down his own glass and shuffled off after the departing figures into the night.

So you see, my dear, I appear to have done the wrong thing.

I was so sure I was right, that your place was with your wife. That I could never be accepted by your friends and colleagues.

I suppose you will say that once again I have been frightfully old-fashioned, steeped in propriety. And hypocrisy.

Will you believe me if I say that I was concerned for your career? Of course you won't. And I don't think I was, over-much. It was all pure selfishness on my part. I didn't want to give up what I had. I was afraid of change. I suppose I should have been a Tory really. How would that please you, Stuart?

You see, darling, I've been very lucky. Lots of love. An easy life. Julian Winchester said today that my life was glamorous. I hadn't really thought of it like that, but naturally he's right. A life where everything happens sedately but beautifully. All superbly arranged, presented and reviewed.

I've never committed myself because it's been me that's been getting the best of all possible worlds. No one in their right minds would give up what I've had, especially when they've been able to claim they're women of independent means.

Even though that's never been true. The independent part, that is.

What happened at Gidleigh frightened me because I could see it was the end. Not the end in the way I first thought, but an end to my contentment with that sort of life. I've been feeling something of a parasite since I last saw you. Something of a waster.

Perhaps I'm no longer in my right mind, then, because I repent. I reform.

In total contrast to what I've just said, I slept with Julian tonight.

Do you mind? Are you shocked? Hurt?

I don't think I've asked you before.

I thought I should tell you so you know what kind of a woman

174

you're dealing with. Not very dependable but with the best intentions.

I don't think it will happen again, Stuart.

It wasn't terribly good, but that's betraying his confidence. (Something I seem to be doing a lot of recently.) I won't be sleeping with him again: not because the sex wasn't up to much, but because I am writing you this letter.

There. A commitment.

My dear, I think I've decided that perhaps I am ready for change.

Of course you may have reconciled yourself to my absence. You may have found another floosie. (I'm sorry, that was cruel. I know you never saw me in that light.)

Perhaps you and Jannine are away now, on a second honeymoon? Giving it another try?

Or perhaps you are utterly devastated, as I am.

There does, after all, appear to be a difference in the way one can love, not just in intensity, but in the very quality of that emotion.

I think I could marry you. Is that insulting? I'm sorry – I mean I know I would marry you.

Will you ask me again? Will you play Darcy to my Elizabeth Bennett?

Ooh, I've missed you so. Three weeks. A lifetime.

Can you have changed in that lifetime? I pray you haven't. Telephone me, write to me, fly to me if only you're still the same and still love me.

Veronica signed the letter and folded it into an airmail envelope. There was no light anywhere on Nelson Plantation. Julian Winchester had gone back to his own bed. She, normally sleepy after sex, had woken up as soon as he'd left her, as though it were already dawn.

She rang the night porter to summon champagne to her room. Major decisions deserved a celebration, even if she was alone to toast herself.

'No champagne on de island,' said Fransis, yawning. 'But I can bring you ah bottle of Mateus Rosé.'

'What the fuck are you talking about, King?' said Karin as the lights at Doctor Doom's were finally shut down.

It was three in the morning, and King was still high as a

175

kite. 'I just think you ought to be nice to Terry, that's all. He's a great guy.'

'I am nice to Terry, but I'm not going to put out for him, if that's what you're thinking.'

Terry came back from the lavatory and handed a joint to King. He took it and inhaled deeply, holding his breath till he felt his heart racing.

'Let's go, kids,' said Terry, rolling towards the Ferrari.

'Where's Jewel?' said Karin, taking the joint from King.

'She must've gone with Hope and Ned,' said Terry.

A little kid, no older than seven or eight, was curled on the bonnet of the Ferrari, fast asleep.

'Up you get, sunshine,' said Terry. 'Rise and shine. Time to go home to beddy-byes.'

The child was instantly awake. 'Ah bin watching de car, Meestah,' he said. 'I stop de mudders from messin' wid it. Dey threatened to slash de tyres, mahn, an' I stoppin' dem. You give me a dollar.'

'Get lost,' said Terry.

'I lookin' after de car, mahn,' whined the child.

King handed him a fifty cent coin. He took it without thanks and ran into the darkness, disappearing, merging with the trees in the uncanny way the Nevisians had.

Karin said: 'I'm just going to powder my nose.'

'She won't play ball, Terry,' said King. 'She won't screw.'

'Now you look to me like a man of honour, King. You'll fix it.'

Back at the Sugar Mill, dawn was about to break. Terry dropped Karin and King at the car park, then drove the Ferrari to the place on the beach where Hope had left her Jeep. 'I knowed what that means, Miss Parnell,' said Terry aloud.

He climbed out, and after carefully locking the door, floated along the beach, eight miles high and completely out of his head. The crabs ran ahead of him like messengers broadcasting his progress.

He sneaked through the coconut groves, under the

arbour, along the open walkway to Karin's room. It was a long way.

'This is going to be so-o-o good, baby,' said King, stretching her legs apart that little bit further and tying them to the bed posts with belts he'd raided from her wardrobe. Her arms were already fastened at the head of the bed. He lent forward to nibble her incredible tits, plant a kiss on the shaven pussy.

'Ooh, yes, King. Yes,' she moaned, trying to wriggle but unable to do so.

'I'm going to blindfold you, baby. You're completely in my power. Say I love you, King.'

'Ooh, I love you.'

'King,' he prompted.

'King,' she said, willingly, enough. Words were cheap.

'You're so wet,' he grinned, and removed his hand to fasten a scarf around her eyes.

He beckoned to the door where he could see Terry lurking outside and it slid silently open. On stockinged feet, Terry crept up the galleried stairs. King nodded, and watched Terry unzipping himself.

What a waste, thought King. That's never going to satisfy this hot little cookie. I should stick around. She's gonna need me when he's through.

Terry mounted her carefully, touching her with just his angular prick. One cock felt the same as any other once it was inside and he wore the same aftershave as King. Maybe she wouldn't notice the difference.

She moaned as he entered her and skilfully wound his cock around her vagina, tickling her insides and making her groan with ecstasy.

'You're good tonight, King,' she said huskily, approaching orgasm in record time. 'The absolute best ever . . . '

Terry flashed a grin at King through white, white teeth. When it was over, he'd tell the producer some home truths about quality versus quantity.

Maybe he could use a few tips.

The alarm by the side of Esme Little's bed rang. She kicked

the lump that was Oz Lennox and said: 'Go fix my breakfast, honey.'

He stirred reluctantly, lifted one leg out from under the duvet to do as he was told. 'This is one bossy woman,' he said to her as he hunted for Bill's old dressing gown. 'No wonder Bill finally pissed off. What time did you set that alarm for, slave-driver?'

'Five,' she replied, huddling back under the covers. 'You leave at six, remember. You have to get back to Nevis for a hard day's flyin'.'

'Have a heart, woman. I've had a hard day's night. Flying's going to be a vacation in comparison to what you've put me through.'

'We aim to please. And it's time you moved in with me,' she added. 'Hope wouldn't mind you bein' based in Barbados instead of up north. Doan't get the wrong idea, Oz-boy. I just like company is all.'

Oz was easy going. There was no one else in the world he liked as much as Esme. Maybe he could think about it. In time.

Dr Wilding said to his agent: 'I'm sorry I've let you down.'

'It's not me – it's the Party and the people you've let down, Stuart. You were the bright boy. You might have got to be leader one day,' said Derek Watson.

'No, I was too unfashionable,' said Stuart. 'I disagreed when I should have held my peace.'

'That's why your majority was so high,' said Watson. 'We all knew that you wouldn't say anything you didn't really believe in. I suppose that's why I have to accept the situation now.'

'Thanks, Derek. I knew you would.'

'Pig-headed sod,' said Watson. 'Well we have to work out how we're going to break it.

'You can't say too much about Veronica Marston while things are, shall we say, in a state of flux between you two.'

'The News of The Screws doesn't seem to think *it* can't talk about Ron and me. Though the only thing I've given away to them on that score is that I was her lover, and that I intended to marry her as soon as possible.'

'Now that was thinking with your arse,' said Watson. 'You told me you didn't have the faintest idea whether the woman would agree – and that's *if* you can track her down.'

'I told them the truth,' blustered Wilding. 'I do intend to marry her.'

'You don't have to go broadcasting it, do you? There's a question of timing. First you announce your resignation . . . pressures of work. Then you announce your separation, by which time everybody's forgotten your name. And when – if – you get around to marrying Veronica, nobody gives a toss. That's the way you should have played it. You can't call a press conference to disclose your love life, Stuart. It's too much like a Confessional. A public sackcloth and ashes.

'So now you're going to have to go through the motions of regret-regret, work, blah-blah. And the Screws can still scoop on Sunday by revealing the real reasons for your departure from politics. "Love Tangle of Labour Party Trio – Exclusive".' He shook his head. 'I don't understand how an experienced politician can get himself into such a fuck of a mess.'

Wilding had been through this over and over again. In the sleepless hours. 'What time's the Press conference?' he said.

Watson checked his watch. 'Two hours. Eleven o'clock.'

'We've got to have the true story out now *before* the conference. And you've got to leak it, Derek. I can't announce it, as you say, but I can answer questions, honestly and openly.

'I won't make any statement at all other than to confirm my resignation. I'm sick of all the pretence. All you have to do is to ensure the right questions get asked so that the full story comes out. So that there are no new revelations to shock the nation later on. I'm trying to retain some sort of dignity in all this.

'If I'm doing it publicly, nothing can be distorted to become more shocking, more sensational.'

'*Even* more sensational,' Watson said. He paused. 'You could be right, but it will need careful handling. No

179

emotion. It's got to be done cold-bloodedly. Are you sure you can handle it?'

Wilding nodded. 'I have no alternative.'

'And then what? Are you going to chase her to the West Indies?'

'I need to, Derek. I want to be with her before the story goes national, which means I've got to try to get a flight out tonight to Antigua. God knows whether I'll make it, but she needs to know what I've done from me rather than from the papers. I don't know how she'll take it. She'll probably never want to see me again, but I want the chance to explain it to her. Face to face.'

The hall was crowded. Cameras popping, sound-men, national reporters, local radio, the BBC. Wilding stood alone on the podium. Watson merged with the Press to get a feel of reactions.

'Dr Wilding, how long has this affair been going on?' The woman was someone Wilding recognised from the Lobby. Friend or foe he couldn't remember.

'Four years, but it's not "going on", as you put it, at the moment.'

'But it *was* while you were in the Cabinet, wasn't it, sir?'

The microphone was thrust so close to him he could bite it. 'Yes it was.'

'Don't you think that posed a threat to national security, Dr Wilding?'

'No, we never discussed politics. We were lovers, not political opponents.'

Derek Watson sucked in his breath sharply, that was a bad one. Lovers. Quote.

'And Mrs Wilding has left you, sir?'

'Yes.'

'When did she find out about you and Miss Marston?'

Might as well be hung for a sheep as for a lamb: 'She always knew. I kept no secrets from her.'

'But she didn't leave you before?'

'No.'

'Isn't that rather strange, Doctor Wilding? That she

180

accepted your affair with Miss Marston without a murmur. Rather unorthodox?'

'Perhaps it is, to some people.'

'So why did she go yesterday, Dr Wilding?'

'We decided, *we* decided that our marriage was no longer meaningful.'

'Why did you announce your intention not to stand at the next election earlier this week?' The man from the *Guardian* was becoming exasperated with all the trivialities.

Pressure of work? His mind had gone blank – he couldn't remember what he'd said at the time. He took a deep breath. 'I felt that I was no longer able to give my full, undivided attention to Party work.' Nice and cagey.

'So why have you now announced your immediate resignation, sir? What has changed? Surely you must know that your seat in a hung Parliament is crucial?'

'I decided that it was unfair to my constituents to leave them represented by a man whose mind was on other things. My earlier decision was an error in judgement.'

'Have you announced your decision to the Party Chairman?'

'I have.'

'And has your resignation been accepted?'

'Yes. Apparently with regret.'

The reporter smiled and wrote shorthand notes.

'Did you resign at Miss Marston's suggestion?' he asked innocently.

'Certainly not. She bears no blame whatsoever for what has happened.'

'When do you expect to announce your engagement to Miss Marston?' asked a motherly-looking journalist who sucked on her pen-top thoughtfully. The scandal-monger in sheep's clothing.

'I don't necessarily expect to do so at all. She may not have me. Also I do not intend to become bigamous.'

There was polite laughter, but the tension remained.

'Do you want to marry Miss Marston? You don't feel this is another error of judgement that you will later regret?'

'Of course I want to marry her! I love her!'

'And will you? Will you marry her, sir?'

'I don't know. I will if I get my own way. But Miss Marston has not yet given me an answer that I am prepared to accept.'

Derek Watson looked over the reporter's shoulder to see her doodling the words 'public proposal'.

Suicide. That was the only honourable way out. For both of them. The ex-Member of Parliament and the agent. They could make it a three-some. Veronica Marston could come and do it with them, if she liked. She'd probably want to when she saw what the papers did to her. Watson rose from his seat.

Wilding was a madman, insane. He should remember he was still legally married to Jannine. He had cut his own throat. He'd warned Wilding to stay unemotional at all costs. To remember to be aloof and evasive, remember the tricks of the trade. Never to answer a question directly.

'Is your political career over Doctor Wilding?'

Derek Watson knew the answer. He didn't need to hear it. He looked at Wilding on the podium and snorted with contempt. Truth, huh. Sick of this pretence. My arse, he thought.

He'd always managed the wallpaper technique on national and international issues in the past. Yes, he'd spoken his mind, but he'd done it in such a way that he could never be accused of lying or of betraying the Party. But now he'd blown it.

Well they'd murder him in the papers, and the Party would undoubtedly lose the by-election. Politicians must be seen to be above emotion. They must be cool, logical and absolutely incapable of accepting criticism. They shouldn't have mistresses at all – what did he think he was, royalty? The only reason MPs had pricks in the first place was to produce some nice little Party converts.

Damn his honesty. Wilding was ruined.

Derek Watson left the room unnoticed as reporters erupted into an excited babble. He walked slowly upstairs to his office and dictated his own letter of resignation to the secretary.

Chapter Thirteen

THOUGH THE telephone rang persistently, Hope slept on.

Ned turned to her and kissed her forehead. Unusual for a woman to sleep on her back like that, so open and vulnerable.

'Wake up, Hope. Phone's going.'

She opened her eyes.

'You don't want me to answer it, do you?' he asked innocently.

She grinned at him, pleased he was still there. 'No way. If it's Zeke he'll have a fit at the sound of your voice.' As she reached for the receiver, it stopped abruptly. There is nothing so frustrating as a phone that stops just at that moment, when you'd decided you would make conversation after all.

'How are you, first thing in the morning?' said Ned. He was warm and sexy, she could feel his rampant cock against her buttocks.

'Rampant!' she cried, diving under the sheets to take him again into her mouth, to caress him, absorb him. Their time was so short, she wanted to enjoy him as much as possible.

But she was stopped by the banging on the oak doors downstairs.

'Damn!' she said, climbing swiftly out of bed and wrapping herself in a cotton gown.

It was Pansy. Her bosom heaved impressively to show there was indeed a major crisis, as Hope had known there would be.

'Hoape,' she quavered. 'Thank Jesus you is heah. I thought you doan't come hoame last night. De Jeep isn't in de parkin' place, and you not ans'rin' de phone . . . '

Hope patted her arm. 'What's the problem?'

'It's de Canadian womahn. De one who dined here. She die in de night.'

'Oh my God,' said Hope. 'Not here? Not at Sugar Mill?'

Pansy's face looked as though it was trying to decide whether to beam at all the excitement or cry with the worry. 'She was gettin' into her taxi. Here at de hoatel, sure enough. She bein' a big womahn, Hoape. Bigger den me. Den she starts breathin' in dis way dat doan't sound good. An' she clutchin' at her chest like dat. Her husband, Mistah Scott, he say she need to come back inside and rest. She can't take de journey. She havin' a heart attack.

'So we bringin' she back in de Great House an' she lie a-moanin'. An' we call de doctor, but he out at de cockfight. An' after about an hour, she stop moanin' an' she say to her husband: "I want to be buried at sea". An' he say: "Doan't you talk stupid womahn". So she say de same again and Mister Scott he agree. An' den she just die.'

'Oh, God, no. You've got to be kidding.'

'No, Hoape. Dis happened. Elisha say to put her in de freezer till mornin', but Rachel say no.'

'Thank the lord for that,' said Hope. 'So where is she?'

'She in de shade on de verandah, at de front of de dinin' room. None of de guests comin' down to breakfast. Dey all havin' it in dere rooms. So we think she safe dere.'

'Have you called the undertaker?' said Hope.

'No problem. Josiah Newcastle say he comin' to collect de body soon as he arrange de funeral. De Reverend Wilcox have agreed to take de ceremony. It happ'nin' dis mornin' as de weather goin' to be real hot.

'Everybody lookin' forward to some good singin' an' prayers from de Reverend –

'Good mornin' Mistah Murdoch,' she interrupted herself, seeing ankles and legs at the top of the steps.

'Mornin' Pansy,' he called back, not at all abashed that he'd been spotted.

'You heah about de funeral? You comin' to see? De whoale island be dere.'

'Wouldn't miss it,' he replied. 'If Hope's going.'

'She have to. It her responsibility,' she called, then added to Hope: 'Maybe he not so bad. He sleep de night here?'

Hope nodded.

'Okay,' said Pansy. 'No problem. You want me to move in his cloathes from de Nisbett Room?'

'Do that, Pansy,' called Ned, emerging wearing just a towel around his waist.

She grinned at him flirtatiously. 'Dat okay, Hoape?'

'Yes,' she said. 'No problehm.'

It was fortunate for Lottie that the Reuters man arrived when he did. She had watched Veronica walk away to the next village of Lilly, clutching post-cards, not three minutes ago.

It would take Ronnie at least twenty minutes to get there and back.

In the back of the taxi, the Reuters man drove up Upper Round Road from the opposite direction.

'Don't bother sending the taxi away,' she said, cutting out preliminaries. 'Miss Marston's flown home. Bad case of food poisoning. She needs medical attention and there are no BUPA hospitals out here.'

The Reuters man leaned through the window. 'That's a pity,' he said. 'I was over here on another story and I thought I'd bring some flowers for the ailing Miss Marston. And try for an interview.'

Lottie looked down the road towards Lilly Village and hoped Veronica hadn't forgotten anything. 'Well never mind,' she said cheerfully. 'Can't be helped.'

'It would have made a better story,' he continued, not convinced she wasn't somewhere around, though that could be checked. 'Doctor Wilding gave a press conference this morning, eleven o'clock British time. Apparently he virtually made her a public proposal. I'd have liked to get her response.'

Jessica emerged from Julian's office. Hearing the voices, she hovered in the doorway.

'That, Mister Derby, is quite impossible,' Lottie was saying sharply.

Jessica started down the steps. 'Good morning!' she called brightly, looking from Lottie's worried face to the taxi. 'Am I right in thinking you must be Reuters?'

'In a manner of speaking.'

'It's Mister Derby,' said Lottie quickly. 'He wanted to see Veronica. But isn't it a shame? His *missing her* like this. I'm sure she'll be so sorry not having had the chance to speak to you.'

The newsman was estimating the value of the new woman on the scene. 'You're a friend of Miss Marston's?' he asked.

'Yes,' replied Jessica firmly. 'A better friend than some.'

The reporter assumed a bored, matter-of-fact voice. He looked as excited as a glacier, but it wasn't the way he was feeling. This woman had something, he was sure of it. 'Then I expect you'll be pleased to hear that Doctor Wilding has honourable intentions,' he said. 'He's made a statement that will be published nationally by tomorrow. Looks like it's wedding bells. Apparently, this story of Mrs Wolff's has rather forced his hand.'

He waited for a reaction.

Nothing doing. He tried again. 'But I hear that Miss Marston has unfortunately left Nevis?'

'Yes,' Lottie cut in. 'Last night.'

Jessica hovered undecided. Lottie would have kicked her if she could. As it was, even a silent snarl would have been spotted. She concentrated on making her face look relaxed and calm.

'I'm afraid so,' said Jessica. 'She has. Temporarily. But she may want to speak to you when she returns. Perhaps you'd like to give me your card?'

The taxi drove off towards Charlestown, where the Reuters man planned to spend a boozy hour at the Longstone Bar before the next job, the burial at sea. It was really only local interest, though he might make a bit from the Canadian papers too.

But he knew he'd struck lucky with the other woman. He'd get his interview, and he was prepared to wait for it. The Wilding affair was as good as tied up.

'What did you do that for, Jessica?' spat Lottie immediately.

'I haven't *done* anything.'

'You as good as gave it away.'

Jessica looked at Lottie and saw guilt written all over her. Head to toe.

'I knew you wouldn't say anything to her at breakfast.'

'Of course not. Not yet. We've got to let it die down first.'

'You're wrong. And it's not the first time in your life that you've made a mistake so don't look so precious.'

Lottie snapped her head up sharply, like a thoroughbred. Who did meek like Jessica Collier think she was talking to?

'Time's running out,' she was saying. 'Ron's side needs to be told, Lottie. For all we know, she might be on trial back in England, and she's got to be allowed to speak in her own defence.

'If you keep hiding her away, it's a "No comment", and that means she's guilty as hell to the Press.'

'If it's "No comment" it's no story, Jessica,' Lottie snapped.

'Balls. And you know it. If you don't want her to hear what you've done from me then it's up to you to get it straightened out. Fast.'

Lottie swore at Jessica's retreating back then called: 'Jess. Please. Do me a favour. Promise not to say anything to Ron. Not yet. Let me think it out – '

Jessica turned on her heel. 'All right. I won't speak to her about it. I promise. But you've got to tell her this morning. Before it's too late.'

Lottie walked slowly away from the Nelson, heading towards Mount Pleasant.

She was confused. Things that had appeared perfectly clear-cut seemed to be tangling up into the most awful mess. Lottie had a terrible sinking feeling that it might be she herself who was responsible for the chaos.

In the distance, Veronica was visible, taking a different way home from the village of Lilly. She was walking briskly, despite the heat.

Lottie stood absolutely still; like a chameleon she tried to blend in with her background.

Jessica was right for once. She should tell her now. Come straight out and say: *I've sneaked to the press about your affair with a married MP. I've lied to them about him being here with you. I gave them a picture of you together. And because of that, they believed me.*

As a result, my dear, I'm afraid your name is shit.

His career is in ruins and his wife has left him.

I'm sorry, Veronica, but I seem to have prompted a divorce, a general election and the end of your reputation through my stupidity.

Yes. That's what she should say.

Lottie watched the distant figure of Veronica growing. She waved casually, as though she'd only just seen her. Then she turned and jogged quickly away from her, back to the safety of the hotel.

The pier was crowded. Women wore their Sunday best; men wore suits. There were hats decked with net, flowers, feathers and tinsel. All worn together. There were children in good, white dresses, their hair tied up into pigtails with red and blue ribbons, eating icecream. There were old men with spotted handkerchiefs tied over their heads or in trilby hats.

There was a hot dog stall run from the back of a fish van. There were evangelists and tourists, saints and sinners.

'This is very sacreligious, isn't it?' asked Veronica of Julian.

'Certainly not,' he replied. 'It's all very healthy and good for the soul. Societies that enjoy mourning the dead and expressing their grief are much healthier than the ones that repress it.'

'But none of them knew the woman,' protested Jessica.

'That doesn't matter. It's the occasion that counts. Anyway, you didn't know her and you're still here.'

Terry Morelands saw Karin and King in the crowd and waved to them. They waved back. They were arm in arm. Karin looking at King with a new respect. She was never to know it had been Terry who'd bedded her the previous night.

188

Hope and Ned were among the chief mourners, Hope because it was her plantation where release had been granted to Mrs Scott, Ned because he was recognised as her consort.

Rodney Scott, the widower, said to them: 'She had a good life. She'd have liked all the fuss she's causing.'

The Reverend Wilcox read the opening lines of the funeral service. Immediately, a wailing began and ice-creams were suspended in their passage to mouths.

Jenny Smith cried: 'Halleluja!' at the words 'Dearly Beloved'.

'She was a womahn loved by all,' said the Reverend, knowing so little about the body that had been Margaret Scott that he was forced to improvise.

'Through her good works for charity, she had won a place in de Lord's heart, an' He is takin' her for His own because He cannot bear to have His Best Loved Ones so far from He.'

There was much shaking of heads and murmurs of Amens.

'She was a womahn of only fifty-three years.' Rodney Scott shook his head and hissed at the Reverend Wilcox.

'She was a womahn of only seventy-three years,' he said. 'She was taken maybe before her time.

'But dat's in de eyes of mahn.

'In de eyes of God, dat was time enough for He.'

'Amen.'

'Praise de Lord in His wisdom and pray our own time not comin' too soon.'

'Halleluja!'

'Now I cuttin' de words short, for de sun gettin' high and Meesus Scot needin' to go to her restin' place as a mattah of some urgency.'

'Amen.'

Josiah Newcastle, the Reverend and three strong men posted the stout coffin in a rowing boat at the end of the pier.

The boat sank alarmingly a couple of inches and then righted itself. The Reverend and the men climbed in with the coffin and extended a hand to Rodney Scott and the other Canadians.

Then slowly and majestically the boat was rowed out into a current, so the coffin would be taken out into the Caribbean sea on a slipstream.

The Reverend said words no one could hear, and the coffin was tipped into the waters. The men started to row back when the coffin floated again to the surface.

'Praise de Lord,' shouted Jenny Smith, pointing.

The rowers turned back and hoisted the floating coffin back into the boat. Everyone had fallen silent, wondering what the next step would be.

'Gadder de stones, my children,' called Reverend Wilcox through a megaphone in the boat. It was rowed slowly to the pier, where everyone who didn't have an icecream or a hotdog was busy hunting for rocks.

The coffin was hoisted back onto the jetty. Josiah levered up the lid of the coffin to expose the cold Mrs Scott to the light. Rocks were arranged around her, carefully so as not to waken her. Then the coffin was placed back into the boat and for a second time, it was rowed slowly outwards till it reached the currents. The Reverend Wilcox stood, swaying uncertainly, balancing with difficulty as the over-laden boat hung precariously in the water.

This time he used the megaphone so the congregation could hear the words and their spirits soar.

'Oh Lord, take dis, your chile, Margaret Scott to sit on de right hand of our Saviour, Jesus Christ.'

'Amen.'

The coffin was lifted. Slowly. The men's muscles strained till they looked as though they'd been over-blown. The coffin splashed into the water. Nobody cheered.

The boat waited. And sure enough, the coffin floated back to the surface yet again, bobbing insolently on the tide.

This time it was too heavy to be recaptured. 'Bring a net, fishers of mahn,' called the Reverend through the megaphone.

'An' womahn,' giggled Rachel, who'd taken time off to watch the funeral.

Ready for action, two boys sped out to the cortege on sunfish, the waterbikes that deceptively looked so easy to ride. They held a net between them and scooped up the coffin to bring it back to the pier.

Refreshments were called for. Rum and beer arrived from The Longstone and The Rookery Nook. The Reuters man was wishing he had a movie camera instead of the Nikon.

Josiah Newcastle sent an apprentice to fetch a hand-drill from the house marked Keep Yore Ass Out. He was back in half an hour. The crowds now filled the main roads. Traffic stopped. Somebody had phoned Basseterre and warned the ferry not to sail.

Josiah drilled holes in the coffin lid, anger and frustration creasing his brow. 'Shame dis womahn wasn't in de hold of de Titanic,' he said. 'She nevah would of sunk.'

The sunfish boys took the coffin out again while the chief mourners trailed behind in the boat.

'Dear God, is you takin' dis chile or is you makin' a mistake dis time?' said Reverend Wilcox. 'If so, I'm wishin' you would give me some sign.'

The net went slack and the coffin, heavy as lead and with no air inside to keep it afloat, sank beneath the blue waters, gracefully, like a submerging whale. There were bubbles popping to the surface.

Rachel said to Hope: 'Well doan't go askin' for fish in de dinin' room for de next week or so. 'Cos if you do, *I* ain't touchin' it.'

'I thought that was you Mister Derby,' said Jessica, panting from her sudden dash through the crowds on the pier. 'I was hoping I might find you here.' She held out her hand and it shook. 'Jessica Collier, from Nelson Plantation.'

'Ah yes.' He had recognised her immediately. 'What can I do for you?'

'You wanted to speak to Miss Marston.'

Oh Lord, was she doing right? Or was she about to make things even worse? Even now, she could turn back, it wasn't too late.

But Jessica had worried long enough. She knew Lottie wasn't going to tell Veronica about the furore that was currently erupting in Britain, no matter what she'd agreed. She was too stubborn, could never admit that she was capable of making an error of judgement.

Jessica had promised Lottie that she wouldn't speak to Ron either. But she'd never said anything about talking to the Reuters man. She swallowed hard. 'If you want to interview her, you'll find her here in Charlestown. She was outside the bookshop in the main road not two minutes ago. If you hurry, you'll catch her. But please don't mention my name . . .'

Derby grinned. 'Thank you, Mrs Collier. And don't worry about a thing.'

'Mister Derby,' she called him back sharply, nerves giving a cutting edge to her voice. 'I want you to be kind. She deserves that at least.'

'Oh I will, Mrs Collier. Indeed I will,' he smiled.

In Antigua, Miriam Morelands was fuming. 'What do you mean there is no plane ordered?' she asked IN-Flight's airport representative.

'I'm sorry, Mrs Morelands. We don't have any scheduled pick-ups today. I can see if I can get a plane over for you, but it may take time.'

Miriam was disgusted. Why had she married that imbecile? An efficient secretary would have been far more use.

She called Portlands from an open phone booth in the corner of the departure lounge. The staff was shocked to hear her voice, so close to home. The boss-man might have given them some warning.

'So Mister Morelands didn't inform you of my arrival?' she asked in her clipped Oxbridge accent.

'Eh, no mam,' said the voice.

'Has my room been made up?'

'No mam. Sorry, mam.'

'And where is Mister Morelands?' she snorted.

'He not bin in de past two days.'

'I understand,' she said, hanging up, not saying goodbye.

She returned to IN-Flight's desk. 'If you were booked up

when my husband tried to arrange the plane, would you have a record of it?'

'Yes, Mrs Morelands. In case of cancellations. But I've already checked and there is no record.'

'In which case you'd better try to get someone to fly out now and pick me up. Thank you.'

She took a seat opposite the desk so she could watch the girl with the too-red lipstick make the call immediately. Let her know she wasn't prepared to wait a second longer than necessary.

It took ten minutes for her to reach Sugar Mill Plantation. Hope Parnell wasn't available, Oz Lennox was on a flight, Gem Welch was chauffeuring the English cricket team from Trinidad to Tobago for rest and recuperation.

'I have a freelance on call,' said the IN-Flight rep.

'Well why are you wasting time then?' said Miriam. 'Get him.'

'It's a woman, Esme Little.'

'Christ! I don't care if the pilot's a wallaby as long as it's well-trained. Get her.'

The girl radioed through to Esme. She was presently leaving Saba and intending to fly back to Barbados. She didn't mind making the detour. It was all extra cash.

The representative smiled at Mrs Morelands. 'The plane will be here in approximately one hour fifty minutes.' It was a long time for someone as busy as Mrs Morelands appeared to be. She enjoyed telling her.

Miriam tapped her feet in annoyance and frustration. Nearly two hours to wait in the stifling departure lounge at Antigua. Without air conditioning.

After California, it came home to Miriam just how uncivilised the West Indies were. The conditions might suit that husband of hers, but that was because he'd never known anything better. He was just an island boy, no matter what he thought, no matter that he'd made enough money swindling her to buy himself that ridiculous Ferrari. Well, things were going to change.

He'd been away, leaving Portlands in the hands of the servants. And God only knew what they'd let happen to the estate if they weren't watched like hawks.

Of course he'd been womanising. Naturally that went without saying. But from now on, Terry Morelands was going to have to mend his ways.

She hadn't minded in the past, his having sex with every tart he could get his hands on. But when it inconvenienced her, when it disrupted the smooth-running of her slick, sophisticated life, the order of the Plantation, that was different.

Terry would be given the ultimatum. Either he left his prick at home when he went out or he was finished. She'd sue him for every penny he'd robbed her of during their long, tedious marriage.

And that bloody bird that took up so much of his precious time when he should be supervising the estate – that could go too. She'd wring its neck personally and serve it up trussed and roasted. For Thanksgiving.

'Excuse me! Miss Marston, I believe,' said Derby, pushing his way through the crowds in the main street.

'Yes, that's right?'

'I'm so pleased to see you so well. Charming.' So she hadn't wanted to speak to him, eh? Too bad.

'I've never been better. But?'

'I'd heard you had flown back to England. You had a bad case of food poisoning?' Rub it in. Twist the knife a little.

'I'm sorry, perhaps you've mistaken me for someone else?' said Veronica.

'No. I recognise you from your photograph, though – if you'll excuse a personal comment – I must say you've lost a bit of weight.' She must have guessed who he was by now? Surely? But there was no sign of it in her eyes.

'I represent Reuters News Agency,' he said patiently. 'My name is Don Derby.'

'Reuters. I see,' said Veronica. 'And this photograph?'

'The one of you and Doctor Wilding.'

'At Nelson Plantation?' she asked, quite calmly.

'Yes.' Derby was taken aback. He'd expected evasiveness after her earlier 'disappearance'. Was it possible he'd misjudged her? 'Could I speak to you alone? Today?'

Veronica needed time. Time to find out what either Lottie, Jessica or Julian had told this man. 'No, I'm sorry. Not today. I already have plans.'

He began to protest, but Veronica cut him short. 'I will, however, be pleased to see you at ten tomorrow morning. I will meet you at The Rookery Nook. Upstairs, on the gallery.'

She turned to walk away without further conversation.

'Miss Marston,' he called after her. She turned. 'Could I have your assurance you won't speak to any other newsmen in the meantime?'

She considered the question for long enough to worry him. Then she said: 'Yes, Mister Derby, you may have that assurance. Most definitely.'

She held out her hand to him and he took it, though he wasn't sure whether to kiss it or shake it.

He watched her walk away and then headed back to the Longstone Bar. He'd have to arrange for some British papers to be flown over to him before the ferry crossing tomorrow. He wanted to be sure he'd make an impact on the inscrutable Veronica Marston.

Stuart Wilding's secretary covered the telephone receiver and said: 'The first available flight is on Friday. There's nothing sooner. I am sorry. I know how anxious you must be.'

He shook his head in frustration. Friday was a long way away. Anything could happen between now and then.

'It leaves Heathrow at ten-thirty and arrives at four in the afternoon, local time. Shall I book you a seat?'

He had no choice. 'Anything, whatever's going.'

She spoke into the receiver. 'Yes, we'll take that. First class. One way.' She raised an eyebrow at Wilding and he nodded yes. 'And we'll need an onward flight reservation from Antigua to Nevis. Could we leave that to you to arrange with one of the small airlines out there?'

He smiled. The royal 'we', the corporate identity always amused him.

She wrote out a note of the timings and passed it across

195

the desk. 'I think you're terribly brave, Stuart,' she said. 'Very honest.'

He smiled. 'You're the only one who does think so.'

'It's going to be frightful tomorrow, when the papers come out. Do you think you'll be the lead?'

'I fear I may be. This is the silly season when nothing happens. I'm the only thing in a dead week.

'But I've yet to appear in a news bulletin, so there's still a chance I'll escape with a scrape and not with a hanging.'

He looked at the note thoughtfully, and wondered whether he should pack a case or a trunk. If he was going to chase Veronica around the world, he ought to be well-prepared. And there was the other problem: the problem of where he was supposed to stay while he was in Nevis. 'Better phone through to book me a room at Sugar Mill Plantation, Julie,' he said resignedly.

He'd have preferred to stay at the Nelson, but he couldn't risk appearing there, out of the blue.

He was going to have a long, hard task explaining the debacle of his press conference and the ensuing scandal to Veronica. It might be weeks – months – before she'd take him back or before he'd be welcome at Nelson Plantation. Especially if this political storm reached her before he did.

Chapter Fourteen

THE EYE of hurricane Cleo avoided Cayenne by thirty kilo-
metres. It had taken a new course and swept north at
speeds of 120 miles an hour, leaving behind in its wake a
trail of devastation and heartbreak. In the eye, trapped in
an invisible cage, tropical birds, seeds and seedlings
whirled in truly suspended animation, to be finally released
thousands of miles away, wherever the hurricane decided
to die. On the edge of the vortex, frozen tears circulated,
thrown outwards by centrifugal force to melt into
blinding rains as they fell to the earth below.

In Nevis, Zeke sat on the beach, listening to the song of
the sea. It had changed. The change wasn't a good one.
There was an echo, an ominous beat, a thunder in the
waves as they crashed slowly, too slowly onto the sand and
the rocks. The pelicans were taking advantage of the seas
that were moving so uncertainly. They dived for fish
rapidly, surfacing with full beaks, filtering them from the
water, and diving again. It looked as though they were
storing up for hard times to come.

Hope and Ned sat alongside him, arriving breathless and
starry from an afternoon of loving. They too were storing
up for the future when they'd have nothing to show for
their week together other than memories to be treasured,
like a photograph album.

'Lissen,' said Zeke.

They had come to watch the sunset. A dusty one.
Brilliantly red already, though the sun had half an hour
before its disappearance. A cloud like a sailboat shone
crimson and coasted away, southwards, over the edge of
the bay.

Ned was alert to any changes in the sea. He felt a

physical churning at the slow beat of the waves, the strange booming that resounded in his ears, almost slowing down his own heartbeat with its magnetic, hypnotic rhythm.

It was high tide, but the water level was still low.

Zeke pointed to it. 'De water bein' sucked away from de island,' he said.

'What is it?' asked Hope, knowing.

'Wind,' said Zeke simply.

'I haven't listened to the radio reports today,' said Hope. 'Is it the hurricane?'

Zeke nodded. 'It come dis way.'

Ned said: 'You've heard that for sure?'

Zeke didn't need weather reports. 'I know.'

There was that strange booming. Not a sea-sound at all. It was a voodoo drum; the belch of a toad; slow explosions in a distant gravel pit.

'How long?' said Hope.

'Tomorrow, maybe.'

They didn't like to break the silence. They breathed quietly, spoke in whispers.

'They'll want to go,' said Ned. 'Perce and the others. They'll want to run the storm, get out to Puerto. They'll say to sail before the winds come. Tonight, even.'

Hope felt he'd hit her. 'But you won't, will you? Running a hurricane is madness. You think you know which areas are safe, but then something changes the pattern.

'Scientists could seed the storm and deflect it. The course was plotted before – but it couldn't have been right. Not if it's coming this way now.'

'The Maria Juana's fast,' said Ned. 'I wouldn't risk it in any other boat.'

'But you will in this one?' asked Hope. – *And die – just when I've found you –*

'I don't know, Hope.'

They lapsed into silence again, listening. Normally, the waves came in ten or so to each minute. Now they were down to five. Zeke counted, instinctively measuring them. 'Long way away yet,' he said.

Ned reached for Hope's hand and cradled it. It lay there lifelessly, not responding to his touch.

198

She wanted to say don't go. It's not worth it. There are other ways to get to Puerto Rico. What is time? Does it matter to them so much that a missed plane is worth risking lives? Instead, she said: 'When will you decide?'

He said: 'I should tell them. Tell them that the hurricane's on its way. Let them make the decision.'

Hope's expression became blank. Shut-down. Keep those emotions wrapped up safe so no one sees.

That's what you get, she thought. That's what happens when you let someone into those secret places. When you let your barriers break down and in sneaks the infiltrator. And you think here's sunshine, here's rosebuds. And you think he's feeling the same. But you're not strong enough to hold him. There are other things that are more important to him than you are. If it's not another woman, it's the sea. Or it's a deal, or it's his separate life. There's no real fusion of the soul at all, because love never moved mountains. The sea did.

Ned thought: if I don't go, Hope, I have to stay. I don't know whether I want that. Not yet. It's too soon for me to know. I don't want to be forced to stay with you because of the winds. If I stay, I must choose. I can always come back. Afterwards. When it's my choice.

The sun sank lower, now on its rapid descent to its watery grave. It swelled till its sphere seemed to fill a quarter of the sky. It was molten lava, burning coals, smoldering rubies. As it hit the sea, the green flash glowed spectrally, a ghostly line of turquoise fluorescence stretching from the outer edges of the sun to the end of the horizon.

They were sitting on a dead tree trunk, their feet in the hot, dry sand. Ned pushed silver hair away from Hope's face. 'It's all too soon,' he said.

'The sun drops quickly, she replied, misunderstanding him deliberately.

Red cloud-feathers spattered the sky. It was an angry bird of paradise. The frogs began to chirrup, Zeke softly whistled in time with them.

'What about that crapaud?' said Hope, suddenly afraid, torn, almost despairing.

199

'You don't believe in omens?' asked Ned.

'I do now, right at this second. Ned don't go. You know the sea. You know you don't win against nature.'

He put his arm around her and she was melting like a wax effigy. 'So you don't battle against her,' he said. 'You trick her. You take evasive action and you think on your toes.'

'You make it sound like a game! But it isn't. Ned, you are going to have to think twenty-four hours a day if you sail. You are going to have to stay awake and alert all the time till you reach Puerto. Why don't you let me fly them across tonight?

'I've got The Goose. I can outrun a storm better than you can.'

He said: 'It's not my way, Hope.'

She said: 'Who are you cheating? The hurricane or you?'

Zeke didn't like storms. Especially emotional ones. He got up from the tree-trunk and shuffled off through the sand.

'We'll make it. Christ, I've seen hurricanes before. I'm still here.'

Now the sky was liquid. The ripples of feathers that were clouds rolled and bubbled, flowing south-west as though pulled by a magnet into a central point. Everything was pink – the sand, the crabs that scuttled towards the sea and back again, the great house on the hill behind them.

'Come on, babe. Let's go in,' said Ned. 'I have to talk to Perce.'

Veronica sat in the library at Nelson Plantation and looked for a book on West Indies flora.

She had spent the afternoon avoiding everybody until she could get what had happened into perspective. She had dwelled for too long on the problem of the Reuters man and over which of her friends had betrayed her. She wouldn't know any more news of Stuart until tomorrow, so she shouldn't allow herself to worry unnecessarily.

Now she had fifteen different flowers she'd never seen before to identify. She spread the specimens out on the tiled floor and kneeled over them, trying to match them against the coloured drawings in Julian's book.

'Thank goodness I've found you,' said Lottie breathlessly. 'I've been looking everywhere. I thought we might go for a walk.'

Veronica held a thin, green leaf up to the light. It was so translucent you could imagine you could see every cell, every nucleus of its structure.

'Did you have something you wanted to say to me?'

'Me? No! Nothing at all, Ron. Just a walk, that's all. I thought we could go down to the Newcastle Pottery and buy some of those clay birds you like. It's open till eight tonight.' Her voice trailed away. 'Or something . . . '

Veronica looked at her at last and Lottie instantly turned away, afraid to meet her eyes. Yes, of course, Lottie was Judas. No wonder people habitually concealed their private lives from her. Lottie processed and used information as if it was machinery.

'How was the funeral?' Lottie asked casually.

'Very interesting.' She was distracted by a hummingbird whirring against the window pane in a flash of green feathers for a moment before it vanished again, as if by magic. 'And I met someone there. A friend of yours perhaps.'

Lottie stared wildly around the room, as though she was looking for a quick exit. 'A friend? Of mine?'

Veronica could make it easy for her. She tossed a coin, came down against, and looked innocently up at the ashenfaced woman. 'You haven't got much of a tan today, Lottie,' she said. 'You should get out in the sun a bit more than you do.'

'Ron, don't beat about the bush. What friend of mine?'

'Don Derby.'

Neither of them spoke as they measured their friendship.

'Well that's buggered it,' said Lottie eventually. 'I wanted you to be kept out of it.'

Veronica smiled icily. 'Out of what exactly, Lottie?'

'Out of the papers.' Here goes. Bull by the horns and all that. 'You know that photograph? That one of you and Stuart Wilding?'

'Only too well.'

201

'Well I gave it to the Press.'

She paused, saw no response apart from that maddening, empty smile, and went on in a hurry: 'I thought you were hurt, and I put it down to some relationship breaking up. I thought that on the plane. And then when that photograph came up, I realised who had let you down.'

'Let *me* down, Lottie?' interrupted Veronica.

'Well, naturally. And with it being Wilding, I thought I could take the wind out of his sails a bit. You know. By getting in touch with the papers, make life a bit difficult for him.'

'What? Are you talking of revenge, Lottie?'

'Yes, if you like,' she said quietly.

'And?'

'And apparently Doctor Wilding has resigned from politics . . . '

'Directly in response to the photograph?'

Lottie nodded miserably. 'Yes.' She bit her lower lip. 'And his wife's left him. And, I'm sorry Ron, but I've got you terribly involved. They want interviews with you and I expect pictures.'

Veronica was white, tight-lipped. 'Actually, Lottie, you've been pretty stupid.'

'Yes. I'm sorry. I did it for the best of motives. I hated the idea of you suffering . . . '

'And you think what you've done will make my so-called suffering any less?'

'No, but I didn't know all this – ' she waved her hands in the air to indicate enormity, ' – all this would blow up. I'm sorry. I'll do whatever I can to make amends, Ron. Any way I can help . . . '

'Let me tell you something,' Veronica hissed. 'You got it all wrong. *I* finished the affair. *I* was the one. He did nothing to hurt me at all. It was the other way around. But from what you've said it seems that he is the one to be punished. Unjustly punished.'

She looked blankly into space and spoke quietly, as though she was talking to herself. 'I want to know how much Jessica and Julian were involved. I need to know where I stand.'

'Julian knows nothing,' said Lottie quickly, 'nothing at all. And Jess said I was doing wrong. We rowed about it last night. She said I should confess everything to you. But you know how stubborn I am. And anyway, to tell the truth, I was afraid. I was afraid because I was no longer in control. I don't suppose I'd have said anything even now if you hadn't brought it up first.'

Veronica crumpled one of the flowers in her hand, creasing the creamy petals, the pink stamen, the veridian leaf between her fingers.

'I've booked a flight home,' she said shakily. 'I arranged it this afternoon. I still love him you see. More than ever. I made a most terrible mistake when I said goodbye.

'And now he must think that *I'm* the one who's told the story to the papers. He's going to assume that I must have gone mad, that I'm out for his blood. When I love him so desperately . . . When I've only just found out . . . God it's so ironic.'

'Oh my Lord,' groaned Lottie. 'Whatever have I done? I'm so sorry, Ron – '

Veronica could hold back the tears no longer. 'Lottie – what can I do – there isn't a flight out till Friday,' she sobbed. 'I've tried and tried to get through to him on the 'phone, to explain, but he's not answering at home and he's told his receptionist not to take any personal calls at his office. What can I *do*?' Lottie held out her hand and Veronica clung to it as though it were a lifeline.

'It's okay, it's okay. Don't worry, love. It's only two days away. Not much can happen in that short time.

'I'll come back with you. If you want me to. Say yes, Ron, please say yes. Then I'll be with you at Heathrow. And if there's any trouble with the Press I'll be there. I won't let you down again.'

Veronica swallowed and dried her eyes. 'I know, Lottie. I know you didn't mean any harm.'

Lottie looked at her anxiously – how could she be so generous? Though she knew her so well, Lottie still searched for insincerity in her words. But there was only forgiveness. And trust. This time it would not be misplaced. She said: 'So we'll go off together on Friday.

Yes? We'll be a combined force. Okay? Come on, things will be fine now. Nothing that's done can't be undone.' She raised her eyebrows hopefully and her voice was encouraging, rallying. 'So what time are we leaving?'

Veronica nodded and smiled though her lips still trembled. 'I've booked a seat on the three o'clock from Antigua.'

Stuart Wilding's flight, booked by his secretary, was due to touch down exactly one hour after their departure.

Oz Lennox arrived at Sugar Mill just after sun-down.

The time for action was now. Esme was worth the effort after all. He'd decided during the flight, when there was nothing to disturb his conscious mind other than the dials, the crackling radio and the occasional bird that had drifted up to too high an altitude.

He sat in the sitting room, downstairs in the mill and waited for Hope • There were things here he didn't recognise; there were changes afoot. A compass, maps. Men's shoes. Rather a man's shoes

It had been a long time since he'd seen men's shoes at the Mill. A year? Before that, his own had been there in the same place, under the leather Chesterfield.

He and Hope had had a brief affair. Nothing serious Only the comfort of the flesh, not the spirit. It wasn't like that with Esme, where the flesh beckoned and the soul followed. Esme was something special. It was even worth seeing the Bill-things everywhere, to spend time with her. Although they'd have to go. Once he moved in, they were o-u-t.

But what the hell, he was gone. What did his thing mean? Jesus, Oz didn't even mind wearing his old dressing gown, so completely had he replaced him.

Hope opened the door, and came into the mill alone. She looked drained, unhappy.

Oz said: 'Hope, are you too busy to see me?' Giving her an excuse to send him away, a chance to be alone.

'No,' she said.

'Do you want a drink? Shall I fix you a whiskey?'

She nodded. He went to the cabinet and poured her a

204

stiff one, diluting it with just a little water and ice cubes from the fridge next to the cupboard.

'The hurricane's coming,' said Hope. 'We won't be able to fly for a few days. Not after tonight.'

Oz said: 'There were atmospherics over Barbados this morning. Esme landed Miriam Morelands here today. She got a weather report at Antigua and decided not to fly on out of Nevis.'

'Where's she staying, Oz?'

'With me.'

They didn't speak for a while. Oz drank his rum, Hope sipped her whiskey, feeling better, less doomy. Less end of the world.

'How are you, Hope?' asked Oz, finally.

'Okay. Strange question.'

'You don't seem to be your usual self, that's all. Quiet. No problems?'

'Nothing,' said Hope. 'I'm fine. Just wondering why you wanted to see me?'

'I thought I might move in with Esme,' he said. 'I'm fond of her.'

Hope took it in slowly, registering his words seconds after they'd been spoken because the subject was so far removed from her mind. 'Why doesn't she move in with you?'

'The kids. They're at St James School. They'd have to board if she moved over to Nevis and she doesn't want that. The eldest is coming up to exams.'

'So you want to be based in Barbados?' she asked.

'Yeah. We get a lot of runs from Barbados, Hope. The move might even benefit the company. Think how often I have to board there already.'

'Are you getting married?' Hope said.

'Hell no. I ain't reckoning to tie myself down. Just hankering after a few home comforts, I guess. Someone in the other half of the bed.'

Someone in the other half of the bed. Hope had got used to being alone, but Ned had screwed up that contentment, that complacency, in just one night.

'Oz, I'll have to think. I'm a bit confused right now. I

don't know whether I'd make the right decision if I said yes or no – How soon do you need an answer?'

Oz drained the rum. 'Any time, babe. I don't wanna be pushed into it by Esme. I'm ready to make the move, but happy to wait until you say whether or not the situation fits. If it doesn't then Esme's goin' to have to wait a while longer for Boy Blue to come home.'

'I expect it will be all right Oz,' said Hope. 'I don't want to stop you from doing what you want.'

'If I was one hundred per cent sure I wanted this, Hope, I'd have told you *after* I'd done it. As it is, I'm easy. In no hurry. Just mentionin' it, is all.'

'Give me time to look at the flying trends for the last six months. I'll see whether the company can afford to have you based in the south. Here, Oz, we're slap bang in the middle of the Caribbean and it's pretty convenient for flights anywhere.

'Give me an hour.'

'No rush, babe.'

'It's okay. I'll see you in the bar. Stay to dinner afterwards.'

'No thanks, I can hang around for the hour but I won't stay on. Esme's cooking me a Bajan Pepperpot. Can't stand it but I've got to show willing. What would have been on tonight at The Sugar Mill?'

Hope thought. 'Creme de Christophene, Crevettes Creole, Caramel soufflé. That's soup, fish and pudding, to you.'

'Huh,' grunted Oz. 'Frigging Bajan Pepperpot. Have you ever had it the way Esme makes it? Jesus she's a lousy cook.'

'Yep,' said Hope. 'She really is. Shredded corned beef in gravy. Very nasty.' She felt better now. Better and better. It didn't take long to get over a man, not when it was early days. And she'd know better next time. There wouldn't be any early days again. Three times bitten, fourth time shy.

'Give me the hour, Oz. And then you'll have a day or so because of the hurricane to decide whether or not you can live with my decision.'

'You're the boss, ma'am.'

Oz left and Hope picked up the flying records from the drawer.

She had got through to March when the door opened again and Ned came in. He could hardly look at her. Guilty. Knowing he was escaping from her, from the magic that was Nevis, that was Hope.

He sat on the Chesterfield with her, at arm's length, frightened of getting tangled in cobwebs. 'Jewel's missing,' he said, not really caring, wishing instead that he could say they were staying for definite. But just till Friday, the allotted day. An acceptable time-limit.

'What did Perce say?' asked Hope.

'He said to go tonight. He's worried about being stranded away from his homeopath.'

'And you think it's safe enough?'

'There's no change, down by the shore. Still five wave-beats a minute.'

There was no more to be said. He was going. He'd made up his mind – it wouldn't have mattered if Perce had said to ride out the hurricane on the island. Ned would have persuaded him to go early. Hope knew this; just as she knew the sensible alternative, that she fly them to Puerto Rico tonight, wouldn't even have been suggested.

She could cry. She could say – you're taking it all away. You're emptying me. Instead, she said: 'You'd better pack.' It was hardly worth having had Pansy move his stuff over she thought, but she didn't say so. No recriminations. He must go.

He looked around, at the charts, the maps. I'd better go, he thought. I would drown in her. Lose myself. There is the sea and the other islands, the boats and their passengers, the sea-birds and the fish, Keith the Grenadian, the ganja, the empty Grenadines. She is too much like me. It's like looking in a mirror that reflects only feelings and emotions. She is probably suffering as much as I am. She couldn't be suffering more. Does she understand that I must go? I must find out if there's life without Hope. I can always return.

He said: 'I will be all right.'

Would he? 'I'm sorry you're leaving, Ned.' It was as far as she could go.

'But then again, we may not be able to sail after all,' he said, hoping he was wrong, confusing her, saying one thing, then the other. Not knowing what he really wanted, why he was acting this way. 'I told you, Jewel's missing.'

Yes, that was what he had said. Jewel was missing. The child-woman. 'Where is she missing?' she asked, abstracted.

'We don't know,' said Ned patiently. 'She didn't sleep here last night, according to Pansy. And she wasn't at the funeral was she?'

No, she wasn't, now Hope came to think of it.

'She didn't have breakfast here, and King said that Terry hadn't given her a lift home last night, after the cock-fight. He thought you and I had brought her back to Sugar Mill.'

Now he had Hope's attention properly. 'Who was she with?' she asked. 'Last night I saw her dancing with someone, but I can't remember who it was . . . '

'No more can anyone else. And we can't leave her. Not possibly.' Why am I lying? he thought. I have no intention of staying, with or without Jewel.

Karin was packing an alabaster soap dish between her layers of panties in the case. It would go so nicely in her bathroom. The crystal glasses she'd taken from the bar were further down her trunk. They were well-protected, and probably quite valuable. Waterford crystal. Irish.

There were other things too – fuchsia-coloured towels, silver cutlery, even a brass doorknob from the bathroom that she'd unscrewed with her nail-file.

Hope Parnell wouldn't miss them. And even if she did –

Her phone rang.

'Karin Genevieve,' she simpered in her have-a-nice-night voice.

'It's Jewel.'

'Jew-wail! Where on earth are you! We're sailing tonight – because of the hurricane! Everybody's been frantically worried about you. Where've you *been*?'

208

Jewel was on the terrace at Georges Deneuil's bungalow. 'I'm staying, Karin. I'm not leaving with you. I've met a man who's fallen in love with me, and I'm going to stay.'

She didn't mention that though she was at the villa in Cliffdwellers, so was a wife who was currently having hysterics in another room.

Jewel had known she'd cornered Georges, when she'd collapsed in his car last night and he hadn't known what to do with her. He'd simply had to take her back to his home.

It was his own fault. He should have told her about the wife sooner. The wife had been understanding. Kindly even. But Jewel didn't want a wife hanging round their necks, not if she was to spend the rest of her life with the millionaire. No wife: no matter how kindly or how understanding she might be.

So she'd raved deliriously about their lovemaking, just at the moment when Marie had come into the room she'd been laid out in, like a bride, like a corpse. She'd panted and moaned orgasmically, repeating his name, over and over again.

As an actress, she was inspired. And this was her best performance to date.

Well Georges was to blame, reasoned Jewel. He should have got rid of his messy marriage *before* he'd got involved with her. Not afterwards.

So she'd whispered 'Do it again Georges, do it the way you *always* do' as the wife peered in through her doorway. And then she'd deliciously revealed more imaginary secrets. And Marie had taken the hint, assuming more had taken place than actually had, assuming the relationship was long-term instead of day-old.

While Jewel was on the phone to Karin, she could hear them in the kitchen now. They were breaking crockery, but there were still no sounds of cases being packed. Well there would be. In time. Especially if Jewel's friends left her stranded and there was nowhere else for her to go. One of them, the wife or Jewel, would crack and it was unlikely to be Jewel, who had nothing to lose.

'I've been with my lover,' said Jewel into the telephone,

hoping that Marie would hear yet again, feel that knife twisting and turning. 'If you're sailing tonight, Karin, you'll have to leave me behind.'

Karin was put out. Jewel consulted her before she did anything normally. 'Have you made the right choice, Jewel?' she said. 'You're not landing yourself with some half-wit or some *pauper* are you?'

'Of course not,' said Jewel indignantly. Why should Karin think she was the only judge of how suitable a man should be for her? Karin didn't have a monopoly on good sense and instinct, did she?

'You sail,' said Jewel. 'I wish you the best of luck. All of you – you'll need it, I hear. Tell Hope Parnell I want my things parcelled up and sent to me.' She gave Karin the address. 'And I shall want them soon as I only have the gypsy dress with me and the one pair of panties. What time are you going?'

'I think we're going straight to the marina as soon as everyone's packed. I'm expecting someone from the great house to collect my trunks at any minute now.

'Jewel, this all sounds terrifically rushed to me. All your eggs are in one basket. How will you get home if it doesn't work out?' Karin had educated her, guided her, taught her everything in the last ten weeks. No way would she survive alone. It wasn't that it bothered Karin, it was just that she didn't like to feel that she hadn't been consulted. 'You've got the number for the hotel in San Juan, haven't you? You just ring me if you need help. You hear me now.'

Jewel was nonchalant. Things would work out the way she wanted. And if they didn't, then there'd be somebody else, someday, to pick up the tabs, keep her afloat. Whisk her off to Tahiti next time, maybe. 'You needn't worry about me, Karin,' she said. 'I've got things going for me. Didn't you have everything going for you at my age? When you were young?'

'Another one for the obscurity can, then,' Karin said snappily and hung up. Silly little bitch.

No she frigging well hadn't had everything going for her when she was nineteen. Those were bad days. Porn-city days to be forgotten about.

But Jewel's absence would throw the cat among the pigeons. And perhaps some good might come of it all.

They were sailing ahead of the hurricane. Very exciting. And she would be the only woman on board. That would be an experience, out in the wide blue seas with the sunlight blazing on the decks. She could play everybody off against each other without fear of alienating anyone. She'd be in such *demand*. She'd have Ned eating out of her hand, or better, before they got to San Juan, Puerto Rico.

'I'm not coming,' said Hope. 'I don't want a memory of your boat sailing away, disappearing on the horizon, its lights imprinting themselves on my brain like needles.'

'Very dramatic. But I'd like you to,' said Ned. He wanted to remember the woman in the straw hat on the marina, waving to him. He wanted to look back at Nevis and see Hope, not an empty quayside –

'Well I'm not doing,' she said.

Ned said: 'Shall I call you from Puerto Rico?'

'I may not be here.'

'Where are you going?' He was surprised, hurt.

'England,' she said, because there was nowhere else.

'When?'

'I don't know.'

This was spur of the minute stuff, didn't mean anything. 'Perhaps I can call you in England, then?' he challenged.

'I'll be at The Ritz if you want me,' she said, knowing there was no way she'd get into The Ritz in high season without a booking months in advance.

She thought, if he wants me, if he survives, let him find me. I might stay here, and then again I might not. I'll do whatever I please. Once you sail out of Nevis, you sail right out of my life, Ned Murdoch.

Right until you come back.

There was a fleet of taxicabs outside the Mill. All had their radios tuned to weather reports.

There was devastation in St James, Barbados. The east coast, the Atlantic side where Esme lived, was hardly touched. Grenada was appealing for international aid. St

211

Lucia was in a state of alert, ready for Hurricane Cleo's next attack. She was moving north steadily.

Ned said: 'If we sail directly west till we're below Puerto Rico, we'll miss her by miles.' He was very businesslike. Cool.

King shook Hope by the hand and said: 'Bye-bye beautiful lady.'

Karin smiled graciously and said: 'You'll be hearing from my lawyers, dear.'

Perce promised to settle the full bill. She was to send the account to the Hollywood studios. He was gruff, still nursing a grudge against that stupid kid Jewel and blaming Nevis for it.

The trunks were in the car boots, the passengers in the backs of the assorted Morris Minors and Fords. Ned travelled alone, as he had arrived. His window was down. 'Keep those kittens safe,' he said. 'I want the black one.'

'I want, I want,' said Hope cheerfily. 'I think you're insane, but I wish you luck.'

He still had time to say something, he could still make a promise. He could kiss her one more time. Make love to her one more time. 'Goodbye, Hope,' he said.

She was calm. Quite dignified. 'Goodbye, Ned.' Why did she feel as though she'd screamed?

The motors rumbled into life, horns hooted, tyres scrunched gravel, arms flapped like wings from windows.

She stood at the head of the drive, watching the cars' red brake lights disappearing into the dark. Then, as soon as they were out of sight, she went into the cool of the great house. It had been sticky, clammy outside. That was why her eyes felt watery. She poured herself a drink, looking round her at the emptiness, listening to the dishes being clattered in the distant kitchen.

Suddenly she called: 'Back in half an hour, Pansy.'

She ran for the Jeep, snatching up the straw hat, bounding into the driving seat, hoisting her long evening dress up above her knees so she could use the pedals. The motor flicked into life, and she was driving fast after the taxis, keeping out of sight, gradually catching them up by making time on the bends.

They were on Round Road, coming into Charlestown, the lights of the streets ahead like a necklace. She slowed further, not wanting to get to the marina before they'd sailed. She cruised the back roads, the little alleys where chickens scattered, children skipped or played with balls and ropes, where ramshackle homes lined the pavements. She stopped by the pier, looking at the lights of St Kitts, so high they could have been mistaken for stars, and the black pools where the Caribs – or maybe it was only the Rastas – lived. Then slowly she drove round to Pinney's Beach and the marina. The Maria Juana was already sailing, wasting no time, fleeing God's wrath.

She parked the Jeep, cut the lights and climbed out to sit on a bench in the silence. To watch the shadow that was Ned's boat sweeping out into the channel between the two islands. She waved tentatively, feeling foolish, watching the Maria Juana go further and further out of her life; listening to the slow boom of the currents, the waves; seeing the glittering lights of the decks and the stateroom, the cabins and the bedrooms in duplicate as they reflected onto the sea.

And their images, those pinpoints of brightness like a picture out of focus, imprinted themselves like needles in her brain.

Chapter Fifteen

THEY WERE the sea's prisoner; the wind's captive. The Maria Juana, fast though she might be, could not escape the hurricane's shock-waves.

'Ned, come quick, mahn!'

A pool of ooze beneath the engine flowed amoeba-like along the floor of the cabin. 'You want to know why we's not gettin' nowhere fast? Dere's your answer.'

Ned ground his teeth as the green slime reached a gully and flooded it. 'Cut that motor!' he shouted. 'Get that stuff up or we'll be on fire! What the fuck's happened to the Bluebird?' He was sliding over the oil carefully, trying to keep his balance as the Maria Juana pitched recklessly on the swell.

Gonzales said: 'We goin' have to use de sails.'

'In this blow? You've got to be out of your skull.'

'You can't anchor, Ned, and you can't use dis Bluebird. What else you goin' do?'

'It's too rough. It'll kill the passengers.'

'Dat or de sea's gonna do it, mahn. You got no options.'

Ned spun round, losing his footing and crashed against the cabin wall as a twenty-foot breaker cast them into the air and plunged them down again. The hostile Caribbean closed over them, swamping the decks till they rose again in the merciless rolling.

Keith called jauntily: 'I'm hitchin' up de sails, Ned, right?' The seas held no terror for him. He relished each movement like a porpoise.

Ned groaned, resigned. 'Do it!'

The lamps on the deck flickered, the current fluctuating with the generator's uneven power. In the grey shadows, Karin Genevieve stood in her baby-doll nightdress.

'Piss off back to your berth,' spat Ned. 'If you're going to spew up, don't make a mess.'

Keith took time out to look at the jutting cones beneath the silk that were Karin's breasts. As he did so, the boom swung and combed his hair, swaying dangerously with the rhythm of the lurching boat. Ropes spun, uncoiling with the momentum. A cable flashed like a whiplash, striking Karin's chest. She screamed but her voice was thrown away by the wind.

'Bastard!' shrieked Ned. 'Grab that sail or we'll lose it!'

'What about *me*?' howled Karin.

'Screw you! You'll live, if you get out of my way!'

The bow dipped and rose from the water terrifyingly as the wayward sail whipped across the prow, flailing ropes and cables like carnival streamers in its wake. Water spilled over the decks and ran back to drain with the next lurch. Grease and the ocean licked their way over the deck and swamped the men's bare feet.

Cinnamon Hicks made a dive for a tie-rope and got it. Instantly Spencer was behind him, holding on to his body to prevent him from being hurled out into the black waters. They tied it down and the sail was steadied, gravid with the wind but no longer thrashing in agony.

Karin wrapped her arms around her breasts, shielding herself from the spray, the pain, the wind and the fear. It was the only time she felt as though she'd been in any real danger in her thirty seven years.

There was no flirtatiousness about her any more. She felt genuinely wretched. Not really human. If she could have crawled into a corner and huddled into herself she would have done. 'Are we going to sink, Ned?' she asked trembling.

He ignored her, threw quick instructions to the crew and climbed back over to the motor, peering into the grimy darkness with a torch to see what could be done about its death and its resurrection.

'How's the radio, Gonzo?'

'You wantin' to radio?'

'I'm thinking about signalling a Mayday. I reckon we've got a major failure here. I don't want to be stuck here till the winds come.'

Karin, still hovering, still clutching onto the rails, shrieked: 'You mean this isn't wind now?'

Gonzo grinned at her, only his teeth and the whites of his eyes visible. 'Dis a Foarce nine, maybe ten. You waitin' till we a hit a thirteen. Den you *knowed* what wind is.'

Then he said to Ned: 'You doan wanna be gettin' boats out, mahn. Think of de salvage payments.'

And there was the matter of pride. 'You can fix de engine, mahn, or we sail nice in dis blow.'

'I can try. Drop the oil bags over the side so we don't race out of control. Forget the Mayday; radio a distress instead.'

They arranged arc lamps on the motor and Ned fiddled with spanners and wires.

In the blink of an eye, Gonzo was back, panting, his eyes wide with worry. 'No radio, mahn,' he said quietly. 'No connection – '

Ned gaped at him for a moment. Then he flung the spanner down on the deck. Everything was conspiring against him.

The reservoir was empty. A gaping hole at the base of it showed where the oil had escaped. Ned reached into it gingerly, keeping well clear of its burning hot sides. The hole had been padded with some kind of material that had stopped the leak till the cloth was saturated. It would never have been spotted till the reservoir was completely empty. His fingers pried at the rag and he pulled it out. It was unrecognisable: a scrap; a nothing.

He aimed the torch at the hole again. The edges of it were smooth, darkened, blistered. As though someone had been at it with a blow-lamp. Ned frowned – this must have happened while the fitters were on board in Nevis. Any sooner and the engine would have blown before now.

'What's happ'nin' Ned? You fixin' it?'

'Don't reckon so. Look at this.'

Keith squinted into the tank. He ran a finger, hard as leather, around the rim of the burnt-out hole. 'Somebody doan' like you, Ned Murdoch.'

Ned grimaced. 'One of the fitters?'

Keith snorted. 'Dey nevah touched dat engine, mahn.

216

Nor de radio. You so fast an' eager to get out of Nevis, dey nevah had de time.'

Karin stumbled below decks, feeling her way through the dark corridors to her room. There was moaning coming from Perce's cabin: he was retching.

King wasn't. She could hear him snoring from behind his own closed door. King was snoring while they were all going to die. She fell into her room and reached the lavatory just as she started to heave again.

Through the porthole, she could see the ocean rising and falling. Sometimes she felt as though she was in a submarine. Sometimes she felt as though she was dying of alcoholic poisoning. Spinning. Dizzy. She could hear a throbbing, as though the motor was still running, and there was the sickly-sweet, all-pervading smell of the diesel, stinging her throat.

She heaved again. But there was nothing left in her belly. She stood slowly, looked in the mirror and began to cry. The sight of herself was the final straw. Her hair stuck to her grey skin in brassy clumps, her eyes were slits in a puffy face. Her breasts sagged beneath bowed shoulders.

Karin saw how she would be in thirty years. That was an old Karin in the mirror, with mascara stains running down her cheeks, a blur of lipstick missing her mouth. 'Doriana Grey', she sobbed melodramatically to her image before curling up on the floor to rest before the next tide of sickness overtook her.

The boat heeled and pitched, sometimes riding the crests, sometimes crashing into them head-on.

Ned worked in the dismal and soaking engine compartment uselessly, trying to solder metal into the tank to patch up the hole.

'No good,' he announced as he emerged, just before the dawn. 'I need a real mechanic, not a half-assed one.'

Keith sighed. 'We seen lahnd, Ned. St Croix's not more than a half hour away. We can pull in dere an' forget about Puerto. Why doan't you get some rest, mahn? I take her in easy now.'

Ned fumbled his way back to his berth in the cabin he

217

shared with the rest of the crew. He was alone, everyone else – even the chef – was still on deck. He climbed into his bunk and shut his eyes. That was all he needed. Just for a few sweet moments.

It was a strangely silent dawn. A green-gold sky that looked nauseous. Even high-up at Nelson Plantation, the stillness of the air lay claustrophobically heavy, like a damp blanket.

Jessica heaved herself out of bed and ran a hand under her rusty curls. They were sodden at the nape of her neck. Her breasts felt heavy, fluid. She had managed to acquire a couple of mosquito bites on her legs, though none of the insects were supposed to climb so high on the island.

'It's like living in the jungle. It's like a sauna. This is all horribly oppressive this morning,' she said to nobody.

Normally Jessica slept well, but the combination of the tension in the stratosphere, preparing itself for turmoil, Veronica's inaccessibility and Lottie's depression had contrived to make it an evil night.

Jessica was relieved that Lottie had confessed all. It was like a vanishing back-ache to her. Nevertheless, it hadn't made her own private confession later on any easier.

Strange the way Veronica had taken it. As though she'd already guessed the truth about how Don Derby had found her.

So she and Lottie were both flying back to England tomorrow. Jessica couldn't go with them, even though she'd have liked to be on the spot to give extra support at Heathrow. Jessica still had plenty of unfinished business to deal with, and she couldn't waste the suffering she'd endured on the planes purely for a short break away from England. That certainly wasn't a good enough excuse. God, if she needed a few days away from it all, she'd prefer the Lake District any time. Wordworth Country had so many advantages. You could get there by car.

The smell of wet seaweed was everywhere. Breathing felt as though it would give you a headache.

Jessica wrapped herself in an orange sundress that she'd bought in Mahé and sat down on a chair to pull her pants on. Everything was such an effort. She should probably have tried to get some more sleep. Six hours wasn't enough. But that bed felt like a swamp.

She opened her patio doors and walked through her covered courtyard to the bathroom. There was no cold water. No hot water. The lavatory didn't flush. Over the past few days, everyone had noticed that the water had been running more and more slowly. Now there was nothing. The taps weren't even spitting any more.

The Nelson's ancient piping system was just too awful. It would have to be fixed. Jessica picked up the 'phone and said snappily to Fransis on the other end that she wanted coffee very quickly on her terrace, and some water to wash in and no breakfast. Then she slid out to her terrace and sat in a canvas chair, overlooking the cliff face and the ocean.

Lottie arrived moments later and slouched down opposite her.

'Couldn't sleep,' she said. 'I hoped you might be awake.'

'No water,' said Jessica crossly.

'They'll bring up bottled water from the great house if you ask.'

'I have.'

They sat in silence, watching strands of lilac cloud, high in the ether, stream like skinny rivers away to the south.

'Hot, isn't it,' said Lottie.

Jessica felt her mouth was caked with dust, dry despite the dampness of the rest of her body. She didn't reply.

Fransis knocked ineffectively on the trellis to announce his presence. He carried a silver tray and a jug half full of water.

'Put it here,' said Jessica, patting the low table by her side. 'You haven't brought me much water to wash in Fransis.'

'No, Mrs Collier. Dere's not much watah on de island so high. All de watah down dere.' He pointed to the ocean.

'We got a hurricane warnin' Mrs Collier. Dey say de hurricane comin' today. We maybe havin' to evacuarise.'

'Evacuarise?' questioned Lottie.

'Leavin' de Plantation. Go to de safe sheltah.'

219

'Hell. How long for?' said Jessica.

'Few hours, maybe less if de eye passin' us by a long way. Dey say we be a hundred miles out from de eye.'

Lottie had seen tropical storms, but never a hurricane. Was that why her heart was pounding so fast? Some physical reaction to air pressure? She felt almost excited by the thought of that coming all-powerful wind. It would be a purging.

'What will it be like?' she asked.

'It comin' from de south. You see how all de clouds is drawin' together? When dey all ready, dey come back. But den you doan't see anythin' but ah wall of black in de sky. An' de rains. Dis hurricane strange, crazy. She go first one way, den de odder. Grenada get de worst wid two thousahnd dead. Den she swirl around de sea an' is missin' St Lucia. She now nearin' Guadaloupe an' goin' east of Antigua.

'Dere shouldn't be any problehm in Nevis, but dis hurricane a bitch.' He cleared his throat and looked nervously at Mrs Collier, trying to see whether he'd said too much or too little; wondering whether he'd looked as though he was being superior, trying to teach them something about the tropics.

She smiled reassuringly at him. 'Does Julian know it's coming? He didn't say anything last night.'

'He heared a radio warning, but nothing was for sure till about an hour ago. Den de Government sayin' it was comin' dis way official.'

Lottie wondered if the hurricane would have turned around and gone away again if the St Kitts Parliament had refused to acknowledge its existence. Jessica poured herself coffee. 'One for me?' asked Lottie.

'Go and get the tooth mug from the bathroom, then,' said Jessica. She felt as though she could hardly breathe. It was hot damp air, not carrying any oxygen into her body. She felt as though she was suffocating. Perhaps it was a migraine coming on.

'Have you seen Ron this morning?' said Lottie after she'd sipped the strong black coffee. The glass burned her fingers.

'No. Her light's not on yet, so I would think she's still sleeping.'

'I'm rather worried about this interview she's giving to Don Derby you know. We don't know what sort of a man he is at all really.'

'I wouldn't be too anxious if I were you. I'm sure he'll be good to her.'

Lottie's forehead creased. 'How can you be so sure?'

Jessica shrugged. Only Ron knew about the part she had played with the Reuters man.

Jessica kept a lot of things from Lottie. You could never tell what she might do with secrets.

Hope looked at the sky. There was a constant movement, a draining, like a whirlpool. A skypool. She tried to work out how far Ned would be from Nevis. How far he'd be from the storm.

How fast did a boat travel? She wished she knew more about the sea. Perhaps he could already be past St Croix, well away from the predicted path of the winds.

Perhaps he'd been right to go, she thought. A hurricane could have wrecked the Maria Juana in the harbour if it had hit in that direction. Then what could he have done? Of course he'd had to run the storm. Her fears had been groundless. That man was a survivor. He was in no danger at all. She'd behaved ridiculously, letting him see her fears, worrying unnecessarily.

Anyway, what did it matter to her whether he stayed two more days? What had been so great about Ned Murdoch? Only the lovemaking, that was all. And what was that? Simply a release of tensions. Nothing binding. Just physical need. The fact that it had *felt* like a fusion of souls meant nothing. It was just a trick of the emotions; more shattered magic.

Waves washed lethargically around her, rolling back into the sea with far more enthusiasm than they had emerged.

Hope threw a pebble idly into the water. But what about the electricity between them? The charge that shot between her and Ned, rebounded and doubled?

Chemistry be damned. You don't find a soul-mate through chemistry. Attraction, that was all there'd ever been. And it had just been compounded by the fact that they felt the same way about a few things.

He wasn't that special.

She didn't miss him at all. She could hardly remember what he looked like. The only pictures that came into her mind were of him in the pool, holding onto Karin as though he'd been rescuing her from drowning, giving her the kiss of life.

And then there was how he'd looked lying on the beach with his half-closed eyes in St Kitts. He'd been watching her, pretending not to. And his body, how it rippled and shone as he made love to her. Rearing above her like a stallion, his eyes liquid with desire and lust.

There you are. It all came down to lust.

So why had it been so good, smart-ass? Why had it sounded as though the whole of heaven was applauding them as lovers?

Bullshit. He was probably screwing Karin right at that minute. Sinking into her and loving Karin the way he loved her. That was realism. Better to face the truth about Meestah Ned Murdoch. No point maintaining any illusions. That was the way he was, otherwise why had he screwed Karin in the first place? They might even have had a regular thing going. What he said – about Karin being a woman unloved – it was only words.

But wouldn't she know? Wouldn't she feel somehow different – physically – if he was with another woman? Wouldn't there be a telepathic reaction? There ought to be. After so close a bonding.

So now you think you're half of a pair of Siamese twins – she scolded herself. Forget it, Hope. There are other things to worry about. That man is a big nothing. Nothing to you at all. Time to grow up.

A chi-chi bird landed on the foot of the sun bed but saw there was nothing doing. In a flurry of fast little wings, he left her to her thoughts.

Think about something serious, she told herself: the Jewel problem for starters. How much was her disappear-

222

ance Hope's responsibility? She prayed the kid wasn't under-age.

She knew nothing about the man Georges Deneuil. Karin had supplied no information other than his address and 'phone number and the instruction to send on Jewel's clothing. Already Pansy had parcelled them up. They might even have gone off in one of the Mokes by now, during the time she'd spent mooching on the beach, listening to that evil, slow booming of the waves.

They were down to three a minute. Possibly less. They were being sucked away from Nevis by some distant, unquenchable sea-monster.

It was all very unnatural and disquieting. She wished the day was over; that she could go to sleep right now, and wake up and find that the storm had passed and that the wreckage had been cleared up. She wanted no part in this day.

Don Derby took the last sailing of the Island Queen. All other voyages had been cancelled for the day – possibly longer. He now had yet another major story to work on as the hurricane neared the island. What a fertile country this had suddenly become. Ever since independence. Great place to be.

It was eight. He was very early for his rendezvous with Miss Marston, but he could get some breakfast at Ma Johnson's while he was looking over the papers again.

The Wilding story was a real hum-dinger. Couldn't be better. If this didn't provoke the cool Miss Marston into some juicy quotes, nothing would. Look at that headline – front page in all the popular dailies. Only a couple of paragraphs in the *Guardian* and *The Times*, but wow the *Sun* had really done him proud.

He sat at a formica table and ordered ham and eggs, sunny-side up, and relished every mouthful.

The sun was a distant circle low on the horizon as the boat glided silently into port at Christiansted. The Maria Juana flew distress flags and within seconds of her arriva., she was surrounded by little vessels like pearlfish around a sea anemone. She was grimy, as though she'd just done a trans-Atlantic; the new paint was peeling, flayed by the waves and the swirling sands.

Like boarding pirates, the fishermen threw ropes into the boat, calling: 'How much help you needin', mahn? You wan' towin'? You got sick peoples?'

The passengers were dressed, anxiously watching the skies for signs that they might have been trapped, seeing how closely they'd escaped with their lives.

Here the colours were less vivid than on Nevis. The same golden sky presaged a kind of doom, but at last the sea was calm, out of the main ocean drift.

Ned's eyelids were swollen with fatigue. His hands ached from hauling ropes, twisting screws that had been rusted on, gripping rails.

Cinnamon Hicks called: 'We okay, we needin' pahrts for a motah. We sailin' in if dere's enough gustulence here in de harbour. Though we could do wid an escort.'

They docked agonisingly slowly for Karin who was deathly pale, still sickly, swimming through the air. She had no make-up on, had run a comb through her slick hair but that was all. Her tongue felt disgusting. Even cleaning her teeth hadn't made much different to the taste in her mouth.

'You be fine when you get you feet on de steady earth,' said Keith, patting her shoulder kindly.

Karin didn't even have the energy to shrug off his hand.

Perce said to King as he leaned over the rails to watch the fishing boats below: 'I'm not going on to Puerto Rico in this. Never again. I'm flyin' over to San Juan.'

'Suits me,' grunted King. He felt as though he'd had a bad night though he didn't remember a thing.

Ned jumped from the gangway to the dock. He was okay: the cat nap had done him some good. I could 'phone Hope, he thought. But I'd better get this motor going first. And a new radio. The others followed him down with mincing steps like Japanese geishas, hanging on for dear life to the rope barriers.

Perce extended his hand to Ned: 'It was a good trip till

224

last night. You did us proud, boy. You got my address in the States for the bill?'

Ned nodded and said: 'It's been great having you along.' He didn't mean it but it was the sort of thing he felt he had to say.

King said: 'You're a real sailor, Ned. Not one of those yachtsmen we see all the time in the Florida Keys. Nobody else would have got us through it.'

'Know what you mean,' grinned Ned. 'Those boatmen in the Keys don't know a yard-arm from a junkyard.' They missed the joke since they didn't know about his past.

Karin turned her back on him, blaming him for everything. She had no words for him. She just wanted him out.

They went their separate ways, the movie people to find a hotel in their taxis full of luggage, Ned to walk along the promenade to find a mechanic.

It was strange the way he felt. The battle with the sea hadn't ended in victory or defeat. Only survival. Hope had been right. He shouldn't have left, tried to race the storm. He'd risked a lot of lives to prove a point.

He nodded to a couple of guys cleaning lobster in the harbour, their boat bobbing on the tide below. In the boat were the remains, the guts, the useless bits of the fish that now lay beside them in a silver, glossy pyramid.

I wouldn't have been bound to stay on, he thought. I could have accepted the situation gracefully, taken shelter for a while. I just didn't want to feel trapped. Inadequate. Landlocked.

How was Hope feeling now? Did she care that he'd fucked off into the night? She'd probably written him off as a bad job as soon as his waving arm had disappeared back into the taxi cab.

She probably hadn't given him a thought since. Maybe she'd wondered if they'd made it safely to Puerto Rico, but a lady like Hope wouldn't have wasted her time being miserable. She was too much like he was.

So much like him that he could almost hear her calling him back.

Ridiculous. He'd be believing in mermaids soon.

Perhaps he should just put her out of his mind now.

225

Forget about it. Who knows how Hope felt about him. He'd just gone, hadn't he? Just sailed off into a metaphoric sunset.

He felt moody suddenly. Blaming himself.

Soon there'd be another man in her life, another man loving her the way he'd done. No, not like that. Nobody made love the way he and Hope had made love. Nothing could be that good.

He found his way into a bar, already open on the quayside, and ordered coffee. The black man held the mug under a faucet and sticky, dirty brown liquid streamed into it, frothing over the rim.

'Two dollahs, mahn.' He was all smile. Ned paid up, not caring that he was being ripped off.

He took the mug outside and sat on the dirty concrete step to drink it. There were other men there, too, crouching, squatting, sitting on the pavement, their backs against the wall of the bar. They wore nothing but faded shorts and didn't acknowledge either Ned or each other. They were deep-water fishermen who couldn't work the seas today in case the storm switched direction again.

Of course Ned Murdoch couldn't have a permanent relationship. Not while he was running the boats, and no way could he give up the sea. He didn't even know why the thought had suddenly occurred to him. Out of the question. And Hope was no sailor, even if *she* was happy to give up the Sugar Mill. But she'd no more change her life than he would.

They were incompatible. Their lives followed completely separate routes. They were star-crossed lovers.

He thought about her silver hair, her lithe body, her chocolate nipples, but couldn't bring her face into focus. So soon she'd gone from his memory. Perhaps she hadn't made that much of an impact on him. Ships in the night, that was all. All he could remember were those green eyes, emeralds set above that soft mouth and its provocative smile. Her smooth golden skin.

He drained the mug and returned it to the bar. Then he slouched off to find a mechanic who knew something about Bluebird motors.

* * *

'I don't think you should speak to this man,' said Julian. 'If you don't speak, there's no story. Nobody ever wrote an article that was solely based on a "no comment". And there's the storm. You'll need to pack a few things in case we get stuck for longer than expected in the shelter.'

Veronica thought again, though she had given the meeting very careful consideration. 'I must do,' she said. 'I must see him. Anyway, I'll be in town so I can get to the shelter easily enough.'

'There won't be any taxis around, Veron. Not if you leave it till too late. Once the sirens go, you'll be on your own.'

'Aren't we always?'

The taxi she'd ordered to Charlestown was waiting for her and she climbed in, feeling as though she was heading for her own execution. The familiar landmarks passed by the window in a blur. Overhead, the sky was clear and icy, like a frozen pool. Veronica noticed nothing apart from the sticky heat. She was quite calm. She knew whatever happened would be frankly terrible but it was just one of those things one had to go through. It would make her stronger in the long run. Less of a runner, more of a stayer.

She needed to find out how much Stuart had said. She didn't want to create extra sensation, only to pour oil on whatever troubled waters already existed.

'I just want to try to minimise the storm damage.' Her thoughts were unconsciously spoken aloud, and the driver turned round to look at her, amused.

'You can't do that,' he said. 'Not after de storm hits.

'You can take all de precautions in de world *before* it comin' – but once de wind blow, all you can do is take sheltah.'

Veronica looked at his reflection in the driving mirror and thought silently: 'We'll have to see about that, won't we.'

Chapter Sixteen

THE SKY was dark as night, black as thunder around them. They were running out of time. Veronica shivered as the sun finally slid behind the blanket of cloud and winked out. Was it a tear on the newspaper, or was it only the rain?

She wiped it with the back of her hand and looked again at the damning words.

DISGRACED ex-Minister, Stuart Wilding, yesterday proposed to his mistress, despite the fact that he is STILL A MARRIED MAN!

Turning his back on family life forever, father of two, Wilding:

* begged *raven-haired beauty Veronica Marston to be his wife;*

* confessed *that the long-running affair had begun while he was with the Ministry of Defence;*

* revealed *that his wife had shared his guilty secret;*

* admitted *that his bedroom antics could throw the country into the agony of another general election; and*

* wept *when he confirmed that his political career was over.*

Dr Wilding, 45, shocked the world's Press as he told of his sordid affair with society woman, the Honourable *Miss Veronica Marston.*

In an emotional interview . . .

Veronica folded the *Sun* and picked up the *Daily Mail*.

'Miss Marston – ' began Don Derby, but he stopped as he saw her face.

She couldn't hear him. Reality had disappeared. There was only the world of newsprint there for her now, a world of fiction and destruction.

A former Socialist Minister has made a public proposal to his lover, without bothering with the usual formality of first divorcing his wife.

Labour backbench MP Stuart Wilding, 44, yesterday made a plea to his secret mistress, the Hon. Veronica Marston, to come home. Miss Marston is believed to be hiding from a storm of emotion in the West Indies paradise island of Nevis and has so far not been available for comment.

Announcing his shameful resignation from politics, Wilding said: 'I will marry her as soon as she agrees. As yet, Miss Marston has not given me an answer that I am prepared to accept.

'I love her desperately. It is all just a question of time now.'

Wilding separated only yesterday from his wife of 22 years, Jannine, who has gone to stay with relatives. He has yet to obtain a divorce.

After the Press Conference Labour's former 'Bright Boy' said 'This has been going on for years. It was acceptable to my wife, who knew about our affair virtually from the beginning.

'But the situation got out of control and I found I could not live without Veronica.

'Now I have to try to find her and persuade her to be my wife.'

* Mail Comment, page 5.

There was a picture of Stuart, speaking at the conference. He looked hounded, wretched.

Don Derby was watching her reactions, waiting to see what she would say. Veronica had two courses of action open to her; she could dramatically accept the proposal in time for tomorrow's headlines; or she could 'no comment', as Julian had advised.

But where would that leave Stuart?

He'd been made to look a cheat, a liar, a traitor. She glanced at the banner headline in the *Mirror*. 'Marry Me' Says Married MP.

That was enough.

She knew the reports would have been made far more dramatic than the actual event warranted, though there must have been some basis in fact. He loved her. At least she could be sure of that. Some of the quotes were confirmed by the other papers' stories: in the *Guardian* and *The Times*.

'I must try to 'phone Doctor Wilding before I comment,' she said, rising from the table. 'Though he hasn't been answering the last couple of days . . . '

'You'll be lucky to get a connection, Miss Marston,' he called after her. 'Most of the lines are down.'

She returned to the gallery at The Rookery Nook after a few moments. 'You're right, of course, Mister Derby. There are no lines.'

Already there were spasmodic winds, short blasts of rain, then more winds. They had crept up sneakily in the capital, but now they whistled around the open gallery of the café, lifting tableclothes, knocking over salt and pepper pots, emptying ashtrays.

'Ah'm closin',' said the proprietor. 'If you is wise, you get to de sheltah in a dahmn hurry. Ah mean, you guddah get out.'

He battened windows, gathered in the flurrying linen, and disappeared behind a shuttered door, banging it firmly behind him. They heard a bolt being drawn behind it, and then another.

'Yep, we'd better move, Miss Marston. Have you seen one of these things before?'

She shook her head.

'Pretty scarey. You going to the shelter?'

'I don't know where it is,' she confessed. 'I know it's near town, but I didn't listen properly to the directions my friend gave me this morning.'

'Well come with me. We'll try to get a cab.'

They struggled down the outside wooden steps, the wind pushing them back constantly, frustrating their efforts.

On the street, papers whirled like crazy birds, a barrel rolled down the centre of the road at high speed, crashing into smithereens as it hit a lamp post. Then the rain again, pouring in a solid sheet, obscuring the line where the grey sky ended and the roof tops began.

There were no cars, no people. The street looked like a Hollywood ghost town set.

'We can't go out in this, now, too late,' said Derby. 'There were no sirens, dammit!

'We'll have to go back up. Perhaps the barman will let us shelter in there with him.'

They climbed again, getting soaked in the driving rains as tear drops bounced off the wooden rails, forming pools in the centre of every step.

Don Derby battered on the locked door. 'We're stranded, man,' he called. 'We can't get to the shelter! Can we come in with you?'

There was no reply. The bartender was now in his cellar and listening to the screaming wind. They banged again, harder. Don Derby tried kicking the door with his foot and then gave up, realising each second was precious.

They fought their way down the exposed steps, blinded by rain that fell so quickly it left an imprint of shining, slanting arrows in their minds' eye. All the colour had drained out of the world. Only black, white and grey, a fearful monochrome, remained.

Down on the street again, in a moment of calm, they ran through the rain, pausing in doorways. Then there was another sheet of chill needles, falling so hard they were like steel, impenetrable. The wind gave a screech of agony. Veronica was soaked to the skin. Don Derby looked fragile – he was so battered and dirty from crashing into buildings. His hair looked as though he'd just stepped out of the ocean.

'Ready?' he shouted above the noise of the howling wind.

'Ready.'

They ran again, taking what shelter they could from the buildings around the street.

Houses shuddered around them. The wind ululated like a voodoo witch through the alleys and the back roads.

Veronica's dress billowed out around her like a tent. 'Hold my hand,' she cried, and the reporter took it. 'I don't want to get separated – ' They fled past the police station – they'd hoped they might find refuge there, but even here, windows and doors were shuttered against the killer wind.

Rain again, more wind. The intervals were getting shorter, like labour pains. Soon there would be no break until a hundred miles of turbulence had passed them by, or the eye centred on them to give a brief false calm. They stopped, panting furiously, resting in a doorway till the latest commotion had diminished. Each time it returned it was worse than before.

There was a banging, a metallic crashing, and a dustbin hurtled down the flooded street, leaving its debris to become airborne in its wake.

Don Derby had his breath back and he looked at Veronica, asking silently if she could carry on. She understood and nodded. He left the shelter of the porch first.

'Head for the church!' he called, momentarily whipped sideways by a blast of furious air that sent him spinning.

Veronica felt as if she were fighting through a monstrous cobweb – the air kept pushing her the way she didn't want to go. And when the rains came next time, they ran on, knowing that soon there would be nothing but the rain and the wind assaulting the poor earth as a combined force.

The church was an open building – pillars beneath a sturdy roof and spire like a market hall.

They collapsed inside, staggering under the roof. There was no protection other than from the sky. The insidious winds could creep in lower down and they did, scattering bibles, candlesticks, blowing tapestries and posters from the wall.

Veronica and the reporter were not the only ones who had sought sanctuary here. There were whole families, children on their own, old people who couldn't make the journey out to the official shelter because it was too far for them to travel on foot.

They were lying on the floor, under pews, beneath the altar. There was laughing and there was crying. No point God comin' to de earth if he not goin' to get a loud reception.

Veronica huddled into a corner and thought: 'If we come out of this, I shall tell Don Derby my answer to Stuart Wilding is yes, and that I am flying home on the first available flight.'

Don Derby thought: 'No wonder Wilding's gone crazy

for her. Even in this tempest she's kept her cool. She'll survive.'

Terry and Miriam were safe in the shelter. There was no sound of the wind inside the concrete walls. They played Nine Men's Morris for money and Miriam won. Terry thought that it was politic under the circumstances.

Outside, the hurricane was at its peak, hurling cars, houses and whole trees around a devastated landscape that bent low against the onslaught.

'There's one of your lovers, Terry,' said Miriam, conversationally. He looked up, and straight into the eyes of Lottie Wolff.

How she'd changed. She didn't look bad, just different.

He smiled and Miriam threw daggers, poison darts, guided missiles at him. Lottie wandered over, worried about Veronica, needing to talk to everyone.

'Terry,' she smiled. 'Miriam. How are you both?'

He grinned. 'Terr-ific, Lottie. All the better – ' he was going to say for seeing you but changed it to: 'For being inside on a day like this.'

Miriam said: 'I'm well. Thank you. And you, Mrs Wolff?'

'A little shaken by the violence of the whole thing. But it's funny, you know, I felt the effects of this storm before it happened. I was terribly tense. Now I feel almost as though I've been released from some sort of prison.'

'It's perfectly natural, Mrs Wolff. Our metabolisms are affected by high and low pressure. If one is slightly unbalanced, it can send one right over the edge.

'Do you know that arthritics can tell when there's a storm coming?'

Lottie said she thought that was an old wives' tale.

'How very unliberated. Old wives. Actually, Mrs Wolff, their joints are as good as barometers. It's the low pressure they can feel. Are you arthritic, by any chance?'

Lottie felt she was being insulted though she couldn't say exactly how. So she said, 'No.' And: 'Excuse me, I must get back to my friends, Mrs Collier and Mr Winchester.'

Miriam smiled at Terry with satisfaction. 'Whatever did

233

you see in *her* Terry? There's absolutely nothing about her at all that I'd have thought you'd go for. But to be honest, I quite like her. She has such dinky little eyes.'

The ocean looked as though it was making a last mad dash away from the land, sucking at the sand, dragging out with it the little crabs, broken coral, sea-shells, tree-trunks and beach chairs in its strengthening pull. Miles out at sea, flotsam and jetsam whirled, hurled together, smashed and crashed into the growing tidal wave.

Two smokes away from The Sugar Mill, Andrew Dean fought against the gusts of wind that kept him pressed tight against the cliff face. He slipped and rolled, skidding downwards to land in a heap of loose stones on the empty sands.

'Bastard!' he yelled, examining his twisted ankle before staggering onwards. He *felt* rather than knew of the hurricane's approach. It was as though the thunderous sky, the luminous blackness, had somehow got inside his head. The elements weren't simply influencing him – they had *become* him.

Something had compelled him to be closer to Hope Parnell. The distance between them was unsatisfying, frustrating. He had remembered the colour of her blood. Now he wanted to remember the flesh.

Until Tuesday, the memories had been indeterminate, hazy. Only the surface facts, the meat of his trial and events, had been accessible to him. But since that vision of Nick at the undertaker's shed, even the roots beneath the soil had become visible. He could pull characters, motives, emotions out of the hat like a conjurer.

It was the moonshine. It had to be. No one could tell what per cent proof moonshine was: it had no labels, no government guarantee, no Nevis Standards Authority test certificate. That was the beauty of it. It could be pure alcohol for all he knew. And taken with those Largactils it had had a terrific effect on him. He was cured of his cure. He'd even felt a stirring for a couple of black guys he'd seen in Charlestown. Now that was a *real* breakthrough.

The unlocked door of his mind and his passions was like

a draught of freedom. He was close to being his true self again.

He paused to rub at his twisted ankle and, to deaden the pain, took a swig of the moonshine he'd brought with him.

Dean had left his apartment at nine that morning, not noticing that the Maria Juana had sailed out of harbour ahead of schedule. The town had been ominously quiet beneath an ochre sky and he'd walked the five miles to the beach in silence.

When the winds began, he was still driven on, unable to resist the compulsion to see Hope Parnell with her lover.

Ned Murdoch. He spat the name.

Tomorrow, before he used his knife on her, he'd tell her how he'd crippled the yacht. And that Murdoch was as dead as she was.

A blast of wind caught him off balance and he spun round on the sands, losing his sense of direction. Grains of white sand, soft as heroin, billowed like gauze around him. He flipped off the plastic bottle cap and took another mouthful of rum.

If that was what it was. Still, it was hot, sweet and fire-spattered. And that was all that mattered.

He'd been doing some thinking. When this was all over, when he had been redeemed, he'd get back to London and remind a few contacts that he was open to suggestions again. He had a few old scores to settle, he was owed a few favours. Money was no problem – he had made enough from deals in the past to enable him to keep out of the back streets. But it wouldn't last forever. And he had his future to think of now.

He laughed aloud, his voice swirling around him as it was alternately suffocated and broadcast by the winds.

How the hell had that got there? He looked down at his hand. He was carrying the stiletto. The knife with a blade so long and silver it could have been a spear.

He hadn't remembered getting it out of his jacket – must have done it subconsciously, remembering those sharks who'd got away from him for so long.

He tested the sharpness of it against his thumb and watched with pleasure as blood spurted from the flesh. He

235

licked its saltiness as though it were a delicacy. The sea swore at him, but kept on rolling away, afraid to come too close.

Abruptly, the wind paused to take a deeper breath and the sands settled.

There was a woman ahead, where before there'd been nobody.

Was it Hope?

He changed direction to follow her, but she was no longer waiting for him. Her silver hair was piled into a tower of curls on top of her head. She was fair-skinned and dressed in a long, red swathe of silk. Some kind of beach robe, he thought, quickening his stride.

She'd seen him, that was certain, and she was turning away, getting further away from him each second, though she didn't seem to be running.

He began to chase her, he was panting, breathing hard, sweat pouring from his forehead and dripping into his eyes. His feet made deadened padding noises in the sand, his fist held the knife outstretched, high above him. The blade seemed to be leading him while his body dangled from it. It was obvious that the knife had a will of its own: maybe that was how it had found its way into his hand in the first place.

Something didn't feel quite right. The shimmering seascape was making him dizzy. Hope was smiling when she should be screaming. His head was pounding and confused when it should be ice-clear.

This wasn't how he'd wanted it to be. He didn't want an accidental meeting with Hope Parnell – he wanted precision, planning, torture – he was being robbed, deliberately cheated of his rights –

Still the water was draining away, the sand calm and flat as a long dune going out for ever and ever. It was as though his vision was massive, as though his perspective had become gargantuan, God-like.

Now the sea was just a line on the horizon, blending into that grey, billowing thing that must be a cloud.

He looked back towards Hope and realised he'd been deceived.

The woman wavered, shimmered as if she was subjected

to a heat-haze. And as he gazed at her, he saw that her skin was pale and dusty as plaster of Paris, that she was cracking, fragmenting, dissolving, bone fragments spattering as if she'd been exploded –

'Nooo!' he screamed hysterically as, five miles out, the wall of water turned on its heel and rushed towards the shore at breakneck speed, threatening to engulf him with its green glass tides and its mass of broken wreckage.

He saw it approaching, a sheer precipice of white froth and distorted ocean as it gathered speed and height in terrifying seconds.

Blindly he ran away from the trap his mind had lured him into – towards the safety of the cliffside that was now almost in reach. His pill bottle dropped from his pocket and fell unnoticed as he began to climb the steep path between the manchineels.

He was twenty feet above the shoreline, twenty-five. The wind was howling, moaning, forcing him against the cliff-face as though he was pushed there by centrifugal force.

He could hear the wailing of the sea as it swept destructively over the white sands, hear the cracking of the shore trees as the ocean hit its first barrier aggressively, angrily, furious that it should be challenged by such weakling growths, demanding that the earth provide a more worthy champion.

The sea looped. The pinnacle of the wave toppled and crashed forwards, hitting the cliff above Dean and sending shale in a torrent towards his face. Water colder than the Caribbean Sea has any right to be rolled down the rocks drenching him from above. He was trapped in a liquid cage, the massive tidal wave closing in on him from behind, the curving tip enclosing him from above –

Whimpering, his hand sought a higher hold to steady him, and he found a ledge to his right. He inched sideways, knowing that he had seconds before he would be engulfed, sucked into that chaos –

The water hit the rocks as he scrambled frantically for the safety of the cave. It splashed like spittle into the air as liquid tons hit the rocks and the shingle with a roar that shook the land like an earthquake.

He was there, in the hollow, as the sheet of water blotted out the sky like a curtain. Rushing cascades flowed feet away from his eyes.

Exhausted, but safe, Andrew Dean panted on the floor of the cave, blind to the tiny mammals and rodents that shared his sanctuary.

For minutes that stretched into hours, he could hear nothing but the sucking, churning sounds of the sea that had nearly claimed his life.

How long he'd be stranded here, he could not guess. He would have to wait for that roaring wind to die, for the sea to recede, before he'd be able to find his way out.

Quickly he forgot how glad he should have been to be alive. Instead he could only curse that he was trapped in this stinking hole with who knew what foul insects and creatures. He might be here at night – alone – in the dark – with the slithering lizards and roaches.

Already dreading the thought of unseen things touching him, he reached into his pockets to check what had survived. He still had the pistol. And the knife. He had some gum, his lighter and two packets of cigarettes. He'd have to ration them carefully.

His Largactils were gone and so was the moonshine. He had nothing to help him through the black hours he feared. He was a prisoner. Not only of the sea, but of his own mind.

Hope Parnell had caused this. Without her, he'd at worst have been somewhere else when this tidal wave struck; at best, he'd have been in Nicky's arms in London.

That woman had a lot to pay for. Those two years in Broadmoor for a start. The destruction of his relationship with Nick David. And now this. Maybe he'd never get out of here alive. Maybe the bitch had actually succeeded in murdering him – utterly, finally and completely. One thing was sure. If he got out, she'd end up begging him to kill her.

Stronger now, fortified by his hatred, he looked out of his cave through the rains.

And he saw Hope's home.

On the beach, he had walked past the plantation, not know-

238

ing where he was, and he had taken shelter in a cave not thirty feet away from the last of Hope Parnell's cottages.

Ironically he laughed. He had wanted to be close to her. Well, his futile wish had been granted. With a vengeance.

Oz Lennox looked at Hope unhappily. Outside, the winds roared, the sea washed over the tennis courts and darkness loomed like night. Inside, Hope's emotions seemed to be having the same effect as the hurricane. Her sadness was as infectious as her laughter.

'Do you want to talk yet?' he asked her gently.

Hope shrugged. 'I have to sort this out for myself, Oz.'

'You should share it.'

Hope got up from her chair by the window to put on a Vivaldi record. Was there anything less appropriate as storm music?

'Is it the weather?'

Abruptly, she broke her vow of silence. 'It's Ned Murdoch.'

'Ned Murdoch?' Oz sounded incredulous.

'Okay,' Hope said, spreading her hands in resignation. 'I'm being utterly ridiculous. I know it. I spend two days with him and my whole life changes.'

'I feel as though I'm spinning in a vacuum. Pointlessly reaching out . . . to no one.'

Esme wandered over from the bar and sat opposite her. 'I doan't feel like that about you, Oz-mahn. When you goin' all I feel is sheer relief.'

Oz frowned at her to keep quiet. Hope didn't need all that. 'Sounds like an impossible dream, babe,' he said to her.

'I know that,' she sniffed. 'It's really a physical thing. If it was mental, Oz, I could do something about it. Think about something important. Rearrange the schedules for after Hurricane Cleo's gone. Something. Anything. But it's physical. I feel positively ill.'

'Maybe it's the weather, hon,' said Esme, passing Hope a Kleenex. 'Everybody suffer from the hurricane syndrome. And certainly it don't help bein' cooped up like dis.'

239

'What are you looking for, Hope?' asked Oz.

She smiled. 'Wish I knew.'

They ate lunch quietly, Hope pulled herself together on the outside and ignored the queasiness in her stomach.

Lunch together was a real treat for the estate workers, and Robert Lane, the chef, joined them all in the dining room. He was wearing jeans and hadn't bothered with the hat. He looked strange without it, like a man you're used to seeing in spectacles suddenly wearing contact lenses.

Pansy said, 'You know we got another bookin' tomorrow, Hoape?'

Hope had noticed it though it hadn't registered particularly.

'A Member of Parlyment from England. A Minister,' Pansy announced.

Hope said: 'He'll never get here. If he's flying over, no planes'll risk the wind.'

Oz said, 'It could clear, Hope. The radio said the eye had already gone east of Antigua. That means we missed the danger quadrant and it's on its way out. The whole thing could be over by nightfall.'

Zeke looked gloomy. 'Doan't sound on she way out to me, mahn. We may not have much of a hoatel left by de time dis Member of Parlyment come out.'

'Zeke!' snapped Rachel. 'Miss Hoape doan' want to hear dat kinda talkin'! She got enough on de plate widout you.'

There had been ominous crashings since the hurricane first made its horrifying presence felt. Hope wasn't counting the cost, she only wanted to emerge on the other side.

Suddenly Pansy gasped. Her chair flew backwards as she sprang to her feet – 'Dere – out de window. Oahh – no – Hoape! Poor baby – '

They swung around and there was a huge manchineel tree sailing and crashing through the air, ripped up from the grove and thrown at windspeed towards the plantation.

Hope felt her heart slow. A cold sweat formed on her body and she rose in a trance to see the destruction. Before she looked, before it happened, she already knew.

240

As it hit the mill, there was a dull thud, a suppressed explosion.

'Je-sus,' said Oz, watching the great trunk embed itself in the ancient stones.

Hope staggered against him. 'Oz, we might have been in there. All of us. The children and everyone. I nearly said to shelter in there instead of here – '

They stood at the terrace window and watched as stone by stone the mill collapsed in on itself. The weight of the tree dislodged coping stones, keystones. Each crashed inwards, ringing its individual death knell that was clearly audible over the sound of the screaming wind.

For what seemed an age, the mill crumpled like scrunched-up aluminium foil.

The bed where Ned and Hope had made love, the lovely furniture, the pictures, the jade and gold necklace, the books. All were buried now. Everything was lost.

Esme looked fearfully at Hope. How much could she take?

Hope had stiffened. Her face was set and hard, her eyes cold and angry. 'What is the bloody point?' she spat. 'You build things up and something has to destroy it all. Nothing lasts. Not even that bloody mill!' She shook her head in amazement. 'That mill's survived wars, eruptions and earthquakes. Then it's wiped out in seconds by a flying tree.' She almost laughed it was so absurd. 'It's just un-believable. A fucking tree.'

Where the mill had stood only minutes ago, there was just a heap of rubble. Just so much dust. Ashes to ashes. Hope turned her back on the ruin and sat down again, alone at the dining table.

The last remaining relic of the Bussenius family was gone.

That was it, then. There was nothing left to anchor her to Nevis any longer. As soon as there were telephone lines again, she'd ring Nick and tell him her decision.

She was ready to sell out.

Chapter Seventeen

THE HURRICANE died slowly. The rains paused first, giving Veronica a chance to remember what dry was. Then the winds stopped to regroup.

'Is this the eye?' she asked Don Derby.

'No. This is the beginning of the end. The eye has sunshine and blue skies.'

The marble tiles of the church floor were submerged beneath an inch of water. The people lay in pools, glad to be under a stout roof. Singing gospel to keep their spirits up. The children were crying, keening, miserable in their wet clothes. No one took too much notice of them; they knew they would stop.

Veronica felt as though she'd been sitting forever in a cold bath. She was confident enough to raise her head from her knees, but her muscles screamed as she straightened. 'We shall all die of pneumonia,' she said.

'Not necessarily,' said Derby.

None of the church ornaments were still in the building. They should have been safely stowed away before the storm, but it was the sort of thing that got overlooked in the general panic. The rain-soaked walls were bare apart from half of a poster still suspended by the altar. It said: *Suffer little chil* . . .

Then the rains began again, and Veronica buried as much of her body as possible into her soaking dress, pressing against the marble pillar that was her shelter. She made bargains with God, forming prosaic statements in her mind like: My honour for my life, Lord. Twenty thousand to the hurricane relief fund if I survive. If I come through this I will devote my life to Good Works. It amused her. And by the time she'd reached utter silliness – Let me live and I will never wear red stockings again – the grey skies were returning to a guilty blue overhead.

She stretched again, knowing it really was over this time. Feeling a relief in her body that echoed the atmospherics. 'It is finished,' she told Don Derby, and he too was uncurling, his grey pants stained black by the water.

All around them, people were emerging, laughing, shaking hands, Praise de Lord-ing, talking, kissing. Survivors. None of them thought about their homes that might be no more than firewood. They were alive. A neighbour would always help, or maybe they would be fortunate enough to help a neighbour. A minister crawled from under a pew and offered impromptu prayers of gratitude.

'Strange to be thankful to a god that's wreaked this sort of havoc, isn't it?' said Derby.

'Not really,' said Veronica. 'Maybe they've remembered how good life is. That's worth a word of thanks, isn't it?'

A mystic. The woman was a mystic. No wonder she'd not cracked up under the pressure.

'An' for de life of our friends shelt'rin' wid us, we ahlso praise you, Jesus.' The Minister was looking straight at Veronica and Derby. 'Have you a word of comfort to our brodders and de sisters?'

Derby shrivelled. Veronica would have liked to do the same, but she couldn't just say nothing. The people were looking to her, wanting to hear religion from the white strangers.

Religion wasn't her thing either, no matter what Derby was thinking. But she wasn't one to stand there like him with her eyes popping, her mouth gaping.

'This storm shows we are all one,' she said, not knowing whether she might sound patronising, mocking. She didn't feel that she was either, but she didn't know how the islanders saw her. 'Wherever we come from, whoever we are, we are one in the eyes of God.' There were cries of amen and hallelujah. Veronica relaxed.

'These events bring us closer together – the rich and the poor, the strong and the weak. We huddle together for

243

warmth, we seek solace with our fellows.' She'd be embarrassed remembering this, later on.

'God inflicts His wrath equally.'

'An' so He is sharin' His love,' interrupted Jenny Smith from underneath a wet straw hat.

'Exactly, Mrs Smith. Amen. And we all remember the value of our lives – however different they may be – as the sun shines and the waters leave us.'

Praise de Lord.

'We are grateful, that is, Mr Derby and I, for your hospitality. For giving us shelter from the storm.'

'De storm of life,' said the Minister, nodding appreciatively.

She was searching for a way to round it up. Couldn't go on forever. 'And now, we pray to you in the words Jesus Christ taught us by saying: Our Father, Which art in Heaven . . . '

The congregation joined in enthusiastically, glad that yet another bond had been forged between them and the visitors. The strangers even knew the same prayers.

Derby and Veronica sneaked out of the church while eyes were closed and hands pressed together.

'I had to get out,' said Veronica. 'I know it seems awful, creeping off like that. I just have to get back to the hotel and change my clothes. I'm so cold.'

'You were brilliant,' said the Reuters man in genuine admiration. His original opinion of Veronica Marston had changed. 'They won't mind us going, you know. They think white people are very strange. And anyway you gave them what they wanted. You almost had me saying hallelujah.'

'I remembered that ending from school,' said Veronica. Unwilling to let go. Proud of herself. 'I meant quite a bit of it. Though I can't remember exactly what I said. It's probably a good job!'

The streets were already drying in the evening sun. Steam was coming from the tarmac. The flimsy material of Veronica's dress was patchy with the water that was evaporating from her.

'You can come back to Nelson Plantation if you like,'

she said to the reporter. 'If there's any staff around, I'd like you to have dinner with me.'

'Thanks, but I have to cable through the news on the hurricane.'

'You can do that from there. Julian Winchester's very into communications. We even have telephones and televisions that work, though in contrast, you're not likely to be able to run a bath.'

'Okay, lady,' said Derby. 'Getting back to St Kitts isn't likely to be possible today. And it's just *got* to be an improvement on Ma Johnson's.' He felt an overwhelming urge to ask if he could spend the night with her.

'And while you're there in the office,' she said, 'You can announce my decision to whoever you want. I'm saying yes to Doctor Wilding. And for all I care, the whole world can read about it.'

Don Derby grinned. He was glad he hadn't been presumptuous. A good story was better than sex anyway. And now he would be kind, as Jessica Collier had asked him to be. 'I'll need some background information, you know,' he said. 'Okay?'

'Okay, Mister Derby.'

The all-clear was announced at the shelter by three blasts of the siren that hadn't worked earlier.

As Jessica and Lottie emerged, blinking their eyes like moles in the evening sunshine, Julian said: 'See? There's nothing so terrible about a hurricane, is there?'

Lottie said, 'No, it was really just rather boring, being cooped up all day like that.

'But what can have happened to Ronnie? She's so reliable and careful, I'd have thought she'd be here well before anyone else.

'I keep thinking she's thrown herself off a cliff, or been smashed to bits by a falling roof or something,' said Jessica.

Julian disagreed. Nothing would have happened to Veron. She'd have found shelter somewhere, surely?

He opened the door to the Datsun and the ladies climbed in.

Terry and Miriam followed them, and as Miriam went

off to find her imported Jaguar, Terry leaned over to Lottie in the back seat of Julian's car. He needed out, fast. The reins were pulling too tight. And this was his chance.

Maybe Lottie still had a soft spot for him. He could certainly manage to feel something for her, if pressed. Miriam's new rules and regulations didn't suit him one bit. They'd played their game without hassle for years, and just when he'd thought he'd got the hang of how to score, Miriam had moved the goalposts.

'I'd like to see you,' he hissed out of the corner of his mouth, so Miriam shouldn't see. 'Tonight. Maybe tomorrow. Or Saturday?'

Lottie sniffed.

'I mean it, Lottie. I think you're looking terrific.'

'I'm looking older. And I'm going home.'

He straightened and called: 'Just coming,' as the Jag revved impatiently. 'It's been a long time,' he said to Lottie again.

'Too long. Goodbye Terry.'

'Are you still at the same address in London?' he asked, suddenly desperate for some sign of approval, forgetting to wear the just-having-a-little-chat-dear expression for Miriam's benefit. Lottie thought for a while and slammed her door shut. Very positively. His hand was resting on the open window and jerked with it.

Once she'd loved Terry. It didn't matter that he was eleven years younger than she was. He had excited her, pleased her, comforted her during the agonising days of her marriage and divorce. Now she saw him for what he was. He was on the look-out for another rich wife.

But oh no, apron strings wouldn't tie Terry down for long, no matter what Miriam thought.

'No,' she said eventually. 'I've moved away, Terry. Goodbye again.'

Julian took this as the signal and rolled the car forwards. Terry kept his hand on the window and started to trot by the side of the Datsun. 'I might be in London soon,' he called. 'Can I look you up? Can I have your new address?'

Lottie looked ahead, through the front windscreen, and ignored him.

As the Datsun picked up speed, Jessica said: 'That was brave.'

'Brave? My arse. I've got my investments to protect.'

'I knowed it was dat crapaud,' said Pansy, crossing herself fervently. 'I felt it when de creature died.'

They walked towards the Mill, in the sudden silence after the hurricane. They carried torches to light their way once the brief dusk was over.

'By rights Mistah Lennox, you should have bin in dere. It was you who killed de crapaud.'

'You don't believe that kind of nonsense, Pansy? Not really?' said Oz, glad of the chance to talk about something other than the destruction and the chaos. 'Surely you only say these things for the benefit of the tourists.'

'Dat crapaud mean you dead, mahn,' said Elisha seriously.

'Do I look dead?' he laughed.

'You sayin' you ain't nevah goin' die, Mistah Lennox?' asked Rachel.

''Course not.'

Pansy looked triumphantly at him. 'Well dat prove me point, den.'

Oz shrugged. There was no winning against island women.

They circled the Mill, slowly, mournfully.

'De spirits have gone,' said Pansy. 'No life here any more.'

The splintered remains of the manchineel tree rose from the debris like a grave marker. Hope felt nothing. It was as if the Mill had never existed. The coconut grove was stripped bare of leaves and fruit. The stalk-like trunks stood alone, telegraph poles in a wilderness, though the Royal Palms to the west had survived. The arbour of bougainvillea and clematis was down, strands of the clinging plants lay scattered everywhere, like streamers in the morning after a party.

The nets around the tennis courts stood firm: its mesh had trapped pieces of seaweed, branches and stones high above them, like a fishing net. In the swimming pools were driftwood, rocks, a couple of chairs that hadn't been locked away.

Miraculously the guests' bungalows had survived intact. 'We're still in business, Hope,' said Esme.

Hope looked around at the torn flamboyant tree and at the devastated hibiscus bushes lying roots-up in its branches. 'Are we?' she said cynically.

Did they really expect her to carry on? Even Napoloen would have surrendered his empire faced with these odds.

''Course we is, Hope,' said Rachel. 'It all looks so bad now because of de dahrk. An' de ground bein' so wet. You wait an' see. Everythin' will be better by mornin'.'

'Oh yes? Will the world change overnight? D'you think some Obeahman might fix the pools and the trees and everything while we're sleeping?'

'Hey, Hope,' said Oz, alarmed by the shell he could see she was building around herself. 'This isn't you talking.'

They carried on walking through the grounds and out beyond, to the plantation itself where the sugar cane lay in heaps as though it had already been harvested. The top layer of soil had been whipped off the vegetable plots, leaving tender young plants exposed.

The sea looked perfectly normal now, its waves trickled and rolled on to the shore, leaving extra debris behind it but otherwise only licking its lips after enjoying a good joke.

The grassland had receded four or five feet to be reclaimed by the sand. To someone else, the loss of the grass would have been insignificant compared to the damage everywhere else. To Hope, it epitomised her defeat.

Ned said you don't battle with the sea, she thought. But she'd fought a constant battle with it, stealing its shore to turn it into a green and fertile place. And of course she'd lost. How could the alternative have ever been possible?

They walked over the damp sands, looking at the debris cursorily. This was wreckage stolen from other islands. The booty from Nevis would be swept onto beaches far away. The hurricane's own idea of the distribution of wealth.

There was a pile of bottles, mostly broken and a dead

sheep, of all the ridiculous things. 'I get rid of dat,' said Zeke disapprovingly.

'Where de kittens?' piped one of Rachel's children, suddenly remembering the most important thing in the world.

'Dey's safe, honey,' said Rachel. 'All de animals safe. All de cats is in de kitchen. Dey know when bad things happ'nin' and dey come into de warm to hide like we.'

There was a huge piece of boat drifting in, bobbing on the gentle tides. Hope looked at it unemotionally.

'C'mon, Hope,' said Oz, wrapping an arm around her shoulders, assuming it would upset her. 'Don't look.'

'I can handle it,' she snapped at him. 'I'm not about to break down.'

More's the pity, thought Oz. Her stiff control was bad news.

'Dere's a mahn in dat,' announced Elisha, wading out through the waves. He stood staring into the wreckage for a few moments. 'We better callin' de undertaker.'

'Is it anybody we know?' Hope asked, her voice clear and cold.

'It nobody now,' said Elisha, dragging the boat back to the beach.

Damn him and his bloody island logic! She almost shouted: 'Was it somebody we *knew*, then?'

He shook his head, unperturbed by her tone.

They walked back to the plantation, scraping their heels in the whorls of sand. There was no more they could do for now. A sickly moon was high in the sky, still gathering strength to compete with the remnants of the day. Esme said: 'Dere's a strange calmness about everything now. Very quiet. Makes me uneasy.'

There were no birds flying, no traders on the beach lighting fires to barbecue fish, no rustle of leaves, no animal sounds. Their torchlight bounced ahead of them in the gloom.

'What's dat?' called Rachel's child, and she took flight, heading for the glittering thing on the sand by the hill path like a magpie, swooping to pick it up and holding it out at arm's length as she fled back to her mother.

'Wash it in de watah,' said Rachel, and the child riddled the metal in the sea till a heavy necklace gleamed bright as new.

'Look,' she said to Hope. 'Dis what I found.'

The sight of the Aztec necklace in her hands sent shudders down Hope's spine. It was impossible that it should be here. It had been safe in the Mill – it had been in a cabinet in her bedroom.

'That's yours, Hope,' said Esme.

'No – it can't be.' Her voice was trembling, less sure of itself than her words.

'Yes it is,' Rachel argued. 'De wind must have picked it up somehow.'

Hope held out her hands for the chain and took it from the child slowly, feeling the incomprehensible brushing against her mind like a tangible shadow. 'It's impossible,' she whispered, softening with that first touch of the warm metal.

Had something survived the hurricane's attack after all? Something precious? 'Pansy!' She turned to her. 'Tell me – can this really be mine?'

Pansy handled it gingerly, as though it might give her an electric shock, and she nodded. There was no mistake. That necklace was the one they'd found in the cellar, sure enough. 'I said dere was no spirits at de Mill any more, Hoape,' she said triumphantly.

And Oz felt relief flow over him.

Funny, he'd never imagined he could be happy to see Hope cry.

Stuart Wilding sat in the motel room and felt released. It was all over. The papers had come out that morning and he'd refused to look at a single one of them. He hadn't listened to the radio. He hadn't watched the news. He hadn't answered the telephone. After all, he'd given the newsmen all they wanted at the conference. He'd given them blood.

His secretary had avoided the subject of Press coverage, the agent hadn't spoken to him at all. He didn't know whether they were embarrassed about it or whether they'd guessed he simply didn't want to know. They were right. He didn't want to see what the damage was.

Though he was a realist, he didn't need to stare his ridicule in the face. His political life had been wiped out at a stroke.

Ten years of wheeling, dealing, debate and controversy were ended. And it didn't matter to him in the slightest.

He was sorry for Jannine. It would have been very hard for her. And it would be equally difficult for Veronica whether she came back to England as his wife or not.

He looked out of the plate glass window, loose in its rusting frame, and watched a jumbo take off into the night sky. It was lit up by the runway lights, an Air Lanka Tristar. He loved planes like a child. Not for the mechanical beasts they were, but for the places they were going.

Every flight to him was as exciting as the first. That roaring, incredible speed as you approach take-off, then the climbing, when the front of the plane angles so you can't walk properly. Then that quiet, level time when you occupy yourself as best as possible, waiting for the descent and the new air, the new sun.

At last he was escaping to Nevis. The island of flowers and hummingbirds, sun and cauliflower clouds. The volcano with its lurking mists. The thick, tropical forest and the people who smiled and said 'you're welcome' in reply to your thankyou, really meaning it. There was enough sincerity and generosity in Nevis to make you think that the world must be an all right place after all. What a pity he wasn't staying at the Nelson. Sugar Mill was superb of course but Nelson was his and Ron's special place. Still, if everything went well, he'd be able to move over to the mountain plantation later. With her . . .

He hardly dared to think about her, to wonder how she would feel when she saw him. His unexpected arrival. Very dramatic and romantic. On a plane and not a white charger, but he was still chasing her, following her to the ends of the earth. The gallant knight.

But not really so gallant. He was running away, wasn't he?

251

He put that thought out of his head and undressed. How he would sleep he didn't know. There was a very early morning call ordered. He would have hours to wait at the airport but that didn't matter. He would go to the duty-free arcade and arrive in Nevis bearing gifts.

'I don't suppose you'll be coming back for your honeymoon in a hurry, darling,' said Julian Winchester. 'You'll be living in sin for a terribly long time.'

'I know,' said Veronica.

'What do you think they'll do with the story about you?'

She shrugged. 'I haven't said all that much to Mister Derby. Only "yes" really, and that Stuart's decision to leave politics has my backing. I said it was the sort of thing I'd have expected such an honourable man to do.'

' "Honourable"? That's asking for trouble, don't you think?'

She shrugged. 'I thought I'd get it in, anyway. But I hope they play it down for his sake. And mine.'

'There's going to be a lot of unhappy men around when they read it, you know.'

'They'll survive. They were only friends. If they were *real* friends, then nothing will have changed, will it?'

Lottie had already packed and was mooching around, looking for something to do. 'Things have been all wrong, this time,' she said. 'Though I know it's my own fault. I'm glad to be going home early.'

'Nonsense,' said Veronica generously. 'You were doing what you thought was right. And you don't have to travel with me just because I asked you to stick by me, you know. It wasn't a physical demand.'

Lottie laughed. 'I know that, Ron. But I might be some help. And anyway, I feel as though I ought to get myself organised at home. What with you getting into a permanent relationship after all these years and sorting yourself out, it leaves me looking at my own life and wondering what I'm doing with it. You inspire me. You always have done in your own, quiet way.'

Veronica packed her Vuitton suitcase after dinner, while Don Derby cabled London.

252

He pushed the hurricane story, but when it was schemed into the layout for the morning papers, it was used for filling holes.

The *Guardian* used it on page seven. It made a paragraph on the back page of the *Financial Times* because the price of coffee and sugar would be affected. The *Sun* told the Reuters office not to bother filing copy on the hurricane unless there were blood and guts pictures.

He played down the Marston-Wilding story, taking the flames out of it as best he could, for her sake. But despite him, Veronica's acceptance of the proposal from a married ex-MP was earmarked for the lead.

Chapter Eighteen

HOPE PULLED on the flying suit she'd had the foresight to move out of the Mill before the hurricane along with a few other clothes to double her chances of survival.

The sun streamed through the windows of the Victoria room. Feather-shadows flickered through the fronds of the Royal Palms to dance on the marble floor. An electric-blue lizard scurried vertically up the white bedroom wall, flicking his tongue out for microscopic insects only he could see. The air was spicy with the scents of crushed blossoms.

In the light of the new day, Hope felt that maybe she could cope. The warmth and smells around her reminded her forcefully of the reasons why she could never leave Nevis. Her first instinct to run and hide had been replaced by a new vigour, an uncontrollable determination to rebuild what had been taken away from her.

She shook her fist at the sky through the window. 'Drive me out, would you? Send me running home, eh?' she challenged.

'No way, sucker.'

Everything would repair – everything except the Mill. That she would have cleared and removed by demolition men tomorrow. Nothing from the old stones would be salvaged, even if it was possible to do so. The sooner it was out of the way the better.

Perhaps Esme had been right, she thought, flinging open the doors to the terrace. Perhaps the despair she'd felt yesterday was a combination of the hurricane syndrome and the absence of Ned. Now, things didn't seem half so bad.

The living trees would grow new leaves, the plants and the bushes, the grass and the vines; they would survive.

Even the sugar cane would revive itself in the sun, for these were the things of today. They weren't some relic from another era: they belonged to the present.

She jogged along the path to the great house, refusing to see the wreckage, feeling only the sun caressing her.

Nature was furious in Nevis: vengeful of an attack from any one of the elements. Trees that would take decades to establish in an English hothouse would thrive and mature in a couple of seasons here. By next year, even she herself would mistrust her memories of the devastation that now surrounded her.

'Pansy!' she called into the kitchen. 'Any paw-paw for breakfast?'

She started work immediately, going through the schedules that would have to be rearranged to compensate for the lost day.

The telephone began ringing before she'd finished her coffee. The lines had been repaired in record time, further proof of man's supremacy over nature. There were offers of help from the other hoteliers, none of whom had suffered the scale of loss there was at Sugar Mill Plantation.

Julian Winchester said the Nelson was untouched by the storm.

Manor Inn had lost animals – but chances were that they had simply taken the opportunity to stray away. They might be rounded up later for all anyone knew.

Later, Terry rang. 'Portland's been injured, but not fatally so,' he chirruped. 'The important thing is that Goliath's okay. Bit ruffled but settling back into his old ways.'

'What's the damage?'

'Someone left a window open, bloody fool. The room's wrecked inside. Would you believe it – it's Miriam's bedroom!' he chuckled. 'She's going apeshit. Threatening to go and stay down at Manor Inn till it's fixed because she can't bear to look at the chaos!'

'Think she's got problems? Have you heard about my mill, Terry?' How strange – it didn't hurt her to say it.

'Yeah, Jules rang and told me. What a pisser. But you're okay?'

'Fine now.'

'Glad to hear it. Thought I might pop over an' see you – '

'Terry!' She could read his mind. Even on the telephone.

'What?' he cut in innocently. 'It was only to see if I could help with the Mill, Hope. That's all.'

'Honestly, Terry. You're incredible, you really are.'

'I know,' he said happily, and hung up.

There had been word from Gem Welch in Tobago to say the hurricane had missed the island and what was all the fuss about? She'd phoned Nick to tell him she had survived. Hope didn't mention how close a thing that had been. Nor did she say anything about her own weakness of the day before. It had passed.

She'd had a fair-weather report on flying conditions from Antigua but she had heard nothing from Ned.

She looked out of the window above her desk in the great house sitting room and saw the rock of Redonda sparkling in the guilty sunlight. Visibility was good today. Soon, she'd get out to the planes, check them over and be ready early for the taxi-jobs to and from Antigua by this afternoon.

The timing was superb as far as she was concerned. Lottie and Veronica had to be in Antigua ready for the three o'clock flight out, and her new guest, a Mr Wilding, was due in at four. With any luck, she'd have time between the trips to fit in a bit of essential shopping.

So nothing was really so bad as it had first looked. Not even the parting with Meestah Murdoch.

It hadn't really mattered at all.

She walked out to the Jeep and stretched herself, like a cat in the sunshine, feeling better and better as each moment passed.

Oz was anxious to get flying again but it was well after lunch by the time the schedules had been rearranged into a workable pattern. He felt it was time wasted.

He had a troupe of engineers to fly from Guadeloupe to Dominica, workers on the new hydro-electric plant. But, more importantly, there was a shipment of hash to be collected and somehow got to the States. That was why it was essential for Oz to use The Goose on a regular basis. At least once a month there was a stash in the hold that was waiting for the right run at the right time. Hope was not aware of his sideline.

Oz didn't worry about the ethics. He liked a smoke now and then himself. Didn't everybody, including Hope? It was a completely different thing to the hard stuff. It was unrelated. As different from crack as water from petrol.

He didn't stop to think about the fortunes being made by the big boys, or the poverty of the people cultivating the crops. He took his cut, smoked a little weed and shared his good luck with everybody who mattered to him.

Obviously it was a risk, running dope. But the stakes were high and instant. He expected to get caught, sooner or later, but the longer away was the day of reckoning, the longer he had to enjoy his illegal earnings.

Oz was moving fast, running through the essential pre-flight checks, looking over the dials and the instruments with a practised eye. Hope was running through the same routine on the Cessna. *In God we trust, but everything else we check.*

'I'm keeping Esme on for another couple of days,' she called from out of her cockpit window.

'Good news.'

'We lost a couple of flights yesterday and we need to make up,' she said. 'I'm going to Antigua and back in another half hour or so, so radio me when you get to Dominica in case there's anything else crops up in the north.'

Oz was drumming the jets, blasting evil smelling fumes into the air. 'How're you feeling today?'

'Stronger.'

'Over the Ned problem?'

'Completely.'

'Into flying?'

'Can't wait. I wanna soar like a butterfly, sting like a bee.' She punched the air like Cassius Clay.

'Even better news,' said Oz. 'Okay, I'm ready for up. Have you seen this note from Gem?' He scrunched the

257

paper into a ball and chucked it accurately through their open windows to land in Hope's lap. Then he taxied down the runway before turning for the final acceleration that would get him airborne.

Hope read the 'This one gets you UP' message and roared, wiping her eyes with an oily hand. She gave Oz Lennox a thumbs-up though he wouldn't see it.

This was comradeship. This was living. This was the way it should be. The sky was beckoning. There was the smell of aircraft fuel, a comforting, friendly smell. A real smell.

There'd be that wonderful silence up there. Just her and the sound of the engines – but even they disappeared in time into the back of your brain so you weren't aware of them, only alert to the changes. You could hear the wind up there. Look down on the clouds like so many grazing sheep beneath you.

You couldn't give that sort of thing up lightly.

You could jive with the air currents, judge your landings with a precision that left your passengers in awe of you, as though you were some kind of guru. Climb out, dirty and tense from a descent and walk wobbly-legged like a space alien on solid earth again. All the time knowing that nothing was stopping you from leaving the land any time you wanted. Up there, *you* were the magician.

Sometimes the tricks went wrong, as they had with the fireball that had been Tom Parnell. But she knew her father wouldn't have cared: he would have wanted to go out like a young man, with an explosion, a roar, a finality. Sometimes, when it was unbearably good, you even called to death to take you then, for the rest of life was as nothing compared to that moment. That was the way to die, laughing, exhilarated, triumphant and alone, recklessly dicing with the fates, gambling with destiny.

Hope had fallen in love with Icarus when she was seven, staunchly refusing to believe that he was no more than a myth. She had been Amy Johnson all her life. There was no room for a man who was a part of another element. What did the sea have in comparison to the air? How could you compare that ultimate escape with floating on something that could drown you in short minutes, trap you with its currents?

Where was the freedom there?

The sea was a wrecker. It took away your land. It had stolen Ned.

She congratulated herself as she read the fuel gauge and settled into familiar things. Ned was out of her mind. Gone. She hadn't given him a thought since the Mill crashed. Okay, hardly a thought, then. Whatever was happening to him now, it didn't affect her in the slightest.

She'd probably never see him again. Or perhaps they might meet by chance, when they were old and both grounded. See each other across a crowded room. A cocktail party for the rich and successful in one of the remote havens. On Young Island, maybe.

She liked that idea. Would she acknowledge him, or would she stare into his eyes and then turn away? Would he recognise her when she had grey instead of silver hair, her face leathery from the sun and the wind?

Or would the room go quiet, the people merge into a blur?

She pictured Ned middle aged, and he still looked very physical. Weathered with a tan that would never fade. A body in good shape. Eyes that were permanently creased from smiling or the salt water.

Would he walk up to her and take her arm and whisper, 'At last I've found you'. Would she reply: 'I've been waiting for you'?

Yich, she thought. No way. More likely he'd be a brash old drunk and bellow: 'Learned to gut a fish yet?'.

But the image turned sour; Ned suddenly had a child bride with him, a younger, simpering version of Karin, and behind Hope was some vague and out-of-focus toy-boy to keep her bed warm.

Damn it. Why couldn't she let herself dream, even?

She cut the engines abruptly and climbed out to wait for Veronica and Lottie in the shade of the hangar.

Jessica rubbed a dollop of suncream into her arms. They

259

were smooth and thin and brown. A couple of days was all it took for the ounces to roll off again.

'Where's Lottie?' she asked.

'Watching for the taxi.'

Veronica sat down on the sunbed next to Jessica, uncomfortable in her travelling clothes. 'I feel bad leaving you here all alone.'

Jessica pulled a doesn't-matter face. 'Hell, why? You've got to get back and I've still got things to do. Don't mention it to Lottie – '

'Of course not. Would I?'

Jessica grinned and reached for her fruit punch. 'Of course not.' They sat in silence, watching a hummingbird zipping dizzily around an Angel's Trumpet bush.

'It's all right between us, isn't it Ron?'

'Yes. You know that. Don't go over old ground, forget about it. At least you gave me the chance to give my side of the story.'

'Well there shouldn't have been any story.'

'Stop it, you!' Veronica leaned over and poked her in the ribs.

Jessica wriggled away smartly. 'I'll say no more then. But don't go getting media-struck or anything behind my back. You'll be something of a celebrity and you might get to like the limelight.'

'Hardly,' chuckled Veronica. 'I'm going back for Stuart – not for the sake of Fleet Street.'

Jessica hated goodbyes. She wished the taxi would come. 'Pass me that cake while you're there by the table, Ron. The pink coconut one. Thanks.'

Veronica felt the same way. She looked at her watch. Any time now.

'You'd better give me a ring in two weeks or so, because I won't know where to reach you,' said Jessica. 'Then we can go off to Champney's together. Starvation's so much easier when it's done in pairs.'

'Taxi, Ron,' called Lottie from the steps. 'Jessica, I'll pick you up from Heathrow. Call me from baggage collection and I'll be with you soon as I can.'

Veronica turned away from her to hide her face. Her

eyes were swimming and she was ashamed of her senti-
mentality. It was an automatic reflex. She always cried
when she was leaving Nevis.

'Bye, then,' she said, and Jessica waved. 'See you soon.'
When her friends had gone, Jessica fed the cake to the
chi-chi birds and wiped away her own tears.

Ned was caught up in the slipstream of a dare. He was on
his way back to Nevis. There were two Ned Murdochs, one
who had listened attentively to a newly-repaired radio for a
day and a night for news of a wrecked island and one who
had tried to drink himself into a stupor. That one was a real
woman-hater.

One had lost out, but Ned wasn't sure which. Okay, so
he happened to be sailing south. It didn't mean anything.
It was only because there was nowhere else special to head
for at the moment. St Croix was pretty dead, shell-shocked
from Protestant clergymen who'd been there for a conference, so he sure as hell didn't want to hang around there.
Maybe if they'd gone on to Puerto Rico as they'd planned,
there'd have been something to keep him away from Nevis.

Well then, he thought, thank God for that wrecked
Bluebird motor. But he couldn't admit *too* much to himself.
He had to keep that emotional shell around him, just in
case.

There was no hurry to get back, he thought. What was
the rush? They might stop off for a few days on the way at
Antigua or somewhere. Or when Nevis was in sight, he
could just as easily sail straight on past and head for
Barbados. Pick up some cruisers and take them along to the
Grenadines if that's what he felt like doing at the time.

'Ned Murdoch, you is hooked, mahn,' grinned Keith.

'Sod off you bastard.'

Comments like that didn't help. They made him feel as
though he had something to prove.

The schooner rode the waves, giving him that old
familiar I-could-die-and-not-regret-a-thing feeling.

Ned was steering, Keith perched on the side with a
fishing line. 'Pass me de spear-gun, quick, Cinnamahn '

The thin man, Cinnamon Hicks, wiry as a pipe-cleaner,

261

ran for it, and peered over the edge. There were marlin. Masses of them. Petrol blue in the water, so near the surface you could pat one of them. 'Cut de engine, Ned,' he yelled.

Ned was too slow, and Keith dropped into the water too far away from them to catch one of the beautiful, fast-moving creatures. 'What's de matter wid dat mudder,' he called from the ocean.

'Sorry,' Ned yelled back, pleased for the escaping marlin.

The sun shone on the waves, making each ripple look like a shoal of flying fish or dolphins leaping. It was hot, but the breeze singing through the sails kept you cool on the deck.

Somebody put the old Eddy Grant tape on the cassette machine and rolled joints. From below, the smell of sizzling bacon wafted upwards. Mouths watered in anticipation.

'You givin' all dis up, mahn?' said Keith, dripping in the cabin.

'Nope,' said Ned, swaying to Electric Avenue in an easy West Indian rhythm. The end of a joint hung suspended from his lower lip.

'Den why you goin' back to Nevis if you not plannin' to give up de sea?'

Ned felt high. Light. Easy. Cool. No problehm. He shrugged and looked earnestly at the Grenadian. 'I don't know why I'm going back, man. I just feel good doin' it so it must be right.'

That was a philosophy that Keith could accept. It was a 'now' thing. The future didn't come into it.

'How you know she waitin' for you, Ned?'

'I don't. If she's not, we'll sail on to Barbados, or maybe even as far as Grenada. Go and see your wife. How d'you like that idea?'

'I could get into dat. I like to know de house an' de family okay after de storm.'

'You radioed from the ship this morning and the police said Point Saline in Grenada was untouched,' said Ned.

'Sure. But I like to see for myself.'

Ned took a last drag then flung the butt out into the ocean.

'So you manage, don't you? You've got a homebase and the water,' he mused.

'A family an' a boat? Is dat what you contemplatin'?'

'Not necessarily.'

'You is. An' sure, I manage in some respects. But I wouldn't if I had to restrain myself when I was in de odder ports, mahn. When I was too long away from hoame. My judgement goes when I get frustrated.'

Michel the chef called that their late lunch was finally ready, and Cinnamon went down to collect plates of bacon and green tomatoes from the galley. They dropped anchor for a while, just listening to the music, munching the food that tasted so much better for it being eaten in the salty air.

'Dere's Saba,' called Gonzo, and the peaks of the island came at them as though the island had just turned a corner. 'Good blowin', Ned,' he said. 'We makin' good time despite de currents in de watah.'

Ned was silent. Thinking about distances and partings.

'Why is dat mahn so dam' quiet today?' asked Spencer, pointing with his fork at Ned.

Cinnamon shook his head. 'Stars in de eyes. I'm wondrin' if we might get to run dis boat on we own. De way it should be done widout de interference of dis "sea captain".'

'Get lost, Cinnamon. When you get your own boat you can run it your own way. Now haul anchor and let's get her moving again.' Ned rose and headed for the radio. Two hundred missing on Nevis – why hadn't they all gone into the shelter, he wondered. Bodies were being identified. Hope's? There was substantial damage to property. Crops devastated. Many animals killed or missing. Probably swept off cliffs by the wind.

Suppose Hope really was one of the dead? Suppose he'd run out on her only to leave her to die? The only person he'd ever felt as though he'd loved for a moment . . .

He let his mind wander over the prospect of being an unmarried widower. He saw her pale, crushed body being taken from rubble, her eyes closed.

He saw a coffin being taken out to sea – no, she'd be flown home to England, wouldn't she? He pictured a coffin being loaded into a plane, then, himself following it, wearing black, and encased in his shell forever.

The ganja was taking him down. This line of thought was ridiculous. He'd be able to feel it if anything happened to her, he just knew it. Right now, she was probably replanting uprooted crops, checking over the planes. She might even be swimming in the post-storm sea.

He thought about her collecting the shells and wondered if she'd added any more to her collection. They could go out to St Kitts again, and this time they could take a net in which to get the big shells back to the boat. She could come with him to the Grenadines, the tiny, silent pearl islets that had never been counted, let alone mapped. They could wander along the shores of islands where no man had walked; find animals and huge lizards that had never seen a human being before.

He imagined making love to her on a beach on one of the unnamed islands that took just a few minutes to walk around. They could find a dune out of sight of the boat. Grill lobster on an open fire. Hunt for coral. Make love again.

He felt better and cut off the radio. It was hot and stuffy in the wheelhouse. He went up on the deck and on impulse stripped off his shorts and dived naked into the water.

'Mahn gone crazy!' yelled Gonzo, and Keith shut off the engine to let the Maria Juana coast while 'Ned baptisin' heself'.

Ned ducked his head under the water and opened his eyes, though he preferred to swim with a mask. The salt stung his dark brown skin, burned his eyes.

There were turtles, bigger than he was in his fragmented vision, their fins paddling them along in a clumsy ballet as the light shone green onto their shells.

'Greenbacks!' he yelled to Spencer who was hanging over the side, a gun in his hand. 'Don't spear any of these!'

'You gone soft in de head, mahn. Dey is worth a fortune.'

Ned gulped air and ducked under again.

264

He swam powerfully, fast through the warm seas, keeping pace with the greenbacks, reaching out to try to grasp a shell. There were tales of sailors riding hawksbills, leatherbacks and even these rare, endangered beauties. He wondered if he could persuade this one up to the surface, but it twisted away from him before he could get a firm hold, disappearing into a cloud of seaborne sand.

He and the greenback were heading towards a coral reef, the ripples of dune-like sand punctuated by enormous sea urchins, like sputniks with their evil, poison-tipped spines waving in the currents. He dreaded swimming in coral. Thank Christ the boat should be holding a steady course out of it.

The smooth sheet of sea was broken as he bobbed upwards, his appearance heralded by the silver bubbles of air that broke through the water tension.

He'd swum away from the boat, and it was still moving. The seas around the Maria Juana were dark – darker even than the area he was in. Red-brown shadows played around the boat like ribbons of rain. It meant that they were ploughing straight into a reef.

He tucked his head down and race-crawled after it.

'We lost you, mahn,' said Keith. 'Where you went?'

'There's a coral reef,' gasped Ned, gulping air as he climbed the rope back into the schooner. 'It might be low stuff, it might not be. But you're steering into it.'

'Not possible.'

'Oh yes it frigging well is.' He strode over the decks like a bull. 'Michel!' he yelled down to the galley. 'Get up here and take this wheel.'

The crew peered anxiously over the rails, and sure enough, the barriers were rising towards them, like submarine mountains. Bright fish glimmered through the turrets and castles of the skeletal coral.

Great fingers of the bone-like mass pointed at them.

'How is it on de odder side, Cinnamahn?' asked Gonzo.

It was the same. The coral was high. Another fifty thousand years and it would be a new coral island.

They cut the motor and watched the sails that hardly moved. The breeze had dropped. Keith tacked them as the others leaned over to call directions, spotting first one tower of coral, then another.

Ned, pulling on his shorts, felt the sun burning his back. He turned and watched in horror as it began its drift downwards towards the sea. Within an hour, probably far less, it would be dark. And any one of these treacherous columns of coral could rip into the hull unseen and without warning.

'We'll try to find a relatively clear patch,' he shouted. 'Then we'll anchor and hope we don't drift too much in the night.'

'De coral might finish widdin a mile or so,' said Gonzo hopefully.

'It might not.'

There was a respite in the reef, low coral here. Keith jumped overboard and Ned viciously threw goggles in after him. Keith spat on the inside of the glass to stop them fogging up, pulled them over his head and dived under to see what the prospects were.

Then he was back. 'Anchor here, Ned,' he shouted. 'Dere's plenty of room, even if we drift. But we surrounded by coral peaks when we sail tomorrow.'

'Thanks to you! How did you manage to fuck this one up, Keith?'

'I fucked up nothin'! Give me a hahnd to get in. Dis coral where it not supposed to be.'

'You mean it's uncharted? Crap!'

'Dere's no coral on dat map. We was sailin' directly south past Saba. De coral over in de east. Right?'

They stormed into the pilothouse, both looking as though they might fight, and Ned thumped the charts with his fist. 'You have to be absolutely precise going round Saba – you *know* that. Saba Bank – '

'Ned – look at de sun – '

'For Christ's sake – a weather report? Now?'

'Look, mahn!'

It was straight ahead, almost level with them.

'Now look at de compass. De needle says de sun's settin' in de *south west*.'

Ned glared at the needle without seeing it. Then he banged on the glass angrily. The pointer fell and then juddered back to its false north. 'Somebody's been at this ship,' he muttered. 'Who the hell is it Keith?'

It was a strange feeling, knowing that somebody wanted him dead. It wasn't just a question of immobilising the Maria Juana. The instruments were as vital to life on the sea as they were in a plane. If they'd been using the compass on the hurricane night instead of the stars and sextant, they'd have been half way to nowhere when the engine packed in. They might even have headed dead into the storm.

'I'm sorry I blamed you,' he said. 'I should have known better. You're a good guy.'

'Forget it, mahn.'

'Some "sea captain", huh?'

'De best. An' doan forget dat.'

They roped the sails and nobody bothered to put a new tape on the machine as the sun hit the ocean head-on.

Ned resented outside interference from god or from nature. He liked to make his own decisions, liked to be in charge of his own destiny. If the wind had blown him towards Nevis, he'd maybe have wanted to go the other way. And now that the dark was preventing him from returning to Hope, that, in all the world was what he wanted most.

Chapter Nineteen

NELSON PLANTATION was strangely quiet without
Veronica and Lottie. Outside, it was the same as ever: the
bananaquit birds pounced on abandoned sugar bowls and
bleeped enthusiastically about their luck; Jack Spaniel flies,
almost as big as hummingbirds, stayed airborne with
difficulty, dipping heavily as they remembered that flying
for them was an aerodynamic impossibility.

But inside, in the silence, Julian Winchester thought
wistfully of his guests who were even now on their way back
to civilisation. He looked around his comfortable office and
sighed. He needed a break – not a long one, heavens above,
he could never give Nevis up for good. Just a couple of
months back in Oxford was all he wanted.

The rap on the door startled him. He had almost
forgotten he still had Jessica around. She came in without
waiting for the reply that hovered unspoken on his lips.

'I've been thinking, Jules,' she announced. 'What do
you reckon to sending the Bechstein over as a wedding
present for Ronnie?'

He frowned. Disruption loomed. 'She doesn't want any
of that old stuff back, Jess. They're just relics.'

'Old friends!'

'Relics.' He was going to put his foot down. Veronica
liked things the way they were at the Nelson. Anyway, she
and Stuart Wilding could buy their own Bechstein if they
wanted to.

'Well I was only thinking of it as a gesture. Something
else then. One of the pictures, maybe.'

Jessica had always listened respectfully to his advice till
this last couple of days. Now she was on about the water
system, getting transport for the guests to use – everything.

Julian eyed her suspiciously and wondered if she'd attended an assertiveness course recently. She'd certainly changed, but was it for the better?

'Lottie said that I led a quiet life you know Jules.'

Jessica was sitting in *his* leather chair nibbling cashews out of the bowl on his desk.

Julian pounced on the last of the nuts before they all disappeared. 'I'm sure you won't mind my saying that it's your own fault she thinks so. All this hush-hush business about your investments. She thinks you're still living on the fruits of your divorce. An Alimony Wife.'

'Yes,' she said decisively. 'I know. I never told her because I was worried she'd criticise, say I was doing the wrong things.

'And that would have had me doubting myself even more than I already did.'

'No self-confidence, that's the problem with you, Jess.'

'I never really believed I was in control.'

Julian felt a sinking feeling. 'But now you do?'

'Yes.'

He paced around his office, patting his thinning hair and worrying.

'Julian – ' she said. 'I've decided I'm going to take a much more active part from now on. I really should learn to trust my own judgement.' Her face glowed with Enthusiasm and Purpose. 'Fortunately it's not too late.'

She shifted the untidy paperwork on his desk into a pile, stacking the memos, bills and receipts decisively, like a pack of cards.

'And you want to look around too. Change your perspective. See your life from the outside.'

Julian's life was very comfortable, thank you. A bit dull perhaps, a bit in need of variety but –

'You should give Hope Parnell a bit of competition,' Jessica was saying. 'She's got things all her own way at the moment. The Nelson's got bags of potential, but it's not exploited to the full . . . It looks so dilapidated outside, it's enough to put people off. It's faded. Neglected almost

'You want new plumbing in. And a new chef. Simon wouldn't know what to do with a plantain if you peeled it

269

for him. And after all we are in the West Indies – not Indonesia. And, Julian,' she said conclusively, 'like it or not, that Bechstein's going back to Ron. So that's that.'

Julian folded his arms, sat down in the smaller chair opposite her and reluctantly resigned himself to an ambitious future filled with promise and optimism . . .

'Fair enough,' he sighed. 'It's your hotel. You're the boss.'

Lottie and Veronica felt it was time wasted. Sitting in the airport like this. They could have had a few more hours in the sunshine.

They hadn't been told when they arrived that the plane was going to be delayed. There had been no announcements, even when the time for departure was long passed. Once you were on your way out of the Caribbean, thought Lottie, you might as well not exist for all the notice that was taken of you.

'Do you think there's something serious wrong with the plane?' she asked.

'Wouldn't they have said?'

'Well wouldn't they have said if there was just going to be this sort of delay?'

Veronica was hot and tense. 'Don't ask me,' she said.

For the third time, she got up to walk around the departure lounge. There was no air conditioning and it was so terribly stuffy. No air at all came through the downward slanting vents of the windows.

She tried to walk out through the door, on to the sheltered area this side of the runway, but a woman in a brown uniform sent her back inside as though she were a straying sheep. 'More den my job is worth to let you come out heres,' she said.

'I'm not going to get in the way – I only want some fresh air – '

The woman lolled against a pillar, basking in the sunshine, watching the inactivity around the big Boeing.

'Do you know what's wrong with this BA flight?' asked Veronica, keeping her talking so that she might gain a few more precious moments in the open.

270

The woman shrugged, looking at Veronica as though she were a revolutionary. 'Now please go inside, mahdam. It's very dangerous to be out heres.'

Veronica turned on her heel. 'Dangerous? Oh yes, all these planes coming and going with this monotonous regularity,' she snapped sarcastically. 'One could be crushed to death at any moment.' The remark seemed to have gone unheard.

Lottie was also arguing when she got back. 'Well how much longer?' she was saying to the man who strode this way and that, very importantly, a radio to his ear.

He shook his head, not listening to her.

'I said *when* are you expecting this plane to take off? It's been sitting right there on the runway for *hours*!'

No reaction. He didn't even look at her, being far too grand to answer a question from a passenger.

'What is the matter with you, man? Are you blind or am I invisible?'

'Calm down, Lottie,' said Veronica. 'Though I know there's nothing worse than not knowing, not being told anything.'

'It's the being treated like I'm a moron that drives me mad.'

They sat down and propped their feet up on the plastic tables in front of them. Instantly the deaf, dumb and blind official was onto them. 'Get de feet off de tables,' he said. 'You cahn't read de signs? It say No Feet On Table.'

'Right,' said Lottie. 'It doesn't say No Arse On Table.' She stood up and sat down again, very deliberately, on the plastic table.

Then there was the announcement. Very garbled. Only a bit apologetic. There was a problem with re-fuelling. British Airways regrets . . . blah . . . blah . . . The plane could be ready to depart in an hour . . . Maybe.

Lottie snorted. 'We've wasted hours. We could have gone shopping here if we'd known. Gone for a meal or something.'

'Not to worry,' said Veronica. 'I know it's bloody frustrating sitting here and watching the thing standing idly

271

by, but it does sound as though we'll soon be on our way home.'

Hope had gone off to replace her essential clothes while she was waiting for the incoming plane. She took a taxi to the capital, St John's, where most of the island's population milled aimlessly, looking into shop windows where a single pair of sandals could cost them a week's wage, blocking roads to exchange hurricane disaster stories through open car windows, haggling over the price of grapefruit sold from crates on street corners.

The shops in the High Street were crammed with tourist goods at tourist prices; pretty batik fabrics made into unflattering dresses and skirts, warri boards, coral necklaces, Mary hats, steel band records.

St John's had escaped the hurricane's wrath completely. That had been graciously saved for the shanty towns and the matchstick houses in the hills where the people wouldn't notice just one more disaster.

Hope headed into St Mary Street to find the Palm Bay Boutique where prices were more reasonable and the fashion designs were better than anywhere else.

The woman behind the counter looked at her in disbelief as she strode in wearing the leather flying suit and boots. She looked disreputable.

Hope scooped up armfuls of Sea Island cotton gowns, Italian jeans, French evening dresses and shirts, shorts and tops from the racks and the shelves.

'Is mahdam tryin' on ahll dese garments?' the assistant said, raising eyebrows suspiciously.

'Yep. Okay?' Hope fled behind a screen and fabrics billowed as they were thrown on, cursorily examined and accepted or rejected. Two heaps grew on the floor.

She emerged looking ruffled, stuffing the scarf into a hip pocket, reaching for her credit cards.

'These, please,' she said. 'Don't bother with the tissue paper. Just pop them in a big bag for me.'

Then, like a whirlwind, she was out of the boutique and swinging down to a fabric shop to buy materials for Pansy to do something special with. She found glimmering

272

Siamese silks, lengths of embroidered cotton lawn, brightly patterned organza. They were a deductible expense. A hotelier had to look the part occasionally.

With rolls of material and bags under her arms, she raced back to find a taxi. Time sped in the islands, in direct contrast to the way you felt like moving.

'Airport,' she said and climbed into the back of a once-yellow Ford. The driver nodded and put a Darcy's Steel Band cassette into the player, thinking she was a tourist.

There were windswept plains where the cotton plants had been, shattered groves where palm trees had grown before the storm. The low concrete houses looked dirtier than usual. Every so often there was a pile of rubbish that might have been somebody's home till yesterday.

They drove along the dual carriageway to the airport where everything was barren and laid waste. She shook her head with sorrow for the island.

'*Veronica Tells MP I Will*'.

The words swam in and out of focus on the cover of the paper that the man on the other side of the aisle was reading.

At first they didn't register. And then they did. Stuart Wilding closed his eyes and opened them again. The words were still there. He leaned forwards in his seat to see them more clearly. '*Veronica Tells Mp I Will*'.

His breathing was irregular and shallow, his heart was threatening to stop beating.

It could be another Veronica. Any old MP. No it couldn't. This news headline was in direct reply to a proposal he didn't know he'd made. And she'd said yes.

The aircraft hummed as it changed altitude, beginning its descent already. The pilot was apologising again for the slight delay.

How strange to make a proposal through the eyes of the world and to have it accepted in the same way. And not even to know it had happened until it was all over.

The man was folding up the *Independent* and tucking it into the pouch in front of him with the brochures and the menus.

273

Stuart leaned across and said: 'Do you mind? May I see?'

He passed it over, looking at Wilding, recognising him from the photographs, the television.

'Congratulations,' he said wryly.

And so it was confirmed. Veronica told the MP she would, by proxy. The last to know. He had been the last to know. A long-distance love-letter.

He hadn't even known he'd formally asked her to marry him at the Press Conference. But obviously someone – presumably a newsman – had interpreted his feelings accurately and put them to Ron in Nevis.

And she'd accepted.

It was the most impossible, wonderful thing that had ever happened to him. He felt as though he was reeling from a blow or a kiss. He needed his life to slow down, his world to stop turning, so that there was enough time to do everything twice, savour every moment again. He'd wasted so much of it till now. Without Veronica.

'I didn't know,' he said to the man who had lent him the paper.

'Everybody else did,' he grinned back.

He wanted to ask about yesterday's news now, wanted to know how his proposal had been made. But he couldn't. It would be far too foolish. And he had his answer before him. He didn't need the question too.

– She will be my wife –

Could any proposal have ever been made or accepted so publicly before?

He couldn't believe it. What had changed her mind?

He'd been so sure he'd have to face many more rejections from Veronica before he could persuade her that what they both wanted wasn't wrong. That it wasn't wrong to love someone you couldn't help loving whether you were married to another woman or not. Feelings didn't respect convention or signatures on a legal document.

And Veronica had accepted what he already knew. What he'd known for a very long time. She had been able to reconcile herself to one man. Just one. Him. If this hadn't been so, no way would she have made the decision that was

274

here in black and white. This commitment.

Thank God. Thank God.

'He is the only man I love. I accept his proposal. I will marry him as soon as he is free.'

Stuart knew they weren't Veronica's words: they were a reporter's dramatisation of what she'd said. But they were enough to tell him the truth.

Stuart had bought her a ring, a single fire opal set in a plain gold band. It burned his hand reassuringly as he felt for it in his pocket. So the ring hadn't been just wishful thinking after all.

The cabin staff were collecting headphones, empty glasses, exchanging smiles and oozing conviviality at the passengers.

'Any more news about conditions out here?' he asked the stewardess.

Since the announcement at Heathrow, very little had been said.

'Pretty bad I gather, sir. That's why we're late. The pilot took a short detour. But the runway was cleared in Antigua this morning and cleaning up operations are happening everywhere.'

'Any news about the other islands? Nevis?'

'I'll ask the pilot, sir,' she said. 'He can radio through for you.'

She was back a few minutes later and telling him there were over thirty dead or missing. First estimates had been much higher but they had proved wrong.

'Any British people involved?' He knew Veronica would be all right. She was the last person to take risks in a storm.

'None that we know of.'

The fasten seat belts lights flashed and they were coming down through the clouds. There had been so little turbulence as they'd diverted to skirt around Cleo's shock waves that they'd hardly noticed it. The hurricane had meant nothing more to them than a short detour southwards.

It was nearly dusk in that other world down there. Night-time in England. And Stuart Wilding was oh so tired. So warm. So content.

The no smoking signs were switched on, and passengers yawned to release the pressure in their ear-drums.

There was Antigua, now, its frayed edges like fingers in the sea. He could make out boats in the cays, buildings like matchboxes.

The plane circled, went out to sea again, and back over the island, lower and closer. Now he could see palm trees standing isolated instead of in their usual clumps. There was the airport, its lights on already, and that big sun bursting. The runway would soon be looming up to meet them.

The Caribbean steel band music was chiming through the cabin, and together with the rushing of the air it signalled a change for the better in the outside temperature.

Hope walked through to the departure lounge. She was never bothered by the customs men at Antigua who knew and liked her. She'd hardly ever had to produce identification or papers. It made life easier.

'Still here, poor you!' she called to Lottie and Veronica and sat with them for a moment. 'If I'd known about the delay in advance, I'd have flown you over later. I'm terribly sorry for you. It must have been awful – all this waiting around in the heat.'

Veronica looked tired and strained, and very, very hot. Lottie had her lips pinched tight together and was still sitting on the uncomfortable table. It was the principle of the thing.

'I thought you'd be heading back to Nevis,' said Veronica.

Hope shook her head. 'I'm waiting for a passenger on the flight that's due in. That's a bit late too. He's staying at the Sugar Mill.'

They lapsed into silence, Hope looking for the aeroplane in the sky, Lottie glaring at the abandoned jet on the runway.

'You didn't stay long this time, Veron,' said Hope eventually. She didn't mean to pry. It was only conversation.

Veronica smiled: 'Domestic crisis.'

'Actually, she's going home to get married,' said Lottie. 'You've heard of Doctor – '

'Lottie. Don't exaggerate, please,' said Veronica. 'I'm not getting married for ages yet, just reconciling myself to its inevitability.'

'That sounds a bit grim,' said Hope. 'I hope it's not.'

'Veronica's low because she's leaving the West Indies,' said Lottie. 'I've told her she can always come back when things are settled between the two of them.'

At last, lights appeared in the dimming sky, engine sounds roared distantly. The plane grasped the last of the sun to flash at the passengers waiting in the terminal.

'Lucky you. Here's your man coming in. On the other hand, I think we are stranded forever,' said Veronica. 'I take delays so seriously.

'They're almost a personal insult. You feel as though people are trying to thwart your most basic need to get to your own home.'

There was a huge roar from the jets. Birds fluttered suicidally in its path. The jumbo crossed in front of the airport building at eye-level and disappeared to taxi to the arrivals entrance.

'I'd better go,' said Hope. 'Get ready to collect my chap and whisk him through customs. Have a great flight home, you two. And hurry back soon as you can. Bring your medical man with you next time, Veron.'

They watched her race out, feeling finally abandoned.

There was a crackling from the Tannoy, a spluttering, as a voice announced that passengers for Heathrow should now prepare to board Flight BA 630.

Lottie's cloud suddenly vanished. Veronica sighed with relief. The wasted hours no longer mattered.

The new arrivals were climbing slowly down the aircraft steps, stunned, as always, by the heat. Dr Stuart Wilding felt as though he could tear down mountains. He threw back his head and laughed as he remembered this warm, damp smell, the hot winds, the taste of grouper and of Planters Punch.

277

'Mister Wilding?' said Hope to each male passenger travelling alone as they reached the bottom of the steps.

'That's me,' he called from halfway up.

'IN-Flight, sir. Can I help you with your bags?'

Wilding smiled, held a briefcase aloft and said no. 'There's only this. I've got stuff to get from baggage collection, though.'

'Fine. Did you fill in your immigration card?'

He reached into his top pocket as they walked swiftly to the stubbornly silent conveyor belts inside the terminal. 'Here.'

'Oh sorry. I see it's Doctor Wilding. Not Mister.'

When Veronica glanced through the glass partition that separated the arriving passengers from the departing ones, she couldn't see Hope. Around her, people were gathering books, cardigans, handbags and duty free carriers. Veronica began to hunt for her boarding card.

Hope and Stuart Wilding talked about the hurricane, the delayed flight. Hope said: 'I had two passengers from Nevis who've been stuck here for hours.'

Stuart wasn't paying attention. He was waiting for the first of the bags to shuffle through the rubber door at the far end of the conveyor. They were in the centre of a crowd of travellers now. Invisible, like rugby players at the bottom of a scrum.

'Hope Parnell must have got away quickly,' Lottie said.

Veronica peered through the glass wall again. 'Or else she's being crushed. Watch out, we'll be boarding soon.'

'Soon? You mean at last, don't you?'

A black woman was rounding up six small children, wiping noses, smoothing down pig-tails, pulling cotton dresses straight. Officials were striding importantly to barriers, taking up positions to justify their existence. Electric trolleys were buzzing in all directions.

'What a contrast,' said Lottie. 'There's so much activity going on now it's like a cyclone.'

Veronica said: 'Don't even mention the word wind to me again.'

In Arrivals, the conveyor-belt rumbled into life, jerking and thrusting emptily forwards. 'False alarm,' laughed Hope.

It juddered again, spat and then the first of the bags came through in a heap, looking as though they'd faced the Spanish Inquisition.

'Those are mine,' said Stuart, pointing as the two leather cases came out side by side. He and Hope swooped on them, like people who are afraid somebody might steal their dearest possessions from under their noses.

'Great, we'll get off quickly, if you don't mind. Otherwise we'll be stranded until that British Airways monster has taken off.

'It's that little plane.' She pointed to the Cessna across the tarmac.

The frogs were already chirruping. 'That's a welcome sound,' he said as they strode out to the craft. 'I've looked forward to hearing it again.'

'You've been before?'

'Twice. I usually stay at the Nelson, but I'll tell you about it later.'

In Departures, the boarding lights were flashing, and Veronica and Lottie joined the queue.

Hope lifted the hatch at the back of the Cessna and Stuart tossed in the suitcases. 'Do I get to ride in the front?' he said.

'Wherever you like,' said Hope, springing into the cockpit. 'You're the only passenger.' He climbed in after her and settled into the seat. This was the last lap. He buckled on his belt, and looked out of the window to pity the poor stragglers who were heading back to a grey English summer.

Hope was reading co-ordinations into the radio, getting clearance for take-off, going through the pre-flight checks.

Stuart Wilding watched as the crocodile of travellers filed towards the two flights of steps.

Hope boosted her engines and began to taxi past the big plane that was bound for Heathrow

The passengers were climbing now. Hope grinned as she saw Veronica and Lottie waving goodbye to the little Cessna.

And suddenly, there was a choking, gasping sound behind her. She twisted round and the man was taking off his seat belt, staggering around, swaying against the movement of the tiny plane.

'Doctor Wilding – What are you doing? What is the matter?'

He knocked her elbow as he pushed forwards, jerking the yoke so that the little plane swerved towards the runway lights.

'Stop it, stop it, stop it . . . ' he croaked, almost unintelligibly.

'For God's sake! Are you ill? What is it Doctor Wilding? We could have crashed – '

He was nearly crying. 'That's Veronica. My God. Stop this plane.'

He knocked on the window furiously with white knuckles. 'Ron! Ron!' he screamed, but she was stepping in through the doorway. Of course she couldn't hear him.

Hope slowed to a halt, blasting retros, speaking rapidly into the radio so the traffic controllers should know she was aborting take-off.

Almost before the Cessna had come to a dead stop, the madman was fiddling with the door locks. 'What is all this, Doctor Wilding?' she said desperately, though she was beginning to work it all out.

'Later!'

He was out onto the tarmac and running for the Boeing. A spot lamp fell on him and a West Indian voice boomed distortedly through a Tannoy. *'Off de runway. De plane is ready for take-off. Cahn you hear me? Off de runway.'*

He took no notice, desperate to reach the plane before it could take her away. He'd been so close he could have touched her, held her, if only he'd known.

'Get the steps back!' he screamed as overalled workers began to push the ramps away from the doors.

Bolts were being drawn, handles pulled to fasten the doors in place.

The captain was welcoming passengers aboard.

Someone behind Veronica said something about a terrorist at the airport.

'All these crises!' she laughed to Lottie. 'Hope we get away quickly, before anything else holds us back.'

She put down her book and looked out of the window. She looked down into the murky darkness. And she saw him there.

Stuart –

Stuart – and armed guards, and mechanics and uniformed officials . . .

'Oh my God,' she said, and unfastened her seat belt. She stood up, saying, 'Look Lottie . . . '

'Nothing to worry about, madam,' said a stewardess, firmly pushing her back down again. 'We'll be taking off any minute.'

'I have to get off – ' gasped Veronica.

'She has to get off – ' echoed Lottie urgently.

'Nonsense dear. Don't worry about anything. Is this her first flight?'

Veronica felt as though she was strangling. Choking. She forced the hand away from her shoulder and stood up again, swaying into the aisle, past Lottie's knees.

'Let me off.' She said it slowly, punctuating each word with a beat of the heart. There was panic in her voice.

'You'll be fine once we're in the air, you'll see. No need to – '

Veronica clenched her teeth and slapped the simpering, stupid woman's face, hard. A red hand-print flared instantly upon her cheek.

She jerked sideways from the blow and stood open-mouthed, gazing at the tall woman.

'Will you listen to me and stop treating me like a child, for God's sake! I am not hysterical though I soon shall be. That man down there – the one being surrounded, *look*

281

woman damn it! being surrounded by the police – it's Doctor Stuart Wilding. And I am Veronica Marston.'

The stewardess glanced sideways, unwilling to take her eyes off her unexpected assailant.

'Now, will you please, *please* let me off?'

The stewardess backed away and spoke to the other members of the cabin staff who had gathered to find out what was happening. Someone had already pushed the panic button.

Veronica banged her knuckles on the window frantically, and Stuart looked up. Saw her there. Mouthed something. Tried to shake off the armed policemen. Hope was running up to them, waving her arms around like a windmill.

'We've called for the steps, madam,' said the air hostess stiffly.

The door was being opened and Veronica stood there in the opening almost hopping with impatience, waiting to be able to get down to him.

Stuart Wilding looked up at her with unbearable joy, and the restraining arms of the security guards released him as they took in what Hope Parnell was saying.

He was almost climbing the steps before they were secured properly. She was halfway down them before they were bolted into place. And they were in each other's arms, feeling that other life swell inside them, forgetting all the bad things, feeling only each other. Oh the relief, the incredible relief and joy, the rightness of it all.

She was sobbing into his hair, he was pressing her to him as though he wanted to merge with her. And they were kissing. Talking in inarticulate, meaningless sentences, though each understood.

How good that rough chin felt against her face. How tender those strong hands were.

How fragile she was. How she trembled.

When her breath would allow it, she said: 'That was the most romantic proposal in the world, Stuart.'

'Your acceptance could have made me cry. And it's true, isn't it. It really is true.'

'Did you know already? Did you get my letter?'

He shook his head. 'No. I didn't need any letter. I'd

282

have waited for you to work out your feelings. You'd find out, some time, and when you did, I would still have been there. Still waiting.'

She laughed. 'But you didn't wait at all – you came all this way – '

'I know – and when I saw you on those steps, Ron, I thought I was going to miss you. See you taken eight thousand miles away from me again, because of a couple of minutes' inaction.'

Her face fell. 'Has it been terrible at home? The publicity?'

'This sounds silly, but I don't know! And it's not terrible. Not any more. It doesn't matter.' He had his hands on her shoulders. 'This is what matters.' He was absorbing her, clinging onto her lest she slip away, like a ghost, like a dream. 'What made you change your mind?' he asked at last. 'You're so bloody obstinate normally.'

'Loneliness. Nevis. I missed you.'

Lottie was calling to them from the doorway above them. 'Are you coming or going?' she said. 'You can't stop where you are. These people up here are going mad.'

Veronica said: 'Going – I mean we're staying in Nevis. That's right, isn't it Stuart? We'll stay now?'

He nodded contentedly.

'But what about you? Oh Lottie, what about you?'

'Worry about yourselves,' said Lottie. 'I'm fine. Really. I'm well-pleased with myself.'

Yes, thought Veronica. That was the way it should be. 'Will you watch my bags for me at the other end?' she called.

'Of course. But don't you want these things?' She waved Veronica's handbag and hat at her and started walking gingerly down the steps to them.

They hugged and felt close. 'Love you, silly bitch. Your passport's in here. Where would you be without me?' she said quietly.

Veronica smiled. 'Somehow, Lottie, I don't think I'd be here.'

On board a riot was breaking out.

Veronica and Stuart held each other. She buried her head against his shoulder, wrapped her arms around him. His leg brushed hers and he glowed at the touch of her

The storms that waited for them on distant shores no longer held any terror for them. For they no longer had to face them alone.

They walked down the steps side by side, sharing the same shadow.

Chapter Twenty

'RIGHT, YOU prick! You just fuck off back to Hollywood if that's what you want to do.' She flung her suitcase on to the bed and there was a sickening crack as glass shattered inside.

Karin Genevieve still looked shitty. And King wasn't into messes, especially when the mess had something wrong with its once-perfect right tit.

'I plan to. Just as soon as I can shake myself free of this fuckin' albatross that's bin hangin' round my neck this last coupla months!' he bellowed back at her.

He'd had plenty of second thoughts since that boat journey. He didn't like it when people made a fuss over nothing, and getting across from St Croix to San Juan had been a royal pain in the ass. Non-stop complaints. He could have used a full-time Customer Relations Manager on this trip.

He regretted the double room, and he regretted ever having gotten in so deep with the Genevieve bitch. He should have switched to the kid Jewel when he'd had the chance and stopped *her* gettin' herself into trouble.

Karin looked at the space where her right breast should have been. Now how the hell could she get her body insured? How could she sue Hope Parnell if her body was worthless? She lashed out at King. 'You're in trouble, boy, if you run out on me – '

'If you ever thought I was plannin' to take you all the way to Detroit, babe, you have been under a serious misconception. Just 'cause I laid you, it don't mean we're man an' wife for ever and ever amen. Right?'

'You didn't lay me, King-prick, you laid me out, o-u-t. But you owe me.'

He bulged his eyes at her in mock amazement.

'That's right. You *owe* me. I've given you a great time and you promised me – '

He snarled: 'I promised you nothin'. I don't pull the strings with Perce. If he says you're not right for that next movie – '

'You and your big influence!'

Karin walked dramatically round the room, rubbing her head with both palms to indicate the severity of the headache King had given her. She posed in front of the window to let him take in her still-wonderful back-view. 'You took me for a real ride, didn't you King-baby?' she spat.

'Pretty words from the pretty lady,' bawled King. 'But soft talk means nothing from you. You, lady, are a shit-actress. You can't even come without givin' it away you're fakin' it. My wife – for Chrissake, my own wife – is better at it than you!'

'Right!' she screamed. 'Get me on a plane now. Get me back to Detroit. The sooner the better. I don't wanna see your face around here till I'm out of this hell-hole.'

'It will be my greatest pleasure to do this small service for you,' he said courteously. A mock-bow. 'May I suggest Modom takes a drink in the fuckin' bar while I run her fuckin' errands for her?'

'Piss off,' howled Karin as she slammed her way through the door. It bounced open again and King kicked it on the rebound with his foot. He'd have liked to gloat to her about the Terry-trick, but it would have been an own goal since she'd said the sex had been so great. So he picked up the phone and booked Karin a very long trip home. She'd be flying via Jamaica, Mexico, New Orleans and Washington. He'd have made the journey even longer if he could.

An hour later, Karin ordered bags and cases into a car and refused to speak to either of her former colleagues.

Perce watched as the departing taxi took her off-stage to San Juan International. The cab literally bulged with the massive trunks that would cost her a fortune in excess baggage at every airport she stopped at.

Strange lady, that, he thought, a real prima donna

without a cause. Things kept on goin' her way and she kept right on duckin' them.

He shuffled back to the bar for a tomato juice. And forgot her.

Georges Deneuil felt he'd survived a hurricane *and* an earthquake the last week. His wife had gone. Flown home to Canada. And this girl that he hardly knew was still here, cooking his meals, putting her clothes in his wardrobe.

'Shouelle,' he called.

And there she was, materialising out of thin air, ready to give him whatever he needed.

'Yes darling?' said Jewel. She was whirling in a cloud of bliss. How could life work out so wonderfully?

'Where did you repose my briefcase?' he said in the thick French-Canadian accent.

'You mean, where did I put it. *Put,* Georges. It's here,' she said, reaching behind the sofa. 'You aren't going to work now are you? Dinner's nearly ready.'

'No, I do not work. I jus' want to speak to you. I want to see if you are still 'ere.'

Jewel snuggled into his lap and took the smouldering pipe from his lips. Smelly thing.

When he went back to work next week, she'd really get going. Make some changes. Rearrange the furniture. Spray the place with Odorgon. Hire a new cook to replace the one who'd walked out with Marie.

'Of course I'm still here, sweetheart,' she said, kissing him lightly on the end of his nose. She wrapped her arms around his neck till he felt he was suffocating. 'I always will be here. Always and always.'

There was so much she could do with a lot of money. And this placid, middle-aged man would go wherever she wanted, buy her everything, follow her anywhere. She felt sure of it.

He was the best thing that had ever happened to her.

'And we will get married, won't we Georges?'

'Shouelle,' he said, frowning. 'I 'ave a wife.'

She cuddled up to him and smiled reassuringly. 'Yes, but not for long.'

287

Should he tell her? Should he confess that he was a Catholic and that he would never divorce Marie? Some other time would do.

She dropped another kiss on his cheek and one for luck on his forehead. She had already written a long letter to Mommy, telling her of her good fortune. She hadn't mentioned the problem of the wife, but she had gone into great detail about the bank she was planning to marry.

'We can fly my folks over for the wedding, can't we Georges?' she mused. 'I don't want to get married in the States. In the rain. In winter. And I guess it will be winter by the time everything's sorted out.'

Georges said: 'Of course, Shouelle.' Another one for Confession.

How the hell had he got into this situation? It could only be the rarified atmosphere of Nevis, he decided. It made one wild, irrational. And now the girl was talking about air fares for her family! Ha! It was *incroyable!*

Georges Deneuil thought about his bank account. He just about had enough ready cash to get himself back to Quebec, should the worst come to the worst. And how long would this woman stay around if she knew that?

It would be a pity to see her go. A tragedy to break her heart. For the time being, he would let her be happy in her ignorance. He owed her that much. She deserved happiness, this pretty young thing. He would give it to her. He would see to it that she shouldn't be hurt, for at least a month.

The night was noisy with the sounds of the screaming tree-frogs. Hope had planned to have an early night – even though she'd woken up so late that morning.

But she kept on thinking of Veronica-and-Stuart. Stuart-and-Veronica. How could she ever sleep with the memory of the two of them so fresh in her mind? She didn't envy them – on the contrary – it gave her hope. From what Stuart had said on the flight back to Nevis, their relation-ship had appeared impossible. And yet now they were together.

Was there any chance the impossible might become a

288

reality for her, too? It wasn't just Ned, it was the lack of love, the lack of companionship in her life that had left her wanting.

She put aside her book and poured herself a whiskey from the replenished drinks cabinet. It was hot tonight. Clammy. Maybe she should have another bath before she finally settled down.

There had been men before in her life: of course there had. A few of them had meant a lot to her. But none of them had immediately appeared to *fit*, the way Ned had done. In the past, she had loved, she had hurt and been hurt, but it was something she could exclude from her emotions. She could draw down that shutter so easily . . . except, for some reason, this time.

Ned was her absolute opposite: the north to her south. And her attraction to him had been irresistible. But perhaps she had misread his feelings. Maybe he hadn't felt that same magnetism, that same *completeness*.

She should have gone out with Esme tonight, she thought, annoyed that she'd refused earlier. They could have gone down to Rick's Bar or somewhere; she shouldn't have made excuses and sloped off to her room. She gazed out on the colourless gardens below, seeing only black and white in the light of the fierce moon.

A man's shadow moved across from the arbour and was gone. It startled her because movement was unexpected. It couldn't be Zeke: he'd be down in Charlestown with the others. She walked over to the wide windows and stared out. Nothing stirred. Perhaps she'd been mistaken then. Or perhaps it had been one of the goat boys, raiding her ruined vegetables.

Well that was okay. He didn't have to be sneaky about it – he could help himself. She pulled down the blinds to close out the night and wandered back into the bathroom.

With annoyance, she spotted that the alabaster soap dish was missing. That damn Genevieve woman.

Jack Spaniel flies, black as night, crashed crazily against the netting across the vents. Hope listened to their thudding for a few minutes and then pulled the slats closed.

Without the lamplight, they'd soon lose interest and head instead for the stars.

The stripes of light reflecting on the terrace outside disappeared, and Andrew Dean dropped to a crouch, squatting like a toad in the corner. In complete darkness, he waited. Invisibly, he hovered, listening to the water running, to the sounds of Hope stepping into the bath. He heard gentle splashes as she rubbed soap over her body, then rinsed it off.

She needed someone to talk to. Isolation wasn't good for her; Hope was a sociable animal. The only silence she loved was the silence of the air, when you were a mile high.

Soapily she reached for the wall-phone, planning to tell Esme she'd changed her mind about that late-night drink down at Rick's bar after all. There was a crackle as the connection was made slowly and then the ringing tone. It kept right on ringing and Hope eventually hung up.

Damn, she thought. But there must be someone else who wanted company – Hearing Hope's telepathic cry, Honest Joe trotted down the stairs from the sleeping gallery, ready to offer what companionship he could. 'They tell me friendship's a gas,' she said to him. 'I used to know but now I'm believing.'

He stretched up, hunched like an old man, putting his front paws on the edge of the bath, shaking them as he discovered the wetness for the first time. 'Don't you jump in you daft old sod,' she warned him. 'You don't like water.'

There was a rustle outside and Hope froze, listening. 'Ssh,' she said to stop Joe purring.

The night sounds were all so familiar, anything unusual was instantly discernible. Puzzling. Worrying. She stood up, making waterfalls, reaching for a towel. There it was again. Footsteps. Was it that bloody goat boy, turning into a peeping Tom –

God! – Or was it Ned?

The thought – the hope – struck her like lightning.

She jumped out of the bath and rushed for her cotton robe. She pulled it on, hurrying, panicking.

Maybe, maybe . . .

She was running to the door leaving wet footprints behind her on the marble. It could be Ned – he could be back! In fact, it *had* to be Ned. There was no one else. They were *his* footsteps. It had been *his* shadow!

He'd felt the same. He'd turned around at San Juan and come straight back to her!

The lock was stiff and she had to use both hands to force the key. Damn thing needed oiling. Jesus, it was gritty, the hurricane must have blown sand into the mechanism. 'Hang on!' she called. Through the filtered light of the rattan blind across the glass, she could see his outline.

She saw what she wanted to see.

She saw Ned.

Honest Joe tangled between her legs, ready to make a quick dash.

She threw back the bolt and, her face alive, hungry, wanting, she heaved back the door.

'Mahn, I got too much to worry about, widout callin' a whoale man-hunt for a missin' dronk. De whoale island in uproar after de blow yesterday an' you is goin' on like he de most important mahn since Martin Luther.'

Josiah Newcastle had not seen hide nor hair of the man he knew as Alan Walker since the night at The Rookery Nook. Something told him he should have done. 'You knowed I guddah sixth sense. Dis mahn causin' trobble somewheres. You de police – it your duty to locate he.'

'Go an' have anodder drink at de bar, mahn. Come back in an anodder hour. See somebody else. Not me.'

'C'mon, Mollina. I want to know what happnin'.'

The officer sighed exaggeratedly and reluctantly shuffled papers out of his desk drawer. He flicked through them to see if there were any unused missing persons reports left. There were. Unfortunately.

'Why is you so ahnxious to find dis boy?' he asked suspiciously. 'He got somethings you needin'?'

Josiah didn't really know why he was so bothered. 'Put it down to me bein' an Obimahn.'

He liked to keep tabs on things. Knowing what was

happening in an island where Events were usually few and far between was good for his image.

'Haven't you got too many bodies already on your hahnds after de storm, Joe, widout you wantin' more of de same?'

Josiah set his face resolutely. 'If dis mahn missin' den de police have a re-sponsibility to find out where he is. An' I filin' de report.'

Officer Mollina resigned himself to the task. All this fuss, when at home his brother and his sons were mending a roof that had been stripped away from its walls by the hurricane. It was late. Dark. He should have been off-duty by now, helping them.

Instead, he had the island crazy in the station. Just his bastard luck.

For a moment, time stopped as they looked into each other's eyes. There was a silence around them like a fire blanket, a darkness in which only the two of them were visible.

Then Andrew Dean lurched towards her, his mouth gaping, his hands like twisted branches reaching for her throat, his hatred oozing like quicksand to suck her in and suffocate her. The force of his attack sent her reeling backwards as she slammed against the door jamb and felt the sickening blow of the wood against her spine.

'No!' Hope screamed. She was up again, scrambling to her feet, running away from him, panting, crying with shock and terror, back into the bathroom where she could lock him out, keep him away from her.

The tiles were wet and she skidded, catching the edge of the door and slamming it to, just as he reached her. All her weight was against the barrier between them, but he was pushing from the other side, ramming into it, charging it, and it trembled and shook. The key, the key –

She looked around her desperately – not that too – Karin had taken everything – everything – even the bloody key that was no use to her but life or death now to Hope. She couldn't take her weight from the door to reach for a chair, a dresser, something to keep the door wedged shut. If she did, he'd be in here –

The door shuddered against her and she could hear him roaring, howling outside.

'What do you want Andrew?' she screamed.

'You!' he shouted and the door rammed back into her, knocking her away with its force.

'What his name?'

Josiah settled down comfortably in the chair opposite the desk. 'He Alan Walker. He address on top of dis sta-shun.'

'Date of birth?'

'I doan't know. He maybe thirty-five. Forty.'

Mollina wrote NOT KNOWN very slowly.

'What he do for a livin'?'

Josiah shrugged.

'Yuh doan' know nothin' about dis mahn, right, Josiah? You wastin' me time, an' I gettin' mahd. Passport number?'

'No.' Josiah wiped his nose on the back of his hand. 'Why we gotta fill in de forms, officah? Why doan' we just go an' look in de room upstairs. He could be dyin' right over our heads.'

They both looked gloomily at the ceiling and saw the rotting corpse of Walker.

Instant decision, that was what Station Officer Mollina prided himself upon. 'You winnin'. I get de key, mahn. It at Ma Johnson's.'

The officer was back quickly, shaking a massive bunch of keys on an iron ring.

They climbed the outside stairs, watching their feet in the dark, wondering if the wooden steps would bear their weight after the hurricane.

Hope staggered backwards, trying to get as far away as possible from him, looking for a weapon to hit back with. There was nothing – not an ashtray, not a bottle – nothing.

Dean was in front of her, hitting her, hating her and throwing her against the shower screen, snarling, hurling her back through the door and out into the room beyond.

She lost her balance, toppled and fell onto the sofa, her

293

gown coming apart, her cheeks flaming with the force of his blows.

His hand was around her wrist, using it as a lever to twist her further down, onto the floor. She screamed and his hand flashed again, striking her mouth.

'Bitch!' he spat, kneeling beside her, examining her eyes for fear and finding it. 'You knew I'd come back for you. You knew I wouldn't let it rest.'

He pulled off his belt and wound it around her wrists, ignoring her struggling as though she was a rag doll. His strength doubled as hers was halved.

She winced as the leather was pulled tight and she fought frantically to regain some control of herself. 'Why?' she screamed.

'You know,' he hissed, looking at her body contemptuously. 'Jesus, you're obscene. You disgust me.' He had to force himself to touch her with his bare hands. Her flesh turned his stomach.

'You're going to pay, Miss Parnell. This time you're really going to pay.'

She shook her head and her hair fanned around her like billowing silver seaweed. 'Andrew, I had no choice – '

His mouth gaped incredulously as he pressed the mirrors of his sunglasses inches away from her face. 'You destroyed me.'

She was shaking uncontrollably. 'No – no – it's not true.'

'Truth, bitch?' he howled. 'You and your truth. You *use* truth. You used it against me, to destroy Nicky's *love* for me. Jealous bitch! He loved me more than he'd ever loved you, and you couldn't bear it – '

'It's not so, Andrew – I had to tell him. It wasn't to destroy your relationship, you *know* that! I was never jealous – I had to stop you flying – you were dangerous – '

'Oh yes, Hope Parnell. I was dangerous. And believe me now. I still am.'

Don't let him think about the violence, about the blood . . . 'It wasn't just the deals, Andrew! I couldn't risk it. You were a killer in the air – '

Dean put a hand over her mouth to silence her. He didn't want this bullshit. He knew why she'd run back to

294

Nicky with her tales and her *truths*. She wouldn't deceive him again.

Hope tried to breathe and couldn't; her lungs refused to work while his hand was there. *Oh God* she screamed inside, *help me*. This time, she *knew* he was going to kill her.

There had been one lie.

Deception had brought Andrew Dean back to London. But it was Nick David's deception, not Hope's.

'Don't try to handle him on your own. Fly back with him, Hope. Keep him smiling . . . Tell him I can't live without him any more.'

Had Nick known, even then, what Dean was capable of?

The penthouse office was flooded with winter sunlight, the polished rosewood table reflected the lines of the Venetian blind. Nick, very civilised, very sophisticated, leaned back in his leather chair.

His face was blank and cold as he looked directly at Dean. There was no sign that there had ever been anything between them. Hope could hardly believe it. She'd always seen him as a sensitive man, someone who loved as deeply and passionately as she did. But maybe in his other life – the life she'd never understood – he was a different person –

'Methadone? Are you crazy?' he asked calmly. 'Are you completely out of your mind?'

Hope looked at Dean and saw how near the mark Nick was. She held out her hand in warning to him. 'Don't.'

Nick David turned on her. 'You've got to be kidding, Hope – after what you've told me?'

She was as angry as he. She had just as much right to be resentful. More, if anything. For months she'd had to watch Dean like a hawk till she was sure of her facts. And then she'd had to pretend there was nothing wrong till she could get him back to Nick. The sham had sickened her. But it was Nick's affair – he had the controlling interest in IN-Flight and she'd had to play it his way. Hope had argued they should go straight to the police – but Nick was so afraid of scandal, of being linked in any way with corruption –

'How many people know about this stuff?' said Nick angrily.

'Only Oz,' she replied. 'And Pansy.'

'Well, that's that then. It's going to be round the island in no time flat. It's the end of ₁N-Flight after all.

'You've ruined me, Dean. How is anyone going to trust the company when they find out that you've been drug-running?'

'No one knows!' spat Dean. 'I was never caught – only by your bitch-sister – '

'Huh,' he snorted. 'They soon will.'

'For God's sake, Nick!' shouted Hope. The loss of money, the loss of face was more important to him than anything. Was this what the world of high finance had done to him, or was it something that had come from his having led two lives for so long? 'Get it into perspective!' she snapped. 'What does it matter about the deals? That's over, and there won't be any repercussions, I promise you. It's more important that he was taking the stuff himself – he could have crashed into a school or houses or a hospital – '

Nick lit a cigar, oblivious to Dean's expression. 'You are a bloody fool,' he snorted. 'You told me you were all over that.'

'You've got to prosecute him, get rid of his pilot's licence,' Hope went on. 'If you do it here, there'll be no scandal that will reach the West Indies and harm IN-Flight.'

He knew she was right. He knew that he would have to publicly confess his affair with this hideous man. Sooner or later, he'd been bound to make a mistake. But he'd never seen that it could be so great a mistake. 'What was the matter? Wasn't the pay-off big enough for you? Wasn't I generous enough with the redundancy money?'

Dean's eyes narrowed to slits. They were the eyes of a reptile. 'Redundancy money?'

Nick spelled it out as though he were talking to a child: 'To compensate for the *end* of our relationship. To ensure your silence.'

Andrew Dean's face seemed to curl away from his teeth. He was trembling; his hand was inside his pocket, turning something round and round . . . 'There's no end, Nicky.' His voice was like steel. 'It's the beginning, not the end. We have our partnership to consider.'

'Partnership?' Nick laughed spitefully. Whatever gave you – '

Dean was crossing the room, his eyes wild. The blade flashed as he raised it. Not at Nick, but at Hope.

And the searing pain that struck through her was a dull ache, a blow. It had none of the sharpness of a burn or a cut . . . it was as though he'd struck her with his fist, with a hammer. His hands were round her throat and she was being dragged backwards as in turn he was being hauled away from her.

. . . And there was no pain, only rational thoughts, an interest almost, in whether or not she would die.

Hope's face was white as chalk, grey as parchment. Dean chuckled. Soon it would be redder than before, when he'd only managed to scrape at her –

This time he'd turn it into a radar screen.

Beneath his hand she struggled, moaned, but it was useless.

'Bitch!' he spat. He pressed his face close to hers. He could feel her hot breath, smell her fear. This was good. This was what he'd wanted.

She gasped, he was so close, so invasive, and he took away his hand to hear her rasping more clearly –

'Everything's come back to me, you see, Hopie. It's all clear as daylight now. I remember how Nick wanted to see me that day in London. How he was missing me. He loved me and he wanted me home. Till you made him angry with me.'

He knew she wouldn't move. She was rivetted to the spot. His captive audience. Slowly he released his hold on her to light a cigarette, holding the match flame dangerously close to her eyes, watching the light washing all the colour out of them.

Mesmerised, she stared at the yellow light till it burnt. But even when she closed them, the flame played on in her brain.

Almost tenderly, he stroked the planes of her face, feeling for the scar that had nearly disappeared. There it was, running behind the curtain of her hair. And there were the indentations on her throat that he'd made with his fingernails.

Almost conversationally he said: 'He loved me so fucking much he gave me my own plane.' He wagged his head, still marvelling that love had run so deeply.

'But you told him I was an addict, didn't you, that I wasn't fit to be a pilot – '

Hope shrank away from his snarling mouth. Did he really believe that? Was he really so far gone, so besotted with his crazy memories? And despite her terror she summoned the last of her strength to scream back at him: 'Nick gave you that Cessna to get *rid* of you! To get you out of his life!

'He ended up *hating* you!'

Oh God – what had she said?

'Liar!' he screamed. 'Bitch-liar! That blind eye, Hopie, the one you turned for so long. I'm going to cut it out. That's what I'm here for!'

'No!' she sobbed. 'Andrew, no!'

'Oh yes,' he smiled. 'And there's more. I was two years in Broadmoor because of your testimony!

'You pay for your deceits with your eyes. And you pay for those wasted years with your life!'

Josiah Newcastle flicked on a lightswitch; a shadeless bulb glowed reluctantly.

There was a rush mat on the floor, by the side of which was a dead cockroach. The unmade bed, the open wardrobe, the kitchen with green stuff in a mug on the sink, all had an air of abandonment.

'He simply gone, Jo-mahn,' said the policeman.

'No. Das impossible. Here his clothes. If he gone, he takin' clothes. English men not goin' wear de same suit for more den a day.'

'So maybe you is right after all. Or maybe you is wrong an' dis a wild goose chase. What you got dere?'

Josiah had his hand in the snakeskin bag. 'Passport.'

'See heah.' The picture was of the man Mollina remembered for being drunk and disorderly. But the name inside
was Andrew Dean's.

'Anodder,' said Josiah.

He passed him the Alan Walker passport. 'So dis is he,'
said Mollina. 'An' dis ahlso is he.

'What else in dat bag?'

Josiah held out six shredded photographs. 'You know
who is dis?'

Mollia's jaw dropped. The identical pictures had been
heavily scored with the point of a knife, till the images were
uncertain, fragmented. Only the last one was intact,
recognisable.

'Je-sus Lord,' he said. And he was running down the
wooden stairs, climbing into his patrol car before Josiah
could even ask who the face had belonged to.

Mollina was half an hour away from Sugar Mill
Plantation. He prayed it wasn't already too late.

There was a sound outside, a whisper, an echo, a memory.

Oh God, Hope thought, let it be Zeke or Elisha . . . But
there was nobody on the estate and she knew that in her
heart of hearts. They were in their rooms in the great house
or in the bars in Charlestown. There was nobody.

Dean reached into his pocket and the blade of the stiletto
knife hung over her face, glinting in the light like a
pendulum.

'I want you to know about Ned Murdoch,' he said.

There was the rushing of blood in her ears, she was deaf,
she was blind, she was already dead.

His words bounced around her head as though they were
fragments of a nightmare, leeching away her will to live,
seeping at her one hope, magnifying her fear until she was
screaming – 'You couldn't have killed him – you liar – you
bastard – you were never on that boat – it's not true – '

But it was and she knew it. And there was no escape, and
even if there was, there was no-one now to escape to –

'Liar!' she screamed again.

The knife was quivering, trembling, tracing the lines on
her face that would turn into cuts.

Andrew Dean tried to decide whether he would remove her left eye or her right eye first.

Terry Morelands slid into the room silently on his panther feet, his heart pounding with fear. He had to help her somehow – had to get that lunatic off her.

But Terry was no fighter. The knife, the blade, Andrew Dean's hands trembling, ready to strike, made him pause, not knowing how to stop him. Then he was moving, inch by inch into the room till Hope saw him at last. 'Terry!' she screamed, giving him away. 'Christ! Help me – help me – '

Goliath would do it. Goliath would go in for the kill, never mind the opponent's spikes and spurs, he'd go in there and he'd fight with everything he'd got – he'd fight till his eyes were ripped out and he was lying bleeding and shredded like an old feather duster. And so would Terry.

His arm whipped around Dean's neck, from nowhere, hauling him backwards, pulling him away from Hope. Dean cried out, his head snapping back as he twisted to avoid the man's forearm. He whirled around and under, ducking the blow aimed at him.

Dean was small, but size didn't matter. You could turn your opponent's strength back in on itself if you used the right leverage.

Terry took aim and lunged for him – like the Ol' Mahn he'd make it. He'd come on through. He aimed a blow but Dean went with the force of the punch, swaying, thrusting it back at him with the same momentum and catching Terry below his ribs.

He bent double, winded, in agony, and Dean was up on his feet, whipping round to face him, crouching with the blade sparkling like glass in his hand.

His mirrored sunglasses fell to the floor to leave his eyes naked. They were empty eyes with pupils that had swallowed up the irises. They were holes in his skull.

Dean laughed because he would win. He feinted, playing with him, nicking Terry's arm with the knife, toying with him, watching blood, darker than the man's flesh, seeping across his skin.

Dean was a power-house, a tactician, a generator.

What was weight or strength against an electric eel, a piranha?

'That's it – ' Terry spat. 'Now you is dead.' His hand was wet with his own dark blood.

'Maybe I am,' chuckled Dean. 'So how're you going to hurt me?'

They were circling, sizing each other up, looking for the weaknesses, displaying their strengths.

Main On! yelled Doctor Doom inside Terry's head.

He see-sawed, ducked and dodged, going first for the left, then the right. He was snatching for that weapon, for there lay Dean's advantage.

Dean was quick, slashing at his face with his blade, spitting insults and venom.

Terry's fist lashed and flailed erratically – there was no technique, only instinct. He was kicking, clawing, butting, finding weapons he'd never known he'd had in his own body. Suddenly his hand caught hold of Dean's wrist – it was pure accident, luck, that he caught it and held onto it, twisting and gripping with a strength that might have cracked Dean's bones.

The hand opened slowly, slowly, and the knife clattered to the ground, ringing like a bell on the marble. He'd done it, he'd done it –

Andrew Dean relaxed his hand, went limp as a jelly fish. Terry relaxed subconsciously with him.

Dean twisted and jerked away from him, twisting and turning and pulling the gun out of his pocket. He took aim at Hope who was half-lying, half-struggling to get up off the floor and fired. The shot missed her, burying itself in the sofa inches away from her head and she screamed. Terry was startled into action again. He was after him again. Like Goliath, he'd go for his opponent's legs, take him to the ground . . .

In Dean's head there was music roaring, shrieking, he was crowing, shouting something – what was he shouting? Why wasn't he breathing? He had forgotten how – it was this room –

The black man's face was changing, mutating, turning to dusty grey plaster of Paris –

'No!' bellowed Dean. His attacker was a hallucination – there was no one here – he'd been deceived by his treacherous mind again, and there was no way to fight a figment of his imagination –

He had to run – run – get away from this monster that would grow and swell and explode in a fragment of bone –

Terry lurched for the knife on the ground, it was his spur, his talon, and it was in his hand, an extension of himself. Then he saw Dean. He saw the horror in his face and was stunned into immobility for a split second.

Dean was running, out into the night, stumbling –

Terry looked at the space where he had been and paused, knowing that he had seen something shocking and terrible . . .

Then he was chasing after him. For Dean was still a lunatic with a gun. A lunatic who would return.

His breath was louder than the sound of the waves below, his heart-beat stronger than the rhythms in his head.

His feet punched the ground and he glanced back over his shoulder.

Dean's feet crunched into the scrub grass as he took off away from Sugar Mill Road, disappearing into the sloping hills that led to the sands.

That music from The Crooked Mile was echoing round his head like his skull was a cave. There were men at his body, prising him open, torturing him with their hands and their mouths. And he was doing the same to other men in a circle of rage and pain. Pounding into them, splitting them, ripping them, wreaking havoc with their flesh, wallowing in his revenge.

It was his brother lying in front of him, screaming. It was his mother, his father. It was Nick who'd rejected him, banished him, thrown him away like soiled linen.

The sparse, broken trees seemed to be closing in on him. No lights were shining and the moon was sinking fast into the sea. There was still enough light to show him the way, enough to cast shadows that could have been tarantulas, hands, oil over him and the ground.

There was a wailing, a shrieking siren, but it had

nothing to do with Andrew Dean. Car headlights shone in twin beams behind him, going in the opposite direction.

Tree frogs were screaming at him, wolf-whistling him. There were rattling, rustling sounds from the groves, shrieks of small mammals, the crunching of teeth on bones. The ground seemed to shake, the moon to laugh. A cloud momentarily covered it again and the shadow, the oil, the hands, the spiders were everywhere. He stood stock still, panting, terrified, not daring to move a step in case his foot should find one of the pits in the scrub, waiting for the light again.

An unidentifiable night bird – or maybe a bat – fluttered softly near his face and he waved his hands madly to frighten it away. 'Leave me alone!' he screamed, for he hated things he couldn't hurt.

His voice gave him away. Terry pounded after him, tracking him into a long run-up to the cliff's edge, knowing that he was chasing madness and death. Like a distant echo of his own feet, he could hear those other footsteps ahead of him. He was getting closer each second, but he had to face him with only the knife while the creature had the gun . . .

The bird or bat returned, Dean could hear the swishing of wings, feel the air circulating wildly around him. He dreaded the feel of the creature becoming entangled in his hair, going for his eyes, clawing at him, sucking his blood. He dropped to the ground, covering his head with his hands, almost crying, almost screaming in terror.

He'd shoot it and damn the noise. He'd kill it for coming so close.

He fired wildly at it, but the creature was still there, its wings whirring and moving the air, fanning his face and flap-flapping and swirling and rustling his hair . . .

'Fuhhck!' he screamed into the night, and he felt stronger for it. 'Fuhhck!' he called out again. And the cloud, terrified by the intrusion of his voice into the stillness, fled, leaving the moon to light his way for him.

He ran on, calling 'Fuhhck!' as his battle cry, as he weaved this way and that through the brambles and the rocks.

He reached the point on the cliff where he could see the sea below and the skeletal trees gave way to emptiness. He could hear the crashing of the breakers on the rocks as they swirled in the currents' confusion, feel the salt and the dust in the air.

He stopped and turned, knowing the monster of his mind would be there, waiting to destroy him. Already, he could feel the slowing of his heartbeat, the thudding of distant drums, the tangling of wires in his head that would scatter in confusion and manifest externally to create the faces he dreaded.

Slowly he opened his eyes.

And they were all there.

Faces coming at him from all directions, rushing in on him, shrieking, screaming obscenities, with spittle tracing lines between their lips, their faces white as statues, hard as marble, dropping pieces of flesh around them as they emanated emotions beyond human comprehension.

The black man was one among many, wavering, shimmering, holding on to the knife that was his. He took aim at the vision, his hand trembling, shaking –

But the other faces were coming close and he screamed and knew there was no escape. No escape from the horrors that he had created with his addiction and his cruelty and he turned the gun on himself, laughing that they would never terrify him again.

He tried to call out 'Fuhhck!' once more, but the rushing sound in his ears drowned his voice and the battle cry was forever imprisoned inside his head, competing with the music of his insanity.

And Terry watched in horror as the man fired the gun and his face exploded like plaster of Paris . . .

'Here, drink dis.' Rachel held the glass of brandy to Hope's lips. 'You soon be better, hon. Dere's no damage. Only inside.'

Hope was still weeping uncontrollably, the shock leaving her weak and empty. Pansy wiped her face with a damp cloth, cooing, soothing her, calming her fears.

'We have de entire foarce out lookin' for he, Miss

Parnell,' said Mollina. 'Dere'll be a guard here till we find dis Walker-Dean.'

Then Terry was back, his chest heaving with exertion, sweat streaming down his face, blood pouring down his arm to leave sticky pools by his feet. 'She okay?' he panted.

'Terry,' she sobbed. 'Oh, Terry – '

'You come in heres Mistah Moahlands,' said Rachel. 'You bleedin' to death.'

She took hold of his arm and examined the deep cut. 'Bahd,' she said. 'You needin' a hospital.'

'I'm okay,' he snapped, pulling away from her. 'How's Hope?'

'Bit weird,' she said, almost apologetically. Her voice was very far away. Pink marks banded her throat.

'It's okay Hope. Don't worry about a thing.'

She shook her head. What could she say to him? Thank you? You were terrific? I'd never guessed you were a hero?

'Hush,' he said again. 'It's okay.'

She looked fearfully at the door, seeing Andrew Dean lurking there like the watcher on the threshold.

'He's gone, Hope. He won't be back. He shot himself.' He shook his head, sickened by the memory of the violent death he had seen.

Station Officer Mollina sat up sharply: 'Killed heself?'

Terry writhed. 'He could have fired at me – I thought he was going to – then he turned the gun back on himself – '

Hope rocked on the sofa in misery and Pansy clung to her.

'He said he'd wrecked Ned's boat, Terry – he said that it would go off course. And Ned was sailing in that wind – and he'll be dead and I never told him I loved him – '

Terry was with her, cradling her face in his hands, tenderly, as though she was a bird. 'Hey,' he said. 'He was mad that guy – don't believe it – '

'No, Terry! I know he was telling the truth – I could feel it – '

'You'll check it out, won't you Mollina?'

'Sure.'

'We'll know, soon enough. You've got to rest, get this stuff out of your head, Hope.'

Hope nodded and took more of the brandy. The world was getting hazy.

Rachel started to make up a bed for Pansy, so that Hope wouldn't have to be on her own. As time passed, Terry began to strut again, filled with the realisation that he was a Hero.

'It was a good thing you was heah, Mistah Moahlahnds,' said Mollina. 'Odderwise who knowed what might have happened. As a mattah of int'rest. Why *was* you heah?'

Terry looked guiltily at Hope. No way could he say that he'd been trying to score, knowing that the plantation was empty, knowing Hope was on her own and, maybe, lonely. He couldn't admit to that. It would spoil everything.

'I was expecting him,' Hope said quickly, her voice slurring with the brandy. 'He'd promised to come over and give me a hand with the Mill . . . after the hurricane . . .'

Okay, thought Mollina. If that was the story, he'd not question it too hard, though he could guess at the truth.

He checked his watch and looked again at Terry Moreland's arm. 'We makin' a statement in de mornin'. After you bin to de hospital. An' after we collect de body.'

'Need scrapin',' said Terry, grinning with relief.

Hope winced at his words and Rachel said: 'It better dat way.'

'Miss Parnell – ' Mollina warned. 'No flyin'. We got to check dose planes of yours first. We doan' know what Dean may have done before he attackin' you.'

Hope nodded, understanding, realising the danger.

But Pansy's face fell. 'Oh, Lord,' she said. 'Meestah Lennox is flyin' The Goose, an' maybe it all too late for he.'

Chapter Twenty One

DAWN BROKE on a calm sea. The distant lights of Saba were obscured by the competition in the east. The ocean looked empty. Thousands of miles of nothingness apart from a few peaking bits of earth, so remote from Ned that they might as well not exist.

He'd never seen the water as a desert before. The two things were so contradictory. But now, with the occasional ripple of a wave like a sand dune, he could see where opposites became one and the same.

He was the sea's prisoner. As powerless to escape the confines of the boat as he would have been to escape the directionless Gobi desert.

It was days since he had slept. He'd cat-napped, that was all. First there'd been the flight from the hurricane, then the day spent drinking and listening to the radio in St Croix. Finally this terrible wilderness of coral.

No wonder he hadn't slept. He counted his waking hours as though they were medals, trophies to prove his endurance level.

His fatigue took him from peaks of frenzied activity to a state where he was aware of nothing but the terrible ache behind his eyes. That glare on the water would soon be back, and unbearable it would be. They would be sailing directly into the sun, once they had found their way out of the tangle of coral, which was as lethal to the boat as a series of mines. That thought had kept him awake throughout the night. He felt as though they were becalmed. Ancient Mariners all.

Irritably he stood up to ring the ship's bell. Get those bastards up and moving. He was awake. Why should they dream on in the sleep of the innocent when he was a condemned man?

There would soon be enough light. Already the world was taking on form and colour. He rang the bell again.

'Get that cook in the galley,' he roared as Spencer emerged, the first. 'We'll work out what we're doing over food.'

The boat had drifted, not too far, but far enough for Ned to be able to spot the next dark band of sea-urchin coated coral, twenty-five yards ahead.

He went over the same old questions in his head. Who was wrecking his boat? And why? How could he have aroused so much hatred? And why hadn't someone seen that saboteur at work.

Either one of the Nevis marina men had something against him or else someone had been about while the crew was off ship one night.

Okay, he himself should have checked out the turbines and the compass, and he'd left port before the fitters could get around to servicing the engine. There was no getting round it. It was his responsibility. He was nothing but an asshole. A jumped up sea-captain.

He joined the crew at the table in the dining room. 'We should have gone back, Ned. Once we knowed we was in de reef,' said Keith.

Okay, another error of judgement. One more in a long line. There was no reply so instead he snapped: 'What's this crap, Michel?'

'Crepes,' barked the chef from the other end of the table.

'For fuckin' breakfast, man?'

'You 'ave a choice of crepes or waitin' till one of you lands a fish. Or you could 'ave 'ad a dried egg omelette. We 'ave what we 'ave.'

'So what's happened to the food stocks? Don't tell me. Someone's poisoned the food, right? We've dumped the freezer as ballast because we're sinking.

'Well?'

'You say you don't want to know, Ned, but I tell, *hein*? On St Croix, food prices were high. You say we go to Nevis or Antigua. I think I buy in food there. How was I to know

308

we would spend a day-trip cruisin' the lagoon? We should 'ave been in port by zis time.'

'Okay,' said Ned wearily, forking up the last of the bland pancake. 'Even more reason to get moving, eh boys?' He grinned at them but all his teeth showed.

'What de plan, Ned?' said Keith.

'If I swim ahead, can I trust you buggers to steer in exactly the same direction? Keep me in sight all the time? Not to sail over me by going too quickly, and not to fall so far behind that you lose me?'

They punctuated his questions with nods. The situation was indeed desperate if they had to eat crepes. Real men *never* eat crepes. Let alone for breakfast.

Ned stripped on the deck and wet his goggles. 'I'll go ahead, Cinnamon, to check that I'm not leading you into a dead end. Then I'll come back and you follow me. Keep the sails furled and use the motor. Very slowly.'

Keith was ready to take the next swim in the relay that might be necessary if the situation didn't improve.

Ned climbed over the rails and dropped naked but for the mask into the cool water. Instantly his mind was alive, wary for the sharks he knew wouldn't be around. On the alert for giant squid. Every sea monster he'd ever read about. His mistress, the sea, became his enemy in crisis, nurturing his nightmares, populating his imagination with terrors.

The sun reflected through the water and he stayed near the surface, weaving his way towards what looked like a break in the coral ahead. He came up to gulp air and swam on through the channel. It was low enough here for the Maria Juana to sail through as long as Cinnamon Hicks was accurate in his steering.

He somersaulted in the water and swam back, calling for the boat to follow. They were doing it right. Keeping him in sight, trailing him between the ridges and the peaks.

Now the sun was on his left. They were heading south. His limbs felt so tired, but he carried on, snaking along the cliff ledge. And then there was another mountain of the stuff dead ahead.

Turrets of white spires that looked like rock-solid

sponges; flame coral spattered with the red flecks of brim-stone or whatever the hell the stuff was that burnt you on contact; fan coral as delicate as a leaf's skeleton. A breath-takingly beautiful but lethal world.

He kicked at a fan and felt it snap with satisfaction. It had taken thousands of years to grow to that size.

There were gigantic sea urchins everywhere – black and purple against the hard, white coral. Some of them had bodies bigger than his head, spines longer than his body. Get one of those in his foot and it would take more than lime-juice or that age-old remedy of piss to get it out. Thank sweet Jesus they couldn't jump out at you.

He turned in the water to fight his way through the shoal of neon-coloured fish that had been tailing him. They were bumping him with their mouths, trying to nibble at the hairs on his legs and his chest like bait. He decided he'd be as well to get back into the schooner and get some pants on in case any bigger fish came along.

He waved the boat forwards and waited for it to take the same path as he had. He was gasping, gulping oxygen into his lungs.

Then he was hauling himself up the ropes to collapse on the sun-warmed deck. 'I think you'd better play scout, Keith,' he groaned as his body slumped and refused to move a muscle.

Blood trickled from hairline scratches all over his legs and arms to blend palely with the water droplets on his skin. Cinnamon blotted him with a towel. 'Dese coral scratches a bitch,' he said. 'An' dere's anodder bad one on your chest again, Ned.'

'If that's you Hicks, who the fuck's drivin'?' moaned Ned, seeing him through half-closed eyes.

'It okay, mahn. Gonzo drivin'.'

Cinnamon and Spencer dragged him to his berth where they dried him and spread antiseptic cream on his wounds.

An hour later, Keith knocked on the door and went in when there was no reply. He stood dripping pools of sea-water.

'We through it, Ned,' he said. There was still no reply.

'De coral's bin gettin' less an' less.' Ned didn't move. 'Mahn, dere's bin' no big reef for thirty minutes.' Was he still breathing?

'Murdoch? You livin'?'

'Sleepin',' mumbled Ned, and drifted back into Hope's arms.

There was no problem with The Goose. Oz arrived back in Nevis well pleased with his night's work. He'd just have a quick check to see who was on customs, then he'd whip the dope through to the Jeep and drive off home to snuggle up with Esme.

He'd been making deals in Dominica all night and flown most of the morning. He was shagged. Shit, it was a real blazer today. The sun was making up for the time it had spent out of action on Thursday. The sooner he could get this heavy suit off . . .

Uniformed policemen were coming out to meet him. Christ, a tip-off, it had to be.

'Ev'rythin' okay wid de plane, Meestah Lennox?' said Station Officer Mollina.

What was this? A trap? 'Sure,' he said, grinning confidently. It wasn't the way he was feeling.

'No problehms, sir?'

'What sort of problems?' Don't over-react or they'll know you're guilty. You can always claim you knew nothing about the stash.

'We guddah mechanic, here, Meestah Lennox,' smiled the Snake. 'We wanna check de plane okay.'

'Of course the plane's okay. I've just flown her back from Dominica - ' But they'd know where he'd been, wouldn't they.

Oz knew nothing about Mollina's fears for Hope's safety, nothing about Andrew Dean or the threat of sabotage.

'Well we guddah know for weselves dat dis plane have not bin monkeyed with.'

'Look, Mollina,' pleaded Oz. 'I'm really tired. I can't hang about - I've been up in the air for what seems like days. Can't it wait? Please?'

311

'We not needin' you. We know what we lookin' for,' pronounced the Jackal.

'Okay,' said Oz wearily. 'I'll come.' He nearly added 'quietly'.

He led the way and two policemen, Bardram, the customs official and the mechanic, specially imported from St Kitts airport, followed him.

The March to the Scaffold . . .

Oz opened the doors, released the side plates, and reached for the brown paper parcel in the back. The mechanic climbed into the cockpit as Oz stood stupidly with the package in his arms. His mouth hung open.

'We leave he to it,' said Mollina.

'What's he doin?' said Oz. Why the hell aren't you arresting me, putting me out of my misery? 'Is it really necessary to tear her apart like that? There's no more – '

'I tole you. He checkin' for monkeyin'.'

They reached the customs house. And here it came.

'What you got dere, Meestah Lennox?' asked the Fox.

Oz heaved a sigh and dumped the package on the search and destroy desk. Three years. He'd maybe get three years. Lose his job of course. Hope wouldn't stand for dealing.

'Five kilos of marijuana,' he said, resigning himself to his fate.

'Doan' you be cheekin' de officer!' said Bardram. 'Or I have you openin' dat.'

Mollina gave a belly laugh. 'Dat de first time someone tell me he guilty when he innocent! You makin' a good joke, Oz Lennox. An' I hoape you have a drink wid me, mahn, some time. Okay?'

Oz couldn't make out what was happening. Were they playing with him or what? He looked from face to face and decided – Jesus Christ – they weren't. They knew nothing about the dope. And he'd nearly confessed, laid it on a plate for them –

'Okay, man,' he said with more enthusiasm than he'd felt for anything before. 'I'll give you a call at the station, all right? Sure. I'll ring you. Very soon.'

- Grab the parcel, saunter out, very casual, turn and wave –

'Aw-right,' beamed Mollina.

And they swung round to watch the sweating man hurrying to his Jeep in the car compound.

'What he say he have in dat parcel?' said Bardram, as Oz started the motor.

'He didn't,' said Mollina. 'You needin' to know?'

Bardram shrugged. 'I guess it doan't mattah,' he said.

So it hadn't been so bad, watching the stones being cleared. It hadn't felt as though she was having her arm cut off or her heart surgically removed at all.

Hope watched as the last of the loose rubble was loaded into the back of the truck.

There was nothing left of the mill. Just a cellar full of broken bits of wood, dust and stones. She'd have liquid cement poured over it on Monday. Turn it into an outside dance floor where they could have barbecues in the evenings, have a steel band, limbo dancers in high season.

She might put up a plaque saying: This is the spot on which stood the oldest of Nevis's sugar mills, destoyed by Hurricane Cleo, and a flying tree.

The men had done a good job. They'd worked hard, even though it was a weekend. She'd forced herself to stand and watch it all so that she could be under no false illusions, occupying herself so that she couldn't think about Andrew Dean. Couldn't think about Ned.

Everything was different, strange. Where was the loss, the grieving for the Mill she'd expected to feel? It simply didn't exist.

Dean had given her a new perspective. In time she'd feel nothing about the attack. She'd blank it from her mind so that it wouldn't ever have happened. Just like before. *But would she ever get over Ned?*

Already, last night seemed a fantasy, a nightmare, unreal. She was still in shock; she was thankfully numb. Dead.

Like Ned was.

Before they'd checked the planes, Mollina had confirmed that the Maria Juana had failed to reach San

Juan. Even now, planes were searching the area around the Virgins. But she knew it was hopeless. Useless.

She glanced at her watch. Hell, it was only two. Time was playing tricks with her, she'd thought it was much much later. She'd have to get out of here. Go for a fly. Escape.

She took one last look at the clouds of dust and then ran. Back in her room, she threw water over her face. There were marks on her neck, shadows in her eyes, but her face showed no other sign of the attack. Thank God. She didn't want people looking, noticing, asking.

She pulled on jeans and a shirt, and trotted back down the path, stopping in the kitchen to call out: 'Back before dark!'

She ran on quickly before Pansy could try to stop her and jumped into the Jeep. The policeman on the gate snapped to attention and saluted her. Why Mollina had insisted on maintaining a guard she couldn't imagine. It was like the men in the garden, hunting for explosives. All way over the top, all unnecessary, and all irrelevant, she thought.

She drove down through the Plantation, smiling with her lips but not with her eyes as she greeted people she knew. She took the long way round to the airport.

She was shaking, dammit. What had she done with her time before Ned? For the life of her, she couldn't remember. How had she filled her empty days?

She parked the Jeep in the airport compound and took her cotton scarf from the glove compartment.

Amos Bardram growled at her as she passed him by, but she couldn't be bothered to reply.

The mechanic had finished checking The Goose and had gone.

She took the oldest of the planes, the 1960's Islander, deliberately flirting mildly with death. No absolutely reliable instruments on this one. She didn't need them. She only planned a joy-ride. Or a joyless ride, maybe.

No landings anywhere but back home. This was just to get grief out of her system in the only way she knew how. She pulled off a clod of baked-on mud from the propeller shaft and kicked it away.

Hope listened to the engine as it began to whirr and rumble. She checked the fuel tank visually and decided there were three hours flying at least.

Then she was cruising out onto the runway, taxi-ing, faster and faster, lifting the wheels from the tarmac and feeling that soaring sensation, that heady exultation as she defied gravity. Despite the hurt, despite the sadness, she was still the magician.

She aimed directly for the volcano, leaving it to the last minute to lift the nose and cheat death. The cows hurried along beneath her, knowing her for the crazy bird in the sky that she was.

Then she was up, high above the island, looking down on the earth dwellers, scorning them while she hovered on the wind, feeling those air currents making love to her and her plane.

There were tears streaming down her face, but she didn't know it. 'Ned,' she called. And again. For this would be the last time she let herself go, let down her barriers.

She headed the little plane towards St Kitts in an agony of morbidity, wanting to plumb the depths of her despair and her loss. For once she hit the bottom, she knew she could begin to climb again.

Ned finally awoke as the boat docked in Nevis. He was awake in a flash, ready to move, his whole body alive and electric with tension and desire. Soon he would see her.

He dashed up the stairs and called to the men to wait for him. For however long it took.

'We goin' to Grenada if she not dere, Ned?' said Keith.

'Sure, but she will be. Get this boat checked top to bottom while I'm gone. And find a real mechanic, not some joker from the marina.'

Charlestown was quiet, almost deserted. Where were all the bastard taxis in Nevis? He jogged round to the war memorial by the tourist office, where the cabs sometimes parked, and found one.

'Sugar Mill Plantation,' he said to the driver. 'Very quickly.'

The driver turned slowly to him and said: 'Why you in a

315

hurry mahn? What you goin' do wid de extra time you savin'? Lay on de beach a while longer? Catch anodder two fishes?'

'Come on,' grinned Ned. 'I know island ways. I'm not a tourist. Take your time but be sharp, eh?'

The taxi cruised out of Charlestown, managing about three miles an hour more than it usually did. The driver felt as though he was breaking all known speed records and looked for Ned's approval.

'Very good,' said Ned. 'Yes indeedy. It takes courage to drive at speed.'

But things had changed at the Plantation. The lushness of the ground had gone. The Mill was demolished. There was nothing left of it, but levelled stones. Marble chips on a shallow grave.

There were no gardeners around, few birds. Instead there stood an armed policeman on the gate, looking as though he was expecting a terrorist attack.

The gardens were being swept by men with metal detectors. What the hell was going on?

He paid off the cab driver and ran inside. The door to the great house stood open, but nobody was around. He didn't know what he dreaded to find –

The room was empty. No sign of life.

Then he heard Hope calling his name, twice, and he spun wildly, looking for her. 'Hope – I'm here,' he called back. But it was a trick of his imagination. There was no-one, nothing.

'Hello dere, Meestah Murdoch,' said Pansy breathlessly, coming out from the dining room, almost running into his arms. 'I is so glad to see you! We bin' expectin' you a long time.'

'Where's Hope?' he asked.

'Hoape not bin' expectin' you. Only me an' Rachel has.'

'So where is she – ' he cried, bursting.

'She gone for a fly, Mistah Murdoch, when she in no fit state – '

'What d'you mean, Pansy? No fit state?'

Pansy shook her head, damning herself for speaking.

Hope would be angry if she told him what had happened. She shouldn't have said anything. Sometime she'd learn not to interfere. Quickly she sidestepped, pressing her knuckles to her mouth.

'She never *said* she was flyin' Mistah Murdoch. Maybe she ain't. Maybe she drivin' de Jeep. Anyways she said she be back before dahrk.'

Hell's teeth. Sunset was an hour away or more.

And what was wrong with Hope?

He sighed, exasperated, knowing he'd need to have to work hard to get anywhere with an island woman who had decided to say nothing.

Hope floated over the cove where they'd stopped in St Kitts. She could taste him, feel him there with her. She took the plane down lower and recklessly skidded the fixed wheels against the water.

There it was, the place where they should first have made love. The cove where the sand glittered bright as shards of glass, as bright as the sea itself. Tiny diamonds.

Hesitantly, she took the plane in closer, and considered landing, after all. But already the sun was dropping behind her and it would be impossible to take off again in the dark.

She turned the plane out to sea again, watching the swirling waves, the leaping fish below her, the endless blue. She was flying low, well beneath the clouds that streamed towards the sun in the west.

In the distance, the peak of the volcano was jagged, moss-covered. She could already see the glimmering lights of the houses shining out now night was falling.

Her eyes were dry. There were no more tears. In time she'd be able to pull that shutter down and forget her grief.

She was flying over the marina.

Some time, there'd be another Ned, one who'd love her, stay with her –

Subconsciously she registered the schooner in the harbour, its pinpoints of light reflecting against the water –

For a moment she lost her concentration on the plane. It dipped, falling, as she lost control. She was back in a flash, grabbing the yoke to hoist up the nose. She was back in the present, in the air, in the cockpit. The plane had tried to take her like a wayward horse and failed.

She glanced fearfully at the marina again in case she'd been mistaken, in case she lost the Islander a second time.

Yes, she acknowledged to her vaulting heart.

Ned is alive. Ned is home. And he's come back for me.

He spun round as she ran through the great house doors.

'Where in hell have you been?' he shouted, worry making him angry with her. Crazy.

She looked wild and dishevelled, too vivid for real life. 'Flying,' she said lamely.

'Pansy said you'd be back before dark!' he accused her.

'I'm sorry,' she said. 'I didn't know. I saw your boat from the air, so I stopped off at the marina. I thought that's where you'd be.'

His hair was matted with the sea. There were new scratches on his face. He shook his head: 'Christ, Hope – I've been frantic with worry!'

Hope's emotions boiled within her, bubbled, burst – 'You've been worried? What about me? Why didn't you 'phone?' she cried – not that it mattered any more – not now he was here, with her again.

'I don't know, I just wanted to get back to you.'

'I thought you were dead – '

His irrational anger at her absence evaporated. 'I know, Pansy told me.' He swallowed hard. He'd thought she'd never come home, that he'd lost her too soon. But she was here. With him. Against all odds.

'It's been a long time,' he said. A few days, a lifetime.

'Yes, Ned. Too long. I've needed you so much . . . '

They were still apart, measuring the distance between them. Then there was none. No distance at all. She moved or he did, or maybe they both did.

'Christ, Hope, I don't think I can live without you,' he said brokenly. 'Because I love you.'

He was holding her, caressing her, rubbing her back as though she was his baby. And she was holding him, loving him too, breathing in his salty skin.

He pressed his lips to hers and they were one and the

same. The desert and the sea. The air and the rock in the second that spans eternity.

'Stay with me,' she whispered, too softly for him to hear, but he knew. He needed no words. They wanted the same thing; they were meteors held prisoner by the same sun's gravity.

'You came back,' she cried suddenly, letting go at last. 'It's incredible! Wonderful – and I can't believe it!'

The terror, the fear, the sorrow, the numbness – everything had gone, shattered by having him there with her now, wanting her, holding her –

He was holding her so tightly she might break.

His eyes were swimming, glistening. 'Of course I came back,' he smiled, amazed she could ever have doubted he'd return. It had been inevitable.

'Anyway,' he went on, 'I wanted a ship's cat. A big black one.'

'But they're only kittens, Ned. New-borns.'

'Then I'll just have to wait till they grow.'

They walked across the cobbled path lit by the Chinese lanterns, hearing the singing frogs, smelling the scents of the night-flowering blossoms that had survived. As they had.

'Yes,' he said thoughtfully, swept away by the magic that was Nevis, by the magic that was Hope Parnell. 'I could definitely stay in a place like this.'

His hand closed around hers and he held it to his lips. His midnight eyes were wicked, laughing.

'Or maybe I could sail you to the Grenadines.'

She smiled back at him, knowing there was no way to forever ground a bastard cheat. Or a magician.

'I'd like that,' she said.

Beneath the gauze mosquito net, she was soaking him up, drinking him as though he were the sea itself. She was swept up on the tide of their love, floating, drifting, coming home.

He was rising into her over and over again, loving her so much he could have died, never regretting a thing. She enveloped him gently like the air, taking him on her breezes God knew where. The cloud lady and the ocean man.

And above Sugar Mill Plantation, pelicans soared in a V formation like ace pilots, returning to their cove after the storm.